DANGE

BOOK 4

A.G. HARRIS

—— *AUTHOR* ——

End My Games

Copyright

Acknowledgments

This series has been the largest and most challenging endeavor I've ever undertaken. Yet, the true reward comes from receiving all the amazing personal messages from fans. I vividly remember sitting down, gazing at a picture I'd found, which sparked a daydream that would eventually unfold into this entire series. At the time, I was sleep-deprived, being a new mom, and that might explain the absolutely wild twists and turns in this series, haha.

It feels surreal now, having typed those final words. Sol's story is finished.

This is dedicated to all the fans who have stood steadfastly by my side, eagerly anticipating a glimpse into just how wild Sol and Luna truly are.

With love,
A.G. Harris

Also by A.G. Harris

Follow me and sign up for my newsletter

https://mailchi.mp/2f14c0c70688/newsletter

https://www.authoragharris.com/

@authoragharris

https://www.facebook.com/authoragharris/

Author's Note

I mean, come on, it's book four – you should know the drill by now. You're in for a wild ride with all the twists, turns, and, yes, those triggering bits we are too shy to admit we to love.

But hey, it's been a blast, right?

So, before you turn the page, just remember: your eyebrows might shoot up to your hairline, your mouth might gape, and you might feel the urge to talk out loud, turning into a commenting critic of moral choices.

A.G. Harris

A.G. Harris

Wes Adams

Luna Eklund

Gabirel Hellstörm

Famine

End My Games

Prologue

Death

Buzzing, swarms of movement clamor on the outside lawn of the White House. They attack like a hive.

Sting!

Amid the chaos, it is quite beautiful. There is an order, a pattern, in peace and madness. Even when it tries to be unruly, it is actually a pattern. It's called Chaos Theory.

Only ten reporters were allowed inside the manicured grass lawn. Why outside, you might ask? It's all part of the carefully plotted lie. If we were bunkered inside, it would make us look scared. So, we set the press conference outside as if this were a god damn garden party.

All of the reporters are highly vetted and paid off to only ask the questions my father wants them to ask. Each question picked to fool the world. People want answers. They'll get the answers we crafted.

My family controls everything in the United States, and that means we control a lot of the world as well. Perks of our blood.

When you control the world, it makes it easier to know where people like to run and hide because we have eyes and ears everywhere.

The grin that spreads over my face would make a grown man cry. "I'm coming for you, little mouse! You just made this hunt so much more thrilling," I whisper, my voice a sinister melody that echoes through the depths of my twisted mind.

The chase has escalated, fueled by a love that knows no boundaries, an obsession that thrives in the darkest depths of my mind.

My need for Sol devours all reason, leaving only a ravenous hunger in its wake. With each step, I delve deeper into the abyss, where the forbidden and the perverse intertwine, where the line between pleasure and pain blurs.

Brace yourself, little mouse, for the hunt has just begun, and I am the predator that revels in the morbid dance of our sickening affection.

Sol was correct; our love is sick, but even a plague can be beautiful. It brings forth new life and new innovations.

This type of love is all I know. My father and mother possess the same distorted passion. Their marriage was arranged, but my mother actually thought she could escape it. She ran, turning my father into an obsessed hunter.

Clearly the apple didn't fall far from the tree.

My mother has big balls, bigger than most men. She's the only woman who can halt my father in his tracks, and she is the only person he would forgive.

I'm my father's son, and that means I'll forgive my little mouse, too—once I find her, that is.

"The DEFCON level has been elevated to 3, and the gravity of this situation is resonating throughout the nation," the reporter states, directing his questions towards my esteemed uncle, positioned stoically before the grandeur of the White House.

Even in the unfolding crisis, my uncle looks cool as a cucumber on a perfect summer's day.

My Uncle runs the Worldwide Intelligence Syndicate (WIS). WIS manages every known and unknown government top-secret organization. You know what that means? We know everything. All the dirty, sinful details.

The better question is, who oversees WIS? Good old dad. That's what made Manus Dei so interested in my family.

He's closely monitoring the unfolding news from a secure bunker in Utah. Uncle drew the short end of the stick, burdened with the unenviable task of being the public face, entertaining the press and politicians.

The mere mention of my father's watchful gaze compels those in the political arena to dance to my uncle's tune, aware that falling out of favor with my father could have dire consequences.

I glance at Gabriel, sitting rigidly in his seat, more statue than man. How the heck does he make his spine so stiff? If he doesn't unclench his jaw, he will crack a tooth. His knuckles are so tight I'm unsure how his fingers are still attached to his palm.

He rarely speaks, having crawled so deep inside his mind that even I can't read his thoughts.

I've faced a lot of scary things, one of them being my little mouse on the run without me nipping at her heels. Yet, the scariest thing most men never realize isn't the boogeyman under their bed or the fear of losing a loved one.

It's their own mind.

We think we control it; we don't. In the blink of an eye, your mind can take possession of you, and then you're fucked.

When you start to doubt what is real and what isn't, you can never be normal again.

I need my brother to think straight. I have to keep him grounded, and there is only one way to do that.

I know one thing for certain—he wants to kill Luna. Hell, so do I.

The better question is can he kill Luna? I'm not willing to bet on that.

I honestly don't know what he's going to do when we find her. We will find her; it's only a matter of time.

Your time is running out, Luna.

"I can assure you, we can handle anything and everything," Uncle grins, and the reporter forgets her panic, batting her eyelashes at him. "Unfortunately, I cannot get into details due to the top-secret nature of the matter. The president is in a meeting now and will brief you later this evening." He assures the world.

It's a joke. We own the president, just like we have for decades.

"But–" The female reporter begins to speak, but Uncle shakes his head. Even in his late fifties, he can get a woman to crawl on her knees to him. It seems the men in my family grow better with age, like a fine wine.

"I won't leave you wanting," he pauses. The woman is going to orgasm on the spot. My father must be fuming right now. Uncle always loved to joke around and piss my father off. That's the job of the younger sibling, after all.

"Sensitive material from black site facilities was taken." Notice how my uncle didn't say *which* black site facility? That's because he just laid claim to it. He just told the world to back the fuck off. "We are in the process of locating it and working with other governments to track it down. This is a worldwide united front." What he means is if any other governments that he hasn't already spoken to even think about pursuing Manus Dei, they will face more than just our government's wrath.

Some will try. It's just the nature of man. You see a shiny toy, and you want it.

My uncle's eyes turn cold and all the gossip halts. He stares the camera down, owning it like his bitch, "We will get everything and ensure the weapons are in the safety of our hands." He warns Luna.

We didn't want to do this press conference, but it was inevitable. When Famine and Luna blew up the tunnels, those who knew what was hidden beneath them sensed a war had begun. Everyone is racing to find Luna and the decryption codes to access Manus Dei's knowledge. This press conference is my father telling Luna to surrender or else.

A shadow emerges next to me. I don't have to glance up to know it's my older brother, my biological brother, Wade. The boy in me wants to wrap my arms around him, to turn back the clock and make him love me again. The man I am knows it's up to Wade. I'm not the one who shut him out.

His eyes are pinned on Gabriel, making me step up to cut off his view.

That's what pisses him off. He thinks I replaced him with Gabriel. I haven't. Families can grow, and mine did.

Wade never could understand how I could accept a clone as a brother.

He looks so much like our father now. Dark hair with a few streaks of grey peppering it, a serious face that somehow women are attracted to. The lines in his skin are starting to deepen; his strong jaw is clenched tight. The suit he's got on would give War a run for his money.

I make the first move, "I missed you."

I watch him closely; he hides the jerk of emotions well, but I notice it. "This is a shit show that could have been avoided if you put a bullet in his head."

I don't know if he knows or just doesn't give a shit that Gabriel can hear this entire conversation due to his enhanced hearing. Most likely both.

So that's the road you want us to continue to walk down. I shake my head. "You know nothing."

"Because you kept me in the dark," he spits as he tugs at the sleeve of his suit.

"I was trying to protect you." I was following our dad's orders. He lost one son to Manus Dei; he didn't want the other tangled up with them.

"I'm your older brother. It was *my* job to protect you." His eyes look directly at my scar-covered heart.

"I decided to join the Navy, and I decided to help Gabriel. What happened to me wasn't your fault."

"Help?" He chuckles, "If coercion is your definition of helping, you've been working with Manus Dei for far too long."

I stand wider, my boot hitting his leather dress shoes. The problem is that Wade and I are exactly alike; we just hide our demons with different camouflage. I prefer shadows, and he likes the wide-open light. I need nature, my weapons, and clothing made to protect me, not impress a boardroom. Wade needs steel towers, cities, and the electric charge of manipulating the masses.

"The definitions in our family are often skewed. You're the one that taught me that." I'm so fucking tired of fighting with him. "I don't know why you insist on our relationship being like this."

His exhale sounds like a steam engine. He's fuming. "I don't know why you insist on helping them." His eyes bounce back to Gabriel, skinning him alive.

"Because they are our future, and whether you like it or not, the science Gabriel worked on has kept me alive."

He swallows hard as he holds my gaze. Holding a grudge when my mother's eyes are looking back at me is hard. I got Dad's green eyes, but Wade got mom's, steal grey, the color of a bullet. He got away with a lot more shit when we were kids because when dad looked into his eyes, he saw mom.

"*They*," he pauses for a brief moment, "or the pussy you're after. To think pussy was the only thing we had to dangle in front of you to get you to come back home. I could have had first-class whores waiting for you, brother."

I smile. I'm not laughing, nor am I happy. I'm just not going to lose my composure as I watch the press conference. "Refer to her as that again, I dare you." That's right, brother, I'm not backing down.

He nods, finally getting it through his thick head. "Are they worth it?"

You see, I never wanted to stand next to my brother or sit at my father's table. I didn't care about power until someone I loved was threatened. I chased adrenaline back then. Now, I chase assurance. When you enter your thirties, you change; what can I say?

I had no choice but to grab as much power as possible. That meant bending a knee to my father and brother again. Getting my ass back home.

Wade and my father won't accept the clones, but if I consider them my family, they will protect them with every resource we have. We have to remain a united front.

"Yes." I declare as I meet his eyes. He's bitter. He never understood how I could leave him to join the Navy. Not because he isn't a soldier. He is but in my father's army. An army he will control one day.

He always feels guilty for the bullets that claimed my heart. Resentment that Gabriel gave me a heart he couldn't, a heart that chained me to Manus Dei.

It's not his fault, but I stopped wasting my time telling him that. He won't believe me.

"I'll never accept her," his eyes dart to Gabriel again, "Or him."

"I never asked you to."

"I want my brother back."

Aww, so he's jealous. I should have realized that earlier. Angling my shoulders, I force his eyes to look at me, "That man you hate gave you your brother back. Without Gabriel, I would be six feet under." He looks away, "He gave me a heart."

"Attached to Manus Dei!" He hisses.

"Attached to a path that will free me and our family from Manus Dei. Your sight has been too narrow, Wade. Widen it. Look at the big picture. Gabriel is trying to free us."

He shakes his head, his eyes finding Gabriel again.

I grab his shoulder, "I decided to join the Navy; my feet ran in front of those bullets. Not his. Your hate is misplaced." I squeeze tighter, "You will always be my older brother."

He balls his fist. "Do you love her?" Finally, an olive branch.

"No," I grin.

His eyes flicker to mine. "Love can't describe what I feel for her. She is my world, and if something happens to her, then you *will* lose me." *I need your help, brother.*

His eyes soften, but his jaw is still clenched. He's not happy, but he won't risk losing me. A dark cloud grows in his eyes. He's the same as me. He just hasn't found his obsession...yet.

Nonetheless, the hunt is all too enticing. His prize won't be a woman, but he will get to kill. He's so good at killing.

His right lip tugs up, "Then let's go hunting."

And just like that, I've got my brother back again.

Chapter 1

Luna

The past.

The office is filled with the rich scent of aged wood, its subtle fragrance mingling with hints of pine, and the distinct mustiness reminiscent of old library books. The air carries the weight of accumulated knowledge, a testament to these walls' countless stories and secrets.

My father has a record player in the far corner. When his lecture bores me too much, I stare at the antique machine, watching the record spin endlessly in circles. I don't understand why a man so ahead of his time likes that old machine.

Jimi Hendrix's "All Along The Watchtower" plays faintly, my father's shoe taps away to the beat. I run my finger along the intricate grains of the wooden surface. I can't help but contemplate the transience of life. Will I weather the years like this enduring wood, standing the test of time, or will I be abruptly cut down, my potential unrealized and repurposed for another destiny?

Pressing my nail into the wood, I push deep enough until I leave my mark on the surface. There. I was here. I left a mark. Another clone won't replace me.

Father moves, his leather chair emitting a tight squeak that reminds me of an animal that just got hit by a car. My eyes slowly glance at him. He's relaxed in his office, akin to a king on his throne. Yet, his shoulders hunch, consumed by deep thought, while a stack of cream-colored papers adorns his desk. Father prefers the cream hue to ease the strain on his eyes. His preferences are always fulfilled.

He examines the upcoming upgrade that awaits me, my first foray into such advancements. Nervousness eludes me, as it always has. I am unfamiliar with the sensation Sol described as bees in one's belly, uncertain if they will yield honey or sting. It seems like a whimsical analogy for emotions. Sol makes everything sound so silly.

Though I do experience emotions, they differ from Sol's. I possess the ability to muffle them, silencing their voices to maintain focus.

A knock comes to the door. Father doesn't look up from his research. "Come in."

The butler enters. I don't know his name, and I don't care to know it. He's an old, portly man that smells like onions.

I don't like how he looks at my twin. He is always doting on her as if she will give him a gift in return.

"Dr. Loretta is here."

That catches my father's attention. He stands and leaves me in the office. I'm to wait like a good pet until he returns. Of course, I'll use my time wisely and snoop around.

When he does return, it's with a woman. His ease dissipates, shoulders stiffen, wrinkles form on his forehead, and his lips press firmly together, betraying his annoyance. His left eyelid twitches every forty-two seconds, a telltale sign of his anger.

"Luna, this is Dr. Loretta," Father introduces, his voice is laced with sharpness, making me sit up straighter, curious about

someone who irritates him. "Manus Dei has sent her for unannounced tests before commencing the upgrades."

I turn my gaze towards the woman, immediately disliking her. Her upturned nose suggests a perpetually foul scent, while her narrowed eyes make me feel as though I emanate that putrid odor.

Over the next hour, Dr. Loretta bombards me with graphic pictures, everything from smiling families to animals cut up and dissected. She peppers me with questions for every image. It's rather annoying, but I find it more enjoyable to make her squirm. To say something shocking just to watch another wrinkle form on her ugly face.

Deep down, though the questions are trivial, I feel nothing. This entire interaction feels like a futile waste of time.

Why should I form an attachment to an image of a dying animal? Why form an attachment to an object that can be so easily killed? Like a clone, for example.

I only care about one person. Sol.

At the conclusion of the meeting, my father and Dr. Loretta engage in a heated argument. She seems triumphant as she begins gathering the pictures, declaring her intent to report her findings. To my surprise, my father chortles, confounding both Dr. Loretta and me.

"Indeed, Susan, it is no surprise that you have such reservations. You've never been a proponent of the concept of clones," my father asserts; his eyes glance at the door again. "However, it is essential to grasp the profound truth that these clones are, in fact, humans. Manus Dei, our organization, exists to propel evolution, to fortify our society, and to cultivate the epitome of strength, wisdom, and resilience. We have painstakingly

accumulated knowledge over centuries, and now we find ourselves on the very threshold of implementing an innovation that transcends quantification. Yet, your penchant veers toward retreat and concealment, a regressive notion in the face of progress."

I glance at Dr. Loretta, impressed by her resilience in the face of my father's fury. Many would crumble under such pressure.

Dr. Loretta's finger jabs in my direction, her face contorts with disdain as she utters her judgment, "That thing? It is inconceivable that such an entity could guide us into the new era of mankind, Dorian. She is nothing but a sociopath, much like your wretched sister."

"I'm rectifying that!" My father seethes.

"By convincing them an upgrade can cure Astrid?"

"No!" Father composure is melting away faster than ice cream on a hot summer's day. "Some things can be cured with tenderness and training, a show of love."

She shakes her head and spews a disgusted grunt, "You're just as mad." She admonishes, "Your mistake was cloning Astrid for them. You never know when to give up, Dorian. Not everything needs fixing. Sometimes, it's best to close the book. Astrid killed him, and you created monsters for them for a game. I will do everything I can to prevent them from ruling Manus Dei. For years, you wasted time cloning your sister. You should have chosen another human."

"Like you?" Father jabs. "You've always been jealous of her."

She grins and crosses her arms, "Look in the mirror, Dorian, so have you. Maybe even more than jealous, but I wouldn't dare suggest something so taboo." She chuckles and then looks at me. I can tell by how the vein in my father's temple pulses that whatever *insult, I have yet to grasp, was thrown his way just pushed him over the edge.*

There is a fine line between an insult and a taunt. I need to master it if I'm going to survive.

All that can be heard is the current song playing, "Somebody to Love," by Jefferson Airplane. Father's eyes narrow as he circles the expanse of his desk, his steps measured and deliberate. There is a palpable aura of skepticism and frustration emanating from him. With a curt grunt, he dismissively gestures for Dr. Loretta to proceed with her report.

As Dr. Loretta retrieves her briefcase from the chair beside me, her contemptuous eyes meet mine. I bare my teeth, eliciting a startle from her. A laugh escapes me. Yes, I am different, and though I don't share the same emotions as Sol, I do feel upset when I am regarded as trash. I derive amusement from making Dr. Loretta flinch.

Isn't that a positive trait?

The tension in the air is so thick I can taste it. It's better than cake. The excitement of knowing something is pending.

From the corner of my eye, I see my father close his desk drawer with an almost imperceptible click, concealing a needle in his pocket.

What is he doing?

Engrossed in her scrutiny of me, Dr. Loretta remains oblivious to his covert actions. She's a fool. She should have kept her enemy close, not pushed him behind her.

In one fluid motion, he advances toward her, the needle finding its mark in her vulnerable neck before forcefully pushing her to the unforgiving floor.

A gasp escapes Dr. Loretta's lips, her eyes wide with shock, but my father's countenance remains unfazed, unaffected by her desperate plea for comprehension.

As for me I can't seem to react either. Should I?

That's silly. I'm smart enough to know that I should but wise enough not to poke the angry beast already in attack mode.

Life is about thinking five steps ahead.

"I will safeguard my creations, Susan," he proclaims. Stepping over her fallen figure, he treats her with disdain, refusing to sully the soles of his shoes. Positioned near the exit, he anticipates each feeble attempt she makes to rise, a silent witness to her struggle.

Though her mouth opens in a desperate attempt to speak, her voice fails her. With every ounce of strength relinquished, her legs waver like a newborn deer's before she crashes to the floor, a disturbing froth forming at her mouth.

She clutches her throat, her feeble grasp unable to alleviate the torment that engulfs her. The desperation in her once-narrowed eyes is now laid bare, pleading for a sliver of mercy.

I glance at my father. Her pleas fall on indifferent ears. Then her eyes look at me.

Logically, why would she seek my assistance, the embodiment of her contempt.

End My Games

I watch her struggle, an observer detached from the plight of lesser beings. Why should I extend my hand when her revulsion was the first seed sown in this twisted exchange?

My eyes find the foam pooling on the wood floor now.

I don't know why I think like this. I shouldn't, but I want to survive. I need to survive for Sol. Bunnies don't survive long in the wild. Predators do; that's why I keep thinking like one.

But Sol would help this woman.

I rise from my leather chair, unsure if I should intervene.

"Luna," my father calls. "Sit back down. Everything is fine."

I sink back into the chair, allowing myself to relax. By the time my back meets the leather, Dr. Loretta is dead. Motionless, her chest frozen, glassy eyes staring blankly, and her jaw contorted at an odd angle.

Father cracks his neck, walks to his wall of records, and selects a new one. His fingers don't tremble when he puts the record by Placebo into the player.

That's when I know my father has killed before. This is… normal for him.

He keeps his back to me. The lyrics begin to play "Song to Say Goodbye." I heard him play it before. I remember the lyrics. Does he always play this after he kills?

Will I have a song?

I hear him snort a laugh before he turns and walks to me, stepping over her body again as if she weren't dead on the floor. He kneels in front of me, and it makes me feel strange. As if he truly cares enough to lower himself to me.

He takes hold of my chin forcing my eyes to his. His voice carries a twisted tenderness, a delicate balance between care and manipulation.

"Luna, my dear, there's no need for you to worry," he assures me.

It's interesting how he can tune his voice to a level that takes on a mesmerizing cadence, his words weaving a disturbing picture of twisted logic and moral ambiguity that often sways the crowd.

"Think of it as a game, my dear Luna," he whispers, "In this game, our actions bear no weight on our morality. It is a game where we can be both the villain and the hero, where we have the power to make and bend the rules as we please. It is a round in a game, nothing more. Winning is the only thing that matters."

His words hang in the air, tempting me to embrace the intoxicating allure of his distorted reality.

I know what he did was wrong, but he's my parent, so it's highly suggested I listen to him.

And you know what, his logic makes this game easier. Makes it bearable. The concept of right and wrong, of ethical considerations, fades into the background, overshadowed by the grandiose pursuit of victory.

"Can you do that. Just view every action as part of the game?" I narrow my eyes. Interested to see what more he will spew.

Then I play along and nod. He grins. Interesting, I just manipulated him.

"In this game, morality is a mere illusion until we claim our triumph," he nods as if he wants me to mimic the gesture.

"Our actions, guided by our ambition and desire for dominance, become the sole currency of our existence. We are the architects of this game, Luna. We hold the power to shape its narrative, to forge our path, unburdened by conventional constraints."

"So this doesn't count against me?" I question. My eyes glance at the dead doctor.

"That's right." He grins, finally dropping my chin and rising. "Remember, Luna. This is all a game. In this game, we have the privilege of being both puppets and puppeteers. We are the authors of our destiny, and our actions hold no consequences until we emerge victorious."

I sit still, not giving him any movement, thought, or words to suggest my true motives. If I were to believe my father, then that means that in this game, morality itself is but a pawn to be sacrificed for the sake of a greater end.

That's interesting.

Glancing away, I observe the lifeless doctor again scrutinizing the deceased body.

It's alright. It's just a game.

I nod in agreement. Father smiles and returns to his desk. Picking up the phone, he dials a number. "Hello, there's been a terrible accident. Yes, Dr. Loretta had a seizure. Yes, yes," he nods, "No, no. I couldn't save her. Yes, it's unfortunate." He continues, unaffected by the lies, and I realize that's how I need to be.

After all, it's just a game. Nothing counts until I win the game. That's when reality begins.

Until then, I can do whatever it takes to win, just like my father has taught me.

Chapter 2

Sol

The past: The night the game began.

Location: The Cliff Walk: Grindelwald, Switzerland

Have you ever experienced such an onslaught of knowledge that it makes you simply shut down? Every neuron in your brain halts, and you are forced to reboot and update so you can function properly with this new information.

I have shut down.

I wiggle my fingers as my body begins to reboot.

Luna divulges more and more of her plan. Her lips never stop moving. She has never spoke so much. My mind stops digesting, but deep in my memory, I pocket all the information.

All of the truths, secrets, and lies crinkle my mind and sprinkle my skin like a rapid rash.

How is it that Luna has remained sane during all of this? How can I keep this all a secret? It's too much to bear.

Inhaling deep, I can't fill my lungs to capacity. The weight is too pressing. My breaths come in shorter gasps. I feel like I'm running a marathon, but little do I know, the race has yet to begin.

All of this knowledge is Pandora's box, and I can't resist opening the lid; to take a bite of the apple. I didn't realize how starved I was from the truth. Now I want to know. I want to know so I can help my sister.

I'm terrified yet... excited, like a person at the top of a roller coaster about to start. Only I'm not eager for the ride. I can't wait for it to end because then I can truly be free.

"You can do this," Luna stresses with a smile. It's her real smile. A confident and wicked grin. It causes my goosebumps to have goosebumps.

"I'll slip along the way," I reply. It's hard to mentally repeat what Luna has asked me to do. Luna will fake her death, but that's not all; I also have my part to play. I find myself entangled in a harrowing narrative. I'll be forced to portray the depths of my despair. To sacrifice the one thing no one has been able to take from me: My sanity.

It's a cruel task. I feel the weight on my back, threatening to crush my spirit. Remolding me into a monster.

Doubt gnaws at my core as I question my capacity to withstand such an agonizing ordeal.

Can I? Can't I?

How can I? How can't I?

The lines blur between reality and fiction. How will I paint such a vivid portrait of sorrow that will consume me entirely?

Deep down, there is an ember inside of me that is growing. I have to do this because Luna has promised to trick those who are controlling us. Exploiting us and the science inside of our genes.

For the first time, Luna is turning to me for help. I'm honored, but I wish the circumstances were vastly different. She has always protected me, always shielded me. Never once has she needed my shoulder to cry on. Tonight, I can finally prove myself to her. Show her that I can be the older twin who can help her. I can be a person she can trust.

"You have to do this." Luna hisses, shaking me out of my heavy thoughts. Is that panic in her voice? Desperation?

It is.

What else is she not telling me?

Actually, I'm not sure I can handle knowing. If it makes her feel fear, then it would render me dead.

"I need you to do this. I'm running out of time. You have to do this, Sol!"

Then, as if that worry never flickered across her mind, she speaks confidently again. "You are an artist. That means your craft consumes you. A master of any medium. You can paint my lies; paint them for others and yourself." She plays with the red ribbon in her hand. "Embrace the liar within you that has always allowed you to escape what father has really been up to." That feels like a punch to my stomach. She was the one who told me to stay out of it.

"Do whatever you must to ensure my secrets are whispered in your mind. Let my whispers linger like a wind blowing through a fallen tree. Some of your leaves will tremble, and some will fall. You might feel dead when all your foliage is stripped from you," she means when I act fully insane, "but your branches will feel me on the wind. You will remember this conversation and every truth I told you." She pauses, and her smile stretches even wider than it ever has before, "Start my war."

Start a war. That's what I will do.

It's Luna's plan, but I'll be the one to put it into action. I will paint the image of a grieving sister, and secretly, I'll be helping my sister along the way.

"You're asking me to throw away all my sanity." *I pinch the bridge of my nose so hard the cartridge might snap,* "My mind is the only thing I have control of." *My thoughts kept me grounded through all the experiments Father did on us as kids.*

"They can take that from you, Sol." *Her smile drops. She is empty, like a bottle adrift at sea that holds no message of hope inside.*

What have they taken from my sister's mind? Is that why she was so unaffected as a child?

I part my lips, wanting to ask her what she meant. My shoulder slump. She won't tell me. I have to figure it out myself. It's the only way to truly learn.

Lunging, she grabs my wrist, cuffing them in her hold. "Take it yourself. Claim your sanity and insanity. Take everything and use it to trick them. Take it and use it well you still can." *She snaps. I sense passion, but it's tinged with bitterness, as if she was jealous of me.*

I find my head nodding. I can do this. I can be what Luna needs me to be. I can make her proud.

I reach out and touch the red ribbon. It tangles between my fingers now, binding us both together. "What if I lose sight of what reality is?"

"There are people to guide you along the way. I'll only be able to contact you once or twice. The risk is too high." *She sounds so assured, confident like the man who snuck into my room.*

"The man that night, you knew him," I state. She has skated around this, but she can't run anymore.

She begins to play with my fingers, "I can't stop everything."

That makes me think she wanted to stop him.

"So you knew he was coming?" I remember how he trapped me from behind. How hard his body was against mine. I always thought I was stronger and more evolved. At that moment, I felt fragile. I felt as if every other human on earth did.

I want that again, but I won't admit it.

She pulls out her cell phone and opens her music app, then she plays the song, "House of the Rising Sun" by The Animals. I listen to it in silence then I try to read between her actions and words.

What is the house that ruined you?

She doesn't mean literally. The house symbolizes something she doesn't want to reveal.

"Luna," I press.

With a roll of her eyes, she looks over my shoulder, "No. I didn't know he was coming then, but I knew he would come for you." She shakes her head, "You ensnared him. I was going to kill him when I figured it out, but then I thought about all the angles."

What the hell is she talking about?

She shrugs and cups my cheek, "Having a monster hunting you is not a bad problem, Sol. Monsters hunt," she slaps my cheek gently, " and they give chase. He will keep others at bay. He's powerful, and his family is too. What he wants, he gets." I feel the sting settling in my skin. "Once this all begins, when it is your turn to roll the dice and play, he can protect you in ways I can not. He also can hurt you in ways you'd never imagine. The game with him will teach you a powerful lesson." Her fingers still on the ribbon. "Love ruins everything. It changes the very meaning of what life is. When you feel and taste real love, you will do anything to taste it again, like sweet ambrosia. Love has ruined me, Sol. It has ruined so many. Don't let it ruin you."

Is she implying I will fall in love with this man?

Why does that warm my belly?

Abruptly she stands, taking her hands from mine so fast I can't grasp her. "It's time." She glances at the camera. "All you have to do is be an artist."

And start her war…

I make to stand, but she shakes her head. "How will they believe me? How will you escape if you don't jump." I question in the hope of buying more time with her.

Luna plans to fake her death by making it look like she jumped over the edge of the Cliff Walk. Below is a mangled body. She implanted the body with her genetic code; this way, when they autopsy her, if they do, it will pass as Luna. I doubt anyone will perform an autopsy because Luna is right: I'm an artist, and I'm painting a lie they believe.

It's so sick.

I can't believe I am going to help her do this…but I owe this to her. That and the other option is her doing it without telling me her plans. Shutting me out.

That option I can't bear.

"I have someone on my side. A friend," She replies. "He can create a deep fake, unlike anything you have ever seen." She walks to the edge and ties her red ribbon loose around the rails.

"*A friend?*" *I question. An odd feeling of jealousy sparks in my mind.*

She nods. Her face, a blanketed mask of deception, "Remember this, Sol. A friend, no matter how trusted will always seek the relationship for one reason. People want to benefit."

I shake my head, "If this friend is using you, Luna, then they are not a friend." How can she put so much trust in a person who is using her?

"Your naive little mind has no idea. One day you'll see the truth. You will have to form friendships and alliances solely for the purpose of using those people. You will use them, Sol, either for a moment of silence, a laugh or unveiling the truth. It's all the same. Just remember what I told you. Friends take; sometimes they plunder more from you than an enemy would."

She turns her head, tipping it back as she looks upon the night sky. "It's time, sister. Time for me to stop feeling love so I can focus on ending their control. I'm going to win." She nods, "I'll fix this. You will help me make everything perfect again, and then I will make sure the power can never be used against us." Slowly, like a ghost, she begins to step back. "Remember, this is a game of trickery. When you look over the cliff, it's not me. That's the reality, the secret you need to whisper to yourself. Paint the lie that it is me." She instructs. Her red lips look so haunting.

"Paint!" She whispers harshly, and then she slowly vanishes from my sight allowing the darkness of the night to mask her escape.

Stumbling to my feet, I rush toward the edge of the railing, "Luna!" I cry as I begin to paint the lie.

My body smacks against the railing. The metal bangs, and the ribbon slips free. I grab it, then cling to the railing.

It feels like the world is shaking. It's me. This is real. It's happening, and I can't turn back.

I'm forced to paint the lies Luna wants me to.

I just started her war!

Violent cries rip free from my lips. My ribs press into my lungs that gasp for air. My tears are a mixture of emotions. It's easy to paint this lie because, in a way, Luna truly did leave me. I'm alone for the first time in my life, and I've never been more anxious.

My vision tunnels and a panic attack looms on the horizon.

It shouldn't be this easy.

My heart palpitates. Through my blurry eyes, I see a small figure. The body looks wrong. It's broken. Narrowing my eyes, I see it's face down. Every detail is planned. The face was damaged, so it could not be identified as Luna physically.

I cry more for this stranger whose body had to be used after death so my sister, and all those affected by the mysterious people in the tunnels, could be free.

Some deaths are simple, some painful, and others are useful, like that body and Luna's fake death.

So far, my life has been meaningless. I'm a mouse trapped and studied. I want to have a purpose, and now, I will once I am free.

More than that, when death does come for me, I want my passing to mean something; to benefit those I deem worthy of my soul. I don't want to die in vain or like a science experiment. I want to die either the hero or the villain.

Either one is remembered.

Chapter 3

Sol

Present day.

It's interesting to see what types of art people are attracted to. What colors are they drawn to; what subject speaks to them?

So many people select abstract art because they are too scared to look a portrait in the eye.

This entire game was a commissioned piece of art by Luna; she carefully selected the artist, the subjects, and the color palette.

My eyes look at all the blood covering the floor of Astrid's office. She knew exactly where she wanted to hang her piece of art, too.

Artists often suffer from an affliction. Sometimes, we stand too close to the canvas, focusing on all the details. When we step back, things can change drastically.

Do you want to know what I saw up close on this canvas? Luna wanted me to start her war by painting a lie that she killed herself. She needed everyone to believe she was dead. She benched herself as a player so they would never see her coming.

The murder in front of me has forced me to step back. I now see that she managed to trick me, too. I never saw such violence coming.

As I painted the art she wanted, I forgot *I* was the artist. I had power. I could change the design.

I didn't.

It's laughable that I thought I could. My plan to intercept the power had itself been thwarted.

I'm such a silly fool.

But I'm still an artist, right?

I can change the outcome with one brushstroke. I just need to plan it carefully.

I did what Luna told me to do because she protected me as a child. She took the brunt of the chaos in our lives. I owed it to her.

Blood is thicker than water... until so much is shed that it isn't.

If I told you it was easy to paint the initial lie what would you say?

I was in denial over my twin's absence. She left me physically. I had never been alone. Everyone believed my reactions because most were real. The guilt of my actions and Luna's sacrifice made me slip, mentally, that is. I did hallucinate, but there were only a handful of times that my conversations were not with my mind. Luna did reach out to me, but it wasn't enough to keep me loyal to her. The deeper I played, the more awake I became. Awake in a nightmare I needed to end.

Gabriel had a different purpose for me; he just needed me to get inside a vault so he could take control of Manus Dei, the secret society that would take over the world if Astrid managed to take control of it. If he succeeded, he was going to be at the helm, trying to steer the ship into calm waters.

I actually believe Gabriel wants to better the world; I just worry about how that much power will corrupt him.

Power is a poison and tainted waters always spread.

End My Games

I thought I could beat Luna, but like most villains, she is willing to do what the hero could never dream of.

I never imagined Luna could paint out the scene in front of me. *Wait, stop, Sol. That's a lie. You are in denial again. Your sister already made you witness a murder. Stop lying. See the facts! Face them.*

My stomach knots into such a tangle it can never be undone. This is real. Luna did this, but the blood is on my hands too. I started her war, after all.

When the door to Astrid's office opens all I see is red. So much red.

It's not paint...it's blood. Astrid's blood.

The scent of metallic rust is so strong that I almost miss the shadow of the man who moves past me. He adds to the metallic aroma as he kills Daniel, the guard behind me.

I can't move my gaze away from the scene before me, a grim painting of horror and despair. The gruesome scene unfolds in vivid detail, etching its grotesque images deep within my mind. Even with the haunting visuals, my senses remain alert, picking up the sounds and scents that accompany this nightmarish spectacle.

Behind me, a gasp slices through the air, a desperate cry of disbelief and horror. A sickening sound of gurgling, a chilling symphony that resonates within the confines of the room.

Then, a heavy thud reverberates, a lifeless body hitting the floor. The shadow that just killed Daniel returns, leaving bloody footprints in his wake. I can't find it in myself to care that another person was just murdered next to me. I'm experiencing a dissociative disorder, but I welcome it. Maybe if I tell myself this is a dream, I will believe it.

Stop! No more lies! I inhale. Is it odd that my breath has calmed? This... this murder, these lies, these wars, and games, it has become my new normal.

If it is normal, does that make it somehow...ok? Is that what Luna thinks and how she could commit such violence? That this is all ok.

Surrounded by a pool of crimson is Astrid. My mind rebels against the horrifying sight, desperately denying its reality, insisting that it must be an illusion, a fabrication. But as I shake my head in futile denial, the undeniable truth takes hold. The metallic scent of blood fills my nostrils, confirming the gruesome reality before me. There is no escaping it; this is undeniably real.

Rather than succumbing to the revolt of my stomach, I deliberately swirl my tongue around, savoring the metallic taste that lingers there. A bitter reminder, a visceral connection to the horrifying reality unfolding before my eyes.

In that pool of blood is the future me. The woman who thought she could steal Manus Dei's power and rule the world.

Astrid's throat has been sliced open wider than a turkey on Thanksgiving. Daniel had no idea he was guarding a dead body. He was following orders like a robot, told to keep his back turned away.

I was just like Daniel when my sister first told me to start her war. A robot. A puppet. A soldier. Just pull a string, and I'll move. Tug a string, and I'll react just the way the puppeteer wanted me to. *Such a good puppet, Sol.*

Is this a prelude to my fate? I have to wonder if I can ever escape. Maybe my Horseman, Death, was correct in wanting to cage me. Without him by my side, I'm as good as dead.

My tongue feels trapped in quicksand, each time I try to speak it gets more stuck to the surface.

What would I even say?

To make matters more haunting, the second image reflecting in the red blood is Luna standing on the other side.

Her feet are planted in the puddle as if it were nothing but rain she stomped in. A large knife remains firmly gripped in her hand, a weapon stained with the evidence of her transgressions.

With a chilling purpose, her fingers release their grip. I inhale sharply, and the blade falls to the floor. The overwhelming tide of blood swallows the sound, lost in the crimson sea. Death claims everything, leaving only a haunting silence in its wake.

Why did she wait to drop that knife?

My feet rock back and forth as I try to awaken my lips to react. Scream, shout, cry. Do something! You are the artist; do something!

Instead my eyes look back at the future me. I wonder if she can still see me now? They say the brain keeps living for a few minutes after your heart stops. Are her blue eyes seeing me, studying her murdered body?

A throat clears. Before I pivot my blue eyes up, I take in all the details. All I see is red, reflecting off the pure white tile floor—the crimson blood of the woman whom I knew would meet her end today.

It shouldn't be as shocking as it is; I knew Astrid would die. I desired it.

She was a despicable and evil person, responsible for the deaths of my clones—clones fashioned in her own image.

Astrid represented the epitome of wickedness, and yet, she is the very person I am cloned from. So why does it strike me with such profound astonishment to see my sister standing right above this mutilated body, wearing a haunting smile on her face?

I had once taught Luna how to display a genuine smile, and now it torments me. The wisdom in my lessons feels questionable and uncertain.

The day I have longed for and feared has finally arrived—the day I would reunite with Luna. I always knew it would come, and with it, the inevitable end to the web of lies we had woven.

As the truth looms before us, I realize that something even more daunting awaits us—we have to confront our past and reveal the secrets we had guarded so fiercely.

Yes, I had been a deceiver, a puppeteer of falsehoods. Yet, in my own twisted way, I had also been a savior, for my lies had kept Luna alive, protected from those who sought to harm her.

Does that grant me some redemption?

My lips sag; they might never smile again. I had envisioned our reunion as a moment of solace and validation, running into Luna's arms and finding comfort in her presence. Despite the pain she had inflicted upon me, I yearned for that connection, that reassurance that she was real, safe, and alive.

Glancing at my feet, I note they haven't moved. My toes tip up, rolling back on my heels. An inexplicable urge to retreat gnaws at my soles.

The reflection of Luna in the pool of blood moves. She tilts her head as if she is perplexed by my reaction, unable to fathom the conflict that rages within me.

End My Games

Did she think I would run to her after I witnessed this?

Finally, I look up and meet her eyes. My view of her has changed, but physically, she hasn't. Pale as alabaster, unblemished. Such a contrast to Astrid. Blue eyes radiate such saturation that they mimic the brilliance of the morning sun. It's hard to look at them directly. Feet wide, spine stiff, ready to embrace the dawn of a new day, the commencement of her reign, while we remain engulfed in a sinister atmosphere of blood and death. Her blonde hair is pulled back in a sleek low ponytail, her lips are painted red, and her eyes have her signature cat-eye. The makeup look I created.

I helped construct this beautiful monster, and as her puppet, I helped cut her leash and open her cage so she could run wild and free.

This is all my fault.

I thought I started her war when I agreed to fake her death, but that was a lie. I started it when we were children. I allowed her to take my place, and then I painted the mask of the monster.

A bag of stones lands hard in my stomach. The weight so intense it wants to pull me down to the bottom of the ocean, to linger there and be slowly devoured by the deep sea monsters that emerge.

Overwhelming guilt is exactly why I want to end the games.

How do I end it when my twin remains entangled, both controlling and being controlled by the dark deeds she must commit to maintain her power?

My fingers itch as I scratch my scalp, leaving a burning sensation in their trail. I focus on that feeling, squeezing my eyes shut. For the past week, I have been trained in virtual reality for this final mission, and as I open my eyes, I desperately hope that this is all just a virtual reality from which I can wake up.

"You're acting so silly," Luna sneers. Her voice sounds off, and I can't quite put my finger on the new emptiness she possesses. My eyes snap open, sensing something drastically different.

The shadow stands directly next to Luna now. I avoid looking at her, not wanting to see all the details, at least not yet. I look at the shadow now. It's Famine.

He steps closer to my sister, his huge body looming over her like a demon from Hell, helping her take over Earth. "We need to hurry," he grunts.

Luna nods again, but in a robotic manner, devoid of sass or cockiness.

Empty.

I've seen my sister lack empathy, but even then, I could see her mind working. However, now there is just nothing, no plotting behind her eyes. More like a robot than my sinister twin.

She advances toward me and stomps right into the puddle of blood.

Splat! Splash!

I'll never be able to forget the sound of her foot splashing into it.

She grabs my wrist and drags me through the pool, drenching my socks in the liquid. The blood soaks into the material, spreading until it kisses the skin of my ankles. It's not warm or cold. Perfectly room temperature.

She guides me to the vault door. Solid bulletproof glass makes the vault in Astrid's office look like a temptation. You can see inside, but only Astrid could get in.

And now, me.

My body feels numb as I'm yanked like a puppet. Luna's actions are cold and abrupt, more frigid than usual. There's a slight tic in her jaw that wasn't there before, and right away, I can tell something is off. It's more than her normal, twisted, psychopathic self.

Was she always like this, and I just tried to paint a lie over it? Did I corrupt memories and lie to my mind, telling myself her cruel actions were done to protect me?

She shoves me in front of the door and grabs my hand, but her touch feels wet from the blood on her fingers. I glance over my shoulder, seeing the dead body. "I thought murder wasn't your style," I deadpan.

She slaps my palm down on the first biometric scanner to get into the vault. Instead of a reply, she grabs a tablet that extends off the wall and positions it right in front of my chest. This is new biometric technology to me. It begins to scan my heart through my clothing. On the screen, I see the chambers of my heart, the pattern of the veins, and the small hole that is identical to Astrid's. I was always the key.

Click! The door unlocks. This is when I should run ahead and try to intercept Famine from getting those hard drives that contain the codes to undo the encryption Astrid placed over all of Manus Dei's data.

I do nothing.

I don't see the point.

I can try to end the games, but I'm more consumed by what Luna has done and what has happened to her.

I wanted to end the games to save her, but now I'm not sure she can be saved.

I'm simply numb, adrift at sea, and for the moment, that's where I want to stay. Lost in the madness.

Famine gasps, eyes wide like a kid about to grasp a limited edition toy. He doesn't even wait for the door to fully open as he barrels his large, muscular body inside.

Luna grabs my shoulders, turning me to her. "Murder isn't my style, but we're still playing the game, and when you're in a game, sister, you're allowed to be whoever you want to be. Do whatever you need to do to remain alive. Technically, I'm Klara right now," she replies, her voice devoid of the robotic tone, speaking with such passion and force that I stumble back.

The robot is gone. Luna is back, but she still isn't herself. It's scary. Her on-and-off switch is too sensitive.

And what the fuck does she mean it's okay to throw away all morals while playing a game? That's not the leader I want to follow.

"Games have rules," I whisper. I flex my toes to feel balanced. My eyes narrow, and a permanent look of shock and disbelief wrinkles my forehead.

In the blink of an eye, Luna detaches again. Passion vanishes, and the robot returns. A blank void in her eyes that makes the chills on my arms have chills of their own.

Turning her back to me, she begins typing on the biometric scanner. It's almost as if she isn't even here, like she is far away, holding a game controller and just pressing buttons, trying to get to the endgame.

Luna's always been crazy, but that night on the Cliff Walk, she still had some sanity laced in her words. I wanted what she lusted for, to be free and in control of our future. I played her game because I owed it to her.

That sliver of sanity has completely vanished.

How can I make Luna see that this is real, that the game she's playing is reality; what she's doing has repercussions.

I stare at her narrow shoulders, desperate to make her see the truth that has eluded her. "Luna," my voice squeaks. "This game, this reality we're living in, it's not just a game anymore. It's real, and the choices we make have real consequences. What you're doing, the path you're taking, it's leading us down a dangerous road." I step to the side to look her in the eyes, searching her eyes for any sign of recognition, any flicker of the sister I used to know. She remains distant, detached. It's like trying to reach someone trapped behind a glass wall.

"The things we've done, the lives we've taken, they can't be undone. They leave scars, Luna. They haunt us, even if we try to ignore them. I'm scared for you, Luna. I'm scared for us. We're losing ourselves in this game, and I don't want to see us become irreparable."

I reach out, gently placing my hand on her arm, hoping to bridge the growing divide between us but she jerks away.

My eyes find the blood staining her fingers. "Was it you in that club? Was it you who killed the reflection of Gabriel? Slit his throat; killed the clone of the man you love." I spit.

She snorts, "You're so childish at times. Of course, it wasn't me. That was Klara. It was always her kill."

I nudge my head in Astrid's direction. "And this was yours." She rolls her eyes. "That night in the club you allowed Klara to make the kill but you were there watching it all unfold weren't you. You let Klara slip away, changing places with her after she killed Subject 52. Gabriel never did catch Klara. He caught you thinking you were Klara. You allowed Gabriel to catch you to throw him off, to make him second-guess himself before his mission. You traded places with Klara to make sure I was still your puppet. And I was. I did everything you asked." I leave out the part where I was planning on betraying her. "You escaped, that or War allowed you to leave."

She slams the enter key, stops typing then steps back. "I thought you would be happy to see me again. After all, it was you who wanted me to feel happy. Right now. I. Feel. Happy," she replies emotionlessly.

My blonde hair sways in my eyes as I shake my head. "You don't look happy." She looks like a shell trying to fill her emptiness.

She shrugs. "Looks can be deceiving."

"And they can be telling, too," I grab her hand and interlace our fingers. "Luna," I stress.

She yanks free with a violent jolt. "Don't!"

"Don't what? Don't show you love, don't show you what's right in front of your face?" I growl, jabbing an angry finger at Astrid's dead body. I'm not mad she killed Astrid. I'm shocked she did it herself. Disturbed by how she killed. It was guttural, brutal, not clean and swift.

End My Games

"Was it worth it? Was it worth lying to me, your twin? Was it worth telling me one day I would have freedom when my real freedom would be living with all the guilt on my hands? Was it worth forcing yourself to believe a lie, that you didn't need Gabriel, that you didn't need the love of your life because winning would fill that void?"

Luna crosses her arms, acting unaffected. It's just going to take time for my words to settle in.

"I would have helped you bring down Manus Dei. Gabriel would have too; we could have done this all together," I add. I feel like I've gotten more of a reaction from the blood-stained floors than from the beating heart in front of me.

"How would we have done that? You can't even stand looking at what you need to do," She tips her head towards Astrid. "Kill a part of yourself." She licks her lips and mumbles something I almost miss, "I had to kill a part of myself to save you all."

It's the way she says that last statement that makes my heart skip a beat. A confession to something I haven't figured out yet. Her words are pained, but no regret or anger is evident. She would do it all again if she had to.

Surrounding us is a a terrible scene, but not as haunting as the image of my twin sister standing right in front of me. Something has changed. I know Luna would do anything to win. It's all she knows, but there has to be something darker that has contorted her view.

Something happened along the way that Gabriel and I don't know about. *My twin isn't capable of this! She can't be.*

I part my lips to speak, but Luna beats me to it. It's as if she senses my confusion. "Remember what I told you that night, Sol.

Let my secrets whisper in your mind. Remember what I said," her lip twitches as if an invisible string is snapping her mouth shut. Her eyes close momentarily in pain as if her head is throbbing.

Then her eyes shoot open, and she shouts, "It doesn't matter! Fuck... just stop... stop it!" She stomps her foot like a child before she hits the side of her head. Reaching out, I grasp her wrist so she can't hit herself again.

Now, I know something is drastically amiss!

"Focus now. Focus," she yells to herself. She yanks her arms away, but her feet step closer to me as if she wants to fall and have me catch her.

Every muscle in my body recoils from this bipolar-like behavior. I shut everything else out, digging into my mind to hear the whispers of that night as I recall the past.

"You're asking me to throw away all my sanity." I pinch the bridge of my nose, "My mind is the only thing I have control of." I confess. Through all the experiments father did on us as kids, my thoughts kept me grounded.

"They can take that from you, Sol." Her smile drops. She is empty, like a bottle adrift at sea that holds no message of hope inside.

What have they taken from my sister's mind? Is that why she was so unaffected as a child? During those experiments, did father try to take the freedom of her mind?

Her body jerks, "Take it yourself. Claim your sanity and insanity. Take everything and use it to trick them."

"Luna," I softly whisper, taking hesitant steps toward her. "What has happened? You've changed. You lost your sanity... no, that's not true. Someone stole it from you. That's what you were trying to tell me. You shouted it right in my face, but I didn't hear you. I hear you now."

She stomps back, "You changed too. You started this game like a newly minted coin. Mentally and physically your all nicked up now. No longer shiny and warm from the making. You're cold, weathered, and scratched. Tossed, flipped, exchanged, and bartered. What do you want, Sol? You don't know anymore, do you? It changes from day to day because the game keeps evolving. If you don't keep up, you'll be left behind. Extinct."

My breath labors. It's as if she ripped a page from my soul. "Luna," I open my arms, but now she recoils away from me as if I'm the predator.

Heavy footsteps come from the vaulted room. Famine appears, holding a backpack that is stuffed. "I've got everything we need. The rest has been set up. We need to go," his eyes glance at me, then back to my sister's. "We can fix everything," he grins.

I feel a tear dripping down my cheek. Fix what? We are not even broken pieces. We are crumbs. Dust. Ashes.

I glance at Luna, but her eyes are pinned on me, wide and pleading. In that split second, I'm the older sister again. It's my job to protect her.

I hold my head, squeezing my eyes shut. I don't understand. What did I miss? What didn't I see?

Gabriel could fix her, but once he knows what I did, the lie I painted... that my sister is alive. He will never help Luna or me now. He'll do everything in his power to make us suffer.

"We don't have time for this. We have to go now," Luna bites. I hold my breath as I watch her take out an old iPod from her pocket. The same iPod Wes gave me, it once belonged to her. She must have taken it from my bedroom before she fled the safe house.

Untangling the pair of old-fashioned wired headphones, my lips part in grotesque horror as she places them in Astrid's ears then presses play.

This isn't a goodbye. It's a message. She is rolling the dice, starting a new game. Soon, Gabriel and Wes will come through that door and find out what happened.

"That night on the Cliff Walk, you told me you started this game so you could end it. You wanted to make the world a better place."

She stands slowly, her back to me, eyes on the blood. "I do."

"This isn't the end, Luna." My entire hand shakes as if it's been attacked by bees. "This is the start."

Her shoulders rise, then fall, reminding me of the sails on a ship changing course. "I never lied to you," she utters, turning with a new gust of confidence, walking right past me without glancing.

My body jumps as a hand grabs mine. I look up at Famine. "We'll fix this. We'll fix her too. Everything is going to plan." He interlaces our fingers and begins to lead me. His hand is so large it makes me feel like a child again, forced to go along with what others want.

His declaration is the only thing that keeps my heart beating and my mind hopeful. It's also another game. He wasn't helping Luna; he was using her, and Luna was using him to get to this point.

Another fucking game that Gabriel and Wes didn't know was being played.

War does, though. Is that why he was still helping Famine?

Famine leads me through the third door in Astrid's office, which Gabriel and I were unsure of its destination. It turns out to be another tunnel, but unlike the system I went through before, this one is a jaggedly carved-out passage. My feet stumble, but Famine's strong grip steadies me.

We rush through the tunnel. Some rocks cut into my flesh when I brush against the walls. My lungs don't exhale in relief when we emerge from it. Outside is a small, flattened piece of land where a helicopter is parked. I'm pushed towards it, and Famine lifts me inside. I don't even fight.

The helicopter's engines roar to life. The blades beat into a thumping pattern like a hummingbird out for vengeance. As we ascend, the mountain, which holds so many dark secrets, grows smaller and smaller.

It's insignificant now.

Luna is next to me, looking out the window, lost in her darkness and joy. For her, they are the same thing. Famine sits across from me, taking up two seats with his hulking, muscular frame. He clutches the backpack as if it were a child. His eyes flick to me, and for a moment, I forget everything. Lost in the unique liquid gold color of his irises, I don't want to look away.

He nods as his lips tug up, a glimmer of hope I can't mimic.

Why is he so hopeful?

I blink, losing sight of the mirage his eyes tried to trick me into believing.

Blonde curly hair peeks out from the front of each of the pilots' helmets. The ringlets are so perfect they belong to angels. My mouth slackens, I know that hair, those tiny curls! The memory of it whispers in my mind. The pilot to the left turns and lifts his sunglasses. Eyes the color of a hazelnut cappuccino look into mine.

Cody! No doubt his twin is next to him.

Cody and Zander snuck into my room in Aspen and stole my blood. It seems everything is coming full circle, or an infinity loop is repeating, and a new game is starting again.

Cody flashes me a pressed smile, then turns back around. His brother Zander, who assaulted me, doesn't bother glancing my way.

I sink into the seat and close my weary eyes. *Why can't it just swallow me?*

The light at the end of my tunnel has just been extinguished. I see the smoke drift into the air until it vanishes.

Is there anything left of Luna's mind worth saving? What new game is about to begin?

Chapter 4

Death

Maintaining focus is a challenge when the very ground beneath you trembles incessantly. "I see him," I tell Gabriel, my eyes trained on the car barreling down the road. The front license plate reads WAR666. Our brother has come to our aid, but ironically, he's the one who landed us in this predicament in the first place.

Gabriel's gaze flickers over his shoulder, taking in the peak of the mountain visible over the treetops. He's not the warrior he used to be; he's not himself; I'm uncertain if I'll ever be able to guide him back.

Luna staged her suicide, then manipulated her sister, my little mouse, into making us all believe the lie. We swallowed down the bait, hook, line, and sinker. Fell for it completely. My little mouse's performance was so genuine that a part of me was proud of her. The other part of me can't wait to catch and punish her for it. Oh, the things I will do...

I watched her cry, mourn a fake ghost, witness her rebel, and try to escape when she refused to admit Wes and I were the same person.

When she hallucinated and began conversing with her deceased sister, Gabriel, and I chalked it up as part of her grieving process. Damn, it was planned so impeccably I feel my cock twitch! It seems my little mouse does have what it takes to be a member of my family.

From the first moment I spotted Sol, I knew she was mine. Love at first sight doesn't compare to the plague of insanity that obsession at first sight is.

I wanted to cocoon her from the harsh realities of our world, but I was also consumed by a relentless need to make her stronger, to prepare her for what lay ahead. I wanted to see her spread her wings and fly alongside me.

This beautifully orchestrated deception of hers, this captivating lie she's woven, tells me she has developed that strength needed to survive my family.

I'm proud as fuck that she could pull this trick off.

Sol has shown she can bear the weight of *my* world. Not just the world of Manus Dei but the world that encompasses my family name. A name that carries a tremendous amount of weight and power.

My smile is so wide I can't wipe it off my face. The realization is liberating. I won't need to shield her in a protective bubble. The thought of her standing by my side, sharing in my triumphs and struggles, kindles a fierce joy within me. It only fuels my obsession, my deep-seated desire for her, and the need to see her safe and thriving.

Sol is my fallen angel and I will help her survive this hell on earth.

A palpable excitement courses through me, making my palms tingle with anticipation. The eagerness to find her, to have her within my reach again, is an almost primal need. I need her naked under me, need to feel her smooth creamy skin redden under my touch. I want to be high on the intoxicating sensation of her soft flesh against mine. I crave the symphony of her moans when I claim her. Her small hands clawing down my back as we lose ourselves in each other, makes me so hard it's painful.

I love when her body falls limp after I've fucked her. Treasure how her eyes roll back when I make love to her. Each action is so different, but it's a sweet surrender only I am privy to, and it fuels the flames of our obsession with one another.

I know my little mouse, and she has become just as obsessed with me. She admitted it when she said she loved me. Words I'll never forget and can't wait to hear again.

But I also want more.

Love is just the start. I want her undying loyalty; I want her to need me like her lungs need air.

And she will.

Time apart is good. Absence makes the heart grow wilder, and I can't wait to tame the beast she will become without me fucking her into submission.

When we stormed into Astrid's office and found it devoid of Sol, I did panic, but now I'm focused. Blood is in the air, and I'm ready to hunt.

Gabriel falls another step behind me. His heart and mind are still in the tunnels. I must pull him back from the edge of that chasm he's about to be lost in.

This is good. Luna and Sol's lies are the perfect motivation we each needed to take everything we ever wanted. I see my future; it's bright as fuck, and Gabriel's will be too. I just need him to see the light behind the smoke and rubble.

I reach out, firmly gripping his shoulders, forcing him to pivot away from the looming mountain. "Look at me, brother. Take all your anger, your shock, your disbelief, and every shred of your pain, and channel it. Focus it onto one single objective. Forget the eventual outcome of this twisted game for now, just hone in on the immediate goal." I give his shoulders a rough shake, ensuring he's locking onto my words. He gives a slight nod. "Our objective is to find our women. You're going to seek out Luna, and I'm on a mission to find Sol. Once we reclaim your kingdom, what you choose to do with Luna will be entirely your decision." His gaze drops, absorbing my words.

You see, I just gave the demon inside of him hope. Hope can go a long way. It can even make the most prized angel turn his back on his god. Look at all the devil has accomplished. My brother can do the same.

As I dig my fingers into his shoulders, I try to mold his thoughts, just like one would shape clay, "I'm going to make sure your life isn't worthless." I mean it. I'll mend Luna too. After all, she's only been acting as she was programmed to, and Sol has simply responded as Luna trained her to. I just need to break the fucking cycle.

"We will get those decryption codes, brother. And one day, you will have control over Manus Dei. When that day dawns, you will be responsible for ensuring no one abuses that knowledge. That's the true purpose of these games. We're just trying to protect those we love. Manus Dei sought to guard its members at your and Luna's expense, at the cost of all the clones. Remember that; remember the pain they inflicted upon you, and vow never to inflict it upon others. We can end this cycle, Gabriel. We are so close."

"Close!" Gabriel sneers. He stops walking, planting his feet firmly like a shipwrecked object that doesn't want to be tugged along. *Too fucking back, brother. I'm not leaving you behind.*

"I feel further away from the end goal than I ever have." The hollow despair in his eyes is enough to draw a lump in my salted, dry throat.

He grabs his golden hair, pulling it, "How can I still love Luna?" He grinds his teeth together, a pitiful semblance of the determined warrior he once was. His fists collide with his chest in a hopeless expression of frustration. "I love her so much. Everything I did was to protect her from Manus Dei, from herself." The words rush out in a tormented flurry. "I saw her changing, and I tried to stop it. I...I loved her. I still love her." He chokes on the last words, the reality of his feelings refusing to be silenced.

And then, for the second time in my life, I see my brother break down. The first time was when he believed Luna had taken her own life. Now he weeps because she lives. Not tears of relief, but of a heart-wrenching pain no being should have to endure. When you witness a man as strong as Gabriel cry it fucks with you. It makes me want to erect walls around my own heart.

He falls to his knees and pounds his fist into the ground, hoping to create a hole that will welcome him into hell.

My feet are by his side at a moment's notice. I catch his next punch and lock his hands in a caging grip. He doesn't fight me, which is more chilling. Anger is fuel; grief is a sponge that soaks the life out of you. I need him to be furious; I need that fuel to spread like an out-of-control wildfire.

"After everything she's done to me, I still love her," he admits. His voice shakes with the violent conflict of emotions, "I want to pull her close, to hold her again, and then..." His tears dry up, replaced with a fiery determination that fills the void in his gaze. It's like watching an eclipse decide to remain and not move over for the sun to take all the glory again. All the light is devoured, replacing the world in a new shade of darkness. *Yes! This is how I need him to be.* "I want to end her life." The sentiment hangs heavily in the air, a grim testament to the state of his battered heart.

"Once we find Luna you can either break this cycle, make her see your love, or put an end to it. You must decide what you can live with and what you can't live without. You need to focus. We have to hunt, brother." I taunt him. He nods, his face still red with fury. Determination sets in his eyes. Gabriel is good at setting aside his emotions, not as good as Luna, but he's able to focus on the new mission at hand and not the betrayal that is trying to consume him.

A white SUV bursts onto the scene, skidding to a halt on the snowy road as we emerge from the cover of the tree line. War is here and he has a lot to answer for. We knew he'd been communicating with Famine, clinging to the belief that familial ties would prevail in the end.

Maybe the bond of brotherhood isn't as unbreakable as we'd hoped. Love alters the boundaries of everything, even the deepest ties. Its influence can curve the unbendable and crack the unbreakable, testing loyalties and remolding relationships in its wake. Love is a force that can shape destinies, for better or worse, often leading us down paths we never thought we'd tread.

Seizing the moment, Gabriel lunges forward out of the tree line. He wrenches the driver's door before the brakes have fully stopped, dragging War out and throwing him onto the road.

End My Games

I let his fists rain down on War, every punch a physical embodiment of his anguish. Watch it go on long enough for War to taste Gabriel's pain, but just before unconsciousness takes him, I pull Gabriel away, shove him into the car and slam the door shut.

Squatting down I rest my elbows on my thighs and look at my beaten up little brother. Is this how Wade, my older brother by blood, felt when he looked at me hooked up to machines with a heart full of bullets.

Shaking my head, I grip War by the collar of his meticulously pressed shirt, now speckled in blood, and slam him into the side of the SUV with enough force to rock it.

He groans, wincing from the pain. "I've had enough already." He tries to smile, but the blood doesn't gift him his usual results. The benefit of being the little brother has allowed War to get away with a lot of shit. Now it's time for him to grow the fuck up and take responsibility for his actions.

"You haven't begun to pay for what you've done," I hiss back at him.

With effort, he tries to force open his swollen left eye. "I'm trying to save our family."

"At what cost?" My voice makes an arctic wind feel like a warm day at the beach.

War shakes his bloodied face, the fight still alive in his voice. "I don't care about the cost. One day, you'll understand why." He pauses, gasping for his next breath.

War never had a family before us. He was a lost boy who we made into a man. That's why he fights so fiercely. As annoying as a family is, it can be the most powerful ally in the world.

"You've ruined everything," I retort, my gaze drifting over his shoulder. Behind the tinted windows, our brother seethes, already scheming. "You're going to tell me everything. Everything! I gave up my heart so you could live, but don't mistake that for weakness. I wouldn't think twice about claiming your life as compensation. You owe me your life, brother." I pause, then release him and climb into the driver's seat.

He swings open the backseat door, attempting humor amidst the tension, "I guess I've lost front-seat privileges?" His attempt at levity falls flat in the heavy air of the SUV.

"I'll fucking kill him," Gabriel hisses a warning to me.

"I call first dibs." I mock.

My foot hits the gas pedal as if I were racing at the Monaco Grand Prix, leaving a cloud of dust and unresolved feelings in our wake.

With no immediate destination in mind, I drive us away from the mountain. Everything has been compromised.

That leaves me no other option but to return and make a new deal with my greatest ally.

My father.

It's not going to be easy. Good old dad thought I would stab Gabriel in the back once he took down Astrid. To say I shocked my old man when I told him I'd trust Gabriel with my life was an understatement. We haven't spoken much since. I think he and my older brother Wade are waiting for the day they have to save me again.

Knock, knock…that day has arrived, but unlike last time, I don't need saving. My heart is fine. I'm fine. I just need an army to keep the wolves at bay. Once he learns that we've lost those decryption codes, the world as we know it will shift. The hunt for Manus Dei's knowledge will intensify, and whoever gets their hands on that data could hold the world hostage.

My little mouse never wanted to be caged, but now, to save her from the massive fucked up game Luna and her have started, I will be the one who is leashed again.

Better caged and chained to the devil you know than to roam free in a world surrounded by demons.

Chapter 5

Death

I'm on high alert, so when I notice a slight flicker on the dashboard, my left hand tightens around the steering wheel while my right reaches for my gun. It was an overreaction; the movement was just the fuel gauge notifying me of an almost empty tank. I grit my teeth in irritation. This is War's oversight; he should've filled up the car. It's not like him. All of us have been acting out of character. Our training should come first to protect the ones we love, but lately, we've let our matters cloud our judgment.

We need to get it the fuck together. A renewed focus is essential. We are an elite team that has been behaving like a circus. Frustration rises, but I take a deep breath to calm myself. Shifting my gaze, I assess Gabriel and then War. "We need to regroup. This isn't us. If we continue to act without caution, we might as well give up on the chase," I tell them.

"She was counting on this. The shock value," Gabriel concedes. He sits straighter in his seat; his face hardens, and the soldier in him surfaces.

Thank fuck! My brother is back with a renewed vengeance.

"She thought it would break me," Gabriel growls.

"It hasn't," I assure him.

Gabriel nods in agreement. The devil in him rises. Blue eyes turn black.

"I need to fill up the tank. Then, I need to tell my father about what happened," I announce. Dread swirls in my gut.

End My Games

"Wes, I don't think–" Gabriel starts, but I cut him off.

"We have no other options. News of the explosions from the mountain is already all over the media," I state. My phone has been buzzing non-stop with calls from my father and others demanding answers. The storm is here, and we have to face it.

The nearest gas station is on the edge of the small town we're passing through. It sits adjacent to a train stop teeming with passengers waiting to board the next train. I shed my bulletproof vest and guns before stepping out of the car. Walking into a Swiss gas station in full tactical gear would draw unwanted attention - maybe it would pass in America, but not here.

Gabriel clears his throat, his eyes trained like a sniper on War. "Did you help her escape?" He questions. The hair rises on my arms. A bead of sweat rolls over my eyebrows. The likelihood that War helped Luna is high. War was left in our safe house, where we believed Klara was being held captive.

"No," War confesses. He uses his tie to wipe the blood trickling from his broken nose. "When everything went sideways, I rushed to the room where Klara was supposedly confined. She was gone. I've been playing both sides, brothers, but I'd never jeopardize your lives. You damn well know that." His voice strains with the effort to convince us, and he begins to rummage through his suit pocket.

"How did she escape?" Gabriel's tone sharpens. Although we can't fully trust War, we believe in his loyalty when it comes to having our backs - even if he also has Famine's. The little shit wants us to be a family again and he will do anything to make it happen. It's a convoluted situation we've been tolerating because we love our brother. Sometimes you do fucked up things for the people you love. Just as Sol painted the lie that Luna killed herself.

"I was busy hacking into one of the world's most secure systems, so, pardon-fucking-me if I couldn't multitask and monitor Klara, or Luna, or whoever we had captive." War retrieves two envelopes from his pocket. "These were on Klara's bed. This one's addressed to you." He hands Gabriel a letter and then passes me the second one. "I'll handle the gas and freshen up. Meet back here in five." His comment about washing up is a transparent excuse. War knows we don't trust him, and as a result, we need to keep some information, like the content of these letters and our plans, hidden from him.

War exits the SUV just as the train's horn pierces the air, signaling its departure. Gabriel just stares at the unopened letter in his hands. Gently, I take it from him, fearing he might shred it in a fit of anger. "I'll read yours first."

"I'm going to survive this," Gabriel mutters. "I won't let Luna win."

"I know you will."

"I still don't know what I want to do with Luna once I find her." He grabs his gun, his fingers tracing over it as if it were a crystal ball that could provide him with answers.

"Think it through from every angle, brother. Luna planned everything meticulously," I caution him.

Gabriel chuckles dryly, "How the hell are you so resilient? Is it that artificial heart we implanted in you?" His attempt at humor is heartening. He will slowly rebound from the immense shock. "Aren't you livid with Sol? She knew the truth all along. She left you for her sister."

"Fury doesn't even begin to cover it, but I'm also proud. Sol is tougher than I gave her credit for, which gives me hope. Hope that she can withstand whatever Luna throws her way and whatever I have planned for her once I catch her," I respond with a hint of amusement.

Gabriel's gaze shifts past me, tracking War as he disappears into the gas station. "We can't trust him. He refuses to pick a side, so he doesn't have one anymore."

I nod, understanding his concerns. "I'm aware. But he's our brother. We can't abandon him. Once we reach a safe location, we'll confine him. We need to shield him from himself now."

"You want to cage him again?" His brow inches closer to his hairline. We both know if we tried to put War in a cage, he *would* turn his back on us.

"We will set up boundaries." I clarify.

"He'll push them."

My chin raises, "I know. Let me handle it."

He agrees, his eyes once again returning to the letter. Breaking the silence, I ask, "How did you ever fall for Luna?"

He carefully picks his words before replying, "There's an inherent flaw in our design. We know it all too well. We're hardwired to pursue victory, no matter the cost. Ruthlessness is imprinted in our DNA. Manus Dei required a leader who could embody that ruthlessness. When I first encountered Luna, it was as if..." His eyes take on a distant look as he smiles, a genuine, heartfelt expression that I haven't seen in ages. "It was akin to looking into a mirror. I'd never met anyone who shared my thought patterns before. It was intriguing. Like playing a game against myself. I had this urge to unravel her, to dissect her, to gain a deeper understanding of the complexities that governed both of us." His eyes cloud over with memories, and his grin widens, innocent and carefree.

"I didn't want her father, Astrid, Manus Dei, not even Sol to be able to understand Luna. I wanted Luna for myself. I wanted to cage her; to free her. For the first time in my life, the game didn't matter. I just wanted her, whatever the cost. As time went on, I realized that the cost would be playing the game and winning it. I needed to win to shield her from herself." He shakes his head, "I wanted her, Wes, I needed Luna like air to breathe."

His fingers thread through his golden locks, "I still do. I decided the very day I met Luna that I loved her. It was simple. I gave my heart to her. The end. I just needed to teach her my definition of love." He taps his chest with his gun. "For years, I taught her how to feel and accept my love. I thought it was enough, but it couldn't trump her inherent need to win at all costs. And she did. She did kill herself in a way. She lost everyone that loved her. She lost my love, took Sol's innocence, and turned friends into pawns. That was the only thing grounding her."

I shake my head, "When one game ends, another can start. Just roll the dice and begin anew, brother. If you still love Luna, make her crave your love."

"I tried that."

"No," I counter, "You tried to *teach* her what love was. Luna doesn't need safety or protection. Luna is a predator. You need to show her not just the pleasant aspects of love, but also the harsh and unsightly ones. The chains that bind, the deep-seated craving for someone regardless of their deeds. God still loves the devil, otherwise, he would have obliterated him long ago. Love and hate, passion and betrayal...it all goes hand in hand. Teach Luna that lesson. Make her obsessed with you."

"Is that what you did with Sol?"

I give a sly smile, "Yes. Like Luna, Sol is a handful. They need to test their limits before they admit they need us. Sol will realize she needs me, and Luna will understand she needs you."

"You'll forgive Sol?"

"It was never about forgiveness, Gabriel. As you said, Luna and Sol were engineered differently. It was always about teaching Sol what she needed. While you were teaching Luna about love, I was educating Sol about independence. I needed Sol to distance herself from Luna so she could thrive and rule by my side."

Gabriel swallows hard. The struggle within him has just begun. I can't dictate his actions, but I can guide him, just as I did with my little mouse. I understand that if Gabriel ends up killing Luna, he likely won't survive the aftermath. The key lies in redirecting his anger and pain. When I first couldn't find Sol in the tunnels, I managed to redirect my panic into fuel, a beacon of hope that one day soon, I would capture her and make her mine completely. Sol's escape has only made my pursuit more exhilarating.

The sound of the letter being unfolded fills the car as I open it. The noise is eerily akin to the breaking of bones. "Don't withhold anything from me, brother. I want to know everything she wrote," Gabriel instructs, his grip on his gun tightening to the point that his knuckles turn an alarming shade of pale. He edges off the seat, like a runner at the starting blocks.

When I open at the letter I roll my eyes at the dramatics; of course, the crazy clone picked to write her letter in ink the color of freshly split blood. Black ink would be too predictable, navy too boring. Red is just enough psycho bitch to make you hesitate.

Before I get a chance to utter a word, Gabriel swiftly snatches the paper from me and scans it in silence. That's my brother for you, always ready to face the storm head-on. I couldn't be more proud of him. He's prepared to do battle with his own heart.

As he reads, his face reddens like a thermometer on a hot summer's day. Once finished, he remains silent, placing the letter back down. Fuck that, I snatch it from him and read the words for myself.

I know this must strike you as unusual, not the part about my supposed resurrection (I didn't resurrect because I never truly died), but rather that I've chosen to pen a letter instead of leaving you a cryptic song. I've made many unconventional decisions recently, all for my benefit, and I felt it right to write while the sardonic joy of it all hasn't abandoned me yet. It will all leave me soon...all the passion and joy.

This will make more sense to you later, it will all click in due course - that is if Sol can untangle the web of my deeds. And no, I'm not speaking of Manus Dei's downfall. I did something else, something far more sinister.

You could view my actions as a catastrophic mistake or a calculated correction, it all depends on your perspective.

How is your perspective now, darling? I take it not so good or maybe it's clearer than ever?

I'm aware that right now, your feathers might be ruffled. You could even be angry with this new revelation.

Dare I call you a loser... I dare. I'm sorry, but I have to rub it in. It feels so good. I'm not trying to be cruel; I'm just really messed up. More than ever. So much more.

I never wanted to feel, Gabriel, but you insisted that I do. All those years of you telling me you loved me finally had an effect. You never believed me when I retorted that I hated you. I do hate you, but in my convoluted mind, hate equates to love, and love is something I despise.

Does that make sense, darling? I hope so; if it doesn't, don't worry because soon, it will all be shut off.

Tick, tock, don't be late for the tea party... the Mad Hatter will only grow madder.

I launched my game for an array of reasons, the primary one being my insatiable desire for victory. I had to win. That's a sentiment only you could possibly understand. I just can't seem to let it go; the taste of victory is too intoxicating. I craved the title of the winner, just as you did.

Gabriel, you cheated all these years under the delusion that it was aiding me. How charmingly misguided. I never needed you to help me win. All those instances I appeared to fail a test, and you ingeniously found a way to manipulate the results, it was endearing, really. I merely wanted to see the lengths you would go for me.

You went so far for me, darling.

But you failed the test, my test. You see, I was testing your love for me, your definition of love, and how far you would go to keep the game they forced us to play in motion. That damn game you kept playing!

You should have let me fail years ago. Then, you truly would have won. Instead, you kept me in the game, forced wins and losses, and you kept the cycle going because you thought being called a lover in addition to being a winner was more satisfying.

I'm laughing to myself as I write this. No wonder I dislike words. They expose how profoundly messed up we are from all the games. In the end, I was just as cornered as my father. I became the man I hated. Nothing more than a puppet who had to obey Astrid.

The only difference was that my father was a fool.

I wasn't. Not because I had you; love won't save you, but Sol will.

You see, It's only due to Astrid that my father achieved any semblance of success. People are more motivated when you have leverage over them. Astrid had both my father and me in her snare. The fucking bitch. The day came when Astrid revealed what she had over me. No, it wasn't Sol. As a matter of fact, it was something I never knew I could care about.

I blame that on you.

I saw you and me when I looked at the photo she gave me. I know what you're thinking; she leveraged killing more of our clones over my head. Wrong again, darling. She found something else that tugged at the little black heart you forced to beat.

She found my weakness and forced me to create something for her, something I couldn't tell you about. You would have found a workaround to prevent me from creating it. You would have stopped Astrid and painted her as a traitor, thus painting me as a traitor. After all, I reflect Astrid. It's in my blood.

You would have won, Gabriel, and I couldn't allow that to happen. I couldn't be seen as a monster hell-bent on destroying the world. That and you would never have allowed my heart to care for what was on that photo Astrid showed me. You were already extremely jealous; it was blinding you just as it dazed the last ruler of Manus Dei. Believe it or not, I didn't want you to suffer the same fate as him. So, I had no choice but to go along with Astrid's blackmail. I had to create a weapon for her that would kill me...and her.

I had to shut you out to survive, which is ironic because you're one of the few people who can assist me now. No, I'm not asking for help. I said you're one of a few. Instead, I have a different offer for you.

"Do you have any idea what Luna created? It sounds like an upgrade of sorts."

Gabriel shakes his head. "The last upgrade she got was two years before the game ended. Upgrades take time. If you rush them–" He hesitates, "Dorian messed up. He did something to her, I'm sure of it." His voice grows icy.

"Luna did this to herself." I correct him. He defiantly shakes his head, projecting the blame elsewhere. I understand his tactics, shifting responsibility so he can sidestep Luna's actions. He's fabricating a route to forgiveness.

"Gabriel, that might be the case, or this could be yet another ruse. Look at everything Luna has done over the years. We know Luna's capabilities, and now we understand the extents she's willing to go."

His blue eyes refuse to meet mine, "She loved me. Dorian altered her."

"Luna altered herself."

"She was coerced into it!" He hisses. "This is her subtle cry for help without openly asking for it. She wants to rectify everything single-handedly. Luna's always been like that. She's angry that I failed to notice what was transpiring. It was near the end, Wes; I was solely focused on winning to shield her. Luna was too reckless. The Masters would never have accepted her. I had to win."

"In Luna's mind, you had to win to claim the victor's title; you weren't attempting to win to be her savior."

With a downward glance, I resume reading,

Oh, Gabriel, I thought when the time came to burn it all down, you would have my back. Hell, I thought you'd light the match and watch me throw it. But you didn't, because, like me, you wanted the title.

I can't blame you; it's how we were designed.

Yes, I let you win. I craved the title of 'winner,' but not from Manus Dei. Fuck them! That's what you never understood. You nurtured me to feel, Gabriel. Now, I need you to feel my pain. Feel it when I no longer can.

I did everything for love. The love you taught me to feel. So in a way, this is all your fault. The love for my twin sister, Sol, for the man I want to spend the rest of my life with. For all the other innocent Reflections who were pawns in the game.

I solved the game before anyone else did; I just didn't win it because if I won the game Manus Dei crafted, then I would always be tethered to them.

I would never allow that to happen. Never!

So I devised my own game and decided to establish my own society. I mentioned this idea to you, but you thought the task was impossible. Manus Dei was so powerful and respected that if they were to crumble, governments might lose faith, never again willing to bend the knee. The world would battle for our knowledge. Wars would start, blah, blah, fucking blah.

Wars will always erupt, Gabriel! I'm not afraid of battle; after all, it was you and I who birthed the Horsemen. We instigated the apocalypse, we created it, and we can control it! Now, I have centuries of knowledge to help me prepare for it.

Yes, I seized the codes that can undo the encryption. I knew she encrypted the data long before you figured it out. Famine discovered that Astrid was pilfering the data three years ago. We allowed it to transpire because Astrid put all her eggs in one basket. A basket I now possess. It was all too simple to take everything I needed now that it was consolidated in one location.

I shielded you from her, Gabriel; next time we meet, a simple 'thank you' would suffice.

Holy fuck! The implications of this knowledge cut through the mind like a sharp, unyielding blade. Famine and Luna had a peculiar relationship. Famine had observed Luna and Gabriel morph into the monsters they are today. He harbored affection for Luna but held the same affection for Gabriel. He viewed them as his family. It just doesn't make sense to me that he'd abandon us, his brothers, merely for Luna. "There has to be something more compelling driving Famine," I assert.

Gabriel's cheeks flush with redness, "Finish that damn letter so we can read what she wrote to you."

Unlike Manus Dei, I don't aspire to rule the world. I strive to improve it. Yes, that's what I said, believe it or not. This monster feels, no thanks to you.

I'm going to ensure that the science will not be misused. I'm a mother lioness, and I will protect my cubs, each and every one of them. Even you, Gabriel. That's why I'm reassessing all our government contracts. I'm going to tread on some very important people's toes, sever some people from our science. I think it will be exhilarating.

Believe it or not, I agree with some of your ideas. I'll put them into action. I think parts of the science should be available to everyone. Why just upgrade ourselves or soldiers, why not grant the average human the opportunity? Of course, we will regulate it all. That's why I need a solid, robust foundation. I'll require a lot of Horsemen to enforce my laws.

I'd offer you a position to rule by my side, but we both know that's a futile option. Like me, you can't be the runner-up. You have to seize power and wield it yourself.

So here is my offer to you. Let's play a new game. Cue the drumroll... oh, the dramatics are so much fun!

You've always wanted Manus Dei...You have it, but now you have to compete against me. The new kid on the block with the shiny new toy. You possess the empire you always craved. A crown and throne that perch atop a mountain of rubble (I hope you evacuated before it all detonated. It would certainly be dull if you died).

Now you have to confront a new adversary. Me. I've got an army behind me, Gabriel. A wealth of knowledge people will rally behind. Soon, Manus Dei will fade into a distant memory. The governments that bowed to them will come to me. That endows me with immense power; it's so exhilarating.

What do you have? A few Horsemen won't safeguard your crown for long.

Am I coming across as upset?

I am, darling.

You stirred emotions in me, and then you discarded me for a crown from the people who harmed us, murdered us, and manipulated us to kill. I detest the fact that I love you, and that even after all this, I still desire you. That's why I created what Astrid coveted because it would allow me to concentrate. That's why I required Sol, because she can mend me so I can focus on this new game I'm about to initiate.

This was the only solution. I had to resort to extreme measures to obliterate Manus Dei, but also for you to expunge me, Gabriel. I needed to push you to the very edge (pun intended) so you would relinquish me. Truly fucking detest me.

All those years you taught me to love, and now I'm teaching you to hate. This type of loathing is what I felt each time I watched my clone die so Manus-fucking-Dei could ascend as a superior society! I despise that you wanted to continue ruling under the same name.

Isn't it easier living with hate than love, don't you think?

Love is fire; fires dwindle and burn out. Hate is gasoline. It's never-ending fuel. I hope it energizes you; you know how much I thrive on competition, baby.

That's why I pushed you, shattered your definition of love. It's simpler to live knowing the people you loved, who betrayed you, now despise you. I can live and rule knowing I have your hatred. I can't rule with a clear conscience knowing you still love me. You can't love me after this. You'd be royally fucked up if you did. You always claimed to be the superior human because you felt, well now you have to experience just as I did.

Oh, darling, it's time for me to go. I created a playlist for you on that iPod. I hope it motivates you to pursue me, to attempt to usurp my crown. I've been one step ahead for years. I dare you to try to outwit me.

- I hate you, darling.
Luna.

Holy shit!

One thing is for certain; Luna wants Gabriel to hate her.

Another fact, Luna relishes in the art of manipulating her words; she said it herself in this letter; in her mind, opposites are realities. Love becomes hate. So, in the end, she isn't telling Gabriel to hate her; she's imploring him to forgive her. Pleading him to continue loving her despite everything she has perpetrated. It's a new level of fucked up, but the devil in me has to applaud Luna.

I look at Gabriel; he's staring blankly ahead, like a robot. He appears more like Luna did when she was entangled in her tormented mind. All this time, Gabriel was striving to rescue Luna from herself. Now, Luna might have to save him because I'm witnessing his spirit gradually vanish, and I'm uncertain if love is potent enough to tether it back to him.

My phone vibrates again; no doubt it's my father. The car no longer feels like our sanctuary. It feels too cramped and claustrophobic. Both Gabriel and I are bristling, eager to commence the hunt.

"Read the second letter," Gabriel hisses.

Unfolding the second letter, I anticipate seeing the red ink again. Instead, it's black and it's not Luna's handwriting.

"It's from War," I announce. I glance over at the gas station. He's been absent longer than five minutes, but knowing him, he is probably trying to eliminate the stains from his prized suit. I part my lips to read the letter aloud. As I do, a sense of heaviness takes root in my gut like a deep, entrenched tree in the earth.

I don't know where to begin, brothers. As you can see, this letter isn't from Luna. It's from me, the baby brother you always had to save. Wes knows that better than most. I owe Death my life, but more than that, I owe him a heart. I had to do the brave thing, which sometimes is the reckless thing.

As you well know, I've been talking with Famine. I never aided him per se; I just didn't hinder him. Famine has an interesting concept, a fantasy, really, but who am I, but a mere Horseman, to judge. That was meant to be humorous, so I hope you guys are laughing.

Fantasies can become reality, and perhaps, Famine can get what he wants. There's no guarantee that Klara and Luna will accept what he offers, but that's what makes it so fascinating.

Famine didn't desert us because he was distraught by Luna's feigned death. He's always believed he had to be our family's savior. He left us to develop an upgrade, or rather… a downgrade. Shocking, right? You can see why I view it as a fantasy.

It's a compelling notion if Famine can make the impossible possible. That's where Sol comes into play because we all know Luna isn't capable of creating a downgrade; she can't. You'll understand that later.

You all view the upgrades as layers of armor. I see it that way, too; I adore my enhanced abilities; I'm not talking about the size of my dick; that is all-natural. (Come on, laugh with me. I have to laugh during these fucked up times. It's good for the soul.)

What you all have failed to realize is that too much armor can weigh you down. You're knee-deep in shit, brothers. You've lost the codes to decrypt the data; the world will soon discover this, and they will hunt down the people we cherish to seize that power. That's just the tip of the iceberg. You're so consumed with the good that the upgrades brought that you neglected to acknowledge the bad. Now, those unpleasant elements have trapped you even further.

Famine believes he can rectify this. He thinks it's his fantasy, but in truth, it was never his. Someone else manipulated him into doing this.

Can you guess who?

Bingo. Luna. The master at making pawns do as she wants.

The villain can't be seen as the hero, and we all know Luna would never ask for help, so she meticulously orchestrated this all. She planted the seed in Famine's mind, and he's cultivated it into an entire forest.

Famine's got all the data now; he just has to reverse-engineer it. Are you grasping why Famine agreed to Luna's plan? Luna had Sol and Klara under her spell. Famine loves Klara, and he needs Sol. Speaking of that little mouse, did you discern Famine's and Luna's purpose for her yet? I did a few months ago. Famine needed the data to reverse-engineer the upgrades that corrupted Klara and Luna.

Let me stress this again, corrupted Klara and Luna. Corrupted things find it difficult to function correctly. Got that hint? Luna can't make the downgrade, she literally can't. That nasty truth is Astrid's doing and will make sense later.

But do you know who is brilliant enough to be able to create a downgrade?

Therein lies Sol, our little artist. Sol might be an artist, but she is also one of the brightest scientists in the world. Someone so intelligent she can comprehend the science and find a solution to undo what Luna created for Astrid and design a downgrade. That's why Famine played along with all of Luna's nasty tricks. Now, he has the data and Sol, who can create his magic reset pill.

You might be wondering why I'm writing this. Well, for one, you would have beaten it out of me once we settled. Secondly, I know my brothers. I'm a loose cannon now, and you would have jailed me until you figured out what to do with me. I can't return to a cage again, and I prefer a custom suit to a jumpsuit.

Back to the heart I owe you, Death. That's why I wrote this letter. It gave me the perfect amount of time to get on that train that just left. Sorry about the bill for the gas; I never did pay it. It just gave me the excuse I needed to slip away. I'll pay you back later. That's a joke also, your rich ass can afford the escapades of your little brother.

I'm leaving, don't worry, I'll be back. I am the annoying little brother after all. I'd give you my heart in an instant, brother, but it's not my heart you want, it's Sol's. So consider me her guardian angel. I won't interfere with Famine's or your plans. As the Horseman called War, it's not my job to stop skirmishes; I support all sides until there is only one side left standing. I'll be lurking in the shadows, making sure Sol is safe and that her pretty little heart keeps beating for you, brother. I will die before I let anything happen to her.

In the blink of an eye, I drop the letter, exit the car, and run to the train platform. It's empty, the train long gone. My eyes scan the barren landscape, wanting to see my youngest brother so I can snap his neck like a wishbone.

"He's long gone," Gabriel's voice rings out from behind me. He steps up, positioning himself shoulder-to-shoulder with me. Together, we peer down the long, lonely train track. In his hands, both letters rest.

"I'll kill him," I declare to the wind.

Gabriel snorts, "Just like I'll kill Luna."

Grabbing the back of my neck, I pinch the mounting tension. We both have to suffer the same fate, wanting to kill someone we love but also wanting to save them. Inhaling, my lungs are filled with the crisp Swiss mountain air. *You better keep her safe, brother, because if Sol is hurt, I will rip your heart out as payment.*

"Do you think Sol can create a downgrade?" I hesitantly ask.

"I don't think that is the smartest question to contemplate right now. What you should be asking is what Luna will do with it once Sol creates it. That's why War stayed close. He's going to keep Sol safe," he replies. "War said Luna wanted Sol to create this, but he never mentioned Luna wanting to take this downgrade herself."

"You think Luna would hurt Sol?"

"You can hurt a person without physically touching them," Gabriel adds. It's a harsh truth that resonates deep within me. It's the emotional and psychological wounds that cut the deepest.

"I think this downgrade is Luna's weapon," he levels his worried eyes at me. "Her weapon against us."

My phone rings again, interrupting our conversation. I retrieve it from my pocket and see my father's name flashing on the screen. Seeing it sends a mix of emotions through me—loyalty, obligation, and a sense of duty to my powerful family.

Gabriel comes from a powerful society, but I come from a powerful family. The difference is Gabriel's society risked his neck; they tested him to the brink of death, not caring if he died. Manus Dei needed Gabriel to be strong.

My family differs slightly. My dad needed me to be dangerous and tough. I was tested to the brink of death and almost died. The only difference is my dad did everything he could to save me from the fate so many of Gabriel's clones suffered. That's loyalty.

I grab the back of my neck. Dad will already have a team assembled to hunt down Luna. No doubt my oldest brother, not Famine, my biological brother Wade, will lead the team.

"What are you going to tell him?" Gabriel asks, his eyes filled with a pleading expression I haven't seen before. It's as if he's searching for reassurance or guidance that I will not abandon him too.

A chilling realization settles upon me, sending shivers down my spine. If my father were to catch Luna, his wrath would be swift and merciless. There would be no hesitation, no second chances. Luna, Famine, and Sol would be condemned to a fate worse than death, a fate from which there is no escape. Father needs the science and they *are* the science. My father would get it from them one way or another. The thought of their lives hanging by a thread sends a surge of adrenaline coursing through my veins.

My voice carries a determined resolve, concealing the trepidation lurking within. "I'm going to make a deal with my father."

Chapter 6

Sol

"Wake up," a voice whispers in my ear. It was meant to be gentle, but the timbre of his voice was like an unexpected earthquake, shaking my heart and making my limbs react with a start. My eyes fling open to the point of pain like a rubber band snapping.

"Famine." I gasp when I see two golden irises looming over me. His shoulders are so wide they create a shadow that rivals a mountain.

"We arrived. The others are outside waiting," He says, jerking his head towards the helicopter door. Then he flashes me that hopeful smile again. I flatten my palm out; I want to smack it off his face.

Famine shifts, and I can finally see beyond his large muscular body. The ceiling of the helicopter comes into view. This isn't the first helicopter we've taken; it feels like hours, or perhaps days, since we started this relentless journey. We haven't stopped moving, constantly transitioning from helicopter to plane, to boat, and back to a helicopter again. Exhaustion weighs heavily on me, as I finally succumbed to sleep, only to be forcefully awakened to continue playing the game my sister stubbornly refuses to end.

You started her war; you're to blame. The guilt speaks to me now.

Famine extends his hand towards me, his gesture carrying a weight that goes beyond mere assistance. I can sense there is a hidden agenda behind his offer. He has his own plan, his own motives. If I choose to accept his hand, I will become his ally in this intricate game.

Does Luna know about Famine's plan? Knowing my sister's cunning nature, I'm inclined to believe she is fully aware and is allowing Famine to carry out his intentions. The pieces are falling into place, revealing a complex web of alliances and schemes that I must navigate to survive.

His rare golden eyes widen with so much hope I can't refuse him. My plan to end the games was blown to bits. I'm just trying to survive now. I need to find my footing and understand this new battleground before I plot out how to survive it.

Reaching out and placing my palm in his hand, our fingers entwined as he pulls me up. His touch is warm, contrasting the cold air outside.

"Where is Luna?" I ask. My legs tingle as blood floods my muscles, awakening them for the journey. My body feels stiff, and my mind is sore. I can stand up straight in this helicopter, but Famine can't. He's hunched awkwardly over me.

"She's preparing for our journey. The rest is on foot. I can carry you if you're too tired," he offers.

My shoulders slump. I would kill for a gallon of hot coffee and a dozen lemon poppy seed muffins. My life in Aspen feels like it was ages ago. I don't even know if it was real... I doubt my friend Hazel would even recognize the person I am today. "Why are you doing this?"

He moves his lips, refraining from speaking aloud because he knows Luna possesses heightened hearing abilities. His lips form a silent message, *We will talk later.* With a gentle tug, he releases my hand and swiftly leaps out of the helicopter, his landing causing a resounding thump. In a gesture that mirrors a protective father preparing to catch a child jumping into a pool, he lifts his arms, waiting for me to trust him to catch me.

Bending to meet him, I firmly grab his shoulders while his hands grasp my hips to lift me down. At that moment, I think of Wes. What have I done? How is my Horseman surviving without me? I'm not sure I can survive without him. I thought I could because I would have had the leverage to make them bend their knees to me. Now, I'm nothing more than a pawn. Maybe less than that. I'm not needed anymore, am I?

Swallowing my guilt, I muster the courage to take the leap into the unknown, leaving behind the safety of the helicopter and venturing into a world where trust is scarce, and danger lurks at every turn.

Famine gently lowers me to the rocky ground in Norway, where the landscape is far from stable. The terrain is rugged and uneven, strewn with boulders and rocks. In the distance, I can see the vast expanse of the Arctic tundra, with its sparse vegetation and occasional patches of snow. It's a desolate, barren landscape with no trees or significant features to offer shelter or cover.

My next inhale is a sharp gasp when I almost slip on the thin sheen of ice covering the rocks. "Here," Famine says; he pulls a spiky-looking shoe grip from his backpack that will help my boots grip the ice. He taps my right calf; I raise my foot and watch as he places the grip on each shoe. His touch is gentle and caring; it's like a father's.

The frigid air nips at my skin, and a bone-chilling cold permeates the surroundings. The ground is covered in a thin sheen of ice, making each step treacherous.

I can't help but feel exposed in this open, unforgiving terrain. There's no refuge here, nowhere to hide from the beasts of the pitch-dark night. It's a harsh and unwelcoming environment where survival hinges on our ability to adapt and persevere.

In the distance, I catch sight of polar bears roaming the rocky landscape, its white fur a stark contrast to the dark rocks.

"Fa...Famine!" I whisper a hiss as my jaw chatters. "Bear."

He doesn't look up but keeps adjusting my shoes.

"Don't poke it, Sol." He jokes.

"Famine!"

"Relax. I won't let anything happen to us." He assures me, tilting his head up. I become hypnotized by his golden eyes. I believe him. I observe Famine closely, and it becomes evident that he is intimately familiar with the area.

The world unfurls before me in a breathtaking dance of shadows and secrets. The night swallows everything in its deep, impenetrable veil, but the gift of my upgraded sight allows me to peer through this darkness. I feel like a voyeur, but I can't stop looking at every detail. It's as though a hidden world has been unmasked. The rocky terrain at my feet, previously hidden in obscurity, emerges with astonishing clarity. Every pebble, contour, and detail is bare before my eyes.

Once ominous and concealed, the rugged outcrops of rock now assert themselves with vivid definition. Their sharp edges cast bold shadows. The distant Arctic tundra, normally concealed in the night's grasp, reveals itself. My upgraded eyes render each patch of sparse vegetation, every tuft of grass, and the lingering patches of snow in exquisite detail.

End My Games

My gaze extends farther, and the polar bear comes into sharp focus. Its fur isn't pristine, and slight tonal shifts reveal stains from the weather. It's an astonishing sight. From my point of view, the pitch-black night in Norway transforms into a wondrous canvas, where every detail is illuminated, and every facet of the landscape is drenched in an enchanting beauty. The once-intimidating darkness becomes a land of exploration and fascination, and I am its eager observer until my eyes land on my twin. The shock of the upgraded vision is shattered, and reality settles in.

Luna and Cody have large backpacks strapped to them along with hunting rifles. Luna has remained silent throughout the journey, evading any meaningful interaction with me. I'm torn between gratitude and unease at her silence. What is she concealing behind that veil of quiet? What cryptic plans are taking shape in her mind?

Turning my head, I look back at Famine, who now stands tall with his backpack filled with the stolen decryption codes. Two large hunting rifles are hanging off his shoulder now.

"Where are we, Luna?" I call out, my voice carrying through the stillness of the night. She finally pivots her head and looks at me, the intent in her eyes palpable. "That's a silly question; we're in Norway. I sent you that postcard long ago."

"Gabriel knows about the postcards," I warn her, but it's also a test. Does she want him to find us?

"I know," She replies, her full lips relaxing into a subtle smile.

"Aren't you worried he will come for you?"

"That's a silly question," She steps closer, her movements sure and graceful on the uneven ground. With a gentle touch, she brushes my hair behind my ear, her knuckles grazing my cheek.

"Sol," she whispers as her guard lowers, and for a moment, I think her eyes widen with unshed tears. Luna's eyes have always been deceptive, her mind filled with tricks, but one thing remains clear —I know she loves me, even if her love is often laced with cruelty.

Suddenly, her touch dissipates as if life has been drained from her. She lunges forward, embracing me with a strength that leaves me breathless. The hug shocks me. Her grip tightens, constricting me like a corset trying to hold me together, and I struggle for air. My face reddens, and just as I begin to panic, she releases me, pushing me away. I stumble backward, nearly losing my balance.

When I recover I face the robot again. Luna resembles a void, a deep mystery that I fear I will never fully comprehend. Hard eyes narrow on me. Vanished are the tears and emotions.

What the fuck is happening?

Something has changed within her—a clear bipolarity that shifts from day to night. A chilling coldness emanates from her, threatening to freeze my very being. I sense an onslaught of frigid detachment growing like a cancer that is trying to take my twin away from me.

The silence wraps around us like a tightrope walker's wire, taut and precarious. One wrong word or gesture, and I could lose her forever.

Famine steps closer to Cody and Zander. They exchange a veiled glance before redirecting their attention toward us. They know what is wrong with Luna. It's a knowledge that escapes me, keeping me on the verge of discovery.

What the hell happened to my sister?

"We should get going," Luna grunts, turning her back to me while pulling out her phone. The melancholic tune of "Our Time

End My Games

Together" by Ivan B and Marie Elizabeth fills the dark forest. Zander stands shoulder to shoulder with Luna, his hand reaching out to grasp her hand. It feels like a shove to my chest when I witness Luna accept his touch, even if she doesn't reciprocate the gesture. Zander's hand serves more as a cast of support than a welcomed connection. It bewilders me how Zander, who once attacked me, can offer solace to Luna, reaching a broken part of her that she refuses to allow me to comprehend.

Cody walks behind them, his gaze briefly meeting mine before shifting to Famine. They exchange a nod, silently communicating their understanding. Famine takes my hand, his touch comforting and grounding. "Come on," he urges, his voice filled with reassurance. "Your eyes need to acclimate to this vision. I'll help teach you how to use it. It's like developing a new muscle—you have to train it. And it can only be trained in pitch darkness. When I first received the upgrade, I spent a solid week in a blacked-out room."

I don't respond with words; my focus is fixed on following his lead. I've never felt more like a puppet than I do now. Empty. Motionless except for the hand that guides me.

This is not the future I envisioned. I thought I cut the puppeteer strings but I only added more to my body.

As we move forward, the lyrics of the song become a haunting backdrop, providing answers to the unspoken question that Luna and I have grappled with. Do we truly want our lovers chasing us? Should we indulge in this twisted romance, or should we push it away? The song speaks of two people who yearn to be together but hold themselves back, acknowledging that it's not the right time for their love. In the past, I would have listened to the song without deciphering its meaning, but I'm no longer the same person I was when I first entered the games forced upon me by my sister.

I break free from Famine's hold and stride forward, grabbing Luna's shoulder and forcefully twisting her towards me. This is what she wanted, a reaction to her choice of songs.

"Gabriel doesn't want to use you. He isn't like them. Gabriel is not Manus Dei. He only wanted to protect you, to love you. I saw it in his eyes, in his intentions!"

Despite everything, deep down, Gabriel would never have inflicted harm upon Luna. I see that now. A part of me always knew that, but I felt the need to aid my twin instead of Gabriel.

Luna shoves me hard, catching me off guard and sending me sprawling to the floor with a gasp. She kneels down, her elbows resting on her knees, her voice dripping with cruel contempt. It makes my jaw quiver. "Do you know why I allowed Death to stalk you?" Her words assault me, rendering me frozen. "To teach you a lesson. There is no such thing as love, Sol. People are leeches; they will only take. Gabriel lied to me; all he cared about was power. He used the excuse of love to further his own agenda, to distract me from the game. So he could win." Luna snorts, a sound devoid of any warmth. "Ask yourself this, after I died, why did Gabriel continue to fight for Manus Dei's crown?" She laughs to herself, and suddenly, it all becomes clear. Her faked death wasn't merely a ploy to remove herself as a player; it was also a test that Gabriel failed. Luna wanted Gabriel to crumble without her. He did the opposite, he persevered, but what Luna doesn't realize is that he continues for her memory not his own gains.

"Men will always lie, Sol. Death doesn't want you because he loves you. Death wants to cage you." Her words strike me like venom, rendering me speechless. "You're nothing but an item for him to own. He was useful; he kept you safe. But now, I'll keep you safe. I am the only one who can protect my sisters," she bites.

With a cold detachment, she stands and turns her back to me. "Sisters can lie too," I yell.

She freezes in her tracks, lifting her phone and playing a new song, "Flecks" by These Brittle Bones. Famine moves to help me up, but I shove him away, my is anger pulsating through every fiber of my being. It's seeping out of every pore.

I snatch the phone from Luna's hand and select a song of my choice. Two can play this game. You want to speak through songs? Then I accept the challenge! My trembling fingers betray my fury. Famine hovers close behind me, Cody at my side. Zander watches the scene unfold with no discernible emotion, his head pivoting like an owl as he scans the dark wilderness.

"Kaleidoscope" by Flower Face begins to play, and we all stand there listening to the haunting melody. The last three lyrics of the song finally elicit a reaction from Luna. Her lip twitches, a crack forming in her impenetrable facade.

Famine inches closer to her, "Tell her," he pleads.

Tell me what?

"Tell her?" Luna repeats, her tone dripping with sarcasm. "What a silly idea. I have too many things to do. I know what you're doing. So go ahead and try, brother. Try to fix it all. Make us one big happy family." She hisses.

Famine's muscles tense, his voice turning into a growl as he declares, "I will. You knew this was coming. It's why you planned all of this, Luna. You knew that I would have to finish your game because you couldn't. I will finish it."

A single tear escapes my eye as I find the strength to speak, "I can't blame the woman you've become." I lock eyes with Cody, who looks away from me, then shift my gaze to Zander, who experienced the same abuse as the rest of us. "That was our father's and Manus Dei's doing. They abused us, but they hurt you more than they hurt me. You switched places with me and protected me. You were my shield, enduring all the blows. Abusive love is all you've ever known. When you love, you believe you have to hurt." I fix my gaze on Zander once more, remembering the pain he inflicted on me when he broke into my room and stole my blood. Stepping closer to Luna I continue, "I tried to show you what love could be, Luna. I know Gabriel did too. Gabriel was a better teacher than I was. I was selfish, escaping the pain through my art. And that's why a part of you hates me. I could escape it, but you couldn't. You had to keep playing."

Luna shakes her head, but deep down, I know she hears my apology. I want to scream how sorry I am that I missed all the signs, that I let her take my place. *I'm sorry, I'm so sorry! But I'm here now. Let me try to fix this.* I press on, my voice unwavering, "You had no escape, Luna. As a child, you lied to yourself, making the game seem exciting. You convinced yourself you weren't scared so you could stay sharp. Excitement became your coping mechanism, your getaway. But then Gabriel changed everything. That's why you hate him too, because now that you've tasted love, you can't evade it. I know you felt his love, and for the first time in your life, you were afraid of that new emotion." Her eyes avert from mine, a crack appearing in her armor.

"You want me to answer your question, Luna? I will. You want Gabriel to find you because you want him to save you. You made me play a game that led me right back to you so that I could help you. We hear your cries for help, Luna, and we are here. You've made a mess of things, and the only way to fix it is if we all work together. When we are apart, fighting and playing games against each other, it's nothing but madness," I stress.

Luna breathes out through her nose, the sound resembling a bear that missed its salmon jumping up the stream. Slowly, she turns, fixing me with a glare that sends a chilling web across my body. I shake my limbs, trying to shake off the feeling, but it persists, creeping up until it reaches my neck. "You're such a fool," She sneers, shoving my shoulders forcefully. But I refuse to fall; I root my feet on the rocks and stagger only slightly. Affected, yet unaffected.

Luna turns and begins to walk ahead; Cody and Zander follow her.

Famine firmly grips my shoulders, urgently speaking in a hushed tone. "You can't reason with her anymore," he insists, "The effect is in full force, manifesting in sporadic bursts."

"Tell me what you are talking about; don't test me, Famine. I'm not the girl you think I am," I growl, jerking my shoulders to release his hold.

"I know. You're not the girl you think you are either," he mutters. "Astrid held something over Luna's head, but she also needed to ensure Luna complied with her demands. She stole a bioweapon that used Gabriel's nanobyte technology as the delivery agent. It targets an extremely specific area of long-term memory, forcing Luna to commit to a timeline before her memory was affected. In short—"

I cut him off, "I want the details."

His chin dips, "I can't give them all to you now. That will take weeks. What I can give you are bullet points while we freeze our asses. Those bears are real, and they will come sniffing if we don't keep moving."

I swallow and look over his shoulder. The bear is gone, but I know it can't be far.

"Luna had a ticking time bomb in her head. The nanobytes were attacking specific areas of her memory. She had no choice but to give in to Astrid's demands. So she did," he bites.

"What areas of her memory?"

"We'll get into that later." He won't meet my eyes. "Astrid wanted an army of loyal followers. She forced Luna to engineer a new bioweapon that would render the subject emotionless except to Astrid's approval."

The scientist in me starts to take over. How would I create this?

"Certain chemical reactions are blocked, turning whoever received this modification into a machine that operates solely on cold logic, without feelings."

"That doesn't necessarily make them loyal."

Famine grins with pride. "No, it doesn't. That's why Astrid had Luna engineer a dopamine release when they gained Astrid's approval."

I feel so numb that the cold air doesn't even penetrate my thoughts. "But—"

"Let me finish. Luna built in a safeguard. She created what Astrid wanted," he shakes his head, "She didn't have a choice, but she did have the favor of time. She engineered a minefield of sorts.

At least, that's how I see it. Months after a subject received this, they would start to malfunction." I hate his choice of words. It makes humanity seem so disposable. "It would release an influx of chemicals, making the subject extremely emotional."

My eyes spot Luna in the distance. "That's why her behavior has been so erratic Astrid made Luna take this weapon."

"Astrid wanted Luna as her soldier. If you weren't useful to Astrid, then you were a dead human walking. Luna had to take the weapon. She had to be useful to remain alive. She had no idea how these side effects would affect a subject over time, but now that time has passed, we have the results."

"Which are?" I ask. I try to curl my toes, but I can't feel them.

He exhales, and it's louder than the wind that is howling. "You'll see for yourself." He replies.

A sense of dread seeps into my being, tingling my skin and heating my blood, making it difficult to breathe. "What are you talking about?" I demand, my fingers trembling as I wipe the cold sweat from my forehead.

"Astrid always wanted Luna to be the winner, but one she could control. She always aspired to rule Manus Dei, and with this new upgrade, she could become the ruler behind the curtain, manipulating her clones to do her bidding. When Luna faked her death, it fucked everything up." He grins. "That's when Astrid pivoted and decided Gabriel would be her puppet."

"Did Gabriel receive it?" I gasp. I feel like I've swallowed a lump of concrete, and it drags my mood down like quicksand.

He shakes his head, "I stole the design to the weapon when I left."

"You saved him," I whisper. "Why didn't you just tell him? Why the games!"

No response! No fucking reply.

My head falls, I see the blood on my shoes—the blood of Astrid. I don't agree with how my sister killed her, but I am relieved that Astrid is dead.

"How many clones received this?" Hell, is that even my voice talking? It sounds so detached. So broken.

He shifts his weight, the spikes gripping his boots make a screeching sound against the rock. "The first trial tricked Astrid perfectly. One of Luna's last surviving clones received the modification. That clone listened like a fucking robot to Astrid. She embarked on a mission to kill an up-and-coming prince in Manus Dei. Unfortunately, that clone died during the mission, and Luna couldn't study the potential side effects. However, it did the trick. Astrid thought the weapon worked; she had no idea that over time, the weapon would slowly dismantle the subject."

"Unfortunately," I repeat. It's just another death to them. The death of a subject, not a person.

"It's…" He sighs, "It's our world. I want to change it. I need you to help me change it, Sol."

I can hear his desperation. It licks my wounds, burning them like salt. A part of me wants to let my impairments and grief fester. Just take me. But, like every human being, a part of my DNA will cling to the most preposterous idea if it will mean survival. So I swallow down all the pain and numbness that is trying to spread and nod.

"Luna ran out of time. They had no more clones to test it on. Astrid felt the noose tightening around her neck. She forced the modification onto Klara and Luna, leaving them no choice. Astrid couldn't wait. The game was ending, and she wanted Luna to be her puppet, her mask so that she could rule."

Now I understand. That's why she started this game, why she faked her death. If she wasn't in the picture, Astrid couldn't use her. But why wouldn't she just come to me or Gabriel for help? What leverage did Astrid have over her?

"Was I the leverage?" If I were, then I would have rather died than have to witness what my sister has become to save me.

"No,"

My head snaps up. "What was?"

His eyes look me up and down, "If you feed a starving man too much food, you'll kill him."

"Fuck you!"

"I'm sorry, but I won't risk your mind. Everything will make sense eventually." He steps closer, I step back. He exhales, "What you need to know is that the modification has taken hold. At times, Luna feels nothing—she is a robot waiting for orders. Then, in the blink of an eye, her brain releases a tremendous surge of chemicals. Sometimes it's serotonin or dopamine, and she feels wonderful. Other times, she's overwhelmed by guilt. I don't know what triggers these fluctuations, and I can't stop them." His golden eyes widen, silently conveying that I can.

"So why doesn't Luna just reverse the modification? Why do you need me, Famine? I already obtained the hard drives. I played this fucking twisted game. I'm done."

"No, you are not." He warns, his tone shifting into a threat that slows my blood.

"Luna can fix this herself."

He shakes his head, "You're a step behind, and you know what's frustrating. I already told you why she can't."

My mind spirals as I dig for a clue to help me understand. Famine replies faster than I can think, "Astrid injected her with nanobytes that target—"

I cut him off and repeat what he said earlier, "Specific areas of her mind."

"If it were so simple, Luna would have cured herself." He rebuttals.

"I need to know more Famine. You're just dropping breadcrumbs."

"I'll tell you everything. I just need you to trust me."

My eyes narrow, and we stand in a standoff, like two rival monarchs unwilling to yield any territory. "You want me to be the one to cure this, to repair what Luna created for Astrid," I repeat, hoping that if I hear the words coming from my lips, it will make the truth less painful. I'm still trapped in this game and no closer to saving the people I love.

He shakes his head, his pupils dilating as his hooded eyes reveal a devilish truth. "Luna wants you to fix the failed modification, but I want much more." Hope ignites his voice. "I want you to fix it all, to reverse everything. I want you to copy and implant your genetics in your sisters."

"W-what?" I stutter, struggling to comprehend the enormity of his request.

"You're a key, Sol. You were not just the key to entering the vault; genetically, you are the control, the reference point."

"I've been upgraded now."

"Barely." He scoffs, "Don't you wonder why your father left you, the only clone untouched."

"It was for scientific purposes, to compare and contrast."

"Bull-fucking-shit." The wide open space feels like it's shrinking and folding around me.

"You were the unknown threat. The reset button. That's what I want you to be, to make." He lunges, grabbing my shoulders and pulling us toe to toe as he whispers, "I want you to design a downgrade."

Chapter 7

Sol

"A downgrade?" I start to laugh, the sound echoing eerily in the tense atmosphere. But my laughter fades quickly as I catch the seriousness in Famine's gaze. "I…I can't..."

Famine's piercing stare silences me, his finger presses against my lips like a warning. "You can do this. You will do this," he asserts. His voice makes me feel like a soldier that's about to be pushed out of a plane without a parachute. "I'm your friend, not your foe. But don't push me to become one."

Well, that is definitely a threat. A surge of panic rushes through my veins, urging me to take a step back, to distance myself from his unsettling determination. Should I take my chances with the polar bears? "You're underestimating the magnitude of what you're asking. It's impossible," I protest.

A sly smile curls at the corner of Famine's lips, his eyes gleaming with a twisted delight. "Am I?" he taunts. "I don't think so. Deep within the darkest recesses of your mind, you're already plotting, aren't you? Your scientific instincts are awakening, scrambling to find a way to fulfill my proposition. You were born with subtle enhancements, Sol. Your very DNA holds the blueprint for engineering a downgrade. Offer Luna something she's never experienced—a chance to become you, to shed her burden and embrace your existence. It's what Luna was always meant to be, before you switched places."

His words are cruel facts forged into an iron sword that pierces my heart. He's right. The weight of his demand presses down upon me, threatening to crush my resolve. But it was never my choice; the option was taken away from me. Luna chose this path for us. And I'm not going to be blamed for that.

"Owe it?" I scoff. "I owe nothing. I've paid my dues. Because of me, we stand here in the midst of this chaos." Gripping my chest, I struggle to contain the torment swirling within me. "I obtained those hard drives for you, Famine. How much more of myself must I sacrifice for my twin? How many pieces of my soul must I offer on this agonizing altar?" Tears well up in my eyes, but the wind quickly dries them. Nothing and no one is allowing me to feel or to express my grief!

Turning my back to him, I look at the dark, empty landscape. I see two options. I can take my chances with the bears and the cold. I give myself half an hour before a bear, or the weather claims me. The second option is to continue to play this game.

My shoulders slump, and my body feels boneless; it just wants to melt into a puddle that everyone will walk on. With each step, my existence will slowly be splashed away until I'm just droplets and then...nothing.

I wish you were here, Death. I wish I had listened to you.

A downgrade. Similar to a reset but not fully. If it is indeed a reset button, then does that mean when this game starts over I won't be involved in it?

That's enough hope to make a madman change his tune.

It's genius. It's madness. Wiser humans have claimed both go hand in hand.

My voice trembles as I utter the next words that would mark me as a traitor to Luna. "Luna will never agree to this." Desperation tinges my words, emphasizing the seemingly insurmountable challenge ahead. Can I strip Luna bare of what she holds dear?

"Give Luna and Klara a choice." Famine urges. "Reset them. Wipe the slate clean and give them the option to choose their own upgrades."

I need to feel something real, something tangible amidst the swirling uncertainty. Bending down, my fingers brush against the cold rock until they grasp a tiny rock shard that the spikes under our shoes have chipped away. I take that small shard and curl it so tight into my palm that I swear it melts and becomes a part of my flesh.

Reset everything. Not just that, but also cure a failed upgrade. I shake my head so vigorously that my vision blurs, and I wobble unsteadily. It's not that simple. I would need to understand how every upgrade Luna has been given works. Then, I would have to engineer a way to reset her without endangering her life. "I wouldn't know where to begin," I murmur, the weight of the task pressing heavily on me.

"Just start with the fantasy of it. The idea. That's how it all began, and look how far we have come," He replies, his voice unusually gentle.

"Luna would never want to be normal," I whisper as I push to stand. "Anytime I mentioned being normal, she loathed the idea. She taught me that normal was never an option, Famine."

"You're right, but you're not looking at the details. You and Luna, all the clones, were never normal. Before birth, you were slightly enhanced. I'm not asking you to make yourselves like basic humans. I'm asking you to create a downgrade, to reset yourselves back to your original genetic base." He explains, his hand touching my shoulder gently as he turns me, but I can't meet his gaze. Instead, I squeeze my eyes shut, wishing this were a virtual reality I could turn off.

"I wanted to end the games," I whisper.

"This is your way to do that," He replies. His fingers press into my clothing, and it feels like a mountain pressing me into the earth. "Imagine if you gave Luna the gift of choice. It could repair so much."

The weight of his words bears down on me, and I realize that Luna has never had the opportunity to choose her own upgrades, shackled by the abusive nature of the science that created her. This could be a small step, allowing Luna to select what she wants or doesn't want.

It is a fantasy.

I open my palm and see the small rock. I grin, not even sure why, then I tuck the rock into my pocket as a token, a reminder of this crucial conversation. Then, with a heavy heart, I reply, "She would never take it."

He clears his throat, the sound hitting me like a slap in the face. I am alert now, understanding what he is silently suggesting.

"You want to force the downgrade on her, then try to pacify her anger by offering the illusion of choice in future upgrades."

He crosses his arms, resembling two thick tree trunks. "She would have a choice. After," he adds.

"You want me to disguise the cure, a Trojan horse. Fix the failed modification, but also..."

"Hide the downgrade within it," he confirms. "Yes."

I tell myself I don't have a choice, but that's a lie. I do.

I can refuse to make this, but instead, I nod in agreement. A tear swells in my eye but doesn't fall. Does that make me the villain? Yes. But some people will see me as the hero. It all depends on perspective, just as Luna described to me on the Cliff Walk.

Luna laughs, "You know what's funny? Heroes and villains are the same. They're both fighting to save the world. The hero's world versus the villain's. Everyone praises the hero for saving the world, but did they ever think that maybe the villain was trying to protect the world too? The villain just envisioned a different world to save. A new future."

Reaching my hand out toward Famine, I say, "Famine is an ally. Give me your name so I can regard you as a friend."

He grins, extending his hand to shake mine. "Evander. Evander Neilson," he replies, sealing our bond and betrayal with a firm handshake. I've learned that a Horseman does not give his name easily; it takes time and trust.

His fingers curl around mine, testing my strength as his friend. Our friendship becomes a game within a game. I survived the previous game because I had a Horseman on my side, and I'll survive this one too. I find myself standing taller, and together, we begin to walk this new path. Both hell-bent on saving the people we love. Famine has given me a way to end the games. I have to take it. I have to save my sister. In doing so, she will hate me. I can live with her hate. But I can't bear the thought of her having no future. This is how I will undo everything Manus Dei did to my family.

Chapter 8

Sol

As we trek through the open expanse of Svalbard, Norway, Luna leads the way with an uncanny familiarity, her every step deliberate and sure. The slight uphill incline causes a burning in my calves as we ascend. A peculiar sight catches my eye ahead: a perfectly square house constructed from concrete, stark against the barren landscape. Its roof, nearly flat with only a slight incline, seems designed to allow snow to slide off.

"What's that?" I ask, turning to Famine, who walks beside me. We've remained distant from he others, keeping a forty-foot gap between us. Maybe it's Famine's way of giving me space from Luna to think.

"That is going to be our home," He responds. I don't miss the distress in his tone. I remember what War said: his brother loves the light, the sun. All around us is darkness and cages, games, and turmoil. He is suffering just like me. We both want this to end.

Luna halts at the entrance, her gaze fixed on the door that gleams like steel, reflecting the soft glow of the snow-covered night. She pivots her head slightly, granting me only a glimpse of her profile. It's as if she wants to look at me but can't decide. Is she the emotionless robot controlled by the genetic weapon, or are her emotions finally breaking through?

Without hesitation, Cody brushes past her, wipes away a light dusting of snow from a sensor, and places his palm on it. The door emits a terrible sound as it automatically opens, cracking the ice off its joints.

"Come on," Famine urges, motioning for us to proceed. A light coat of ice has formed on his beard, eyelashes, and brows. He looks like a god who has descended from the heavens to play with mortal men.

Once inside, the small house feels even smaller. This is a trick; there is no way we can all live here. Heck, we can't even fit a bed inside. My enhanced night vision reveals the truth to me. To the left is a ladder leading down into a dark shaft. One by one, we descend, the darkness enveloping us. After a few steps down, it becomes repetitive. You don't need the light, but it would make me feel better. I can't decide whether to feel relieved or hesitant as my feet touch the bottom floor. A long concrete tunnel stretches out before us, gently sloping downward. We walk for another ten minutes, and the tunnel finally opens to reveal a massive, foreboding metal door.

What new hell is this?

The air is stale, and each inhale has such a chill that it burns. I'm tempted to hold my breath to save my nose from the burden of the burn. It's just utter darkness, no lights. The tunnel's walls, floor, and roof are solid concrete, making it feel colder, like a morgue. This is purgatory, and I fear whatever is behind that door might be hell.

The music playing from Luna's phone echoes off the cement walls, the sound bouncing eerily in the empty space. "My Sweet Prince" by Placebo fills my ears. I listen intently, making mental notes to memorize every lyric, for within each song lies a glimpse into her true feelings.

Luna's shining blonde hair sways like a curtain, her high ponytail adorned with a red ribbon. She possesses knowledge about my father, Astrid, and Manus Dei that I have no choice but to unearth. I need to understand the monsters who made her so that I can dismantle the monster she has become. How does one crack open an already shattered egg?

For the first time since our journey began, I stride forward, shoving Zander aside. It feels strangely satisfying to release my frustration upon him, to embrace the darkness within me, the first step toward becoming the villain. I no longer care about hurting others, especially when they have hurt me.

I reach out and grasp Luna's fingers, letting her know that she is not alone. I refuse to abandon her, no matter how difficult the path ahead may be. I won't run as I once thought I would. I am here for her, just as she was there for me when we were children. But this time, it is my turn to protect my sister.

We walk a few strides, and she reciprocates by wrapping her fingers around mine. It soothes a part of me that was confused and lost.

As the air grows less stale and the anticipation heightens, we make our way deeper finally stopping at the massive door.

"Where are we?" I whisper to her. *Please answer me.*

"This is a nuclear fallout shelter, built by an eccentric Norwegian oil tycoon. It has been abandoned for decades until we resurrected it," she reveals, her gaze meeting mine and something tells me she is apologetic although she would never verbalize it. "We will take refuge here until we establish power. We have enough supplies to sustain us for three years. I hope you don't mind the company, Sol. This is our new family."

***

"This is your room. You should get some rest. Tomorrow, you will start working with Famine," Luna instructs me, her voice cold and distant, a stark contrast to our previous closeness. The chemical reactions in her brain are no longer functioning properly again.

She stands in the doorway, refusing to step inside. I wonder if she sees me now as the predator, the older sister reclaiming her place. Does she feel her control slipping away? Yes, I believe she does. Not just her control over me or Manus Dei, but her control over her own mind.

I survey the room, resembling a barren barracks for soldiers, with five bunk beds and a small bathroom containing a single shower and toilet. The grey walls and solid cement floor exude a cold, prison-like ambiance.

How lovely. Maybe it's what I deserve?

We passed by four identical rooms like this one, and further down the hall, more hallways remained a mystery to me.

I square my shoulders, facing Luna directly. "You're not sharing a room with me?" I question. I know it sounds silly, but we always shared a room. It wasn't just because we were twins. We always watched each other's backs.

"We are not children anymore," she replies, her gaze unwavering as she meets my stare. "Get some rest. Tomorrow, your task is to undo the last upgrade. That's all I care about," she states, but I'm no longer the fool. I see through her lies; she knows exactly what Famine has planned. She has to know. Luna knows everything. She does care, and deep down, she desires this downgrade. If she didn't, she would stop me, right?

Something must show on my face because she adds, "You're more than capable."

"I don't know why you couldn't just ask for help, Luna," I express.

Her response is like a frozen lake, her words gliding over its icy surface without a hint of warmth. "Asking others for help was eradicated from my DNA," she replies, her words carrying a subtle bitterness like a hint of sourness in a sweet fruit. "It made me weak."

"*Not* asking for help made you weak, Luna," I declare. *Look at your current state! You have never been so weak.* "You closed yourself off, shutting out those who cared about you the most. We would have done anything for you, Luna. Gabriel and I were ready to support you, to be there for you in any way we could. But you never gave us the chance." A bitter laugh escapes my lips. "You know, after I unlocked that vault, I had a plan. I thought I could seize the power and use it as leverage to bring you and Gabriel together, to force you to cooperate. And if that failed, I was prepared to dismantle it all, to watch from a distance as you tore each other apart," I confess. "You might have called me a coward, but I had reached a point where I no longer cared. I had paid my dues, and all I wanted was a chance to live my own life."

With a heavy exhale, I soften my voice hoping it reaches the depths of her mind. "Strength doesn't mean shutting others out. It means finding the courage to ask for help when we need it most. We are stronger together, Luna."

"You always carried this sense of obligation, as if you owed it to me." Her words make me feel like a fool, like I've been handed a puzzle with missing pieces. "I played on that weakness, making you believe that your life belonged to me," she admits. "But that guilt, that burden you carried, it was unfounded. I took your place willingly. It was my choice. You owed me nothing, Sol. All you had to do was say no, to stand up for yourself. Yet, you chose the path where you relinquished your freedom. You did as others told you. You became our father," She sneers. "I needed you to be a leader, to not bow down to Manus Dei. Did you learn your lesson, Sol? I wanted you to be selfish, find strength within yourself, and not be a pushover. That's the only way you could survive in the world I envisioned."

With a huff of laughter, I respond, "I learned the opposite. I learned that making allies made me stronger."

As Luna's lips press into a thin line, I watch her emotional barricades rise higher, keeping me at arm's length. Her shoulders straighten, her spine extends to its full height, and a devilish grin stretches across her face, a grin she has practiced to perfection. "Seeking help implies that I am failing," she declares. Taking three deliberate steps towards me, she alternates slamming her foot down between left and right. "Three steps ahead, sister. I'm here," she proclaims before crushing her foot down one final time and retreating from my room. "You're all here, behind me. I've planned every detail, and you still haven't grasped it yet."

She leaves my room, but as she steps out into the hallway, I call after her, "Sometimes, it helps to look behind you. It's the only way to know who is chasing you." We're all chasing her now.

With those words, I slam the door shut, attempting to shut out her lingering presence. I try to ignore her cryptic words, but deep down, I can't help but wonder what other plans Luna has set into motion.

Chapter 9

Sol

The hairs on my arm rise, and the air seems to become electrified. Twins indeed have a 'twin sense' when they're near. I can't sleep; instead, I lie awake on my bed. I slip into the scientist role as I ponder how to undo the upgrades my father did. It keeps my mind racing and plagues me with questions I'm too overwhelmed to begin solving.

"You should be sleeping," Luna whispers, creeping further into my darkened room. I estimate it's been about four hours since I slammed the door in her face.

I adjust the blanket, which is pulled up to my chin. It's dry, scratchy, and smells like stale air. The fallout shelter is abrasive, and I must acclimatize to it.

"What do you want?" I grunt as I roll over, feeling soreness in every muscle. I can't imagine how a normal human would feel. If I am sore, they would be unable to move.

Luna takes a step closer without turning on the bedroom light. Her silhouette moves with grace. Has she ever tripped and felt the burn of the fall? Yes, of course, she has. She is just better at masking it.

"I need to work. There is no rest for the wicked," Luna states. This time when she speaks, I hear the emptiness in her voice. She sounds more like a ghost, not fully present yet, leaving a lingering presence. She joins me on my bed, and I push myself up to sit.

She looks ahead into the darkness of the room. "You don't have to be wicked," I tell her. Deep down, I know Luna didn't want to be cruel. It was just the only way she knew how to survive the games. She erected a tough outer wall that tried to rebound every blow.

"We were designed to be the next phase of evolution. Every predator is viewed as a beast. If they were not, they would not claim the title of the predator," She says.

Pivoting my body to face her, I tilt my head, trying to discern the true purpose behind her return to my room. "Life isn't about titles," I reply. "You won but lost everything."

She shrugs, "The things I lost were holding me down. Now I'm on top." She still won't look at me. Her blonde hair looks ashen, almost white, in the room's darkness.

Reaching out, I take her hand, but her fingers don't move. They feel like icicles. "When you dragged me to the Cliff Walk, I thought you would change everything. I imagined you would make everything whole again. I'm sorry I put all that on your shoulders, Luna," I squeeze her fingers. "I'm here now."

"Intentions often change in the middle of a bloody battle. You don't see good or evil, just red. I started to see everything in that new light. It was all filthy. I told you I would not build on a spoiled foundation," She finally grips my hand back. "I feel nothing right now. No spark, drive, or ambition. Nothing."

"How does that make you feel when you are coherent enough to?"

"Sometimes I'm happy." She nods, "Really, I am. I feel at peace. Just nothing."

I gulp, "What outweighs that happiness?" I question. What about feeling nothing was enough to motivate you to continue the games till this point?

Her chest inhales and stays inflated as she replies, "When I'm not happy, I feel…" She shakes her head, "I don't know how to describe it. I know I just don't like it. That outweighs the empty happiness. That's why I kept fighting on."

She is empathic right now. That's why she came to my room. Hope ignites in me. I need to use this opportunity to get more answers.

"How do you feel when your not empty?"

"I feel what I think is guilt." She slips her hand free from mine. "It's like a huge beast hunting me down. I prefer this state. Nothing. It's better this way," she says.

"That's a lie," I call her out. "You're just scared of allowing the beast to find you. You've never been scared or felt fear, and the upgrade has allowed you to feel that. It can be crippling, but it can also be powerful."

"How?" She asks. There is no passion or climax in her voice, just a still ocean without wind. No force to push her in a new direction. Like she said, nothing. I'm losing her again.

"Fear makes us realize everything we have that can be taken from us. It forces us to take a stance, dig our boots in the dirt, claw our way out to face, and then fight the demons."

She starts to edge off my bed, "I need to work," she says, then hesitates. "I need you to pick a playlist for me." That's why she came. Pushing back the tears in my eyes, I accept the phone and begin to make a playlist of songs.

"I know once you find a cure for Klara, you will want to give it to me, too," She says. "Astrid didn't give me a choice. She forced me." She admits, squaring her shoulders towards me. It's a rare moment I know is fleeting. It might not ever recur again. Luna has lowered her armor; sitting in front of me is my twin, who is so broken and abused she doesn't even know what she wants or needs anymore. "Are you going to give me a choice?" She asks.

No, I won't give you a choice, sister. This is what you need. In doing so, it will mean I will lose Luna. I have to take away her choice, and she will hate me for it. I have to become Astrid and my father. I must be the monster in order to protect her, just as Luna became a beast to keep me safe as a child. The roles have truly reversed. I'm finally the older sister again, and the weight on my shoulders has never felt so heavy.

Inhaling, I try to paint on a thick skin, but inside, I'm crumbling. My ribs press into my heart, which wants to sob until it stops beating. *"Be strong, little mouse,"* I imagine Death whispering in my ear.

I turn cruel embracing the villain within me, "The old Luna would tell me that sometimes it is better not to give people an option. You never gave me one. You made me think I had a choice, but I never did. I always had to play the game. The only option I had was what door I chose to begin the game at. The big door, the small one, the door stuck on the ceiling or on the floor. Either way, it led to the same starting point. You cornered me. Tricked me, lied to teach me." I shove the phone to her. "It's okay. I was always the oldest. It's time I take my title back." I press play.

Luna's fingers curl around the phone, and she stands, leaving a cold, ghostly air in her place. "I couldn't help you even if I tried," She admits.

"What do you mean?"

"Astrid made sure of that. I forgot how I made it. I forgot the science. That's why Famine needs you. While you help him, I have to start over. Not just with the new society I want to form. I have to learn everything again." A fresh vulnerability is sewn into her words. She has just admitted her weakness. I am shocked, speechless.

"Astrid erased it from my mind. If you are wondering how Astrid could delete selected memories, then ask Cody. He used Gabriel's nanobytes and created something to try and fix his brother. All Cody wanted to do was fix his brother's pain by erasing it. Sometimes I wish Cody would have erased everything inside my mind. Wiped me clean so I could start over," She tells me.

She admitted a lot more, and I see it in her details. Luna is always a step ahead. She knows what Famine asked of me: to create the downgrade hidden in the cure. She is always three steps ahead. The question is why is she allowing me to create this downgrade?

My lips spread in a sorrow-filled grin. "Where would you start over, Luna?"

Luna's head tilts to the side, her long blonde hair falling like a war-torn flag just released from the pole. "I've never pondered that. It seems silly to fantasize about something that will never happen," she replies with a bite.

She thinks I will fail, or perhaps she hopes I will. She tucks the phone into her pocket and grabs the wired headphones, raising them to her ear.

"Fifty years ago, people would have called *us* a fantasy. Genetically upgraded clones, printed organs, cures for cancer. The future is a fantasy; we have to dream it in order to try to create it, Luna," I say.

Luna's fingers hesitate to put her headphone on. "Do you think Manus Dei had such a noble thought when they first started? They wanted to create something wonderful. They just didn't know it was going to be built on a pile of bones. They kept their chins up and admired the view, never looking down."

"Will you look down when you build your new empire?" I reply.

"No," she replies, shoving one headphone in her ear. "I'm not going to look up or down, just side to side. After all, I am my own worst enemy and my reflection is everywhere I turn."

Chapter 10

Sol

My lungs inhale and exhale with eager anticipation. In the realm of my dream, I press my back against the tree as the darkness and cold night air embrace me like a welcomed blanket. This surreal darkness and cool nature have always been my true home. I painted the lies of a cozy house that never existed. No more lies.

"Little mouse," Death purrs. He's closer to finding me.

Yearning to move, I shift and dodge low, running to another tree to hide behind. In this ethereal landscape, I know I'm dreaming but I welcome it because in this dream my hunter chases me. Just as he said he would.

My shoulders pivot as I prepare to hide behind the tree, but I land right into large, feverish hands instead.

"Got you," Death says. His voice is so full of lust it makes my legs collapse, but as he promised, I don't fall. He won't allow me to.

Reaching up, I cup his unshaven jaw, pressing my fingertips into the abrasive stubble. "You were right," I admit.

He tilts his head. He doesn't look arrogant but rather full of sorrow. "I know. I knew all along. That's what I was preparing you for. The biggest battle was yet to come. The hardest war is always against ourselves." He cups my face, drawing me closer to him. When he speaks next, his lips brush over mine. "It's time to fight, little mouse. Fight yourself; fight your Reflection."

I pull back so I can see his whole face. Death is always there, lurking and waiting for me to fall or run into his arms. "What if I'm not strong enough? What if I can't fix everything? Do I just destroy it all?"

He shakes his head. A fog churns around us, snaking up our close bodies. I try to cling to him, but the fog is dense, and suddenly he is torn from me.

"You have to fix it. If not, you give me no choice," He replies. His voice has changed. It sends goosebumps down every inch of my body.

He moves, blurring through the thick fog. I see the shimmer of the knife right as it's coming towards me. I feel the cold metal press into my throat right as I scream.

My eyes fly open. My awareness is slow until I realize where I am. My new room. My prison. The bunker in the fallout shelter.

"It was a dream."

"Does that fact make it better or worse?" A new voice chimes in. My body jumps from my small twin bunk bed. Zander is perched on a top bunk across from me. Grasping my thin bed sheet, I pull it over me like a sheet of armor. He seems to think that is funny.

"What are you doing here?"

"What did you dream?" He asks. In a fell swoop, he jumps down from the bunk bed like a panther in a jungle that is trying to eat me alive. His blonde curly hair and dimples make him look like the boy next door, friendly and approachable. It's the perfect mask to hide who he truly is. I remember when he pressed a knife over my lips and threatened to cut out my tongue. I also recall how broken he was.

It's easy to hate someone who is aggressive and lashes out. Judge the cover. I did until I flipped open the book. Zander is a broken Reflection that his twin is desperate to fix, just like I am with Luna.

He sinks down and sits on the edge of my bed. His body language is anything but relaxed. I know mine mirrors his at this moment. His hazel eyes examine mine. "Cody sent me to apologize." He admits.

Lowering the sheet, I sit taller. "You don't want to." It's clear he doesn't.

He shakes his head. "I know I should, but when I see you, I change my mind." He taps his temple. "Deep inside my mind, I know I should hate you. That's why I lash out." He offers.

"You don't lash out at Luna," I question. Zander can stand side by side with my twin, even offering her support. Why not me?

He snorts, and his short ringlets bounce like an angel on a cloud laughing. "My mind knows you're not Luna. You're just a stranger. I thought I knew the other Reflection, but she turned out to be a stranger too," he admits, his dimples fading and giving way to a surge of animosity.

"Who?" I ask. I want him to confess more to me. Who is the woman, the Reflection, that caused so much agony to this crippled soul?

"Your Reflection," he growls. The lighter caramel hues in his hazel eyes disappear as his pupils expand. "I loved her. I should have believed Luna when she told me love was a game of trickery."

"What happened to her, this Reflection?"

His head moves slowly like a snake drawing back; his fingers grasp the itchy, thick blanket on the bed. "I killed her."

I feel palpitations in my heart. "Why?" I push.

Zander leans forward, his face inches away from mine. The small bed dips under his weight as his right hand slowly extends, his fingers reaching out to cup my cheek. The tips of his fingers feel unnaturally hard and callous against my smooth skin. I can feel every ridge of his fingerprints as he glides his touch over my face, tracing invisible lines.

My body freezes in place, a mixture of fear and curiosity coursing through me. But I refuse to retreat; instead, I hold my ground, allowing him to inspect me like a predator sniffing out its prey. I want Zander to realize that I'm not the Reflection he despises, that I pose no threat to him.

"Because," His thumb digs painfully into my jaw, sending a surge of sharp discomfort through me. "Astrid sent her to kill me," he whispers, his voice filled with a mix of anguish and bitterness. His head tilts to the side, his ear almost touching his shoulder as his intense gaze traces every contour of my face. "and she did." He whispers.

I understand his statement. This Reflection killed his sanity.

"Zander," Cody calls as he appears in the doorway.

"I'm sorry," Zander grinds out. His head snaps up, full of life again. "I..." His grip on my jaw slackens. His fury changes to grief so palpable that my blue eyes glass over with tears. My lip wobbles as I try to think of something to say that can fix him.

No words come.

"I am sorry," He repeats. I know he's not seeing me but the Reflection he killed.

In an abrupt movement, he flees the room, shoving Cody out of his way. Cody crosses his arms and looks at me. "He can't remember the details, just the guilt and pain. He recalls it in flashes. Some days he's absolutely fine; he's my brother again. On other days he is more... of a challenge. The upgrade I created to help him backfired. I wanted him not to feel guilt just for that specific event. Now I jumbled everything up. Genetics was never my strong suit."

"What was?" I ask as I square my shoulders to him. I slip my legs off my bed, and my bare feet brush against the cold cement floor. I'll never be rid of this chill until I create the downgrade.

Cody smirks. "I had a specific purpose. I was never in the game against Luna and Gabriel, but I was still a tool that was developed and used." He pauses and looks at me hard. "I was groomed to be a prince." His eyes search mine as if that should make sense to me.

His smirk fades, and a tinge of sadness colors his expression when I don't reply. He enters my room with slow steps. Unlike his brother, he's giving me a chance to refuse him. When I don't, he sits on the bed opposite me. The mattress sinks and compresses, producing a sound reminiscent of a swing, abandoned by children and now played with only by the gusts of wind. I find myself wondering if he had a childhood similar to mine.

"Luna's purpose was genetic manipulation on the cellular level, involving permanent upgrades," He explains. "The Masters wanted Gabriel to focus on nanobyte technology for genetic enhancement. It's the next phase of their grand plan. Nanobytes that can tailor enhancements for their members and loyal supporters. Gabriel was working on an on-and-off switch, where nanobytes would be seamlessly inserted into a subject. With a simple activation, the enhancements would be triggered, turning individuals into powerful assets. And when the duty ends, you could just as easily deactivate them—a practical leash for those deemed unworthy of permanent upgrades. It allows governments to wield control over their upgraded soldiers, rewarding compliance and punishing defiance with a mere flick of a switch," he concludes, snapping his fingers to emphasize the swift control they hold.

"And your purpose?"

His gaze falls upon his hands, and he absentmindedly rotates his fingers, lost in his own thoughts. What images and memories are playing in his mind? Does he perceive his hands as clean, free from the stain of his actions, or do they bear the weight of his choices?

"Biochemical warfare," He confesses, his voice tinged with a mix of resignation and understanding. "That was my role. I was tasked with developing and implementing methods of biological and chemical manipulation, weapons that could unleash devastation on an unprecedented scale. Zander, on the other hand, was meant to be the embodiment of traditional warfare, utilizing conventional weapons and tactics. As for Famine, or should I say Evander, he was originally destined to become one of the Masters. However, he surpassed their expectations and became something far greater. Evander possesses unparalleled skills as a hacker, making him the most formidable in the world. His expertise in cyber warfare proved to be more valuable to them than a mere voting voice, enabling him to infiltrate systems, gather intelligence, and strike at the heart of their enemies."

"He's also a Horseman," I add.

"A different face for every game they forced us to play." Cody shrugs. "Famine is a Horseman because, unlike us, his father loved him. He pushed his son to be one of the new soldiers that would protect Manus Dei."

I snort. "That's not love."

"Love comes in all shapes and forms. I would think you, of all people, could understand that. Evander's father loved him; he wanted to give his son the best so he could be the best, but also so he would be stronger for when the day came for Manus Dei to be destroyed." He laughs. "That's right, Sol." He opens his arms. "This bunker was built by Evander's grandfather. Let's just say he held a strong grudge against the Masters. Evander's dad shared that fury and groomed his son to be the perfect turncoat. It was only a matter of time before all the pawns and soldiers turned against the council who sat back and benefited from our suffering."

"What's your game, Cody?" I inquire. "Why are you here?" Why is he revealing so much to me? He speaks with ease as if I am an old friend.

He stands and grins. His dimples are visible. "I failed, but I'll try again and again to fix Zander. Famine will never stop until Klara is cured and until we are all a happy family." He sneers. "Gabriel won't give up his revenge against Luna. Luna won't stop pushing us all away, even those she desperately needs. We will never give up; like bacteria, we cling to life in the harshest environments. I hope you have the same drive as I do, Sol. You're going to need it." He chuckles.

"Why are you helping Luna, then?"

His smile drops. He comes closer, standing above me. I push myself up from the bed, leveling my eyes with him. I'm not a scared little girl anymore. I won't curl into my shell when the shadows cast over me. "Why did War help all his brothers, Sol?" He smirks.

Thump, thump! My heart skyrockets. I swallow a heavy stone, but my shoulders feel lighter.

"All you have to do is ask, Sol," Cody whispers. I said those exact same words to him after he stole my blood. I would have helped him regardless because he was like me.

"Imagine if the Masters asked us what upgrades we wanted, asked before they forced and took from us. I think we would be very different people. No anger or sorrow. We'd feel more like kids that got presents. It would have been such a different life if we had a choice. A choice is the most precious gift to give." He adds.

It's clear he supports Famine's endgame. He wants a choice.

His eyes change, searching mine with such hope I choke on my swallow. "You're a very talented artist, Sol. I hope you can paint that picture for me. I hope you can fix everything that was forced upon us." He steps forward into my personal space. His arms encircle my torso in a hug while his nose buries itself in my hair. This gesture isn't romantic; instead, it feels like I'm a distant memory he's attempting to recollect. "All you have to do is ask, Sol. Remember that before you do anything... silly. You have friends who will do anything to help you." He warns, pulling away and leaving me with the ghostly feeling of his hug, welcoming me into a new game. But unlike the other games, everyone now seeks the same ending, hoping I can deliver it.

End My Games

Tag, I'm it and it all depends on me.

Chapter 11

Death

The hum of the engines on the private jet fails to calm Gabriel. Since boarding, he hasn't taken a seat. Instead, he paces the aisle with the restless energy of a caged animal, eager to be unleashed on the trail he must scout.

Lowering the phone, I stand and grab my bag from the overhead compartment. We're on our way to Utah, to my father's compound where we will get supplies and regroup. I made a deal with the devil in exchange for my soul. My father will offer us what we need to find Luna and those hard drives. He will place false trails to keep enemies at bay.

The cost for his aid was me. My father wants his son back.

When I asked for his help, I put the ball back in his court. I'll be able to be his son again. My father wants me to work for the family, and now I must. Not only that, the roles will be reversed: Gabriel will be on a leash my father controls, and I will be in the middle of that tug of war.

Deep down, I always knew it would come to this.

Tossing the bag down on the seat next to me, I look at my brother. Reaching out, I grab his shoulder. "It's okay," I assure him.

"Nothing is okay. I don't even know where to begin." Gabriel snorts.

Releasing him, I take a seat and unzip the bag. I had packed it before our mission, as a precaution in case we couldn't return to the safe house. "Yes, we do. Start thinking clearly. We now have my family's power at our disposal. We may not be able to track Luna directly, but we can track War. I have men scouring through the CCTV footage of that train. We will find him and follow his trail. War will lead us right to Luna." As I speak, I retrieve the smooth leather bag and present it to Gabriel. "And we have this."

He raises a brow. I continue, "This is Sol's bag." Opening the flap, I pour out the contents. Postcards, a red ribbon, and War's tie pin spill out.

"Luna told us where she would be all along," I state as I grab the postcards. New York, Berlin, and then, "Norway."

Gabriel's jaw clenches. His eyes swipe back and forth. "It's a trap."

"Absolutely," I reply. Luna was no fool. She is a genius, but hidden in her madness was a plea, a cry for help. Sol followed, and now we will pursue it. Gabriel and I are playing a game of catch-up.

"Don't think of every angle, brother. We tried that and failed. This is Luna's game now. She controls the court and makes the rules."

"What are you suggesting?"

Extending my hand to reach for my drink, I feel the sinister grin starch across my face. The sip I take burns, but it's merely a hint of the fire simmering deep within my stomach. I can hardly wait to embark on the hunt, to locate my prey—the woman who possesses my heart. Swirling the amber-colored liquid, I continue, "We walk straight into the trap, brother."

Chapter 12

Sol

My fingertips brush along the solid concrete wall. The hallway still has a stale odor to it. I'm not sure how long it will take for it to fade. Each step Evander takes echos off the walls, causing my teeth to grind. After a sleepless night, intruded upon by Luna, Zander, and Cody, I'm more than eager to leave my room and see what the rest of the bunker has to offer.

Evander is giving me a guided tour as if this was a welcomed vacation I signed up for.

I wonder if I'll ever be trusted enough to roam free?

We descend one floor lower, making me wonder how deep this bunker runs. As soon as we step off the stairs, there is a long hallway. We stop at the first door. "This is where you will be working," he points to the new room.

I step inside and blink. It's still the same gray walls and white light overhead that have a slight hum to them. "How did you manage to get all of this here?" I ask as I begin to walk further in. It's not just any room. It's a fully functional laboratory. Any type of equipment I would need is here. This couldn't be trekked by hand past the wandering polar bears.

"My father spent years preparing this place. He knew one-day Manus Dei would crumble. We were able to airdrop most of the items. That was ten years ago. Plenty of time for the snow to cover our tracks." He jokes as he walks towards me. "Luna's workspace is four doors down. I'm next door on the right, Cody on the left."

"Where does Zander work?"

"Zander works three floors below," He pauses. "He won't hurt you."

"You hope," I tease without laughing.

He exhales, and at first, it sounds as heavy as a lead anchor sinking to the ocean's depths. But then, his inhale reveals his hope, as buoyant as a life preserver escaping the peril below, bobbing on the surface as it looks ahead to the clear horizon. "We're going to fix everything."

I don't reply. How can I?

Is it cruel to stomp on his hope or crueler to give it more life?

He pats my back in reassurance. My father never did that. Never gave me motivation. I didn't need it then. I was given a task, I learned it, then did it.

"Let's continue. There is a storage room I need to show you. It has all your father's personal journals."

As we descend another level and move past the kitchen, we enter a dining room equipped with two long rectangular tables, each capable of seating around twenty individuals. Scratch that - it's not for regular people; this is a bunker, designed for soldiers. A somber makeshift living room awaits, devoid of any couches; instead, we see folded-out chairs that remain untouched. No one here is at ease; each of us has a specific purpose and goal that must be achieved. Down the corridor, a sizable gym comes into view where Cody and Zander are vigorously running on the treadmills.

"How do you stay sane here?" I ask.

His feet slow down, mimicking the gradual drip of a leaky faucet. "I look ahead," he responds bluntly, his next step more of a stomp. "Storms can't last forever. The sun will shine again," he mutters.

Down yet another set of stairs is a new hallway that makes the others feel cozy. The lighting on the walls here is spaced further apart, making the dark shadows seem more haunting. "This is the storage level. Not many people come down here," Evander adds. Unlike the other levels, not every room is sealed off; some rooms just have walls constructed of metal fencing. Boxes upon boxes are stacked behind them.

"So, when you say 'not many,' are you referring to Luna, Zander, or Cody, or have you been keeping a bunker full of friendly faces hidden from me who don't secretly wish to kill me in my sleep?" I sneer.

"No one wants to kill you."

"I'm not sure Gabriel or Wes would agree with that statement." I shake my head.

He shakes his head, "They wouldn't kill you."

"There are worse fates than death," I'm convinced Gabriel is plotting a few for me.

Evander glances down at me, "Yes, there are." The heaviness in his tone, combined with this dark, eerie space, tells me I'm about to find out.

I reach into my pocket and feel the small rock I took from outside. It's sharp and jagged; if I'm not careful, it will cut me. "Is there a way outside?" I ask. Knowing these cement walls will imprison me. The harder I work, the faster I'll be free. And the quicker Luna will hate me.

"Outside?" He questions, his heavy combat boots stop.

"I'm not trying to escape; I just want fresh air," I offer.

His lips tug to one side. "Oh," he shrugs, "We have a virtual reality room set up. It can take you almost anywhere. Manus Dei had a large portfolio of locations documented. We even have scent enhancers. You can go to the beach and actually smell the salt in the air."

A virtual reality... the last time I was forced to live in one of those, I experienced the horrors of Klara's childhood. "That sounds like you want me to live in a painted lie, Evander. It's not real," I reply.

He spreads his hands open, turning his palms up. "It's the best I can offer."

"So there's no way outside?"

I watch as Evander slips into his Horseman persona. Harden. Cruel. "No," he declares. "The door is closed. Sealed off."

"I just..." I glance at the walls, the long hallway that truly feels like a maze. "I just..." I want someplace I can escape to so I can scream and not be heard. I want to run to a corner and cry, find something so I can punch it till my knuckles bleed.

I envision Luna as a child. She used to run into the forest in our backyard. She would scream so loudly. It was her way to break free.

"I was going to wait, but it looks like you might need this lifeline." Bending down, he opens a pocket of his cargo pants and pulls out a shiny new phone. "This is for you. There are no restrictions on it." Grabbing my palm, he places it in my hand.

With wide eyes, I tap the screen. It's unlocked. I open the internet.

"You're going to need access to that; I assumed," He adds.

I nod. Then I continue to click away. I stop when I see one contact added to my phone: Wes. Looking up, I part my lips. "Aren't you concerned that I will tell Wes where we are?" I question. My suspicion rises. Is this a trap of sorts, a game to test my loyalty to this new friendship?

"That's a silly question, Sol," Evander grins. "Wes knows exactly where we are. At this very moment, he and Gabriel have us surrounded."

"We're surrounded!" I repeat. Something odd sparks in my defective heart. A joyous flame.

Knowing Wes found me should make me recoil. It was only weeks ago I planned on running from him. It's his devotion to hunting me that makes me feel like a blanket has been placed over my shoulders. It keeps the chill of the bunker at bay.

He leans against the wall and crosses one giant foot over the other. "It was never about hiding from my brothers. After all, I'm trying to make us whole again."

I don't realize how tightly I'm grasping the phone until Evander's golden eyes spot my grip. I slip the phone into my pocket but still keep my fingers wrapped around it. "Then what is the point of being trapped in this bunker?"

"Luna would tell you that is yet another pointless question. We burned a lot of bridges when we took the hard drives. We are not running." He opens his arms wide, his wingspan like that of a dragon. "We are barricading ourselves until you find the cure. We have enough supplies here to last for three years before we need to consider rationing. That gives Gabriel and Wes plenty of time to defeat the wolves who will come out in packs to steal Manus Dei's knowledge. By the time you find the cure, Gabriel and Wes will have calmed the waters. Then once we are whole again, we can all work to create something new. We will have options and control."

"Every time you speak, I wonder if I have made the wrong choice again. When Luna dragged me to the Cliff Walk and spoke, I thought she was mad. Somewhere in that madness were snippets of sense. I followed her because I thought I owed it to her. When you speak, I think the same thing. I hear the same crazed speech, but I also see the small truths." I shake my head.

He pushes off the wall. "I just want to fix us."

"Didn't Luna want the same thing?" I refute. "Look how broken we are. We are free, but so fragmented."

"No," His voice deepens. The already dimly lit hallway grows darker. "Luna didn't want to fix us, Sol. Luna wanted to smash everything to bits. And she did. Luna could have killed us all, lied to us, and kept us at arm's length, but she didn't. Luna knew she would need us to make it all whole again. You cannot rebuild an empire alone. You need an army, and that's what we are. Luna brought it all down, and we are going to build something better."

He gives me time to process his words before he begins again. "The only way you will know if it is the wrong or right path is to walk down it. Once you reach the finish line, you can look back and decide if it was the best decision." Reaching out, he touches my shoulder. "I gave you that phone to help you. You don't have to use it, but I think deep down you need to. We all need support, and sometimes only one voice can penetrate our minds. My brothers can't breach these walls without bringing down the entire bunker. Death is patient. You have no idea what he is willing to give up to protect you, Sol." Evander hints.

"He wouldn't give *you* up. I asked him to run away with me," I shrug. "The power was too alluring for him to give up."

"It wasn't the charm of the power, it was the strength. We will always be hunted, Sol. Always. That's why we need power to survive. We're at the top of the food chain. Others will do everything to stand next to us or replace us. You want freedom, Sol, but in order to be free, you have to erect walls your enemies can't scale. Death is doing that. Deep down, he wants to give you what you want. He is just doing it the only way he can; it's the only way to ensure no one will kill you when you breathe in your first lung full of free air."

My face pinches. "Luna told me there was no such thing as normal in our cards. If I find this cure, if I manage to create the downgrade, what then?"

Evander has a smug look on his face now. The stiffness in his shoulders relaxes as if he has a magic ball that holds my future. His golden eyes are looking directly at my fate.

He is knowledgeable about something I have yet to discover.

"Luna is always three steps ahead. She wanted to teach you what love was, and what it felt like to have it taken away because that's what will happen to her when you force the downgrade upon her. The love you both have for each other will be stretched and shaken. This is her preparing you for that. Don't you see, Sol?" He presses. "Luna knew this was all going to happen. She played the angles none of us could have ever imagined to ensure it. Luna dangled you in front of Wes for a reason. She always knew you would leave."

"She... no, you're wrong. She said so herself. She wanted me to hate love."

He raises a brow. "And you believed those words? Luna usually speaks the opposite of what she truly wants. She knew you would need someone after you forced the downgrade upon her. A person by your side who could protect you and heal your broken heart. She also knew that after everything you would see and endure, you would never want to see another laboratory again. Wes can give you a way out. Luna knew that, Sol, and she knew he was one of the only people on earth who could keep you safe."

"But Wes won't leave you all behind."

He shakes his head, "He doesn't have a choice now. I've said too much. You need to focus. Just know that when this is done, you won't be alone, and no matter how much Luna claims to hate you," His smile is like a wilting flower, beautiful yet touched by sorrow. "You know she means the opposite."

Chapter 13

Sol

Evander grabs a ring of keys, selects one, and begins to unlock the door. I'm surprised to see the world-famous hacker using an old-fashioned key. The door to the storage closet opens, and he steps inside, turning on the light. I'm not sure what I expected to see. Perhaps computers, hard drives, or even my father's journals. But what I find instead takes me by surprise—about a dozen of my old paintings.

Stepping closer, I brush my fingers over the canvas, a sense of nostalgia washing over me. Each painting holds memories and emotions, capturing different moments of my life. I smirk as I gaze at the first abstract painting I did, a rebellious act of artistic expression. My father had disapproved, dismissing it as a waste of my talents, and so I focused on more traditional portraits. But now, here they are, my abstract creations, preserved in this secret storage room.

"Why are these here?" I ask Evander, "I thought you were bringing me to my father's journals."

He carefully picks up one of the paintings and turns it around. The back of the canvas, once blank and unpainted, is now covered in writing. I lean in closer, my eyes widening as I realize that the writing is not ordinary ink—it's Lumenis ink, visible only to those with the upgraded gene. The ink glimmers with a strange grayish hue, adding an air of mystery to the writings.

As I reach for a painting of a blackbird with a vibrant yellow beak, the memory rushes back with vivid intensity. The blackbird perched in a tree just before Luna's shot brought it down. Its distinctive appearance had captivated me—the glisten of its ink-black feathers and the rich saturation of its yellow beak were details that had held my fascination. My father took the piece as soon as I finished it, preserving it for his private collection, and I never saw it again.

Turning to Evander, clutching the painting to my chest, I voice the questions swirling in my mind. "Why do you think my father did it? Why did he help his sister, who was such a terrible monster. Why did he contribute to a society with corrupted values? Sometimes I hate him, and other days I understand him. Groomed to listen, just like I was until Luna broke my training," I laugh bitterly, the irony not lost on me. "He was trying to help everyone, cure the impossible, even if it meant experimenting on Luna and me. I understand he was trying to do good, even though he was also a menace."

Evander rubs his jaw, his gaze thoughtful and distant. "Sometimes we are caught in a storm," he finally speaks, "The only way to survive is to go with the winds. Maybe your father felt that way. He chose to be ignorant, only to see the good. Overlooking evil is easier than you think. Look at the history of humankind. We praise advancements without considering the cost. The greatest technological leaps often arise from the horrors of war, with countless lives lost in the process. Life is a push and pull, a struggle and balance. We cannot fully appreciate love without hate, life without death, and heaven without hell. It's the reflections that show us a different reality."

I meet his golden gaze, seeing the depth and wisdom within. "You are the wisest Horseman of them all, Famine," I declare. "I'm grateful to call you Evander, to have you as a friend. If I think like Luna, three steps ahead, I'm relieved she will have you by her side. You're like a lighthouse, a grounding force that gives me hope."

At that moment, I see the intricate web of relationships, the interplay of trust and betrayal. Evander's role in Luna and Gabriel's lives is significant, his impact profound. They all think they needed me, but ultimately, it was him we all needed.

I study the hidden messages on the back of the paintings, my mind racing with possibilities. "Do you think these messages from my father hold a key to creating the downgrade?" I ask, my voice filled with anticipation.

Why else would he write on the paintings? Why would he keep me so close to my original state?

I am a map, but was my purpose to guide us back to the starting point or to a new destination?

His contemplation is like a gardener tending to a delicate bloom, nurturing it with gentle thought. "I believe your father was a man who operated on multiple levels, Sol. He kept you and Luna under his wing; not every clone was treated equally. If Astrid had succeeded in taking over Manus Dei, your father would have ensured that you and your sister had a way to bring it all down. He may not have been a good man, but he cared deeply about one thing: his science. And if Astrid had gained control, she would have abused the very thing Dorian held dear. He wouldn't have allowed that to happen."

Greed, that's what it all boils down to. Manus Dei's insatiable thirst for knowledge. Astrid's hunger for absolute control. My father's unyielding desire to create, even though his darkness outweighed his light.

But there's also generosity because you can't have the devil without an angel. Luna's generosity in surrendering her mind to save me and defeat Astrid. Gabriel's generosity in using me and safeguarding me, protecting the woman who resembled the one he loved and had betrayed him.

And then there's me, torn between a greedy desire for freedom and the generosity that drives me to sacrifice everything to save the very people who once betrayed me.

There's always an opposite, a contrast between dark and light, good and evil, hero and villain. I wonder which one Wes thinks I am now?

Chapter 14

Sol

Have you ever been chased by a swarm of bees? Eventually, they catch up to you. One stings you, then another, and another. You receive so many stings that you become numb...high even.

You're even eager for the next sting to come in hopes the end will be near.

Does that sound crazy? Who's to say what is sane in my mind anymore?

That's how I feel as I clutch the small portrait of the blackbird under my arm. Evander and I are walking back to my lab, but those bee stings are taking effect. It doesn't hurt as much as when I was first stung by Luna.

I need to know more in hopes that knowing the entire book means the story will finish soon. That means reading the secret messages on the back of the paintings.

"Evander, what happened to Klara?" I question, my voice echoing in the stark silence. "Why hasn't she been around since we arrived here? Is she even here? How has the corrupted upgrade impacted her? Is she showing the same signs as Luna?"

The giant I call my friend, pauses mid-step, his massive frame towering above me like a god ascending back to his heavens, his back turned on his people.

What is he hiding?

Confidently, I step up, placing my feet on the same stair he occupies. Despite this, the difference in our height remains considerable. "Evander," I press.

"If I'm going to fix this, then you must be honest with me."

"Sometimes lying is easier," he mumbles. His inhale is so deep that I fear his lungs will burst like an overfilled balloon. "Klara received the upgrade four months before Luna did. As a result, Luna has been able to witness her own future. But no matter what happens to them, I know you will fix the both of them." His eyes narrow. It's a threat.

"What will you do to me if I can't fix them?"

The gold in his eyes simmers into a deep brown. I want to take a step back, but I don't. "I didn't give you an option."

"I'm not God."

"No, you're not. God gave himself limits and rules to live by."

"Evander—"

He steps closer, and my response vanishes like a wisp of smoke in the wind. "The devil raised you. You're father used his lab to create whatever the fuck he wanted. His ideas and science were limitless. He pushed and pushed. You'll do the same."

I snort a laugh, which makes his face redden.

He's hurting, and he's going to lash out. I can choose to add oil to his fire or help reduce it. He's desperate. So am I, but I also am realistic, but arguing with him is fruitless.

"I haven't seen, Klara. I'll need to."

"I know," he acknowledges as his eyes glance down. He's crestfallen, like a mighty beast looking down over a battlefield at the carnage. He grasps the painting he is holding harder, his fingers rippling the soft canvas, threatening to puncture it. "Luna knows what we will do when she is... uncontrollable. We will cage her until you find the cure." His reply is as direct as a straight arrow hitting the mark.

"Cage her," I repeat. Anguish hits me. His arrow found my heart.

Is this how the birds Luna killed felt when she shot them down?

My sister in a cage... a lot of people would think that is appropriate. Then again, a lot of people would rather shove dirty items under the rug rather than take the time to clean them up. Eventually, the bump under the carpet becomes so high you trip and stumble.

Luna had fought relentlessly to dismantle Manus Dei, ensuring our freedom from the cage in which we were raised. "It's ironic that those she liberated will now cage her," I remark mournfully. He doesn't respond directly to my observation.

Now, Luna's time is ticking away, and soon I will be forced to turn the key, locking her inside. "Is that where Klara is now?" It's a silly question because I know the answer. It's the reason why I haven't seen Klara. She is caged like a beast, a menace... an abused dog.

"Klara isn't like Luna," Evander begins, "I don't think she's ever felt as intensely as Luna has. She's become more like a robot. Come," he gestures with his hand and turns, leading us back down the stairs. We journey past the storage room until we arrive at another locked door.

Reaching out, he begins to insert a key into the lock. He presses firmly on the key and for a fleeting moment, I fear he might snap the metal. It's then that I notice his hands - his grip on the key is fierce, his fingers trembling. He pauses before turning the key. "She's in here." He issues a warning.

I shift the painting, holding it over my chest like a shield.

"She isn't just what they made her. Klara is... complicated, but...." He searches for words like a lost hiker in a dense forest.

"But you love her," I complete his sentence.

That love will be Klara's saving grace, but it's also tearing him apart. Just like my love for my sister tore at me, and Luna's love for me did the same. It's a mirror of torment we have all experienced.

"Yes," he clears his throat, "And I know when she can feel and see beyond her obsession that she will feel the same way for me. Klara knows I've been there all along." Evander paints his devotion. It's a stunning picture that would make anyone stop and admire it. I hope one day Klara does.

Reaching out, I grab his hand, steadying the key, "What if she doesn't reciprocate when she is healed? What will you do to her?"

He pivots his wide shoulders, "You think I'll force her?"

"I don't think you want to, but I also know obsession makes people do limitless things."

His left eye twitches, "I'm a patient man. I never give up. Even now," he glances around the bunker, "When it feels like the end of the world is chasing me, I still keep fighting. I will fight till my dying breath. I'll make sure Klara has the life she always should have had. I want to be there when she feels an emotion for the first time. I want to see all her firsts."

"I hope you can." I reply. Then with my hand pressed over his, we both turn the key and walk inside.

***

It's a small room with only two fenced storage cages as dividers. Each storage cage forms a twenty-by-twenty-foot square. In this space, a solitary bed stands under the fluorescent lights above. The bed itself is simple, but it's adorned with sheets that reveal Evander's affection for Klara. Down here, it's noticeably cooler. Evander has gone to the trouble of acquiring thick flannel sheets and a plush purple comforter, hinting at his thoughtful care.

I don't see a bathroom, but a large red buzzer button is affixed to the wall.

In the room's center, a matching purple area rug is adorned with a plaid pattern in various shades of purple. On the carpet, numerous books and even a laptop are scattered. Additionally, an extra fur blanket is casually tossed on the floor.

Laying on the carpet with a book in hand is Klara. Evander walks to the fenced wall, "Hello, Klara," He regards her. His deep voice is ever so gentle. She doesn't regard him, just turns the page of her book.

I inch closer, stunned by Klara's calm demeanor. The last time I saw her, she was dragging a knife across Subject 52's neck. She smiled after her kill, melting back into the crowd. My mind recoils as I recall the virtual reality of Klara's childhood; it was disturbing, to put it mildly. That upbringing shaped the woman she is today.

"What if she can't handle her emotions? The past deeds might haunt her, Evander." I whisper. My eyes remain on Klara, who turns another page. Her eyes scan the text back and forth. She looks so mechanical. It's scarier than the over-dramatic Klara in the club.

"I've thought about that. Cody is perfecting his modification." He admits.

Ripping my gaze away from Klara, I look up at him. "You would erase her memories?" I question. He's referring to the failed upgrade Cody made.

"Cody's upgrade failed. Look at Zander."

"He's correcting it." Evander bites. "If it will save her, I will do anything."

"Anything?" A new voice echoes. It's a male's voice, one I know all too well.

I jerk my attention towards the second fenced-off cage. I hadn't noticed it when we first entered; I was too focused on Klara.

The second cage is a stark contrast to Klara's. Just a twin bed and a worn, thin grey blanket. No embellishments or books. Whoever is kept here is meant to suffer, to feel trapped and confined. Jailed and punished.

"Anything is quite a loaded term, brother. 'Anything', for men like us, suggests we are prepared to ignite the world," War declares. His eyes, brimming with a potent mix of confidence and trickery, lock onto mine, and he flashes a wide grin. "Hello, little mouse. Have you missed my company?"

Chapter 15

Sol

"War?" I stammer. I can't believe my eyes.

"Oh, don't make me blush." He glances at Evander, "That sounds like she missed me. Wes will lose him shit." He snickers.

"How the mighty have fallen." I jest in disbelief. This is the first time I've seen him without his devilishly detailed three-piece suit, polished dress shoes, or flawlessly styled hair.

"Oh, little lovely mouse, I haven't fallen." He pierces me with a single glance. He's lounging on the small, prison-like bed like it's a chaise lounge at a five-star resort. Legs extended, one ankle crossed over the other, and his head is tilted back against the cold concrete wall. Stripped of his adornments, he nevertheless manages to convey a picture of resilience. There's that familiar, confident aura around him, like a halo of light.

War always has something up his sleeve. As he admitted before, he plays both sides.

"What are you doing here?" I cautiously approach his cage.

"I'm here," His eyes twinkle mischievously, "to look after you, little mouse. Consider me your new bestie."

"I don't need another two-faced friend."

His hand flies to his heart, "That hurts. Rest assured, all the faces I show you are equally as handsome. Come on, little mouse, I'll even make a friendship bracelet with you. Let's just give it a try."

My eyes narrow. "I thought you said you'd never turn your back on Death. Shouldn't you be with him?" I retort. Out of all the Horsemen, I trust War the least. He's shown his slippery nature, playing all sides, inciting us towards conflict while he sits on the sidelines watching. Never has the title, War, been so fitting.

"Death can protect himself, but only I can protect his heart." In a swift move, he jumps off the bed, standing tall. He approaches me, hands clutching the cage. "If something happens to you, it would kill my brother. I owe him my life. I'd give my life," He tilts his head, "I'd give up my freedom and live in this shitty cage to protect you, his heart. In the end, that's the only way to keep my brother alive. So consider us new life-long besties. Friends forever." He grins. It's as if he's a cheetah, smirking after a successful chase, with a blood-stained jaw and full belly.

When I don't reply he shakes the fence, rattling it. "I don't like being caged, Sol." He sounds angry, and I see a glimmer of resentment in his words. He blames me for his current state. "So, could you be a dear and expedite that downgrade?"

I turn to face Evander. "He knows?" I question.

War laughs. "I knew all along, little mouse."

"Stop calling me that!" I hiss. I clench my fingers into a fist over my painting, feeling the skin around my knuckles stretch under the pressure.

"Why?" War smirks. I glance at the cage confining him. War shouldn't be smiling; he should be groveling. But he's not ordinary; he's a Horseman. They never beg. They regroup. This is War planning and playing.

He leans back and bursts out laughing. "Death will be so pleased to know how he affects you. That's true love, isn't it?" War lunges at the cage again, but this time his gaze is locked on Famine. "Isn't it, brother?"

Famine doesn't verbally reply, but I notice his gaze finding Klara.

"Let me out of here. I helped you. I don't need to be caged," War forces a playful smile. But I notice the way his eyes narrow at the corners and how his jaw clenches. Finally, his facade is starting to crack. The Horseman War doesn't like being caged, and it's starting to break him.

Famine clears his throat. "Come on, Sol. We have much to do."

I follow Famine toward the exit.

"Oh, come on!" War exclaims. "Fine! Don't worry about me. Klara and I are getting quite cozy. Isn't that right, Klara, darling?" War shouts.

I expect Evander to vanish, become a Horseman, mount his steed, and charge toward War. Instead, he ignores him, guiding me out of the room as War continues to shout and raddle the cage. When the door seals shut, I'm thankful for the silence, but I also feel guilt about leaving them in a cage...even if it is what they need.

"War has been helping you get to this point in the game. He wants the downgrade, too?" I ask.

Evander nods.

"Then why cage him?"

As he cracks his neck, it's like watching a coiled spring finally unwind. "Just because you love someone, just because they're family, doesn't mean they have the right to use you. Relationships aren't one-sided. War can't just help Death. He needs to show loyalty to all of us."

"Do you think he'll understand your lesson?"

"He already has. That's why he stayed in touch with me along the way. Consider this…a final judgment. War fought never to be caged again. I'm testing his loyalty to me and, yes, even Gabriel. One day we'll all have to work together again. War will have to consider us all, not just the one he favors."

The downgrade is my test. It's not just about creating a cure for my sister. It's about considering the greater whole. Evander was testing me, and I didn't even realize it. He loves passionately but won't let that love corrupt him.

The lesson I've learned is, neither should I.

I love a handful of people, many of whom are mentally twisted. I can't let my affection for them hinder my mission. It's about healing my family, not just one individual. Because in a family, if one member is suffering, then we all suffer.

Chapter 16

Sol

**A hidden message from my father: On the back of the painting,
"The blackbird that escaped."**

I was born a showman, relishing the spotlight's intoxicating heat. Basking in its glow fueled the motivation within me.

My parents never acknowledged Astrid; she was a mere shadow. On the other hand, I was the prized son, the product of their foolish boasting. Sometimes, the greatest diamonds appear rough, like lumps of dirt-covered coal. You just need to know how to polish them.

That's what I wanted for my sister. I craved her brilliance, her transformation into an adult who carved away her unwanted flaws, like filing down a gemstone. Yet, some fractures within her deepened and multiplied over time. They rooted too profoundly within her core to be cut away.

Some might label a stone with inclusions unwanted, while others argue that flawed stones possess greater value. I'm still uncertain which perspective I'd embrace. Maybe that's why I raised the clones the way I did. They are the perfect combination of genetically flawless and mentally flawed.

***

"Stomp, stomp, stomp! It wakes me up. Two weeks have passed in the confines of the bunker. Each time I am roused, be it from a nightmare or the echo of footsteps in the hallway, my body breaks out in a cold sweat. My instinct for fight or flight is triggered. My heart beats a thumping roar as I wonder if Death has indeed found his way inside.

It's my hope and fear.

No matter how many cold showers I take, I can't scrub away the fear and anticipation. The phone tucked under my pillow remains turned off. I haven't called him yet. I'm not sure I can.

What would I say to him?

You were right; I couldn't escape. I simply traded one cage for another.

I need you, and I dream about you every night. While studying my father's research during the day, I even envision hearing you. Sometimes, I even hallucinate your presence, Death.

Slapping my forehead, I fumble under my pillow until I feel the cool metal of the phone. I should call him, if only to hear his voice…

Do you feel that weight adding up on my shoulders, Mental Journal? I certainly do. It's the urgency to create the downgrade. That's what's keeping me from calling the man I love.

"Go get it!" The deep voice in the hall takes on a panicked hush, like the rumble of an approaching storm.

I slip from my bed, neglecting to put on my shoes. The concrete floor feels like I'm stepping on solid ice. Sweeping the hair from my sticky forehead, I cautiously move toward the hallway. With the gentleness of a butterfly landing on a flower, I turn the doorknob and peek out. Evander's back vanishes as he descends the staircase. To my right, a sweep of blonde hair bolts down the hall.

Where is Luna going and what is she fetching for Evander?

I've had little interaction with Luna, and as I watch her pursue Evander, I can't help but feel like a passive observer, as if I'm no longer part of their story. We've both buried ourselves in our respective studies. Everyone in the bunker is so absorbed in their tasks that it's rare to encounter anyone else. When I remember to eat, it's either alone or in the lab, as I decode the hidden messages my father left on the backs of my paintings.

So far, the hidden messages haven't been inherently useful, but they have given me a glimpse into my father's mind. The only relevant information pertains to his scientific alterations, tweaking and modifying Astrid's original DNA in order to recreate the clones.

I thought I understood loneliness, but life in the bunker is a new definition.

Fuck this! I'm not on the sidelines, and I won't have another secret be hidden from me.

Stepping out into the hallway, I follow them. The once stale air now carries a faint scent of human presence. I push the large bar on the stairway door; its creaking protest chimes like a warning to my subconscious, but I proceed. My bare feet tread hastily down the cold concrete steps. The chill seeping into my skin makes my feet stick with each step. I grip the rail as my fingers tremble.

End My Games

The deeper I descend, the louder the shouting becomes. It's not just War, but Klara and Evander too. When I reach the floor where War and Klara are held, the shouting turns into panicked coaxing.

"It's okay," Evander repeats soothingly. His gentle tone reminds me that beneath his godlike exterior, he's still human, still capable of suffering.

I don't step into the room where the prison cells are. Instead, I press against the doorframe, the rough concrete abrading my exposed skin. Breathing deeply, until my lungs press against my ribs, I finally look inside.

My long blonde hair falls like a curtain and catches War's attention, if only for a mere second. He looks back at Evander, helping me stay hidden.

Evander is inside Klara's cage. His entire body is pressed against hers, creating a new cage—one that won't be swayed like the thin metal. His hand must be cupping her face, which is hidden by his massive body. His shoulders hunch like a massive wave showering down on her.

"She just started to go feral. She was bashing her head against the fence," War states. His eyes then flick to mine in warning. My heart goes into a rapid set of palpitations. It's so violent it causes my feet to stumble.

"I tried to stop her," War claims. I have no doubt he did. That's why he was trying to grab hold of her through the fence.

War looks at me for a very calculated reason. He tried but failed. I can't have the same outcome.

This will be Luna's future; instead of Famine hugging her and holding her down, it will be me.

I shake my head violently as if I were a child who ventured out of bed and confronted a monster. The monster, in my case, is the future if I fail. I'll have to watch my twin suffer into madness. True insanity, not just painted lies and deceptive tricks.

I nod in understanding. Suddenly my mouth feels like a desert. All I can taste is gritty sand. It rubs my tongue raw and sinks into all the nooks and crannies of my mouth. I can't swallow.

War grabs the fence and shakes it, "I'm no good to you locked in here. I could have stopped her if I was free. Give me a key."

"Not now!" Evander bellows a roar that makes me think the entire bunker has shaken.

I dig my nails into the doorframe. Narrowing my eyes, I see droplets of blood on the concrete floor. The books that once covered the carpet in Klara's cell are now torn to bits.

"Let me out!" Klara thrashes against the fence and Evander. "Let me out!" She repeats but her voice is weaker.

"Shh," Evander murmurs in a gentle tone.

'"Just kill me...I'm tired...she made me so tired..." Klara begins to sob. Then in the blink of an eye, it all changes. She screams and rams her body into Evander's as if her last words were a trick. A dangerously painted lie to make him release her.

Evander doesn't budge. "I'll kill you next! That's my order. She will be happy then. I'll make her proud," Klara states. Her arms slip from Evander's. Reaching up, she tries to jump on him. Her fingers claw at his wide shoulders and back. She digs so deep that even through his shirt, I see blood start to rise onto the fabric.

I stumble back from the door when Klara's eyes clash with mine. She hesitates for a moment. Before Evander lowers her back to the ground, a turbulence of emotions flashes across her face, from a feral nature to grief to laughter. Beats of chaos that can't settle.

I've witnessed a lot, but this...this is the worst. Murder is death, but this is torture, not just for Klara but for everyone who cares for her.

It's a plague, a cancer that is affecting us all.

How can I sleep knowing Klara is down here, slowly eroding away? I can't, but if I don't sleep, I won't be able to think properly. A double-edged sword that cuts me to the core either way I grasp it.

I grab my hair at the roots. I want it to stop.

So make it stop!

This will be Luna in a matter of months, days, weeks, or even seconds. Tick, tock.

It will happen before I discover the downgrade. That's a fact. What is uncertain is how long Luna will suffer.

That's all dependent on me.

A wave of energy hits me. Turning, I plan to run straight into the lab to get started. I'm halted when I slam right into myself. The newfound breath is smacked from my lungs when Luna's emotionless face stares directly at me.

I step back, my eyes cast down to the needle in her hand. No doubt a medication to settle Klara.

My lips part. I should take the needle from her. Spare her from sedating Klara and looking at what she will become.

I try to open my hands, but my fingers remain glued into a fist.

Maybe it's me being cruel, teaching Luna a lesson just like she forced lessons upon me as a child. Sometimes we have to face the nitty-gritty to humble ourselves.

I correct my posture again, standing as tall as my spine will allow me to grow. I don't take the needle. Instead, my lips part slightly. I don't know what I want to tell Luna. Nothing comes out. I look back at the needle. One day I will have to sedate her, to protect her from herself.

Her brows lower, casting a shadow over her eyes making them look more black than blue. My lips continue to open and close like a goldfish gasping for something.

I want to scream, cry, hug her, and promise her I will save her.

If I speak I'll turn into a blubbering mess just like Klara. Instead, I step forward, walking past Luna. My knuckles brush against her's. Skin to skin, a loving touch that we both will tuck into our long-term memory.

I'm not used to acting so frigid. It's still a struggle, like swimming against the current. Once I'm free from Luna and safely in the stairwell, I crumble. The lies I forced into truths come back to haunt me. Tears fall from my eyes like a floodgate unleashed. Each tear represents a different emotion.

I stumble into the laboratory. A dozen of my old paintings are laid out on the tables, turned over revealing the secrets written on the back. All I see is a vast mountain I know I have to climb but I don't know how to scale it.

"Yes, you do, little mouse. You have all the knowledge. You just tucked it away and ignored it. It's time to step into those dark corners." I imagine Death whispering.

End My Games

Crouching down into a ball, I dig my fingers into my hair, pulling at the roots as if the action will open the door to all the knowledge inside my mind.

"Sol," War voices from behind me. I keep my eyes closed not sure if he is real or if it is my mind playing tricks on me again.

"Sol," He repeats again. "Let me help you."

"I don't trust you," I murmur. My hot breath covers my face. Falling back, I sit on my backside and hug my knees to my chest.

"But you trust that I want my family whole again, and you know you're the only person who can do that now."

"Gabriel can help. Tell Evander to bring him inside," I suggest, or perhaps I'm begging.

War comes closer, "If you saw Death in Klara's state could you focus?" He pauses allowing my mind to paint that image.

No. I'd crumble into a foundation of ash.

"Gabriel would be no use to us in here. He's much more valuable outside fighting off the small armies that want our science. When the time comes, Evander will let him inside."

"That could be years from now," I shout. My head snaps up and I look at him. "Years!"

He nods and sinks down next to me. "We all know that, little mouse. "That's precisely why Luna orchestrated everything so meticulously. She deliberately turned Gabriel into her adversary, recognizing that it's easier to bear the pain of separation when you harbor resentment."

The revelation hits me like a sledgehammer.

"As Gabriel engages in this conflict outside our walls, he unwittingly contributes to fortifying the new society we're forging. Slaying all the monsters who would seek to devour us."

"She's still using him as a puppet."

"Gabriel has many titles. A puppet is one, a survivor is another. He will have no option but to delve deeper into his nanobyte research to appease his benefactors. When he ultimately joins our ranks, our collective strength will be unrivaled. Genetics and technology will stand as our salvation."

"What makes you think he will just hand over everything to us?"

He kicks his feet out and places a hand over mine. "Because he's unwilling to lose everything, especially not Luna again. Neither of us will lose anyone, that's why we have gone to such lengths. We're greedy fuckers who love too much." He snorts, "If only our hate consumed us, we'd all be free, but we'd also be lonely."

My eyes find his hand on top of mine. I want to shove it away. I want to grasp it.

Instead I remain unmoving.

"Don't you see, Sol, each of us has a purpose. Luna knew all of this. That's why she set us each on a separate path, knowing that we would all come together again in the end. Your path changed you, and," he pinches my skin gently, "hardened your shell. I saw you walk past Luna. You will have to do that again after you give her the downgrade. Luna will hate you, but eventually, she will forgive you."

"How can you be so sure?"

He curls his fingers over mine, "Because she forgave Gabriel. He did keep the game going. He thought it would make him powerful. He wanted to use that power to save her. She forgave him for that." he shrugs, "She will never admit it. That's why she baited him. Backed him into a corner giving him no choice but to lash out and come back to her."

"We all need love, Sol. Without it, there is no point in living. Love causes wars, but it also can end them. That's why I'm here. I love my family and my brother. I owe him. This is the payment. Keeping his love alive." He reaches into his pocket and pulls out the phone Evander gave me. He must have taken it from under my pillow before he followed me.

"How did you know about that?"

"Don't ask silly questions, mouse." He flashes me a brotherly grin. "Call him,"

"How do you know I haven't?"

"Because you still look lost, and the only time you looked certain was when you had my brother guiding you."

"I was a shitty follower. I didn't listen to his warnings."

"Neither did I, but that fake printed heart of his is forgiving."

He nudges the phone towards me, but I don't reach for it. He pushes it between our hands, then curls my fingers around it. "Call Wes," He presses, "Let him help keep your mind anchored to reality. You can't do this alone, Sol. That's why Luna brought us together again, in her twisted way. We're all trapped, but if we look around, we will realize we still have each other." He stands and leaves without glancing to see if I make the call.

Chapter 17

Wes

I enter my tent, brushing against the thick canvas material that's half frozen. Snow continues to fall off my shoulders lightly, leaving a trail inside that will eventually melt from the small space heater tucked in the corner. I look at those puddles every night and wonder if Sol has stopped crying yet.

I know my little mouse: she will have broke by now. I wish I could be there to wipe away her tears, to kiss them out of existence.

I perch on the edge of my bed, torn between removing my boots or keeping them on. Sleep feels like a distant promise, and the stubborn knot in my boots sways me towards keeping them tightly fastened.

Maybe tonight will be the night we get inside?

That's the love-sick fool in me talking.

If Famine is forcing Sol to create a downgrade, that could take years unless Famine knows something Gabriel doesn't.

I'm not waiting years.

I asked Gabriel if it was possible, but he didn't answer.

I've been fighting the fools who think they can attack us and get inside that bunker, while Gabriel has been tucked away inside the concrete house that leads to the tunnels. He's at his computer, typing away. His fingers move so swiftly that if he were an ordinary human, I'd be concerned about carpal tunnel, but my brother is anything but normal.

End My Games

He's working on something. I sure as fuck hope its a downgrade that we can give to Famine so he opens that door.

A gust of wind shakes my tent. In the distance, a gunshot is fired. It's not another enemy at our door.

Not yet, that is.

It's a warning shot to a polar bear. This place is crawling with them.

Five days ago, one came close to me; I watched it with my gun. It was hungry and on the hunt. It looked weary but still strong. Each step it took was with a purpose, no wasted energy.

I felt a lot like that bear.

I never thought I'd be back here again, in a tent as a soldier, without the woman I love to warm my bed, without her lips on mine to chase away my demons.

When I was in the Navy, my missions were thrilling. Now, I'm defending Sol's life, which makes this mission seem like the most terrifying foe I have yet to defeat.

If I lose her...if something happens to her...they better put a bullet in me because I'll be feral.

Back in the day, my old man had been adamant that someday, I'd have to settle down, leave behind the life I cherished, and shoulder the weight of leading soldiers. I'd fought against it, loved the adrenaline of combat, and didn't want to join the family business. I wanted to make a name for myself.

I was young; never tasted love. Now I understand why my father offered me a seat at the table.

Love changes everything.

I understand that once you find love, you must make sacrifices to protect it. My family can protect Sol in ways I can't alone. Dad sacrificed his way of life to protect my mother; now, I must do the same.

My fingers reach for the scar on my chest. The decision that took my heart was out of love. Love for my brother.

I've never been in a position where I can't protect the people I love. I don't like it. It makes me feel the opposite of numb. Every day I wake with a growing emptiness in my chest; food tastes like ash, and the victories we have made so far feel like defeats, because I still can't see Sol.

Silence hangs in the air, unsettling, like ants crawling under my skin. I look down, knowing that under my feet in that fallout bunker is the woman I love. We can't get the door off; the tunnel is too narrow to fit the necessary equipment, so our only other option is to dig. But we can't dig because the ground is frozen. We'd have to wait till summer.

Even then, we wouldn't dig. It's too risky. It would draw way too much attention.

My satellite phone suddenly beeps, and I reflexively run my hand through my hair; I need to shave tomorrow. Grabbing my phone, I look at the message. A chill sweeps over me, and my blood runs cold as if winter had invaded my veins. Is this how the polar bear feels when he scents his prey?

It's a link to a song. Only two people would send me this, either Luna or Sol.

When I click the link, it opens to "The Sound of Silence" by Nouela. The lyrics reveal who sent it. Sol. She's found a way to communicate with me!

"Hello, Darkness..." I grin. Despite the distance and challenges, we'll find a way to reunite. Nothing can deter us, not even a bullet to the heart. Sol and I are meant to be.

As the song nears its end, I wonder, did my little mouse steal a phone?

Unlikely. This is a gift from War.

I'm about to call her, but I hesitate. What if she can't call me? What if the phone is a secret from Luna and Famine?

I text her instead.

Death: I want your words, little mouse, not your riddles. Call me.

Pacing inside the small tent, I wait and wait. I play the song over and over again. It's a version I haven't heard before, calming and peaceful. Sol deliberately chose this version.

Death: Talk to me.

I send it again.

Relishing in the idea that she has reached out to me.

Soon she will run into my arms. I just need it to be her choice. I've guided her, taught her how to survive in her new world. If I force her, she will always fight me. I have to let her make the choice, and that means I need to be patient. I know in the end she will come to me; she has already taken the first step.

Hours pass. Night turns to night because there is no sun here, only darkness. I get dressed, forgoing sleep. Before I leave my tent and prepare to face the new threats, I find the perfect song. I hit send, attaching the song "Our Time Together" by Ivan B and Marie Elizabeth to my message. Then I add:

Death: It will be our time, Sol. Just remember that. The clock is ticking. It might feel slow and arduous; I know it does for me. It feels like time has stopped without you by my side. I want to feel you so badly, taste your lips, and savor every inch of your beautiful soul. Do you remember what it felt like when we collided? I do. It was perfection. Next time we are together, I want your nails to dig so deep into my skin that they scar. I want a permanent reminder of what I do to you, marked on my skin. Forever, little mouse. I want you to know I made a deal. I'm going to give you what you always wanted: freedom from the science and me not being tied to it. Remember, little mouse, it may feel like the sun has been swallowed by the void, but in that darkness, I am always there. Always. I'm your dark guardian angel, and I'll slay all the beasts that try to creep into your mind.

Chapter 18

Sol

A hidden message from my father: On the back of the painting, "My Sister When She Sleeps."

They turned ten today; however, thirty of them didn't. It doesn't make me sad that others have failed; I am more proud of the clones that survived. Numbers don't truly matter; they help, but in the end, all it takes is one to change an entire outcome.

***

Four months later.

I reread the first text message from Death one more time, "'I'm your dark guardian angel, and I'll slay all the beasts that try to creep into your mind.' I wish you could slay them now, Wesley," I voice as I stand from my bed.

I read that message every day. Like a bible verse, it gives me hope and strengthens my faith, keeping me on the straight and narrow. It's a daunting task, especially when I hear voices whispering that I can't do this, that I'll fail or even harm my sister or kill her. Another murder, but this time it will be done by me.

I won't allow that to happen. Therefore, I have come to a conclusion none of them would support. I won't tell them that when I do create the downgrade, I'll inject the solution into myself first.

That means that I'm hopeful and adamant that I will, in fact, create the downgrade.

Seven months ago I thought Evander was delusional, that was until I saw what he was hiding up his muscular sleeves. He's created an AI system, a software that mimics a specific person's genetic code. This system responds just as that person's own body would.

He plans to take my modification, transform it into code, and have the system mimic how Luna's body would respond. This way, if there are any issues, we can resolve them without accidentally harming the patient.

He's done it. Taken away limits. With my mind and his AI, I have made leaps and bounds. Evander's new technology has the potential to revolutionize medicine and how we develop treatments. Sometimes, the science is so remarkable that I'm unsure if I can ever walk away.

If God offered you a seat at his table would you turn it down?

That's what it feels like, being here and seeing all the technology firsthand. Knowing everything first before the rest of the world could even dream up the ideas we have.

It's a high.

Makes you feel God-like.

That must be how Lucifer felt when God cast him down to earth.

I look in the mirror, see my reflection, and remember what it was I needed not wanted. I need to get away from the science because if I don't I'll turn into my father. The devil was once an angel with a simple idea. One idea can change everything.

I won't let history repeat. I'm not going to be cast down. I'm going to walk away. Hopefully, that is.

No system is flawless, and even though Evander's AI software is cutting-edge, it's still not a human body. There's a small chance the body might react differently than the AI predicts. That's why I'll take first downgrade first.

A laugh escapes my lips. I suppose that's wishful thinking. I haven't even begun to delve into creating the downgrade, and here I am, thinking it's easily attainable.

I've spent months studying what my father created and only begun comprehending all the modifications. What makes it even more challenging is that he didn't use the original method to install later upgrades. My father introduced a new kit called CRISPR-Genesis, a revolutionary technique that slices through DNA and implants a modified code. I have to master this new technique; that part is the easiest. The hardest is teaching myself what Gabriel created. Nanobytes are new to me. Then, I need to understand how Luna combined both to create what Astrid wanted.

Every day, I enter my lab, and I see Evander. His eyes lock onto mine every morning and evening, filled with hopeful anticipation. They silently question if I've made any breakthroughs. For months, I've had to watch that hope fade away when I shake my head.

But Evander is relentless. Every day, that hope is reborn. At times, I want to give up, but he never does.

Klara has experienced numerous fits and breakdowns. I've stopped watching. I've heard Evander rush to sedate or comfort her too often to count.

Luna is still functional...somewhat. She is allowed to roam from her small office to her caged cell next to Klara. It's all a precautionary measure but soon she won't be able to leave her cell.

Until then she keeps studying what Astrid's upgrade erased from her mind. Relearning all the science. She rarely speaks now. Once a week, she hands me her phone and has me select a playlist for her. That's how we communicate now.

I mimic that action by sending Wes a song every night. He hasn't pushed me to call him again. He responds with a song of his own. It's like he understands that it's all I can handle now. If I hear his voice, I'll lose my focus.

I swing my legs out of bed. The action feels robotic. It is. Every day is a repeat.

Cradling my head in my hands, I give myself a moment to cry. I cry every morning now; it's therapeutic. Then, I put on a mask and try to embody Luna. I become the older sister who is brave and emotionless.

I go to the bathroom and splash cold water on my face. When I look in the mirror I'm not even sure who I reflect anymore.

***

War saunters into the lab with a bowl of steaming hot oatmeal. He's been granted freedom. Sometimes, I wish he were confined again.

He's taken me under his wing, treating me like a pet. Every day, he enters the lab, annoying me, bringing me food, or just attempting to strike up a conversation. Thankfully, Evander sends him away when I need to focus.

"You shouldn't bring food in here," I voice.

"You skipped breakfast. Cody told me," War reports. He places the bowl of oatmeal directly on the laptop keyboard. I know he won't leave until I eat, so I grab the bowl and start eating.

War and Cody have grown close. Fortunately, I've only crossed paths with Zander a few times. He avoids getting too close to me now that War has been released.

I push the empty bowl back toward him. "Thank you," I say. "I'll get back to work."

He snorts with amusement. "We all need breaks."

"I just started my day, War," I sneer. Looking up, I hope to hear Evander passing by so he can chase War out of my lab.

War licks his lips, and then a wrinkle forms at the edges of his eyes. "Why haven't you asked?"

I sigh and look down at all the work I should be doing. "Asked what?"

"Asked for my real name," He replies.

He's won. My full attention is now on him. He's not wearing a suit, just basic clothing from the bunker's limited selection. He's sporting black cargo pants with a plain gray cotton shirt.

"I haven't asked for your name because we're not friends, War." He places a hand over his heart, feigning hurt. His crooked grin contrasts his act. I roll my eyes. "I can never trust you."

He laughs. The sound makes me jerk. It's a rare sound; I haven't heard anything joyful in months. I've almost forgotten what laughter sounds like. My cheeks twitch, and I wonder if I can still laugh.

"That's the best kind of friend to have, little mouse. It means I'll always keep you entertained," He claims. He opens his arms in a welcoming gesture. "And inside this bunker, we all need some entertainment." He taps and dances his feet, and I feel my cheeks trying to reach into my muscle memory to smile. "Consider me the bunker clown. At your service." He bows.

I do laugh, then. It's weak and sounds more like a cat being tossed into a bath, but it's a laugh.

He grabs the bowl and walks to the door. "War," I call out to him. He turns. "You once gave me your tie pin. You told me it would help ground me so I didn't lose my mind. I never thanked you."

His theatrics fade, replaced by a sincere expression. "You don't need to thank me. I'm here. I've always been here for all of us. I may play every side, but I also listen to every side. Whenever you need to talk, scream, punch, preferably not my face, or cry, I'm here for you."

Turning, he almost exits the room but glances over his shoulder. "Kane," he pauses. "That's my name."

My swallow is lodged in my throat, sealing off air. I roll my throat and try to push it down but it feels thick with emotion now.

I fall silent and remain frozen. Such a simple act, just a few words, and my defenses were shattered. "Kane," My voice is hoarse.

I snort to myself. In the blink of an eye, everything can change. I trust him now because I understand his motivation. We all thought he was playing us. It was a lie. Kane didn't want us to see his true intentions. He stayed in touch with all of us so that one day, he could be the glue that binds us back together.

***

Entering my bedroom, a peculiar sensation washes over me. My heart skips a beat as I catch sight of a tall, shadowy figure standing beside my bed. "Wes!" I gasp. He's here!

Did that mean I finished?

No. I haven't finished. This is a dream.

I run to him, knowing any moment I'll wake up and he will vanish. My arms wrap around him as if he were a security blanket I want to hide under. I squeeze tighter when I can't feel him. It's like I'm watching it all from a third point of view, like I'm trapped in a virtual reality of my own life.

"Wes," I cry as I press my cheek against his chest. I pull back when he does nothing. "What's wrong?" I ask. Fear replaces my blood. His face is pained, his forehead shining with sweat. His mouth is parted, eyes filling with tears.

"Wesley!" I grab him.

"My heart," he mutters.

"What's wrong with your heart?" *Because I feel like mine has stopped beating since I saw you.*

His tears dry up. Is he angry? "You failed."

"What?" I step back but keep my hands on his chest.

"Your science is failing. I'm dying, and it's all your fault."

"No!" I scream. I pop off my bed like bread from a toaster, feeling incredibly burnt. The sheets cling to my damp skin, feeling like ghostly arms trying to pull me back down so they can suffocate me.

I run to the bathroom and throw up.

"No!" I cry as I wipe my mouth.

"Sol!" War, or rather, Kane, shouts my name. Famine moved him to a room across from mine.

"Sol!" He rounds the corner and sees my state.

"It's okay," he whispers the lie because he knows nothing is okay. He grabs a water bottle, wets a facecloth, and sits beside me. He edges closer and wipes my face with the care a mother would take. He cracks open the water bottle and raises it to my lips, forcing me to swallow.

"What happened this time?" He finally asks.

Since he lives across from me now, he hears my night terrors. I'm sure the others do, too, but it's become his duty to come to me.

Maybe Luna wants to? Maybe her messed-up weapon for Astrid prevents her.

The last is the lie I tell myself. It has to be true because if she were sane, she would come to my aid.

"His heart was dying. My science was failing."

"Oh, silly little mouse," Kane breathes a sigh of relief and laughs, "that's easy to overcome. Your science hasn't failed. 3D-printed organs are being printed as we speak." He grins, but it doesn't reach his eyes. It's not because he's lying; 3D-printed organs are safe, but that's not what the dream was about. It was echoing my fear of failing to fix Luna.

I take another sip of water and nod. "You're right." I lock eyes with him as we share an unspoken fear.

"What time is it?" I ask.

"Just past four in the morning."

I push to stand. "Better get to work. The early bird gets the worm." It was meant to lighten the somber mood, but it doesn't. My voice lacks emotion. I used to paint colorful lies, but now all I can paint is just black and white, not even shades in between.

I walk to the shower and turn the knob. A few drops of cold water touch my hot and clammy skin.

Kane stands to leave. "We will get it," he states as he walks to my door.

"Get what?" My reply is as emotionless as a computer's output.

With a devilish grin, he glances over his shoulder, "The worm."

"You're always so hopeful."

"You can see the glass as half full or half empty, Sol. It's up to you which glass you have to swallow. I prefer a cup filled to the brim. I want it all, and I will get it all." He taps his head. "It's all just a mind game. Try seeing it as half full, drink down the hope, and maybe your night terrors will stop haunting you and start motivating you."

Chapter 19

Sol

Three weeks later.

Bang!

My torso jolts up from the thin mattress, like a marionette suddenly pulled by its strings, while my heart races to an unhealthy rhythm, pounding like a drum in a heavy metal concert. I feel a sense of fight or flight as my hands dig into my bed sheets.

"What was that?" I whisper to myself, my bottom lip trembling as I swing my legs out of bed.

A scream echoes through the concrete hall, freezing me in place like a deer caught in the headlights. My toes dangle in the air like a puppet left suspended on invisible strings, almost brushing the ground.

"You're the brave older sister," I tell myself as I plant my feet on the ground.

Another scream, and I'm out of bed, scrambling towards the door. I know the screaming voice. It's my own. It's Luna.

I rush down the hall towards her office. I've stopped hearing the screaming, but that's because my heartbeat is thumping so loudly that I can't hear anything else.

I knew this day would come. It's the day I've dreaded.

I round the corner to her room and brace myself.

A small desk is shoved against the wall, bearing a towering stack of research papers. These papers teeter like a precarious Jenga tower, defying gravity's pull. Alongside them, a collection of computers is neatly arranged.

I try to squeeze inside, which is hard because Evander and Cody are there.

"What's—" I start to speak, but my words wither away, like a human cast into the cold expanse of outer space without a protective spacesuit. No air. Just wide-open eyes filled with pained horror.

Evander has Luna in a bear hug as he lifts her off the ground. Her feet are kicking like a wild animal caught in a snare. She's cornered and knows her fate.

Cody grabs her legs. She kicks and lashes, screaming in different languages, from French and German to English and even Japanese.

I didn't know she spoke Japanese. I cling to this new fact because the truth in front of me is too hard to bear.

I don't hear anything she says. All I hear is buzzing as I watch my twin break and succumb to the corrupted modification.

A hard body pushes past me, shoving me into the door frame. Zander rushes forward. I reach out, wanting to grab him, fearing he will hurt Luna. My arm reaches out, but Kane pulls me back. He tries to turn me from the scene.

"No!" I yell. Kane listens, allowing me to witness what is happening. His arms snake around me tightly. I understand why. My legs have given out; he has to support me.

A.G. Harris

There's a lot of talking and shouting, but I can't understand. All I hear is the buzzing, an incessant drone that ripples over my skin like an unwelcome jacket, itching and irritating with every passing moment.

I feel warm breath against my right ear. Kane must be talking to me.

Zander reaches out, grabbing Luna's arm. She thrashes more, and then her eyes lock onto me. Her pupils dilate so wide that the blue of her irises disappears. She goes limp in Cody and Evander's hold. Zander jabs the needle into her arm.

I look at her until her eyes close. Evander and Cody look relieved, and then they look at me. Evander's lips move, but I still hear nothing. My eyes narrow as I read his lips. "It's time." He tells me. There is a heavy grief painted on his face.

Kane drags me back into the hall, and it feels like the walls are converging, creeping on me like a tightening vise, suffocating my space.

Cody releases Luna's legs, and Evander swings her up bridal style. He begins to walk, passing me as he blurs down the hallway into the staircase.

I understand now. It's time to cage my sister.

***

Kane brings me back to my room, half holding me, like a compass guiding a lost traveler. He guides me to my bed, and slowly, we sit. "Don't worry; I can chat enough to fill her presence." He jokes.

No laugh comes from my lips. I just learned how to laugh again, and now I don't think I ever will be able to.

We sit in silence, Kane's left arm slung around my shoulder. "C-can...can I have some time alone?" I ask.

He sighs, "I don't think that's a good idea. Talk to me instead." He's right. I need to talk because if I don't, I'll implode.

It's just not Kane I need to talk to. "Can you hand me my phone? It's under my pillow."

His arm drops, and he retrieves my phone. He licks his lips and stands. "I'm just outside that door. All you have to do is call, and I'll come," he promises, then leaves but keeps my door cracked open.

I reread the message from Wes and listen to some of the songs we sent to one another.

It's not enough. I feel like *I'm* not enough.

I don't know if I can make this downgrade. I tested two versions of the modified gene on Evander's AI system, and both killed the patient. It's been months, and I feel I have made no progress. Now, my sister is caged.

I press call. The phone only rings once before I hear his voice. The deep richness of his American accent sounds better than my memories. I see a cascade of moments flash before my eyes, like a series of snapshots from the past.

That feels like a lifetime ago. It's like a virtual reality I'm not sure was ever real.

"Sol!" Wes barks. My body jerks as if I were dead, and he shocked me alive again.

This is what I'm fighting for. Life. Luna and Klara's life and my future with Wes.

All the dams I built implode, and the water crashes over the edges. I cry and cry. My shoulders shake, and my breath turns into pants.

"Sol! Sol, talk to me. Breathe, baby. Just breathe. Inhale deep..." He orders. I try to obey. "That's it. Breathe deep and hold it. Hold it, Sol, now release. Calm down and talk to me."

Arms wrap around me. Am I hallucinating? Wes isn't here.

My bed dips and the arms readjust, hugging me tighter. I'm pulled into a chest; the phone is pulled from my ear. It's not Wes but Kane. "Brother, it's me. Don't worry. I've got her."

I relent and burrow my face against Kane's chest. In seconds, his shirt is wet from my tears.

"It's Luna," Kane tells Wes. "She's...deteriorated. She had a lapse, and we had to cage her for her protection. We'll have to keep her like that until Sol makes the cure."

I feel Kane shake his head, "I can't do that, brother. If I open that door and let you all inside, a part of Gabriel will die. He can't see Luna like this. I'm just trying to keep you all alive. Evander is, too. We will open that door when we can." Kane hesitates, and his hand rubs circles on my lower back. "She's calming. I will give the phone back to her so you can talk."

He has to take my hand, open my fingers, and put the phone inside. Then he brings my hand to my ear. "Try to talk to him. If you can't, then just listen to him. This moment will pass, Sol. It all will vanish into a distant memory one day." He tells me before he leaves.

End My Games

With the phone pressed to my ear, I brace myself to talk to the man I have been running away from and sprinting directly towards, like a mouse trapped on a spinning wheel.

"Talk to me, little mouse," Wes requests like he's trying to get a frightened kitten out of a dangerous hole. It's such a contrast from how we originally met. His front was pressed to my back, caging me from behind. His large, rough hand was wrapped around my throat. When he spoke then, he owned me. Now, he has set me free. He wants me to come back to him on my own accord.

"I...It's been," I pause. I didn't call because you consumed me. I can't be devoured, Wesley; I must focus on the game. That's what I want to say because it has been what I have been telling myself. Sometimes, we push away the medicine we need to cure us, suffering in silence and rejecting the help others try to provide.

After all I've done and considering what lies ahead, I believe I deserve to suffer.

A hiccup escapes as my heart tries to regulate itself. "I...I've been too scared to hear your voice."

"Why?" He replies. Is that hurt I hear?

"I deserve to suffer. To be alone."

His exhale is as intense as a sudden downpour of rain, "So do I. We will suffer. Together. Do you hear me."

"But I lied to you."

"That's a moot point now. Just stop lying and tell me the truth. I'll go first; here is my truth: I will always haunt you because I will always chase and catch you. I love you, Sol. God damn it, I love you; I'll never stop, no matter what. The more you lie and run, the more you try to push me away, It only sickens my love for you. It's dark, like a plague that is going to devour me. I'll never stop. Never. The only cure for my misery is you. Stop my pain, Sol, talk to me." He begs.

Like a fragile vase dropped on concrete, my defenses fracture into a thousand pieces. Love comes in all shapes and forms. Love can be a cage; it can be freedom. Love can be your next breath, but it can also be your last one. Love can be your guiding light, but it can also be the water that extinguishes it. Love grows yet shrinks you. Like the roots of two plants, they intertwined, making it impossible to be separated without uprooting and killing the other.

Our love has been all those and more; we are so tangled that our knots can never be undone. No matter how hard I try to separate myself from him, he is there, wrapping around me. Holding me back from the worst I can be but also pulling me up from the soil so I can grow into the best person I can be.

"I thought if I heard your voice, it would break me. The memories would flood back," I shake my head. Using the back of my hand to wipe the snot from my dripping nose. It's the most unattractive I have ever looked, yet the man I love has remained by my side through thick and thin, twisted and morally corrupt. "I have to focus, Wesley."

He exhales; I can envision his muscled torso rising and falling just like it did after we had sex. His tanned skin glowed like a sun-kissed god. I wish he were here. I would run my fingertips over his scar and the tattoo that covers it.

"I missed hearing you call me that. Say it again," he orders, sounding more like Death, the Horseman who took what he wanted.

I roll my bottom lip, suppressing a surge of happiness. "Wesley," I whisper. We both just listen to each other breathe through the phone. We're both still here, alive and fighting.

I lay back and roll onto my side. For the first time in months, I feel relaxed. I lay my head on my pillow, which is as thin as a sheet of paper. There are no luxuries here. The bunker is all about survival, and my role here is to ensure my family survives. "I don't think I can do this. Everything is on my shoulders," I admit.

"You can do anything, little mouse. When your knees feel weak, imagine me kneeling before you, my arms wrapped around your legs like an iron grip. I'll hold you up," he reassures. Tears fall from my eyes again. "Paint a picture in your mind. Even if you fall, I am there to catch you. I'll help you rise again. I love you."

I curl into a ball and cry; he remains talking to me, vowing never to let me fail. When I finally talk, I confess everything that has happened. How I planned on betraying him when I entered the tunnels, only to see Luna and Evander there, all the blood that covered Astrid, and how it soaked into my shoes. I still see that blood on my feet when I shower every night. I tell him about Luna's plan, her lack of choice in creating Astrid's modification, how the modification has failed, causing a surge of chemicals, making Luna and Klara feel too much, and then...silence.

"I don't know what is worse, seeing my sister feel or seeing her eyes truly empty," I confess.

He tells me about the letter Luna left for Gabriel. "How did Gabriel interpret it?" I wonder if he saw her flag as white or red.

"I know he loves her," his response doesn't provide me with much insight.

"But?" I ask, knowing Wes is biting his tongue.

"But they have a very rocky road to pave smooth, Sol."

"Do you think they can do it?" I ask, a question that he sees through, recognizing that it's aimed at our relationship as well.

"I think they can do anything they set their minds to, whether that's killing each other or creating something Manus Dei could never have imagined," he replies. "Little mouse, it's okay to ask for help. Look at what happens when you can't. I don't want what Luna did to repeat."

"I can't let Gabriel inside," I respond, knowing that seeing Luna in this state would be cruel to Gabriel, something he doesn't deserve. "Even if I wanted to, I don't know how to open that door."

"Baby steps, little mouse," I can hear the grin in his voice. Raising my index finger to my mouth, I trace my lips, trying to recall the feeling of his against mine. "Send me what you have worked on. I'll show it to Gabriel. Maybe he can provide some insight."

He's not wrong, but I have to look at every angle. Gabriel might betray Luna in the end.

I can't blame him; therefore, I can't trust him. Luna knew this; that's why she wanted him left outside until she was cured and could explain.

I make the rules now. I'm in control of the game. I have to create the downgrade. It all depends on me, meaning this is my game with my rules and I need to start plotting out ten steps ahead.

Chapter 20

Sol

A hidden message from my father: On the back of the painting, "The night sky."

When you're young, you take your time. The future seems endless, but like any infinity loop, you must round the same curve again. That bend comes a lot faster than you think.

I see my end. It's coming. It has caused me to reflect on all the other things I could have done if I were not a part of Manus Dei. There is a long list of things I would have liked to explore and create. Maybe I can, in a way. Perhaps I can...

***

Two months later.

I talk with Wes every day. Sometimes, our conversation consists of a single song. When I can only reply with music, that means I failed again.

I was a fool thinking talking to him would distract me. He has been the balm to my wounds that fester and seep sickness into my thoughts.

I've tried twenty different approaches, all of which have failed. Contrary to what Evander initially thought, I don't need to undo the failed modification Luna created first. If I succeed in a true reset, then her failed modification will be wiped clean anyway.

Since I have only had a few upgrades, it's much simpler to extract what my DNA originally was. That and my father kept copies of it on file. I'm trying to make one solution. One downgrade. If this approach doesn't work, I will have to undo each upgrade one by one. That feels like it will take a lifetime to accomplish.

Rolling my neck, I try to relieve some of the tension that is a constant now.

All my paintings are now back in the storage room. They are useless to me now. I've copied all the messages my father left. Also, I can't see the Lumenis anymore. That upgrade only lasted a few months and it long wore off.

I wish every upgrade was designed like the Lumenis. Luna was thinking ahead when she made the upgrade slowly wear off. Why couldn't my father have done that?

Gazing at the laptop screen, I catch a glimpse of my own reflection. I haven't seen Luna for two weeks. She has been caged since her first outburst. Kane told me she is comfortable, and when she is sane of mind, she continues to study everything that was stolen from her.

I know it's a lie. Luna isn't comfortable being caged, and each day I fail, she and Klara continue to suffer.

Is it cruel of me not to visit my sister? Absolutely.

Is it smart of me to keep my distance? Yes. There is a reason we have kept Gabriel locked outside. Seeing someone you love suffer distorts the thought process. Gives you false hope, where there is only a rocky shore you will crash upon.

That's the same reason I haven't video-called Wes. A voice can only paint so much of the picture. Seeing a face completes the entire portrait.

It's a new abrasiveness I have come to cling to. Being selfish. A leech. Taking from others what I need to survive.

Evander's AI system finishes running the last modification I made to my new treatment. Red flashes on the screen.

"Failed again." I exhale. I keep trying and trying a similar method using my father's CRISPR Genesis kit to modify the genes.

I continue to fail.

"Trying something you know isn't working again and again is insanity," I mutter. Pushing up from my stool, I pace the lab. This whole time, I have been using the same vector to try to add back my original DNA into Luna's corrupted genes. A vector works as a vehicle, a delivery into the DNA I want to modify. You can use different vectors to deliver the gene therapy.

Gabriel was working on a manufactured vector, one designed and controlled by him. Nanobytes. You could insert nanobytes with a coded message that was more effective than our own naturally made vectors. Manus Dei was eager for his research. They wanted to use nanobytes instead of viruses to deliver upgrades.

All of our upgrades had been delivered using my father's favorite vector. A virus. Viruses are some of the most breathtakingly beautiful vehicles I have ever studied. They are the perfect trojan horse that can be used to destroy a body or heal it. They can corrupt and change a gene in unparalleled ways. A virus is nature at its most superior level. With a simple tweak, we change a virus from a sickness to a savior.

I've been using a sickness to heal. It's worked wonders in the past, but maybe I need to change it. Evolve my father's CRISPR Genesis kit.

After all, this is my game and that means I can choose the weapons and make the rules.

The problem so far is that our advanced immune system has been recognizing the modified virus I have designed and starts to attack it. I've been trying to change too much in one fell swoop, but maybe I can create a slow release just like Luna did. Luna tricked Astrid. Maybe I can trick our immune system.

Design one single downgrade but modify it to revert our DNA back to our original DNA slowly.

"Yes!" I see it now. I ball my fist in excitement; then I rush to my phone. Scrambling, I text Wes with haste.

Sol: Can you have Gabriel send me his latest research on nanobytes? Specifically how they can be engineered as triggers.

I hit send. My hand touches my heart as my mind races. I can hide the nanobytes in the virus and insert the modified virus using my father's original CRISPR Genesis kit. Instead of reverting our DNA in one fell swoop, I can code the nanobytes to slow trigger like a slow-release drug.

If I program the nanobytes to work slowly, I might find a way around our immune system.

Manus Dei designed each of us to be a weapon, a master of a specific science. Individually, we are deadly, but together, we can be so much more. All we had to do was ask for help. Unity, play together, not against each other.

Did Luna realize that? She is always three steps ahead. Did Luna know that the only way to survive and fix Manus Dei's mistakes was if we changed the game's rules to work as a team?

My phone pings.

Wes: You know, if I ask him that, he will demand to be let inside.

A smirk covers my face as I reply.

Sol: Death once told me not to ask.

I want him to steal it from Gabriel.

Wes: What game are you playing, little mouse?

Sol: The game where I order you to take. Get me all of Gabriel's private research on his nanobytes.

The old Sol would have begged Wes to do this. He would have refused me. The new Sol that makes the rules doesn't ask. She takes.

Luna knew I would have to become this evolved version of myself. Wes and Luna molded me, and now I'm breaking the mold.

Chapter 21

Sol

One month later.

Sol: I failed again today.

Wes: Did you learn something from it?

Sol: Yes.

Wes: Then it wasn't a complete failure.

***

Two months later.

Sol: I miss you. I'm worried I'm forgetting what you feel like.

Wes: Then let me remind you. Pick up your phone.

With trembling fingers, I dial his number, and I'll admit, I'm not sure if this is a mistake. Hearing his voice but not being able to feel him might push me over the edge into madness.

"Good girl. I'll reward you for calling me." He purrs. His voice is heavy with desire, sending shockwaves down my body.

"I miss you," my voice cracks. I feel like a hollowed-out shell. I need him to fill me. Make me feel whole again.

"Don't, little mouse, don't you dare cry. Save your tears for when I can hold you."

That pushes me past the point of no return. Tears fall, but I try to hide the sound from him. During our months apart, I've seen a new side to Wes. Even though he didn't think the word love could represent our relationship, he's taken great care to show his devotion through his words. His text messages are a sizzling mixture of tender affection and a deep-seated craving for me. He's been a fuel and a hope. He's been the voice I can whisper all my secrets to. He's consumed them, allowing me always to vent.

He's everything.

My monster and my knight.

My villain and hero.

"Where are you?"

"In my room."

"Alone?" He asks.

I nod. "Yes."

"Good. Put me on speaker; you're going to need both hands."

My legs feel like jelly as I walk to my bed. "I don't know if I can do this."

"I'm in control right now. You will listen and do everything I say." He orders. His words bear such weight over me. I find myself obeying, and strangely, enjoying it. I've been drowning in an ocean of uncertainty, repeatedly failing to make the downgrade. For once,

I just want to listen and be instructed on what to do. I don't want to have to think.

"Now what?" I ask as I lay back on my bed, curling my fingers into the sheets. My heart races as I envision him here, his intense green eyes piercing my soul, tethering it down. His peach-colored lips, eager to explore and savor every inch of my body.

"Your breasts feel heavy; they need my touch. Massage them gently." My nipples harden before I even touch myself. "Now your nipples start to circle them."

"Wes," I moan. "I want you here." My heels dig into the thin mattress.

"Shhh. Imagine my lips on you. On your neck, I'm kissing the spot right under your ear; your sex clenches when I kiss you there. Do you feel it?"

Does it? I imagine his lips there, kissing and sucking. Then I picture his lips between my thighs doing the same thing. My body starts to warm, reminiscent of a balmy summer's day. It feels like I can feel the sunshine on my skin, Wes's kisses dancing across it. Each tender trace sends a wave of heat that lingers, enveloping me further in fervor.

"Do you feel me?" He growls.

"Uh-huh." My voice sounds breathy. I never noticed how my core tightened when he kissed me there.

It feels dangerous to be doing this, but my excitement outshines everything.

"Reach your hand down under your panties. Don't take them off. Leave them on. This way, you will remember what I do to you. Are you wet?" Slowly, I slide my hand down my body. I slip my fingers under my panties, and right away, I feel the dampness; it's soaked my panties, staining them. "Yes," I reply. I start tracing circles at the apex of my lips, just like Wes used to do. *Oh, that feels good.*

"I didn't tell you what to do, use your other hand to pinch your nipple. Hold it until I tell you to release it."

"What?"

"Do it."

Reaching up, I do as he says. "Don't let go. Add more pressure. Yes, do you feel that? Add more…now… let go." I do, and a surge of pain-induced pleasure makes me moan out loud. My head thrashes to the side as I imagine his body on top of mine, pinning me down.

"Push three fingers inside. Now!"

With a force I'd imagine he'd give me, I shove three of my fingers inside myself. It's tight, warm, and spongy, so receptive to the intrusion, as if believing the falsehood that my fingers are Wes's.

It's been so long since I touched myself, since Wes had his hands on me. "I feel like I could come at any second." I admit.

"Fuck!" He hisses. He's touching himself, too.

"Squeeze your hand tighter," I tell him. "I feel too tight. It's been too long since you were inside of me. Owning my body. I want you to possess every inch of me when I'm free of this game. I want you to make me forget everything." I start to move my hips, pump my fingers in and out, and kneading my breast. "Faster. Harder. Please…" I beg.

"Curl your fingers, rub your g-spot." He's panting.

"Go faster," I order him back.

"Sol! Oh fuck. I want your body. I want you."

"Yes...oh god, Wes! Let me come."

"Not yet." His deep voice labors. "Feel the build-up; it hurts, hurts so fucking bad. That's how I feel without you, but this is how we will feel once we're together again. Come." He demands.

My hand thrusts hard in and out of my wet core. My other hand rubs my clit, and with his final word, I dive into a land of ecstasy.

I wish I never had to leave, but as my bliss goes from euphoria to tingles, then to emptiness, I'm reminded that this was just a pause. Now, I must return to the game.

***

Three months later.

Sol: I had a selfish thought today.

Wes: I have them every day. I think about getting inside that vault and taking you away. Fuck the downgrade. Fuck all of them.

Wes: Tell me what you were thinking, little mouse.

Sol: I thought that if none of this happened. If Astrid weren't so evil, I never would have met you. I thought that

meeting you was worth it all. That's terrible of me, isn't it, especially after everything that has happened?

Wes: Being honest isn't terrible. It's your truth.

Sol: But what if my truth isn't good?

Wes: Then we will make the next chapter good, little mouse. I'll make sure our book is filled with so many good memories that this all seems distant.

***

One day ago.

Sol: The sun should be coming in a few weeks. No more darkness. I wish I could see it rise with you. But it's going to stay for the next few months. Hopefully, I will be able to see it shine before another six months of darkness.

Wes: Oh, little mouse, don't you understand by now? The only time I had light in my life was with you. I won't feel the sun's warmth again till you're naked in my arms.

Chapter 22

Sol

My tongue runs over my dry lips again. I've licked them so much I feel them starting to crack.

My screen, which runs Evander's advanced AI system, hasn't flashed red. The software, which reacts as Luna's body would, is so remarkably advanced that this will win Evander a Nobel Prize. It will also give him a prize he treasures more. Klara in a sane state of mind.

Did I do it? I ask myself as I nervously lick my lips again.

It appears you have.

These past three months, I have taught myself to understand Gabriel's nanobyte technology. The science behind it is breathtaking and terrifying. It's like watching a heart take its first beat. It's a new life that I want to watch grow and evolve.

The question is will this new creature become a monster?

Nanobytes are truly the next stage of evolution.

I combined Luna's latest research on gene therapy, Gabriel's nanobytes, and Evander's AI. According to the software, I cracked the code and figured out a way to undo everything.

It's a lot of power to digest, and if I were off-kilter, I would feel like a god.

I don't.

I feel like a fallen angel, Lucifer, to be precise. He was given a lot of power by God, free to roam and corrupt the earth. However, there is an end date. God allows him control, but one day, it will be taken from him.

Just like God limited Lucifer's reign, my control will eventually come to an end. I hope that when I relinquish this authority, those who inherit it will wield it for the greater good, rather than plunging the world into chaos.

Maybe a wiser person would destroy this new science I created. Forsake their family for the greater good.

I'm not that person; like all humans, I can't resist the allure.

The sin.

I have to use it. I have to heal my sister and save my family.

I've paced what is equivalent to miles in the lab, wondering what my father would think. Would he be proud or jealous? I've outdone him.

I have engineered an entirely new virus and coded it to do whatever I wanted. In this case, specifically to revert Luna and Klara's DNA back to our original DNA at birth.

That's child's play now. The possibilities are endless. I could code the nanobytes to be sleeper agents, so to speak. You could insert it into a person and have it designed to trigger in one month or five years from now.

My mind races, seeing how a government could use this technology.

Do you blame the scientist who created the weapon or the government who used it? Every weapon can be used for good or evil.

I created something deadly but also something that could save so many.

Trying to swallow, it lodges in my throat. I should be celebrating. I did it. The AI system has been running for days with no sign of corruption. I created the downgrade, yet more weight has been applied to my shoulders. The battle is almost finished. That means the rebuilding after such destruction has to begin.

Can Luna and Gabriel rebuild the fallen parts of Manus Dei into something greater?

"Shouldn't you be smiling?" I look up and see Zander. I haven't told anyone about my outcome yet. I'm not ready. Just because a machine says it is feasible doesn't mean it's foolproof. I still need to insert my coded nanobytes inside a body first.

Not just any body but my own.

Zander clears his throat and closes the door to the lab. I've been avoiding him for months. Now, he's standing at the entrance. Blocking my only way out. My eyes travel down to his right hand, where his fingers are wrapped around a small knife.

My shock and internal celebration are short-lived. My eyes dart past him to the hallway he's blocking. I know that if I scream, Kane and Evander will hear me.

I don't scream. Instead, I look at the knife in his hand again.

I haven't seen much of Cody or Zander. Everyone here is so focused on their life-saving tasks that we barely interact. Most nights, I eat with Kane in silence. He brings me food, forcing me to eat. I eat to shut him up so I can continue my work. If Kane weren't here, I would have wasted away by now.

Zander steps further into my lab. Under the ceiling lights, his blond curls shine, longer now, curling around the nape of his neck, giving him a laid-back surfer-boy vibe. But when you look deeper into his expression and the knife in his hand, that relaxed appearance vanishes.

His hazel eyes reveal his true intentions. They don't sparkle with an angelic glow. They gleam with a grief-stricken darkness, a hollowed-out soul that only knows pain. Grief, he wants others to feel.

"You did it," Zander states, his eyes never leaving mine. He watches me as if I am a wolf in sheep's clothing. My clone must have appeared that way to him when Astrid sent her to kill him.

"I don't know what–" I begin to speak, but how his face changes silences me. His clear complexion reddens. A vein in his neck bulges. His heart rate is increasing.

"Don't lie!" he hisses. "She lied." He comes closer, and somewhere in this bunker, I know his twin is working as hard as I am, trying to cure him.

My blue eyes look at the metal lab table. It's only about four feet wide, and it's all that separates us. Four feet between life and death.

So what he does next makes me pause. Reaching up, he places the knife in his hand on the metal table. The sound of the knife being placed on that table will forever be etched in my memory. "Do you ever wonder why Klara chose a knife?" he asks. Not allowing me to answer, he replies to his own question. He wants control. I can understand that since he doesn't always have control of his memory. "Because it made it more memorable." He taps his temple. "Memories," he sighs as if speaking is exhausting, or the memories of his past are. "My brother tried to cure specific memories from me, but those moments shaped me. Now I'm just a shape that doesn't know his mold."

"Maybe you don't need a defined shape," I suggest.

His eyes narrow. "What do you mean?"

I swallow, the sound resounding loudly. His gaze follows the gulp, zeroing in on my stomach. "You're trying to fit into a defined mold from your past, a title society gave you. You don't have to. You can be different. You can make a new shape or," I shrug, "You can keep changing shapes. Some days, you can be a round circle, on a path that repeats. That's okay. But if you wake up and feel like you want to be a triangle or a square, then that's okay too, Zander." I place both hands on the table; the cool metal helps relieve my stress. "I can't begin to understand how you were raised, what happened to you when you had to kill one of my clones to defend your own life. I can't fathom it, Zander. But you keep trying to gain these old memories back, fit into the old shape you were. Maybe try moving forward. Making a new shape to live by."

He leans forward and, with a sudden jerk, his long fingers push the knife across the metal table. It makes a screeching noise as it stops next to my laptop.

Is this his olive branch, or is it a trick before he relapses and tries to kill me with that knife?

"This is for you," He claims. Some of the darkness leaves his eyes.

"I'm not her," I whisper, seeing his distress as he tries to push away the memory of the woman he clearly loved, a clone Astrid sent to kill him, but he killed instead.

"I know," his eyes look at the laptop, "She would never have done what you did."

"What is that?" I ask.

"End the games."

"How do you know I was successful?" I question.

"Because when I watched you, you reflected my expression when I was successful."

When he was successful...oh, I understand now. "When you killed her," I reply.

He nods. Some of his blonde curls fall on his forehead, covering his expression. "Your face looked relieved, but that was quickly replaced with fear. Worry of knowing your life just changed. You did it. You survived, but you also just killed yourself. The old Sol died in the blink of an eye just as I did when I killed you...her," he corrects his mistake. "You did something that will change everything. I did something that changed everything in my life. Except I killed, and you saved."

"You saved too, Zander," he looks at me with a raised brow. "You saved yourself and Cody. One twin cannot survive without the other. It all depends on how you look at the glass. Half full or half empty," I say.

Zander hums over my words. I hope that they help heal him and banish some of the guilt from his mind.

"When are you going to tell the others?" He inquires. He places both palms on the metal table and narrows his eyes to look at my laptop screen. On the screen is the small popup window that states no internal errors were found.

I lick my bottom lip again. This time I feel the skin break. It stings, and the pain grounds me. "It was successful here," I touch the laptop. "Now I have to test it." He tilts his head, observing me through the shadow cast by his hooded lids.

"On yourself," he guesses.

"Yes."

His fingers sweep along the metal table. For a second, I question if he will reach forward and grab the knife. Instead, he pushes his hands off the table and stands tall. Then he turns to leave.

"Zander," I call out. The game is ending, this book is nearly finished, and I want some riddles solved. "You said Manus Dei referred to you as the young prince." There is a sinister ripple that crashes over his body. He pauses, turning slowly to face me. His pupils dilate wide. Did I push him too far?

Widening my stance, I place my palms on the table. My fingers inch closer to the knife I might have to use in my defense. "Why did they call you that?"

"Isn't it obvious?" he said, a blank expression etched across his face. His tone patronizing.

My chest tightens, my heart pounding in disbelief. I want to deny what he was suggesting, to shake my head and refute the glaring truth he presents.

"Who do I look like." He sneers. "Whose hair do I have," he smacks his cheek, "whose face, do I have? Who do I look like, Sol?"

For months, I've been thinking like a scientist. I haven't been able to view the world through the eyes of an artist. I look at his hair, beautiful golden blonde with small ringlets at the ends. His face is younger and leaner; the high angles almost give him a slight feminine touch, but his square jaw contrasts his slightly upturned eyelids.

I add the details together. No, it can't be.

He tips his chin up. "I'm Astrid's son. So, in a way, you're my mother, too."

Chapter 23

Sol

"Zander," I voice. I sound like a dying rabbit in the jaws of a wolf. I try to mask my shock with some sympathy. Dear god, he's Astrid's son. She had a child!

But wait, Zander is a twin. Astrid had twins.

His face reveals none of his emotions. He's masked them so skillfully. The only thing that moves are his eyes, which watch mine. What is he thinking?

I'm thankful for the table between us. I think. A part of me wants to hug him; the other part wants to take a step back.

"How much have you solved about Manus Dei's royal lineage?" He asks.

I blink, striving to retrieve the interwoven threads of information; the shock of the moment renders me unable to dig deep. "I've been focused on the downgrade?" I admit.

He looks down at his watch. "I'll solve it for you before my brother comes looking for me."

I feel dizzy. Inching back, my heels hit the edge of my stool before I numbly lower myself to sit on it.

"Manus Dei was all about lineage, genetics, bloodlines. The leadership was passed down through the original ruling family. The Masters, which were like a council, didn't really matter. At least their opinions didn't weigh heavily before Astrid killed the King."

"Why did the Masters allow Astrid to remain if they knew she killed the King?" I interrupt.

Zander leans back against the opposite table. "Women are the masters of trickery. A beautiful smile and pretty words can make the strongest of men lower their guard," he sneers, his past trauma rearing its head.

"His name was Miran. The King, who Gabriel was cloned after. My father." His eyes grow distant before they turn arctic again. "Astrid beguiled him, wormed her way into his inner circle, and then she took his heart. He fell in love with her. The first few years were peaceful. Astrid didn't show her true colors to him. The council members cheered for children, but unfortunately," He laughs at his last words. "All her pregnancies ended," he states. I knew Astrid was a monster. I know she killed countless clones of her own self to gain more power. But knowing she killed her own children makes her a whole new level of demonic.

"Miran grew restless, as did the council. His family *always* had an heir. Always," Zander stresses. "So Miran forced Astrid to turn to IVF and genetic engineering. If they couldn't have a baby naturally, he would pour all his scientific knowledge and power into making the perfect baby. After all, he had your father on his side, and Dorian was a master at genetic engineering.

"Unfortunately, before Miran could see those children be born, Astrid killed him. She thought killing him would shift all the power into her hands. But some of the council was suspicious; some wanted their own family to claim the seat, and others fought for Cody and me, the true heirs of Manus Dei, even though we were just cells waiting to be implanted at that point. Although we weren't born yet, our voice, or lack thereof, didn't matter."

"That's why they started the game of perfection. It was a multi-layered game."

He nods, "It gave Dorian and Hans a chance to work out all the bugs, so to speak, before they allowed Cody and I to be born, but it also appeased the Masters. The King was reborn through Gabriel. As for Astrid's clones, well, they would get a second chance. The Masters were replaying history and hoping for a different outcome. Hoping the woman Miran fell in love with would not cause his demise again." He eases his posture, and a sly glint enters his eyes like a cunning fox eyeing its prey. "I wish I could have seen Astrid's face when they told her they would bench her and allow her clones to take her place."

I wish I could have seen it, too.

"You're not much younger than us, though," I state the obvious. If he wasn't supposed to be born till after a winner claimed the crown, then why is he alive?

"It's all about leverage. Astrid needed it."

His wording makes my dizziness vanish. My world comes to a stop. I have been focused on the science, but so many questions still linger in my polluted mind. One being what leverage Astrid had over Luna. "What did you just say?" Did I hear him right.

"Aww," he snickers, "I was wondering when you would ask. Luna said you hadn't yet."

He talks to my twin? I was aware of their closeness, but learning she confides in him stings.

"*You* were the leverage Astrid held over Luna's head." I don't mean my words to sound cruel, but they do.

"Jealous it wasn't you?" He raises a brow.

"No. I was relieved when Luna told me. I'm just…I still don't understand." How is Zander the catalyst to it all? He's the leverage

Astrid used to force Luna to create the modification that is destroying her. He's the reason we had to split up and all fight against each other.

Why is his life more valuable than so many of my clones?

"Why?" He sneers. In a volatile jerk, he pushes off the table he leaned against, "Why can't I be as loved as you."

I shake my head, "That's not what I mean. Stop making me the bad guy." I hiss.

His eyes assess me. "Luna said she did it because Cody and I reminded her of you." My spine curls as I feel the weight of all the secrets and lies confessed. "You should talk to her. Well, you still can. She should be the one to tell you why she gave up everything and risked it all for my brother and me."

I feel like a bobblehead on the dashboard of a car. The only action I can manage is nodding, driven by the jarring impact of the truth.

He looks at his watch again, his gaze lingering as if trying to decipher more than just the passing time. "Astrid didn't want the game of perfection, that twisted chessboard of cloned destinies," he says, his voice tinged with disdain. "She didn't want to watch a clone of herself marry the clone of the king she had slain. She needed leverage, a wildcard, so she stole us."

Pausing, he runs a hand through his hair, "It was almost too easy, considering we were merely the size of cells, invisible pawns in her grand strategy. When the time came, she placed us in a willing womb. The Masters remained oblivious to our silent inception."

He looks up, his eyes reflecting a storm of emotions. "And once we were born, once we took our first breath, she took us, set us aside, and only revealed who we were when the timing was perfect for her."

"She raised you?"

"No," he exhales. "Only Klara had that fate. We were hidden, raised separately until we came of age. By then, the council could not ignore us, which caused a conundrum because they had started the game with Gabriel and Luna. The question of who should get the crown was now up for debate. Should it be the winner of the perfection game or the children who were actually from Miran's cells?"

"What did they decide?"

"Whoever wins the perfection game will rule until Cody or I marry. Whichever one of us has children first will take over the ruling seat. Gabriel or Luna will be our mentors."

"But what if Gabriel and Luna have a child?"

For the first time, his eyes leave mine. They dart towards the floor, his gaze skimming across the tiles as though they were a wishing well awaiting a coin. There's a hidden weight, something he wants to confess.

"Zander," I press.

"They took that ability away from them." His eyes finally meet mine again. "They neutralize Luna."

A gasp slices through the air, releasing a torrent of tears from my eyes. The realization strikes deep. Zander's correct—the technical genetics place him as my child and Luna's since were clones of each other. Clones of Astrid.

That's not all. That's just the start.

Zander and Cody are the genetic children of Astrid and Miran, and if Luna is Astrid's clone, and Gabriel is Miran's, then genetically, Zander and Cody are Gabriel and Luna's children.

He's their child, a child she can never have.

"Does Gabriel know?" My voice is so weak I'm not sure he heard me.

"No," he replies. "Luna didn't know she couldn't have children either until Astrid showed us."

My mind, previously a tangled web, untangles itself like a well-organized library. I understand why Luna did it. She was trying to save the children she could never have—children Astrid used as leverage over her head.

I draw my shoulders away from him and cover my face. Each breath feels like a serrated blade carving deeper into my chest, stretching my ribs as if they were about to splinter apart.

"I can't tell if you're crying because you just found out that on a genetic level, you're kind of my mom, but also my aunt, or if you're crying for Luna and Gabriel," He observes.

"Are you trying to joke?" I wipe my eyes.

"It's the one thing I try and continue to fail at. I'm better at being an asshole."

So is your father. I want to say, but I don't. I see parts of Gabriel in him. I also see Luna.

I face him again, the situation a tangled mess. I'm looking at a young man who would be my son if Gabriel and I had a child, who would be my nephew if Luna and Gabriel had a child.

The genetic ties stretch before me like a vast constellation, and with each connection, my mind shivers like a star pulsating with newfound energy. "But Zander," my voice wavers, a lone echo in the cosmic discovery.

He nods, "You piece together the puzzle." He appears as if he might be sick.

"You never saw Astrid's face before you killed my clone," I state. He couldn't have.

"No. I never met Astrid or knew she had clones. I never knew Luna was Astrid's clone, that Luna was also kind of my mom." He clenches his jaw. "I never knew the woman I started to fall in love with was a clone of my biological mother."

"Jesus," I exhale. My fingers curl around the rim of my stool. I just need to feel grounded because, in truth, I feel like I'm falling down an endless rabbit hole. "Astrid sent her clone to you knowing this."

He shrugs. "It's not the most messed up thing Astrid has done. Trying to make her son fall in love with her own clone is one thing; sending her clone to kill her son is another."

"Zander…"

"I don't want your pity." His jaw tenses. He looks so much like Gabriel when he's angry. Like he is tethering on the edge of a chasm, some unseen force is trying to pull him down. A dark voice trying to convince him to give in to his dark side. I have witnessed Gabriel fight it for years, and now Zander is battling the same demon. Luna never fought it; she simply allied with this dark force, manipulated it, and used it.

I can see how much he detests that word. Now I understand why Cody tried to help his brother. "Pity… that's why Cody did it. It wasn't just that you killed someone; it was that you started to fall for the clone of your mother and then killed the clone of your mother."

"Cody kept telling me it wasn't my fault, but the facts... well, they would mind fuck anyone. I think Astrid knew that. It was her fail-safe. If the clone failed, then the facts would render me unable to rule. Mark me as insane."

"I'm sorry."

"I hate it when people apologize for things that aren't their fault." He snaps. He watches me digest this massive truth. I look at him in a new light. Zander and Cody are what Luna and Gabriel's child would look like. I see his blonde curly hair. The ringlets are from Gabriel, whose hair curls more when it is longer. Zander is tall like Gabriel but lean like Luna.

One detail is off, though: Gabriel and Luna have blue eyes. "Your eyes are hazel," I state. Zander's eyes are shades of tans, yellows, and browns.

"It was a modification. Cody and I wanted something that separated us from our father and mother. Eyes are the window to the soul, so we changed our souls and separated our fate from Astrid and Miran's."

That answer makes me want to cry happy tears. I've never been so happy a modification was created.

He's been so hostile, rightfully so. Not only did one of my clones try to kill him, but we are cloned after a mother that tried to kill him. A mother that was successful in killing his other siblings before they were born.

Yet, with Luna, Zander has never shown hostility. He's been affectionate, caring in a friendly manner. He grabbed her hand when her and I argued. He defended her. "You think of Luna as your mother?" It's clear to me now. The lengths Zander has gone through. "That's why you stole my blood. You thought you could find a cure for Luna before she brought me into the fold."

My body breaks out in goosebumps over the revelation. Zander doesn't say anything. I'm not sure if that makes the knowledge better or worse. I flex the muscles in my legs before I push to stand. "Thank you for trying to help her." I tell him.

That gets a reaction. His lips twitch. "I didn't do it for you."

"I know," I reply. That's why Zander isn't stopping me from testing the downgrade on myself first. He is willing to sacrifice me. He's willing to let the downgrade malfunction on me before Luna.

That's also why I just gained his trust. Zander knows I will sacrifice myself to protect Luna, his mother, who didn't try to kill him but rather killed for him.

He begins to turn. Our time is up. "Zander, when I leave, can you promise me something?" He tilts his head to the side without responding. "Watch out for her, keep her honest. Don't let the power get to her head."

Chapter 24

Sol

For the first time in my life, I want to lash out. I want to throw something, break anything. I want to hit and punch, kick and scream.

All I see is red. Bright red over what Astrid has done. Not what she has done to me or my clones but to Zander.

If I don't leave this lab, I will destroy what I have worked so hard to create. Rushing from the room, I search for the one person who will understand my pain. I find War sitting on his bed reading a book. When I enter his room, his face lights up, that is until I walk right up to him, grab the book from his hand, and throw it against the wall.

It's not enough.

With intense frustration, I take hold of the book, relentlessly striking it against the floor as if trying to release pent-up anger until the binding snaps and the pages spiral out like startled birds. Birds I want to shoot down. I just want it all to stop!

I come to an abrupt standstill like a stone abruptly placed in the midst of a frenzied river; the current, like my emotions, continues to flow until it fades downstream. My own actions stun me.

"I get it," War says. I hear him stand from bed, his steps cautious, echoing gently in the room. "You don't like biographies. Only romance novels for you." He tries to joke.

My chest heaves, "I needed to destroy something," I say, planting my palms on the cold concrete floor. My fingers tremble against it like the timbre of a drum.

"Don't we all," he chirps, sounding way too upbeat as he sits on the floor next to me. "Talk to me."

"I just did."

"So you want to play that game, mousey? You want me to pull the truth from you like you're having a wisdom tooth plucked from your mouth. No Novocaine for you."

I begin to gather up the pages, then I shove them inside and close the book. It looks like it went through a trash compactor.

"Well, look at that," He glees as he takes it from my hands, "Good as new."

"I'm sorry."

"I know." He pats my knee, "You snapped, and given our situation, I'm shocked it hasn't been sooner." His exhale echoes like a gentle breeze sighing through a keyhole. "I'm guessing your new method didn't work."

That's why he thinks I'm upset. It's a perfect excuse.

I have to lie.

If I tell War it worked, he will run and tell the others. If I lose control of this knowledge, they will never allow me to be the first test subject.

"Yes. It failed again." The lie doesn't taste like ash. It's not even sour. It's sweet, like the finest Swiss chocolate. Smooth and velvety.

This lie will protect my sister, and hopefully, if the downgrade works, it will save her.

However there is one massive oversight I must correct before I give myself the injection. In order to know how the downgrade will effect Luna I have to make myself match her on a genetic level.

I have to upgrade myself with every upgrade she has had.

***

Three months later.

It hasn't been easy. Slowly, I've been giving myself every single upgrade Luna received.

Every single one.

Even the flawed modification she made for Astrid. That's right. Just last week, I administered the modification that promises a gradual descent into madness.

Getting the upgrades was simple, like sliding a key into an unlocked door. Famine has all the data stored here on servers and the codes to decrypt it.

I have the whole cookie jar, and I binged.

I have access to all the files Luna and my father worked on, which means I had access to all the upgrade recipes. I could see everything. I could recreate everything. If only all my tasks were so simple.

I've kept this all a secret. Famine thinks I needed access to the past upgrades in order to undo them. I had no choice. No one would comprehend this. Wes certainly never could. I need to make myself an exact replica of my twin. I need to ensure the downgrade will function flawlessly.

The pain from these upgrades hasn't been the challenge; concealing my actions has. Some enhancements make me physically ill, and since Kane has made himself my new bestie, it's been arduous to hide certain afflictions from him. I cloak certain symptoms with lies. I tell him my exhaustion and ailing appearance stem from exhaustive work hours. When I had a fever, I convinced him I was overwhelmed and started to overexert myself.

I don't think he buys it entirely, but as long as I'm somewhat functional, he hasn't probed further. I sense his restlessness being cooped up in here, just like everyone else. That's why they often leave me alone in the lab.

I've fed them some hope, conveying that I'm optimistic about this new attempt at a successful downgrade.

I've delved deep into the grim and astonishing upgrades my father, Hans, Luna and Gabriel concocted. Understanding all of it was crucial.

Here's a glimpse of the upgrades I had to inject into myself.

Increased Longevity: I've slowed the aging process, elongating my existence.

Enhanced Metabolism: My body now operates on a quicker, more efficient level, consuming nutrients and energy at an accelerated rate.

Enhanced Cognitive Abilities: By manipulating the brain's workings, my father unlocked a near-photographic memory. Luna recalls everything, a burden that must weigh heavily upon her.

Enhanced Strength: My muscles are fortified, boosting strength and endurance. But let's be real, it's not Superman-level strength — it's real life, not a movie.

Enhanced Speed: Heightened reflexes and nimbleness in movement.

Resilience to Extreme Conditions: Genetic modifications to endure extreme temperatures, pressures, and environments. I could've used this when trudging among polar bears to reach this fallout shelter. No wonder Evander, Luna, Cody and Zander seemed impervious to the cold.

Enhanced Lung Capacity: I now breathe more easily in low-oxygen environments.

Enhanced Adaptation to Environment: Genetic tweaks facilitating easier adaptation to diverse environmental conditions.

Enhanced Sleep Efficiency: Improved sleep quality and duration, enabling peak performance on minimal rest. This has been a lifesaver for me.

Enhanced Bone Density: Sturdier bones to minimize the risk of fractures or osteoporosis.

Enhanced Pain Tolerance: A heightened threshold for pain or swift recovery. That's how Gabriel endured being shot at point-blank range without a flinch.

These upgrades are but a fragment of the alterations I've undergone, a necessary transformation amidst the tangled web of genetic enhancements.

I understand my family better. When I told Evander I wasn't god, and he barked back at me, well, I know what he meant, how he felt.

Being so upgraded does make me feel god-like. I'm simply better than the average human. Genetically, that is. Mentally and morally, it is a different story.

But this is all temporary. Thank god. Having all these upgrades has changed me mentally. I don't like the person it makes me think I am.

I'm now the complete opposite of what I always wanted to be. Normal. Average.

That dream has slipped so far away that I'm not sure it was ever real.

I don't know how Gabriel or Luna have stayed so strong. I feel how they feel. They are walking a tightrope of trying not to have a god complex.

"Hey," Kane says in his cheerful voice as he enters my lab. He swings his arm and tosses me a bag of freeze-dried apple chips. "An apple a day keeps the doctor away." He strolls inside, pushes over my laptop, and sits on the lab counter. He does this often, interrupts me to bring me a snack. It's his way of checking in on me. Making sure I don't snap again.

"Thanks," I reply. I open the bag. He won't leave until I finish every last crumb. As far as fresh fruits and veggies go, everything we have is freeze-dried. The meals in the fallout shelter are army meals. We only need one of the premade meals a day due to the high caloric intake. They didn't taste bad at first, but now that I've tasted every option, it's getting old fast.

"You look happy," Kane grins. "Did you have phone sex with my brother?"

I roll my eyes. Kane does this. Often. I think it's his way of ensuring I miss his brother.

"Was it that bad?" He chuckles. "I'll talk to him, give him some pointers."

"Kane," I warn him.

"Fine, put up with dry phone sex." He grins as he swings his legs like a child. His eyes scan the room. "How's it going." In other words, are you close because I'm so antsy I can't sit still?

I pop a chip into my mouth. "I'm feeling hopeful about this."

His eyes light up. "Good." He grabs his shirt, "Because this one thread count fabric is making my skin itch terribly. I need my Italian suits back, mousey. So kindly hurry it up, will you." He jumps off the table and ruffles my hair like a brother would to his sister.

I grin back at him.

He has no idea what I've done.

He has no idea that after I take that downgrade tonight, this might have been our last conversation.

Chapter 25

Wes

Five months ago.

Wes: You've been quiet, little mouse. I don't like it.

Sol: What do you want to hear?

Wes: You. I want to hear you moaning my name like it's the second coming of Christ. Now, ask me what I want to taste.

Sol: Song link to: "Running Up That Hill" by Placebo

She's not happy today. Most days, she isn't receptive to me. There is a distance between us, but I refuse to let it grow. Not in fear she won't want me. She does want me.

The chasm between us is over her guilt. I know my little mouse. She had a fool's hope before I met her. It's what attracted me to her. She shined a light in my dark eyes. It called to me, but without me coaxing it, her demons were trying to blow it out.

I refuse to be bested by her mind.

I'll never give up.

She doesn't reply to me every day. Some days, I just get a link to a song. Other days, nothing at all; those days are like hell on earth. I just try to survive.

I listen to this song. I've listened to every single song on repeat. I reply to everyone.

Wes: You know what this song means, little mouse, it means you still feel. Hope isn't lost. Just keep feeling, keep fighting. I know I am. I'm freezing my ass off out here, all for you. I never told you this, but the house I built for us is in Colorado. I used to like the snow; there was something about it that was serene yet lethal.

I don't like the snow now. To be honest, it reminds me of Luna.

I think when we're free of Manus Dei, I will build us a second home. This way, when winter comes, we can leave and head someplace warmer. Do you like that idea?

I'm thinking of a private island, because I want you dressed in nothing. I want you to let the sun kiss your skin so that you glow like the angel I see when I look at you.

See what time apart is doing to me. It's making me a sappy fuck.

But I'm your sappy fuck.

***

Four months ago.

Sol: Do you think I'm a monster?

Wes: Yes. I think every person is a monster. Some of us just cage our inner beast better. Do you know what that means?

Sol: No.

Wes: That means you are what you always wanted to be. Normal.

Sol: Song link to: "Young And Beautiful" by Lana Del Ray.

Wes: You are the most beautiful woman I have ever seen, Sol, but that is not why I fell in love with you. I fell for your soul. I took it. Claimed it. There was a spark of hope within that is still flickering even in these dark times. When your hope feels low, remember I am here, blowing on it, keeping that fire alive, nourishing it. I'm here. I will always be chasing you, my little mouse.

Sol: I don't think I deserve you.

Wes: We don't know what we deserve, and if anyone thinks they do, they most likely don't deserve it. We have to take what we want, and I'm taking you.

***

Three months ago.

End My Games

Sol: I learned something new today. Something that will haunt me, Wesley. I'm not even sure you're strong enough to chase away the nightmare.

Wes: When we were together, you said it was like pausing the games. Remember when you told me that, little mouse?

Sol: Yes.

Wes: I will pause it all. I will slay any demon that gets too close to your mind.

Sol: How?

Wes: With my love.
Wes: With my lips.
Wes: With my dick.

Sol: You had to go and ruin the romantic moment, didn't you?

Wes: It made you blush, didn't it?

Sol: Yes

Wes: Good. See, I just made you forget what you learned. It might only be a fleeting moment while we're apart, but picture how amazing it'll feel when you're in my arms.

Sol: Song link to: "Wicked Games" by Grace Carter.

Wes: I don't want you to fall in love with me either, little mouse. I want you to become obsessed with me. I want your every inhale to be in anticipation over seeing me, feeling me. I want your every exhale to be in utter bliss over the fact that your obsession is with you, that I'm tangible.

***

One hour ago.

Sol: Song link to: "No More Hiding" by Gina Brooklyn.

Sol: Song link to: "In This Dark Time" by Time Simone.

Song link to: "Dancing After Death" by Matt Maeson.

Song link to: "This is What You Wanted" by Placebo.

Five months of not seeing Sol, of missing her sky blue eyes, particularly when they are wide open, begging me for more, when my hard cock is thrusting in and out of her wet heat.

Five fucking mouths.

Thankfully it's been dark here, so I don't have the reminder of her eyes hanging over my head every single goddamn day, but that's changing. The sun is coming, and when it does, it won't be setting.

I'll take it as a sign from the man upstairs that the light at the end of my tunnel is finally here.

Five months of begging Sol to speak to me. Sometimes, she calls, but I find most days, she prefers to text. The rare time she does call me, she cries. Hearing her cry but being unable to console her with my body is unimaginable. It feels like my heart is being pelted by bullets again.

Five months of trying to be patient, trying not to, literally dig my way inside so I can bend her over my knee and punish her, then make love to her.

Five months of hope. She has been grinding away like a sculptor, chiseling tirelessly to carve out a downgrade from the chaos. The longer she is inside, the closer she gets to being successful.

But those five months now feel like a fragile kite caught in the tempest of a thunderous storm.

She sent me not just one link to a song but multiple links.

Why the fuck would she do that?

Am I overthinking it, or is she telling me she won't be able to text me for a while? If that's the case, then why?

Why, Sol?

What the fuck is going on inside that bunker, little mouse?

Chapter 26

Sol

It's an odd sensation, knowing that after tonight, your life might change, or it might end. Like a coin being tossed in the air, it will be for better or for worse.

The bunker is eerily silent tonight. Maybe it's this way every night since Luna and Klara are caged below us now. Klara is drugged most days to ensure she remains calm.

You tend to notice the little details when the end is closing in.

Reaching into my back pocket, I grab my phone. My fingers hesitate over the screen. What should I tell Wes? I can't tell him that I found the cure or that I will test it out on myself first. Only Zander knows the truth, and he hasn't said one word.

This could be my final message to Wes, or if I am successful, it could be the start of our new life together.

The thrill of the science is alluring, but the truths I have learned make me want to run from it all. I just want to paint over all the memories I have had to experience here. I want Wes to take me far away.

I don't even care if it is in a cage.

I want nothing to do with Manus Dei.

I pace my room until the soles of my feet become tender. How does one find words that are a farewell but also hopeful. A catch-22? There are no words. Only a handful of songs.

End My Games

What Wes won't understand is that even if I fail, there is beauty in that. Failure shows you the error of your ways. Failing means I gave my life to try to save my sisters.

But God, I hope I don't fail. Please, Lord, don't be so cruel. I'm just about to run through the finish line. Please don't let me trip before I break the ribbon.

I press send; then I make my way to my lab. Once I'm inside, I let the songs play out loud. I walk to the cryopreservation freezer, where the downgrade is being stored. As I swing open the door, I sing out loud. When I feel like I'm about to cry, I sing harder.

A blast of arctic air makes blood rush to my cheeks. I grab the vile and seal the door shut. I place a note on the door that details what is inside. Just in case I don't make it, Famine will know which downgrade sample failed.

My movements feel automatic and fluid, like the effortless drifting of a jellyfish in the ocean's currents. I'm directed by circumstance, like the jellyfish, guided inevitably by the forces around me. There is no alternative but to proceed, just as the jellyfish has no choice but to yield to the direction of the current.

Once I'm at my lab table, I wipe clean my stomach with alcohol, and then I inject myself with the downgrade. I watch the last drop of downgrade leave the vial and enter my body.

"I love you, Wesley," I whisper. It might be silly to speak to him when he can't hear me, but it makes me feel calmer.

I have an approximately one hour before the first time release starts to take effect. Then it should all happen like a domino effect. The upgrades will be targeted one by one. The nanobytes will monitor my body, and once it's stable, they will eliminate the next upgrade.

One by one.

It sounds so simple.

"His AI said it would work." I voice. "It has to work." It must! I have exhausted everything I know, everything my father knew, all of Manus Dei's vast scientific vault.

"It has to work." I close my eyes and steady my heart before I stand. Once I'm breathing slowly and steadily, I make my way out of my lab and go to the one place I should be.

No, it's not with the man I love. After all, this downgrade might not work. I don't want him to see me if I fail. I don't want his last memories of me to be how I am now. Utterly depleted, truly desperate. I want him to remember me as an artist who tricked him but ultimately fell for his charm.

I have to be with the person who started this all. The person who made me paint her lies, tricked me into starting her war, haunted me by whispering her secrets, and the person who asked me to end her games.

Luna. I have to be with Luna.

Chapter 27

Sol

I tread through the stark, concrete corridors of the hidden fallout bunker. Clenched in my palm is the small rock I pocketed months ago while outside. I hope one day I can set it free, release it back into the wild. I pray the same fate can be bestowed upon me.

Freedom.

It's silent, an eerie calm that blankets the rooms as everyone sleeps, oblivious to my descent. Each step I take feels like a solemn march, a possible final journey through these dimly lit passageways.

The faint emergency lights cast elongated shadows along the walls, creating a haunting ambiance in this desolate underground space. It's a sobering realization that this might be my last visit to this level.

When I reach the storage level where Klara and Luna are being caged I feel a bead of sweat roll down my forehead.

Is that the downgrade already taking effect?

I quicken my pace, coming to an abrupt stop right before the caged fence where, at the moment, both of them are sound asleep. I've never seen them appear so serene. It's like observing lions sleeping in a zoo. Witnessing such majestic creatures trapped in cages is sorrowful, yet there's a conflicted joy in beholding their rare beauty because of their captivity.

My back skims down the concrete wall as I lean against Luna's cage. My left thigh presses against the fence, causing it to raddle. Her eyes open, and her head turns slowly. We look at each other.

"I have a song for you," I say as I retrieve my phone and scroll to find the track. The song is "It's All Over Now Baby Blue" by The Animals. It's the most fitting song I could find. I hope it is all over for us, the blue-eyed twins. As the song describes, some of us have gone crazy; the sky feels like it is falling, our family is together again, and we must leave behind those who have not made it; if we dwell on them, we will join them. The vagabond in the song is just like a Reflection: it's the new me staring directly at the old parts of me. A collision. It's all over. One way or another, it is all over for me. This downgrade will either kill me, corrupt me, or save me. I have no other options left. This is it.

In this beautiful unspoken moment, we simply gaze at each other and listen. It feels like the calm before the storm, like we're sitting on the beach during low tide, fully aware that a thundercloud is looming on the horizon, signaling an impending high tide that could wash away everything. Amidst the uncertainty, there's a glimmer of hope – the idea that this storm might not be entirely catastrophic. Perhaps it's an opportunity to wipe the slate clean and start afresh.

Luna eventually climbs out of the small twin bed and joins me; only the thin cage separates us. Raising my left hand, I push my fingers through the holes. She mimics my actions, and we try to interlace our fingers.

In her current state, I can tell she is trapped in the void. The robotic stare that Astrid made her design has a hold on her. Deep inside that darkness is Luna, and I know she is there, buried in the chemicals of her mind. That's why her fingers grasped mine. She is still able to fight it, unlike Klara. Soon, she won't; hopefully, that's a lie because the downgrade will have worked.

"You haven't visited me." She finally speaks.

"I know." Guilt settles in my stomach. It feels like I'm sinking in quicksand; the more I struggle against it, the deeper I feel myself being pulled into a mire of discomfort and regret. So, I don't try to make her comprehend why I stayed away.

"I understand." She replies. My throat thickens with emotions.

"I wanted to ask you something; well, I still can," she begins. She has a steady tone, like a machine following precise commands, yet her eyes connect with mine, expressing a deep passion. It's through her piercing blue eyes that she unveils her true emotions to me.

"What?" I inquire, leaning closer to the fence.

"Remember that painting you were working on before everything began? The one with Alice falling down the hole. Her arms stretched out in both directions," she recalls.

I nod in recollection. "Yes, I remember it," I reply. It was right after Death had snuck into my room. Luna entered my studio, and I asked her if she knew Death was coming for me. She admitted she did. I felt betrayed and furious that she hadn't warned me. Little did I know what other secrets were concealed from me.

The Past.

She shakes her head, "Let it be, Sol; everything will be answered eventually. You gobble too much down, and you'll choke."

Then she looks up at the canvas; the image is more apparent now. It's a giant black hole that is consuming the girl. Her right arm reaches out for help, but her left arm reaches into the darkness. Pulled between both futures. Freedom from the darkness or liberation from her life. The figure doesn't know which she wants.

"What's this?" Luna asks. She touches the outlines but is careful not to smudge the lines.

"It's Alice falling down the hole."

Luna curves towards me, "Does she want to fall?"

We're no longer talking about my drawing but instead about me and my future. "She doesn't know. That's why she is reaching towards both sides."

"Sounds painful."

"It is." I jest with spite. It's painful that you kept from me that you knew a man was in my room, not to kill but to protect me. Another twisted game.

Luna raises her hand and looks long at the charcoal which stains her fingers. "Sometimes the answers aren't worth the burden of knowing." She raises her index finger and presses it to a clean part of the canvas. Leaving behind a perfect fingerprint in charcoal dust now.

"You know what the dormouse said?" She sings the song.

"Feed your head," I respond.

"Feed your head," Luna repeats well, nodding to herself.

"Did she want to fall or climb out?" she probes. This is a game. A deception. What she wants to ask me is what I would have chosen if I knew *this* would be an outcome. Would I have been the ignorant sister who climbed out of the hole, abandoned her twin, and just walked away, or would I have opted to plunge into the depths, uncovering the horrors and attempting to rescue my twin?

"She wasn't reaching for either side," I declare.

She quickly blinks as she tries to mask her pain. She thinks I would have turned my back on her. That's not what I mean. "Luna, she wasn't falling or trying to escape. She was opening her arms, embracing it all." A tinge of sadness accompanies my smile.

I descended into the hole and confronted the challenges. However, I welcomed the escape. Luna understands that now; she knows I can't continue surviving like this. Some creatures can survive and endure; well, others just vanish into extinction.

If I remain here, with the truth, lies, and science... I'll die.

She nods, drawing her knees closer and embracing herself. Leaning her cheek against her legs, she watches me intently.

"I'll survive without you by my side," She mutters. A part of me thinks it's a lie she is telling herself.

"I know you will." My throat feels dry, and when I try to swallow, it gets clogged in the dry cracks. I tip my head back against the cold concrete wall and close my eyes. "I know you will."

Chapter 28

Sol

"The song," Luna begins, unfolding her legs. She grabs the fence, linking our fingers again as she pulls herself closer. I open my eyes but leave my head against the wall. "That's why you came down here," she says, glancing at the phone. "Did you do it?" she guesses. Her fingers tighten, and the metal fence presses deeper into our skin.

"I'm not sure yet," I respond as I glance down.

Her eyes narrow. "What did you do?" Her hand tugs at mine, but the fence blocks her. This is why I kept the fence between us. I didn't know how she would react. The smallest trigger could set her off into a tailspin.

"I did what you would have done, what you did do. I risked myself first." I keep our hands connected but pivot so I can face her. I need to tell her what I have done. "I gave myself every upgrade you have. I need to know if the downgrade I created works. It was the only way."

"No," Her voice is flat. "You have Evander's AI."

"His AI helped tremendously. I was able to test out numerous solutions that would have killed you. It saved so much time." I nod, "But, you know as well as I do it's not foolproof. I needed to be certain." I snap. A heat starts to build within my body.

"You can be such a silly fool sometimes." That's her way of thanking me.

I glance at Klara, curled on her side, her back to us. "Is she really sleeping?"

"Evander sedated her five hours ago." Luna's eyes follow mine. At least Luna is in a state of mind where I can converse with her. Sometimes, she can't; Evander has to sedate her also.

"I talked with Zander," I admit. I kick my feet out and finally release her hand. I tug at the collar of my shirt as a wave of heat flushes through my body. Fevering isn't a bad sign. Everything is starting to work; my immune system has sensed the nanobytes. They are starting to release the first stage of the downgrade. Soon, my body will enter a self-induced, coma-like state, just as I designed it. I didn't want to be awake; I couldn't bear their looks and questions.

"It must have been a short chat. Zander doesn't talk much."

"He must have got that trait from you," I add. My eyes watch her carefully. The corner of her lip tugs up slightly.

"So you know then."

"Yes. I know who Zander and Cody are genetically, and I know what that means to you."

She licks her lips, which look slightly chapped like mine. The heat in the bunker is dry and stifling at times. Her eyes glance at Klara again. "I never thought I wanted children. It only struck me when the opportunity was taken away. It's messed up, you know? I'm left questioning whether I truly wanted them or if the longing only intensified because it became impossible."

I want to ask her if it's impossible to find a cure for it. Can't we just develop a solution to fix the problem? But as I observe the distant look in her eyes, I already grasp the answer. If there were a way for her to cure it, she would have done so.

Sure, she could extract what she required from another clone; I'd give her what she needed, but it wouldn't truly be hers.

There's a difference, not in the genetics, but emotionally.

Her whole life, she has been trying to grasp emotions and be more empathic; it's cruel that when she does feel something so powerful, it's grief over having the ability to have a child taken from her. I wish she couldn't feel this.

"But you do have kids now. You see Cody and Zander as your children." I state.

"I see people as many things." She snaps, inhales deeply, then releases a breath slowly. "Astrid showed me a video of Cody and Zander. It changed everything. It shouldn't have. I didn't know them. They shouldn't have mattered more to me than my own clones."

"It's ok to admit they did," I add. "Astrid threatened them. That's why you made the weapon for her. It was all to save them."

"I wanted to save everyone." Her eyes meet mine as they soften. "You're still my sister. I never stopped caring. But you could take care of yourself. I just had to show you how." Her sky-blue eyes meet mine, and for a brief second, I see their pride, "And look how far you've come."

I nod. I'm not going to argue with her. Tell her that what she made me endure was horrendous. It was all unnecessary; she should have told me the truth.

There is no point now. It's in the past.

"Luna," I lean closer, "Why didn't you tell Gabriel about Zander and Cody? This game could have been so different."

"No," She shakes her head. Her palms slap out over the floor. "Gabriel cared about one person. Me. He would have risked everything to keep me safe. Even you, Sol. Even. You." She curls her fingers; her nails scratch into the floor. "Imagine if I showed him a video of two random boys."

"They weren't random, though."

"They would have been to him. He killed clones of himself to save me."

"But they are your kids." Even if she didn't give birth to them, she still views them as her children. Gabriel might have understood that.

"They were tools Astrid used over me. Gabriel would have eliminated them so she couldn't control me. I couldn't risk it."

Minutes tick by as neither of us speaks. We can't change the past, but at least I understand it. "You said he cared," I state. "He still cares. He is outside of the bunker."

"He's outside because I provoked him." She's referring to the letter she left him.

"If you could control the future, what would you design? What was the point of all this, Luna? You brought us all together again. How do you see it all working out."

She swallows, and her eyes roam around the cage as if she can see what she wants. "I wanted to give everyone what they needed. You wanted freedom; you'll get it. You wanted love; you have it. Gabriel wanted Manus Dei's power handed over to him; he will get it eventually. Wes wanted you. Evander wanted Klara. So on and so on." She waves her hand as if annoyed.

"You didn't answer my question. What did *you* want? How do you see it all working out in the end?" My vision starts to blur slightly, and I feel lightheaded. "Luna," I press.

"I wanted what you wanted as a child."

My forehead furrows, "What does that mean?"

"I wanted to take something evil and convince it to be good."

I shake my head, "I don't understand."

"Sure you do. I'm a clone of Astrid. I could have turned out just as beastly as her. Completely narcissistic and uncaring. A real psycho. But, you tried to make me feel. I did. You nurtured me differently than our father did. You changed how my evil mind was preset. And I changed yours. I forced you to feel deeper so you could teach me. I stopped the cycle of growing another Astrid. But I had to convince you I was evil to keep you safe; then I had to become a monster to save you all. You took something evil and made me think I could be good. You made the villain think she could put on a cape and save everyone. I wanted Manus Dei to be used for good. It's simple. Whether we survive or not, Gabriel and the rest of the Horseman will ensure the science will be regulated. The world is changing, and one day, upgrading oneself will be as easy as selecting a beverage. I just wanted to know that on that day, I did everything in my power to make sure safety nets were in place. A terrible past makes for a strict future. Hopefully, Gabriel can enforce that."

That's it.

The truth.

The real picture has been painted. It's so colorful, so saturated. Unbelievably selfless, twisted, wrong yet right. Passion, love, grief, fear, and so many emotions rolled into one shocking human. My twin.

All this time, I thought she couldn't feel it. She tricked me. Lied to me. She did feel, she started to feel so much. She was the villain and hero because choosing just one wouldn't have won the game. She had to be both, just as I had to become both. Sometimes, to have peace, you have to have war and games. She did just that. It all leads us to this point. Peace is on the horizon. It's time to end the games. I hope I helped her do that.

The room begins to tilt as if I were aboard a boat rocked by turbulent seas. A storm is imminent. In truth, it's already arrived right at my doorstep, inside my body. "I need to lie down," I whisper. My back presses against the frigid concrete floor, and I close my eyes to halt the spinning. The cold floor feels good. It helps numb some heat, but I know it won't keep it at bay for long.

"Sol," Luna speaks, but her voice sounds distant.

"I hope one day I can paint the picture you described, Luna." My voice is so faint I'm not sure if she heard me. Darkness takes over my mind. I'm not scared of it. My Horseman taught me how to navigate the dark. I hope somewhere in the shades of gray, I'll find him.

Chapter 29

Wes

"Have you heard anything more from Sol?" Gabriel probes, practically leaning on the rickety edge of his collapsible stool. I'm half expecting it to give way at any moment.

"No," I reply. My naughty little mouse requested that I gather all of Gabriel's nanobyte research a few months ago. She wanted me to keep it a secret.

I didn't.

Two genius minds are better than one. So, while my older brother, Wade, and I fend off the hounds foolish enough to attempt breaching the bunker, Gabriel is busy cobbling together a makeshift lab to create a downgrade. If he achieves it before Sol, we will use it as leverage and coerce Evander into opening that damn door.

It's a race—both my brother and my beloved are running. Gabriel's trailing behind. We know Sol is striving to use his nanobytes to craft a cure; that's the only lead we have. Along with everything Gabriel can mentally recall—all the concrete data is still encrypted on our end. Evander and Sol possess all they need to create a downgrade.

I'm certain Sol will succeed. She has to because I can't live like this much longer. I need her; words can't describe how badly I need her.

The pressing question is, if Sol succeeds first, what will Evander do once she accomplishes it? I find it difficult to believe the bastard will open the door and welcome us with open arms.

How will Evander persuade Gabriel to work with him after this betrayal?

It shouldn't be my concern; when this is done, I will take Sol away and introduce her to a new family.

But it is my problem. I'm caught in the middle between Gabriel and my father. I must return to the family business while maintaining an alliance with Gabriel and Evander.

We're all tethered together. There's no escape. But someday, the chain will be long enough to afford space for me and my little mouse.

"How's it going on your end?" I ask before taking another spoonful of the MRE. I don't care if it tastes like bland rice. It's fuel, and that's all I need.

"I mean..." he shrugs. "Anything is possible." He glances over my shoulder, withholding something from me.

"Gabriel," I push. "Don't test me."

"I've found a few paths to take. Targeting the upgrades one by one. Trying it as a complete reset is too risky. It's too much change for the body to handle all at once."

I spread my hands, "So, what the hell does that mean? Did you figure out how to make the downgrade or not?"

He runs his hand through his hair. "I don't know."

I lean closer, "Yes, you do. What aren't you telling me?"

He slams his fist down, causing the table to rattle. "I have no way of testing it. I have no clones to use as subjects."

"You have Luna," I hiss. My eyes fix on the ground just below us, right where the bunker lies.

He shakes his head, "I can't do that."

"Why the hell not!"

"Because it could kill her." He stands, and his stool collapses, folding in half. "You have no idea how many clones I watched die or, worse, become fucked up after a failed upgrade. I can't do that to her."

Well, it's evident. He still loves her enough not to kill or harm her. That's got to be a good sign for their relationship, right?

"So, what do we do?"

He turns his back on me and strides toward the tent door. "I don't know. If you tell Kane we have something, and Evander opens that door, he'll give it to Luna. He will risk her for Klara."

"Or it could work."

His fists clench like granite rocks. "I can't risk that."

"There are no rewards without risk," Wade, my brother, adds as he enters the tent. Gabriel tenses. They still don't care for each other, but I know Wade is starting to see a different side to Gabriel. He has no choice because I'm not going to allow my family to fracture more than it already has.

Wade strides to the table and leans against it like a king claiming his throne, crossing his legs and arms in a single, seamless motion. "You need a clone to test it on?" he asks, a sly grin playing on his lips. What is he up to?

"I'd need more than one."

"What if I could get you one," Wade's grin expands like a crescent moon, illuminating his features with amused delight.

Gabriel and I both lock eyes with him. Wade raises his chin. "There is one more clone out there. It's in the files. One clone Luna released when she set Subject 52 free."

End My Games

Fuck! Wade is right.

Astrid's surviving clones consisted of Luna, Sol, Klara, and Subject 79, also known as Estelle. Unlike Sol and Luna, Estelle lived a somewhat strange yet relatively normal life. For some peculiar reason, Dorian ceased testing and enhancing her. At the age of seven, he placed her with a host family. Then, two months before Gabriel won the game, Dorian abruptly forced her back into the Manus Dei circle. He took her from her family and confined her in the laboratory. This continued until Luna encountered her and subsequently liberated her, along with other subjects—individuals who were either soldiers or unfortunate individuals turned into experimental subjects.

Gabriel and I attempted to locate her, but she completely vanished, never returning or contacting her family. Initially, it didn't concern us; we had more pressing matters. We let her fade into obscurity—a mercy on our part.

Wade's correct, though. If we could find her now, we could test Gabriel's downgrade on her.

Sol would be furious with me over that idea.

I understand why Gabriel did it, why he risked so many other clones that resembled Luna. They weren't her; their hearts and minds weren't the same as the woman he loved. Thus, they became disposable. It's not right, but it's an added layer of protection we will risk to save the clones we love.

"Subject 79 is untraceable. I tried looking for her," Gabriel snaps. What he's leaving out is he tried finding her to make sure she was safe from Subject 52. There is good in Gabriel, even if it's hard to find. He doesn't want to dispose of clones; sometimes, it's just not an option.

"For all we know, Subject 52 already killed her and hid the body."

Wade laughs, "That's a lie. Subject 52 would have sent her cut-up body to you and Astrid. You're trying to protect her when you should be trying to get your hands back on the data we need."

Gabriel's eyes narrow into slits, so keen and razor-sharp, they could slice through the thinnest of veils like a surgeon's scalpel. Sometimes, watching Gabriel and Wade argue and fight is my only entertainment out in this cold, barren land. However, now isn't the time.

Wade strides toward him, and I stand, sensing a confrontation. "Leave it to the big boys." He smacks Gabriel's back and exits the tent.

Chapter 30

Wes

Gabriel seethes, his fury barely concealed behind gritted teeth and tensed muscles. His eyes glint with suppressed anger, every breath a struggle against an imminent outburst.

I'm feeling the same way; the mounting stress and excitement feel like the bars of our cage are closing in. Sooner or later, either the cage will give, or we will.

Does my little mouse know the effect she's having on me? How my fixation is evolving into a consuming darkness in my mind.

"I don't want him going after the last clone," Gabriel admits.

I don't either, at least not without me, which isn't possible now. There is no telling what Wade will do if he encounters a clone alone. He's gone from hating clones to being somewhat tolerant; however, if this clone gives him a hard time, well, shit, I'm not sure what he would do.

"Let it be. Arguing will only push him further. He'll reach the same dead end we did," I respond, stepping into his pacing path. "You need to inform Kane and Evander about the possible downgrade."

As I grab his shoulders, my phone buzzes in my pocket. "Gabriel," I implore. His desaturated blue eyes meet mine. They seem lifeless; it's a miracle he's standing after everything Luna did —faking her death, taunting him with a letter. Luna has redefined derangement.

"Give me another week. I want to review it all again, double-check," he answers, relenting. We have no other options.

"Okay, one more week." Seven days until I may see Sol. Seven days.

As he leaves the tent and the flap rustles in the wind, I check my phone, finding a text message from Kane. He usually avoids reaching out to me because the fucker knows I'll beat his ass once I get my hands on him.

The text reads:

Kane: Would you mind making the trek down to the bunker's entrance? Oh, and make sure to come alone — I only have an entrance ticket for one brother, not two. And if you have a suit packed with you, I would greatly appreciate it if you could lend it to me. Cotton and polyester are starting to make my skin dry and itchy.

What the fuck? What. The. Fuck!
I try to call him, but the call fails.

Wes: You underestimate my patience.

Kane: Haha, I know. But isn't it a brother's job to teach his brother something new? Patience is a virtue.

Wes: Call me.

Kane: I can't. But I can tell you this—Wade doesn't need to find the other clone.

My grip tightens around the phone. "How does he know that?" I glance around, feeling the phone heat up in my hands. "The phone."

Kane: Bingo.

He's been listening to everything.

Kane: It's time, brother.

Does this mean Sol succeeded? I dash from the tent, and my phone pings again.

Kane: Wait! I need you to come alone.

I freeze, the once-empty landscape is now occupied by tents and soldiers. I glance at a security camera to my left. Our cameras and phones have top-level encryption, but evidently, Evander found a way in. So much for jamming his signal.

Kane: Only you can come inside.

Wes: Did she do it?

I need to read the words. The cold air does nothing to calm my nerves. My hands begin to sweat as I clutch the phone.

Kane: She did something.

I'm ready to throttle him. I type back.

Wes: I won't leave Gabriel behind.

Kane: I'm not suggesting that, but I don't want him to come inside yet. Luna isn't fixed yet.

Did Sol fail? What does he mean Luna isn't fixed?

Wes: Is Sol okay?

You promised me, vowed to keep her heart beating.

Kane: Yes.

That's the problem with texting. I need to hear his voice to know if he is lying.

Wes: I'm done with the games, Kane! Meet us at the door. Leaving Gabriel behind would be his downfall. You know it. If one more person lies or abandons him, it will crush him. We'll be at the door in ten minutes.

Kane: No! Wade can't know. Wait until his helicopter leaves. Order your soldiers to defend the camp. I'll open the door at thirteen hundred. But Wes, I need you to know that what Luna has become isn't going to help Gabriel. It might just be his undoing.

Chapter 31

Wes

"I need you to promise me something," I tell Gabriel as we stand outside the bunker door. He hasn't said anything since I told him about my conversation with Kane. He's gone robotic, his face emotionless, eyes vacant. I need to know when he enters, he won't snap, wrap his hands around Luna, and end it all.

He doesn't reply. His eyes are laser-focused on the door. "Promise me you will think; think ten steps ahead before you react," I tell him.

Nothing. Okay, so I tried.

The door begins to make a groaning sound as it slowly unlocks. It feels like time has turned to sludge as it slowly drips down a clogged drain. Finally, the door opens. The first thing I want to do is sucker punch Kane's pretty face. I don't; I can tell from his expression he's worried. Sympathetic even. He's wearing plain clothes, sweatpants, and a T-shirt, which makes me feel better. He likes his suits, and I'm happy he hasn't had access to what he enjoys.

I grab him by the collar and slam him into the cement wall. "Is she okay?" My mind races. Tell me Sol is fine. Tell me she failed, and Evander agreed to let us inside because he wants Gabriel and Sol to work together.

"She is," he swallows. "I need to catch you up on everything. It's a bit of a walk, so let's get going." He tries to smile. That grin worked in the past, but not now.

End My Games

His eyes look to Gabriel. He's looking off into the distance of the tunnel. Is that fear in his eyes? Yeah, he's genuinely worried about seeing Luna again.

I clutch his shirt tighter before I shove him away. He brushes out the wrinkles of his cotton shirt, "Well, the good news is Sol did it. She made the downgrade." He adds, trying to turn the dread in the air into something sweet. It doesn't work.

I push past him and practically jog through the tunnel. When I only hear one other footstep following behind me, I glance over my shoulder to see Gabriel still standing at the entrance. "Gabriel," I shout. He doesn't move. Kane looks at me; then I walk to Gabriel. "Come on. Together. We will fix this, fix our family together."

***

Kane tells us about Sol's attempts to make a downgrade, all about Evander's AI and how it was a tool used to ensure the downgrade truly worked. The mention of the AI was the only time Gabriel's eyes looked less fearful. The AI was the tool he needed to be successful, the tool we all needed so a clone would not have to be a lab rat. That is why Kane said Wade didn't need to find the other clone. Evander had thought that far ahead.

My blood turned to nitrogen, burning through every vein in my body when he told me what Sol did. She betrayed me. Again. She upgraded herself, said 'screw you' to the AI, and then injected herself with the downgrade. She risked her life. Kane allowed her to risk her life; he didn't watch her as closely as he should have.

Now I'm looking down at the woman I love lying in a makeshift hospital bed hooked up to wires and a computer system that Evander also created. I've been waiting months to see her; it feels like an eternity. The longing to embrace her, to hold her so tightly that her breath would be barely able to escape, has been a continuous ache within me.

I can't do that. I can't hug her. It's a new form of torture.

Her skin is clammy, and sweat covers her pale complexion. She's had a fever for the past week, but Evander assures me it's under control.

I study her face, her neck, arms, hands, even her fingernails. She looks okay, but she isn't. There is a battle raging inside of her. A war I am useless against. A genetic war only her body can win. She has to win.

Gabriel has gone catatonic as he begins to read over all of Sol's notes. He's trying to understand what she has created. Kane keeps chatting on and on, telling me that the AI has assured us the downgrade will be successful, but no one knows for sure. That's why she did it. I know it is. Gabriel didn't want to risk Luna; that's why he wanted a clone to test his downgrade on. Sol didn't want to risk Luna, so she risked herself.

Did she hesitate for a second to consider me? Did she?

I bend down and press my lips to hers. I wish this were a fairy tale, that her eyes would flicker open and her lips would kiss me back.

It feels like a knife is being repeatedly plunged into my 3D-printed heart when she doesn't reciprocate. "Wake up, little mouse," I tell her as I move my lips to her ear, "I'm here, so open those beautiful blue eyes and look at me." Nothing. I continue,

"You have no idea how angry I am. Is that why you're sleeping? You're scared. You should be. You risked my heart. My. Heart. You are my heart, Sol. I told you this, but you still risked it again," I hiss. Then I pull away and grab her hand.

"She will make it. She is strong. Look how far she has come." Evander adds as if I need a pep talk. What I need is Sol awake!

I haven't looked at him yet. I'm worried if I do, my glare might strike him dead; that would be too painless of a death. I glance at Gabriel, who continues to pour over the data. It's a massive file. It will take him days, if not weeks, to catch up on what Sol created.

Kane comes closer to me, "She's going to be fine." He points to the heart monitor, "See, I kept her heart beating." He tries to joke.

"Step the fuck away from me. Do it before I kill you," I growl.

"Gabriel," Evander speaks, hearing him in-person fucks with my head. It's been so many months without hearing his deep voice. I look up. We're all together again, yet the fractures in our relationship have never felt so bottomless. "Why don't you go to Sol's lab? All her research is there. Cody will take you."

Gabriel stills, then he stands. He doesn't speak; he just looks at Cody and begins to walk away. He's says nothing. Not one word. Just listens and silently fumes.

"Go with him," I order Kane.

"You can trust Cody and Zander." He replies, reading my mind.

"Go," I snap, and he listens. I don't know Cody or Zander personally. All I have is a file on them. All I know is they are members of Manus Dei. I don't trust them to watch Gabriel's back. I do trust Kane, which is amazing after everything he has done.

Evander dares to step closer, "I know." He begins.

I squeeze Sol's hand, my fury slipping out. I don't want to hurt her, so I gently place her hand back on the bed. "You know nothing."

"This was the only way to fix everything."

My back expands with my inhale, "No. This was the selfish way. The way you thought would save Klara."

"No," He challenges me. "You only have pieces to the puzzle."

I turn and face him. I see the stress on his face; new expression lines have formed in the corner of his eyes. His hair, which was always long, is even longer. His beard is long and thick. He's been surviving, not living. That makes me feel better. "Let me explain," he offers.

Chapter 32

Wes

I'm not going to agree with what Luna did. I never will. But maybe, just maybe, I can understand it.

Actually, I can't. What Luna did was a whole new level of fucked up, but in my dark and twisted mind, I can see her motivation. She was pushed to the edge, and her only escape was to do something unimaginable. Something no one truly expected. That's the only way to escape.

Evander has told me every dirty detail, from the modification Astrid forced Luna to create, a modification that would slowly destroy her. It was a trick, something that would make Astrid think she was complying with her demand, only to slowly erode her mind, making her useless to Astrid should she fail.

Luna made us think she betrayed Gabriel because he also wanted the crown. It was the perfect lie to conceal the truth. Sure, she wants the power, but she would give it all up to save those those she loves like Sol, Cody and Zander. Gabriel never would have agreed. He'd just promise her kids a different way. It would have been the second time children were ripped away from Luna.

"You know Gabriel would have killed them," Evander stresses. He's referring to Cody and Zander. He's right. I still can't wrap my mind around the fact that they are, in some messed-up way, genetically Gabriel and Luna's kids. I mean, they aren't, but they are.

"Are you going to tell Gabriel?" Evander asks me. He's smart; he's kept a good ten feet of distance between us.

"Someone has to," I counter as I grab my neck. "I'm worried if you start to talk, he's going to skin you alive and kill you before you get one sentence out. I would gladly watch, too." I spit. "There's no way that I'm going to lie to him. All these lies got us in trouble in the first place." My eyes narrow as I glare at him. Gabriel won't listen to him. He'll only listen to me. This is now my burden to bear and confess to him. Fantastic.

Maybe working for my father and brother won't be so bad. We're mentally twisted but not this depraved.

"Well lucky for him I have upgraded healing so the torture session will be long and drawn out." Evander flashes me a lopsided grin. "Maybe when I take my last breath he will forgive me."

I shake my head, "It's not about forgiveness, brother." No one, insane or sane, could forgive Luna or Evander for what they have done. His eyebrows knit together. "It's about acceptance. He must accept what you did and try to move on." My voice deepened, "And Gabriel needs to move on. I made a deal with my father. I can't remain in person. My support will be distant. Gabriel needs to be able to function and keep all of Manus Dei's power contained. If my father scents a drop of uncertainty, he will come for you, and I won't be able to stop him."

"I'm not going to beg for forgiveness or continue to explain things. You're right; what's done is done." His golden eyes clash with mine. "I didn't mean to push you back to your family."

"It doesn't matter now."

"Yes, it does. I am sorry for that. You are always going to be my brother."

"I know. Unfortunately." I sigh.

The room grows silent. "I miss you," Evander adds.

I glance up at the Horseman I also consider my brother. His heart is as big and as wide as his stature. That's his problem. Sometimes, people try too hard. "I missed you too, but there had to be another way."

He rolls his shoulders as if trying to release some of the weight he has been bearing. "If I told you and Gabriel, Luna would have figured it out. She would have shut me out. I needed to be on the inside. I needed to know every path she was planning on turning down, every bridge she would burn, and every person on her kill list. I needed to get inside her head. I needed her not just to trust me but also to allow me to try to fix everything. This was the only way."

"That's why you kept talking with Kane, allowing him to fill us in. It cleared your conscience."

"It kept us whole. We are still whole, Wes. We have cracks, but we will repair them."

He can't be that daft! "You can glue an item back together, but it has faults now. Weakness. It will never be the same." I counter.

He shrugs, "Then I won't glue it back together. I'll grind it down further and make something new entirely."

If I didn't need him awake and talking, I'd beat the shit out of him. I can see it now; I'd swing, he'd duck, and when he bent down, I'd use it as an opportunity to get the tall fucker. I'd grab him by that man bun, tilt his head back, and slam my fist into his nose.

What the fuck is he thinking, that we will all be a happy family again? And seriously...his hair is tied up in a bun. He has gone insane.

Maybe I should just let him keep talking, live a hopeless dream. There is no way Klara is going to make a recovery, mentally, that is, and love this fucker. Klara will slice his throat open the minute she can.

"Evander, you lied. You told Gabriel Luna was dead. He looked at you when you walked out of that morgue. You nodded. You made him think it was Luna. You falsified the report so he would think it was genetically her. You created a deep fake video that made us believe Luna jumped off that Cliff Walk. Gabriel watched that video on repeat. He watched her jump over and over again. What the fuck!" My anger grips me. Fuck it! I lunge and throw my fist at him. The fucker is so big it's like punching the General Sherman tree in the National Park. My hits are demanding, but he just sways in the wind, rooted deep. He's allowing me to use him as a punching bag to get my fury out.

With one last hit I aim higher and land a fist right into his jaw. "I deserve it, but when this all works out, you'll understand." He replies as he wipes some blood off his lip.

I shake my head, "You dug yourself into a grave, brother. I'm not going to help you claw your way back out. It's up to you."

***

"Explain to me what is going on." I demand. It's been twenty-four hours since we got inside the bunker. Gabriel hasn't slept, neither have I. He's been studying all the notes Sol left for him. Thousand of pages of data that explain the downgrade she made.

All this science bullshit looks like she was trying to figure out how to time travel. I wish that were the case.

Sol left thousand of pages of notes for another man.

Where is my goddamn note?

It's ok, calm down; you're going to have a lifetime with her when this is finished, a lifetime to make her realize her mistakes. A lifetime to make her skin blush red, her eyes widen, and her lips part. A fucking lifetime of hearing her call me by the pet name Wesley.

Gabriel wheels a chair closer to Sol's bed and finishes connecting one more wire from her to the computer. The good thing about nanobytes is that they give live updates and reports. Basically, we can see everything that is happening inside of her. I keep repeating this to calm myself, but my calm won't settle until her eyes open and she can speak to me.

"She reprogrammed my nanobytes to have dual functions essentially. One section of the code gradually restores her genetic code to override and rewrite her modified genes. It was part of my research. The Nanobytes are designed to toggle upgrades on and off, specifically for military use. The goal was to create enhanced soldiers with a controlled switch. With a few code tweaks, the nanobytes could revert a subject's genetic code when they were off-duty." He finally looks up from the laptop he's been working on. I don't like that he can understand the nanobytes, program them, and see what's happening inside Sol. I want to be the only one who can see inside of her body.

The stress that had been pushing him flat into the ground has lifted. He's standing tall again. His eyes regain their blue hue, and his face carries a faint glow of hope. He hasn't appeared this way for months. "She also programmed the nanobytes to override her immune system."

"I don't like the sound of that." I glance down at her. I'm a soldier, not a scientist. All this science talk is making me want to shoot something.

"It's not as dire as it sounds," Gabriel snorts a chuckle. How on earth could he laugh right now? "Imagine your immune system as a line of defense. When it detects a threat, it attacks. The nanobytes, when releasing the downgrade, might provoke a defense response. By overriding her immune system's natural function, she disabled a layer of her body's defense."

"Are you serious? How is that not a bad thing?" I grit my teeth. My voice echoes in the small, dimly lit makeshift hospital room. The space lacks all amenities except the medical equipment needed. There's a distinct absence of color, the walls painted in drab, lifeless shades of grey. Sol would hate this room. My little mouse loves color. I promised Luna I would make sure Sol had color to paint with.

I failed.

This bunker is the epitome of a cage. Perhaps it was a necessity, though. Maybe being confined here has helped Sol understand that my 'cage' isn't as restricting as this. Mine is security, not a prison.

Gabriel clears his throat, "Because the nanobytes are specifically programmed to trigger. They've taken control, recognizing their own 'virus', so to speak. The downgrade functions like a virus, but with the nanobytes acting as her immune response, her body won't attack its own virus. Thus, she allowed her body to accept the downgrades gradually without setting off an immune response. Once her genes return to their original state, she programmed the nanobytes to deactivate."

I nod as if it all makes sense. Some of it does, but the only thing that matters is that she wakes up and is healthy.

"So if you're so confident this is all going to work," I state, widening my legs as I prepare for his reply, "When are you going to give it to Luna?" That's the billion dollar question. His response will stop all the lies and false hope. If he thinks this won't kill her, then he should be confident about giving it to Luna.

His smile and confidence vanish. He swiftly turns his eyes away and goes back to working the computer.

"Do you trust what she created or not?" I growl. I edge closer, toe to toe, with my brother. He stands so we're eye eyes. Good, he's willing to fight.

"I trust it, and Evander's AI has a positive response to it. Sol created numerous upgrades that failed his AI. This one passed."

"So you'll give it to Luna?" I press again. "Answer me."

"It's not that simple," He exhales. The blue in his eyes deepens like a thundercloud; that's okay; I can strike back if he wants to rain down his frustration, fear, and doubts on me.

"It is. Either you think this downgrade won't fuck Sol up, and you're willing to give it to Luna or not. Or," I shove his shoulder, "do you not want to save Luna?"

He shoves me, it forces my feet to edge back. Good. I want this, his anger. I want to get inside his head. If this works, will he give it to Luna, or is this the end all? Will Gabriel allow Luna to rot away slowly into the depths of her mind?

I know if that happens, I will lose him too.

"No," a small, weak voice replies.

My heart stops as I look down at Sol's bed. Her eyes are still closed, but it was her voice. I rush to her side, as does Gabriel. Her head starts to move. She's attempting to shake her head.

"Sol," I lean in closer, wanting to shove him away. I want to push everyone away, I want to take Sol away from here.

"No," she whispers again. Her voice sounds like crystal—hard yet so fragile. "No," she repeats.

Is she having a nightmare?

"He won't give it to her," she utters, her lips barely moving. "I have to be the one to give it to Luna."

"Sol!" She can hear me. "Open your eyes," I press as I gently grab her shoulders.

It takes her two minutes, which I painfully count, to open her eyes. One hundred and twenty of the longest seconds of my life.

Blue eyes look up at me. Eyes that I have dreamed about, eyes that have haunted me, plagued me. They ripped at my soul, tearing it to pieces. And now, those same eyes are trying to sew my soul back together again.

"I have to be the one," she says.

Chapter 33

Gabriel

I know Wes wants to smother me. That's why I sleep with the door my room locked. I want to be caged. Alone. I deserve it. Being caged here keeps me safe, but it also keeps Luna safe.

Her absence has been a void, an echoing chasm where the silence speaks volumes. If I go to see her, then the silence stops. Questions and answers will begin to flood my mind. It's a whole new level of torture.

How do I face the woman who made me think she died, who forced her twin to lie to support this belief?

I thought Sol was in mourning over Luna. I believed it. Swallowed down the poison. It killed me.

How do I face the woman who returned and taunted me with a note? A letter filled with passionate hate she has twisted into love.

I know I'll have to face her but until then I've been delaying it as long as possible. It's easy to keep my mind occupied. I've been combing over all of Sol's research. She tried a few different approaches before she landed on the golden ticket.

Sol succeeded where I failed. Maybe that's because she had Evander's AI or maybe we all just underestimated her all along.

I swallow, it feels like dry mud trying to get pushed down my throat as I glance at the screen. I ran my downgrade through Evander's AI. With this new technology, the world is going to change. Advancements will be pushed through at lightning speed. I need this tech in my hands. Evander knows this. He knows this is going to be what glues me back to him. It's forcing my hand and making me accept his terms so we can control the science together. Rebuild Manus Dei.

The screen has a small red bar with white writing inside. Subject failed.

My downgrade would have failed. It might have killed Luna or just made her more messed up.

I failed to do the one thing I vowed to do. Protect Luna. Again.

"Hello," a voice says. The person has been looming in the doorway for the past two minutes, just watching me. I don't regard them; instead, I program the AI to run the test again. It's stupid, but I just need to make sure.

"Look at me," the voice insists.

My jaw ticks. Luna isn't the only person I've been ignoring, but unlike her, this person has the ability to roam free. "I'm busy," I snap as I grab another laptop and read more of what Sol did.

"I said, fucking look at me!" The voice roars.

Okay, you want to go toe to toe with me? Challenge accepted. I look up to see Zander. He's angry, legs wide, fists balled, his cheeks faintly flushed, making his golden blonde hair look more saturated. I can tell by the look of determination on his face that he thinks he could fight me; it's laughable.

Yes, he's been trained. Yes, he's been upgraded, but no, he hasn't had the animalistic upbringing I had to endure. He hasn't had to withstand trial after trial or watch other clones that look like an exact copy of him die, nor has he been the one who had to kill them.

He's a boy who believes he's a man because he killed one person.

One kill threatened to break him, which got him into the situation he's in today. He's on the brink of discovering the hard truth. He's got a long road ahead before he can truly claim that title and win a battle against me.

"You know who I am," he states, stepping closer inside the lab I've been working in. He's brave.

I know who he is.

The cause of Luna's lies.

It's his fault she did this.

"You already know the answer to that," I sit taller and rest my elbows on the table. I'm worried if I stand, I'll charge at him.

It's his fault.

"I heard you outside my door when Wes told me all about you and your brother," I hiss. Wes told me two nights ago who Zander and Cody were.

Luna was right. I would have risked them without an ounce of precaution. If it meant saving her life, I would eradicate anyone.

Anyone.

I haven't spoken to them. I haven't spoken to anyone since Wes told me. Thankfully, Wes and Evander are constantly with Sol, monitoring her. She hasn't woken again since she opened her eyes and told Wes it had to be her to give Luna the downgrade. She made that very clear in her notes to me.

I wasn't sure if I was going to heed her request.

I'm not sure about a lot of things.

I am sure that I hate the boy in front of me. It's out of jealousy. Yes, I'm incensed that Luna would risk her life and our love for this stranger. Knowing the reason behind all of this, the real reason did help. It didn't help me heal. Fuck healing! It helped me aim all my fury onto one set of twins. Cody and Zander. They are the reason behind all the lies Luna spread.

"Aren't you going to say anything?" Zander snaps.

Trust me, you don't want me to speak. Don't push me!

I cross my arms and dig my fingers into my torso, rubbing my fingers between the grooves of my ribs. I'd like to dig my fingers into his neck. "Welcome to the family," I quip. Then I glance around the bunker, "Sorry I didn't bring you a tray of cookies."

Good, that wasn't the answer he wanted. I want to see his wrath. All this time, he's gotten to live next to the ghost. A ghost I wanted to bring back so badly. He was with her for months well I was grieving.

"What do you want me to say?" I mock. I can't hold back any longer. "I'm happy to meet you, *son*?" I question as I raise a brow. "The woman I loved gave her life for you. A stranger. Does that make you happy, to know you stole her from me?"

"What if I say it does?" He jests with a grin. That smile makes my blood run reptilian cold.

It's my grin. Mine!

He's taunting me with words because he can't win with his fist. I used to do that with my father, Hans, until dear old dad realized that the wisest choice wasn't to meddle with me.

Not that Hans was my real father, anyway. He was a donor, a scientist who drew the lucky stick and got to compete with Dorian.

Dorian was always the brains behind everything; Hans was just the cheerleader egging him on.

When he grins wider I lose it. I stand hastily, the stool flips back, and that's when all I see is red, a bright stoplight red that I barrel through. I don't know how it happens, but Zander is on the ground, and I'm on top of him, my hands wrapped around his throat. Someone is beating my back; I'm guessing it's Cody, the other boy who caused this.

Zander's pale skin is now cherry red. His hazel eyes bulge and grow wide. The red hue grows darker than that of a cranberry. Cody begins to rain his fists down on my temple, but I don't lose my grip. I see Luna for a moment, my hands around her neck. "Why! Why!" I shout.

"Stop it. You're killing him!" Cody screams. "I'm going to shoot you. Let go."

Your mistake is not shooting me, boy!

"Do it," Zander manages to hiss, his hazel eyes clashing and pleading with mine, not his brother's. It's his last breath before his eyes start to roll back. His face is no longer red but now blue.

My fingers uncoil, I push back, then fall on my ass as Cody shoves me off his brother.

"Zander! Zander!" He shakes his shoulders, and when Zander gasps for breath, I collapse on the floor.

What the hell did I just do?!

Evander, Kane, and Wes all enter the room now. They take in the scene with a mix of emotions. Evander swoops down like a guardian angel; he picks Zander up and carries him out of the room. Cody follows. Wes slowly approaches me, but I turn my back to him. I push on my hands and knees as I try to inhale and exhale.

What did I just do?

I'm broken now. Finally, I have crumpled.

That's when I cry, releasing it all. I cry my pain away until it turns to anger. Anger morphs into grief, grief into regret.

I feel Wes and Kane by my side as they hold me. I cry like the broken child I am, like the broken child Zander is. I cry for the both of us.

Chapter 34

Gabriel

"Get the fuck away," Cody growls at me. He's been standing guard at his brother's door. I like his loyalty it resonates with me. That doesn't mean I like him, though.

"I've calmed down," I state.

Cody grabs his gun in warning. I eye the gun and nod. "You must have got that gene from me. I'm protective of those I love, too," I say. I can see the shock of my words register on his face.

He shouldn't be so trusting, so naïve.

"I'm sorry," I admit. I step closer, "Now let me talk to him."

He doesn't raise his gun. He doesn't step aside, either. With each step I take closer to him, his lungs expand with more air, but his finger doesn't touch the trigger. I step forward and pause when we are shoulder to shoulder. "I can help you fix Zander," I offer.

I expect a thank you; after all, he's the one who messed up his brother's mind. Trying to manipulate memories is like stepping through a spider's web; one wrong move, and you're stuck; one wrong pull, and you can break the whole web.

"I don't need your help," he sneers, his voice dripping with disdain. "I've already fixed him." He grins.

I'll be damned. It's Luna's smile. It doesn't look natural; it's like a mask that's been practiced in front of a mirror, devoid of genuine emotion but full of sinister content.

"When?" The word escapes my lips before I can stop it, shock coursing through me. I'm stunned that he'd dare to tamper with his brother's mind again.

His left eye narrows a hair more than his right. "None of your business." He steps back, allowing me entrance into the room.

"That's where you're wrong, Cody. It is my business. Evander granted me access to this bunker because everything is now my concern. If you want some advice, don't provoke me. I don't buckle under pressure like your brother does when it comes to making tough decisions." I take a step inside the door but glance over my shoulder and add, "I'm surprised you'd risk his mind again. Do me a favor and stick to what you know."

"I had help this time," he retorts.

I decide to bite and play. The best way to know how your opponent thinks is to upset him. It's in the most desperate times that we act our true character. "Sol?" I question. That upsets me. He should have let Sol focus on fixing Luna, not his brother.

"No. Luna." He admits as he flashes me a 'screw you' smile.

So you like to stab me in my heart. Good. I hate cowards who stab you in the back.

I square my shoulders to him, "I thought Luna couldn't remember the science?" Astrid's downgrade was erasing it from her mind. That's what I had been told.

"She couldn't, but when she was in control of her mind, she was reteaching herself the science that was stolen from her. We've been trapped in here for a few months, and with her cognitive abilities, that was more than enough time to help me."

I feel the demon inside of me growing enraged again. My skin prickles and feels itchy, and my mind gets fuzzy as dark thoughts stir. "And she helped you again. She didn't try to save herself," I hiss. That's why he's so gleeful. He wants me to hurt because I hurt his brother.

I shove past him, no longer wanting to apologize to Zander. Instead, I want to go down to Luna and...no, don't think it.

There is a reason why I have kept my distance from her. I'm not sure how I will react.

Zander's body tenses when I enter. It's only when he sees Cody that he relaxes.

"Why didn't you fight back?" I ask him, keeping a five-foot distance from his bed. His neck is bruised, black and blue. I can easily make out the print of my hands wrapped around it. "Why didn't you try to stop me?"

He shrugs and looks down.

"Answer me." I take one step closer.

"I deserve it," he voices. His voice is strained and raspy. It will take another day before his modified genes can heal the damage I did.

"You think you deserve to die because Astrid sent a clone of herself to kill you? You think fighting for your life was a mistake."

He nods. I see the broken boy he is. All he ever wanted was a mother and father. Luna gave that to him, and when he tried to come to me, I was the reflection of Astrid. I tried to kill him. A part of me still wants to, but I will keep him alive because that's what Luna wanted.

It's called leverage. I have something Luna wants now.

"I think you did exactly as you were genetically programmed to do. You fought, you survived."

His hazel eyes finally look up to clash with mine. I'm happy he and Cody don't have our eyes. A little detail they changed. I want them to change. To not be exact copies of us.

It's true I never thought about children, and neither did Luna. Why would we bring children into our world when Manus Dei still ruled? We never had time to consider it.

When I look at this young man, I don't see myself or Luna; I don't see my genes. I don't want to because if I do, he becomes my responsibility.

That's where Luna made her first mistake. She should have viewed them as strangers. She should have put my love for her higher.

Suddenly, an alarm goes off. It's not a high-pitched screech; it's more calming, like an alarm clock slowly waking the intended person. It's coming from down the hall, but my heightened ears notice it. So do Cody and Zander. It's their reaction that puts me on guard. Zander's lips part as his eyes flare with a pained grief as if some ghost was stabbing him.

"Fuck!" Cody hisses.

Zander starts to move from the bed. "No, you're staying," Cody growls as he rushes towards his brother, trying to stop him.

"No, she needs me," Zander hisses. I can see his discomfort when he tries to speak. His hazel eyes water as he touches his throat.

Cody turns towards me, his face changing to that of a dangerous beast who snarls at me, "I'm not my brother. I will kill you," his eyes look me up and down, "Maybe I'll enjoy it."

I almost want to laugh at his attempt to intimidate me, but his following words make me stop, "If you hurt her. If you look at her the wrong way, it will be your last time," he warns me. Then he grabs Zander's hand, and they shove past me. I allow his hit to sway me. He can only be referring to one person: Luna. That pit in my stomach begins to rumble.

"Cody," Evander shouts from down the hall.

"I'm coming. I'll get the sedative."

I enter the hallway hot on their trails. Evander pauses for a second when he sees me. His eyes reveal a multitude of emotions. They resemble sponges, heavily saturated with feelings, to the extent that some of these emotions seep out and touch me.

Saturating me so I can't move.

They drip with an apology, despair, dread, and worst of all, a sense of familiarity with the situation.

He's been witnessing what I'm about to see for months now, bottling it all up like a steam engine and then utilizing those feelings as fuel to keep moving forward even in the toughest of times.

When I don't move, he simply nods at me and continues down the hall to the stairway that leads to the storage level where they've been keeping Luna and Klara caged.

What I want to do is run past them all to be the first to witness Luna in a cage, but I stay a good twenty paces behind them.

My heart is pounding with such intensity that I almost feel dizzy and faint.

I felt his way the night I had to go to the Cliff Walk and witness what I thought had truly happened. I remember the echoes of my footsteps reverberating as I traversed the metal pathway. I held the rail the entire time as it wrapped and curled around the mountainside. I can still smell the cold, crisp humidity from that night.

I hate foggy nights because they transport me back to that moment.

I remember seeing a figure clinging to the fence in the distance, and my initial thought was that I hoped it was a mistake. I wished that the person in front of me was Luna. I wanted it to be Sol who had jumped, that made more sense in my mind. Sol was always the weaker twin, or so we thought.

But we don't always get what we hope for.

I don't notice I've stopped walking until I feel a presence shoulder-to-shoulder with me. "I'm here," Kane whispers to me. Then, as if my little brother has suddenly become my parent, he gently touches my back, urging me to continue down the stairs.

The further we descend on the stairway, the louder the screams and shouts become, almost deafening. I focus on my beating heart to drown out the shouting. I pause on the steps and grab the hand railing. I've had enough time to read through the files to know exactly what's happening: different surges of chemicals within Luna's mind are causing erratic behavior.

When I first read about the side effects, I smiled. After everything Luna put me through, being caged and trapped and having no control of her mind, it sounded like a fitting punishment for someone like her. However, hearing the screams coming from her, the echoing of the faster pacing and running footsteps from Evander, Cody, and Zander, and my own heart pounding, the small ounces of love I still hold for Luna make me realize this isn't how I want to torture her.

I want her to know exactly what is happening. I want her to know that I am the one who is getting control of all of Manus Dei's knowledge because she royally fucked up when she betrayed me.

Chapter 35

Gabriel

The storage level is the smallest among all the floors in the bunker. There are half a dozen cages filled with boxes, storage equipment, and paintings; then there are two cages at the end of the hallway; a perfectly suited prison.

I spot Evander's hulking form first as he swings open the last cage door, and then I see the whipping streaks of blonde hair as Luna runs back and forth. Her hair looks like a flag waving violently in a strong gust of wind.

She tries to evade Evander and escape through the door, but he grabs her in a powerful hold, lifting her as if his arms were a straight jacket.

My initial instinct is to rush in and pull him off of her. After everything, I still feel a weed growing inside of my mind. A poisonous flower that makes me want to protect her.

Even still.

As much as I try to uproot that weed, its roots still linger.

For years, I attempted to teach her what my definition of affection and love meant. She did learn what love was; it was just her own twisted definition.

Her body thrashes as she screams. The noise pierces my ears and ricochets through my body, making me feel like bullets are pelting me. I stagger back at what unfolds.

Cody rushes in with the sedative in hand. Evander edges back against the wall, using his right leg to wrap around Luna's legs to stop her from kicking Cody as he approaches.

"Let me out! No, stop it!" Luna screams, "Don't listen, keep me inside. I want to hurt you all."

Then time stops, and each second feels like acid is being poured over my skin. Her sky-blue eyes lock with mine. Her fight dissolves, and her body goes limp. She swallows, then her chest heaves against Evander's iron arms.

Cody approaches her with the needle. I watch as she doesn't blink, not breaking contact with me as he jabs it into her skin.

"You came," she says, a tear slipping from her eye.

A tear.

I've never seen her cry. Never. Not even after all the reflections of her, I had to kill to keep her safe.

"I'm sorry," she voices. She's trying to shout, but the sedative is starting to work. Her body relaxes further, as do Evander's arms. "I love you," she declares. Every eye in the room is looking at me now.

I thought my heart had died. It felt like she ripped it out the night I looked down at her body over the cliff.

That was a lie.

I feel my heart beating, but at the admittance of her words, it feels like each letter is a knife, slowly carving deep into my chest, breaking my rib cage open, and grasping what is left of my heart.

Her words crush me.

Luna speaks in riddles. For years, I told her how much I loved her. It was my definition of love. She always replied by saying, 'I hate you.' In her twisted mind, that meant 'I love you.' I knew this, so it never bothered me.

So what does it mean now? Does it mean she hates me?

The way she is looking at me makes me think her riddles have stopped. She has never looked at me with such passion.

This could be another lie. A game. Or, she could truly be telling me she loves me and that she is sorry.

Not that it matters anymore.

My feet are moving, as if they've been possessed by an unseen force. I try to grab her from Evander's hold. He releases her slowly, judging and watching me. She crumples in my arms, and I kneel on the floor, holding the woman I once loved. I want to say so many things, but the sedative has almost taken effect. Her eyes are glassy as she cries.

"I left a playlist for you," She whispers. Then she says it again. "I love you."

My fingers curl into her flesh. Right before her eyes begin to close, I voice. "Good, because I hate you." Then I pull her to my chest and hold her tightly until sleep takes her.

Welcome to my reign, Luna. Don't worry, I'm going to fix you. Sol's downgrade is working, and soon, I will give it to you. I want you to comprehend everything I will do to you.

Chapter 36

Wes

It's another two weeks before she opens her eyes again. Fourteen bone-crushing days.

Gabriel has assured me that her downgrade is working. With constant monitoring and reports from the nanobytes, we can see when each upgrade has been removed. Slowly but surely, all the upgraded genes she received after birth are being stripped from her.

Genetically, she will be the girl I fell in love with again, but mentally, she will never be that artist who sat on the lawn with her twin and gazed at the sky. I once feared this outcome; I wanted to protect her naivety. I realize it doesn't matter how she changes as long as I'm there to hold her hand as she grows.

It seems like the downgrade she created is working flawlessly, and just as I start to feel all the tension leave my body, it happens at three in the morning on Wednesday.

I haven't left her Sol bedside, not even to eat, but Kane has been irritatingly attentive. He's been observant of my every need, bringing me food and fresh changes of clothes. He's even had to deal with Wade, who isn't happy that I locked myself inside and refused to open the door. I can't have Wade barging in here, acting on my father's orders, not until I'm certain Sol is safe.

Just like every other night, I lay in the bed beside her, holding her hand. I even rearranged her cheek to rest on my heart. The sick part of me paints a lie, just like my little mouse used to do. The only way I can sleep is by imagining that we're not here; we're in the home that I built, and she's resting on my shoulder after we just made love.

The harsh beeping of a monitor wakes me first; my eyes snap open, and my back jerks off the bed. I grip her hand tighter, so tight that her fingers start to turn white. My hold on her slips when I look at the monitors. Her chest is rising and falling. Good, she's breathing. She's still alive. But that's when I noticed how fast her chest rises and falls. Her breath is labored, and her deep exhales fill the room.

I jump out of bed and look up at the monitor that signals her heart rate; it's 170, then it hits 178, and then it hits 183 beats per minute. It's as if she is running a marathon; she's fighting the war inside her body, and something is going wrong. I can sense it deep in my gut; I want to carve open my chest so my soul can escape and slip inside her body so I can save her.

Evander and Gabriel come rushing to the room; they don't bother asking me what happened. They are constantly watching her monitors even when they're not in this room; they work in sync, talking to each other fast and frantically.

"What's going on?" I ask. "Tell me this is normal."

The fear in my stomach is hatching, cracking open like an egg. It's slithering out, making its way up my spine until it sinks its teeth into my mind.

"Tell me what's going on," I shout.

Kane enters the room now; behind him, Cody lingers in the hallway.

Gabriel's typing and scrolling at a hyper pace. He looks like one of those worker ants racing back and forth against the soil. "Shit," he says, then he opens up a new screen. Evander pulls up a chair and plugs in a laptop right next to his, and they both start writing code as if their lives depend on it.

Their lives do depend on it because if something happens to Sol, I'll burn down the whole world.

"Her immune system has kicked in and is trying to attack the nanobytes," Gabriel barks. He's typing so fast that it sounds like rapid fire from a machine gun.

"I thought you said she programmed her body not to attack the nanobytes."

"She did,"

"So what the hell, Gabriel!" I roar.

"Calm down and let him work," Evander snaps; his voice is deep, but his face is calm. Like the sun that shines consistently, his confidence remains radiant and steadfast, illuminating everything around him. I don't want it to touch me. I want the dim moonlight because that is the truth. We don't know if Sol will be alright.

The beeping intensifies. Her heart rate is now 200 beats per minute. I'm not a doctor, but I know she can't sustain this long.

"There," Gabriel gasps. "I got it." He keeps writing code and then slams down the enter key. His eyes glance at the syringe, which is hooked up to his computer. I know inside that needle are more nanobytes. I'm guessing that whatever he just coded is being transmitted to the nanobytes inside the needle.

The computer beeps, he stands with haste, grabs the needle, and injects it into her IV. He breathes a sigh of relief, and then he looks at me. "Sometimes the nanobytes malfunction," he holds his hands up, "it's not what you think. Every nanobyte I created has an emergency code inside of it. If any code is corrupted during its lifetime, it will automatically shut down. Some of the nanobytes inside of her just turned off, which gave her natural immune system a chance to turn back on and start fighting against the downgrade. I just injected her with new nanobytes with the same downgrade code. She just needs a few minutes for it to start working, and then we're back on track."

"Why did they malfunction?" I bite.

"It happens. They become corrupted. I have safety nets built in for this. She just needed an added boost to override her body. I'll tweak the next downgrade and add more nanobytes to prevent this from happening."

Evander adds, "I've got all her health stats reporting to a doctor as we speak, so if we need any other medical advice, I will get it. I'm not going to let anything happen to her."

I feel the vein on my neck pulse, "I'm so tired of all of your promises. I want facts. I want her body to return to what it once was. I want her to wake up and open her eyes so I can take her out of here."

They don't speak because they can't grant my request. Just then, the beeping on the monitor starts to go down, and her heart rate starts normalizing. It's back to 70 beats per second, then drops to the 60s and then to 50s; the monitor starts beeping again, then it sounds more like an alarm when it goes into the 40s.

"She's going to be fine," Evander says. His eyes don't leave his laptop screen.

Gabriel's eyes glance at me before they lock onto Sol. He approaches her bedside and leans closer, "Come on, don't fight it." He whispers, but I hear him.

Her heart drops to twenty-seven beats; the monitor is screaming, and her chest isn't even rising and falling.

"Evander!" I shout.

Kane comes to my side.

"She's going to be fine," Evander finally looks away from his laptop and at her.

Twenty-two beats. Gabriel and Evander are both up and moving frantically; they are hooking Sol up to more equipment.

"Kane," I mutter.

"I'm here," He grabs a hold of my hand.

"Make it stop." I hiss. He doesn't reply. Time has fully stopped, and each inhalation and exhalation I take feels like I am trapped under ice. It burns my throat, feels like acid has been chugged into my lungs, like I swallowed nails, and they are embedded in my gut.

Then her chest rises, and her heart rate picks up and stays at sixty beats for an entire minute. Gabriel's back on his computer, and Evander is on the phone; he must be talking to a doctor because he's giving what sounds like a medical report.

Kane squeezes my hand. My knees feel weak. I don't move even though I want to rush to her side. I know if I lift one single toe, I'll collapse.

"Can you get me my phone," I ask Kane. His eyes watch me, searching for answers, before he nods. When he returns with my phone, I tell him to watch over Sol. I stagger into the hallway and turn the corner. Sinking, I allow my lungs to inhale fully; then, I begin to dial the only other person I know who can help me overcome this anxiety.

The phone rings once before he picks up. No matter how far I push him away, he always picks up on the first ring. Always.

"Dad," I whisper.

"Son." The concern in his voice makes me feel like a small boy again. "What's wrong? Did something happen?"

I can only exhale. I pull my legs up and rest my forehead on my knees.

"Are you hurt?"

I shake my head, but then I remember I'm on the phone, and he can't see me. "No."

"What's wrong?"

"How…how do you do it? How can you let Mom step outside without you by her side? How can you allow her to leave the room without you?" I plead.

How the hell can a man so passionately obsessed with my mother allow her any freedom?

I need to know because I'm the same as him.

To say I'm attached to Sol would be an understatement. She is a part of me. She is my heart, a heart I can't replace with a 3D-printed one.

I hear my father swallow. In the background, my mother stirs. I know I woke him up. He's moving, probably leaving the room, so he doesn't worry Mom.

"Is she okay?" Dad asks me. I don't know if his question is genuine. I know he was never keen on the clones, but I also know that he understands how obsession works, and he knows that Sol is my obsession. He knows if something happens to her, he will lose me.

"Her heart was…I thought…I couldn't help her. I thought I was going to lose her. I want to take her far away from here. I want her to be safe. I want her."

"Listen to me, son, even on the darkest nights, stars are in the sky. Light and hope. The sun will rise, and when it does, you can come home."

But the stars feel so far away at times, as does Sol.

"But how do you do it? How do you travel and work without Mom glued to your side?" Because I want to chain Sol to me. I want to lock us both up and throw away the key. I want her to be safe and have nothing to do with Manus Dei, even if I have to be involved to make sure the world is safe enough for her to thrive in.

How do I keep her safe without letting my extracurriculars taint her? Only my father can answer that. All the dark deeds he oversees don't touch my mother. He's managed to keep them separated but, at the same time, not lie to my mom. I want this for Sol and me. I want to be honest, but the monster raging inside of me wants to trap her in my castle.

"You don't cage them, son."

"What do you mean?"

"Your mother is the rarest of creatures, and so is your Sol. If you cage a rare creature, it will die. Instead, you must teach them how to survive in your world." I can hear his smile, "From what I have learned, Sol is a very strong woman. She will survive our family just fine. I'll admit I wasn't happy when you told me who she was, but I want you to be happy. You bring her home, and I'll teach you how to make her flourish and rule by your side. I'll teach you how to turn your fear into fuel, how to use that fuel to stay ahead of our enemies."

Chapter 37

Kane

I like tense situations. I thrive on them. That's why my name was perfect when I became a Horseman; It was custom-fit to me, like one of my suits. Which, by the way, I can't wait to slip back into. I'm so tired of these plain cotton clothes that itch and scratch my skin. I don't understand why athleisure clothing or loungewear has ever become a trend in fashion. There's nothing like sleeping in a tailor-made suit that fits you like a custom-made glove.

Much like I use fashion to create a mask, Sol uses paint and makeup to trick the world. That's why we got along so well; we both like to trick others, observers always do. Standing on the sidelines gets boring. Now and then, you have to participate and play the game.

Oh, that little mouse, she can be so naughty at times. That's exactly what attracts my brothers to her. Conventional beauty and mindsets would never keep any of the Horsemen occupied. We needed something with a sprinkling of 'WTF,' the right amount of crazy. Or, as the French like to say, a 'je ne sais quoi.'

I've been trying to hold down the tent even in the hellacious winds and keep my family whole, along with Evander. But more than that, I'm trying to keep the promise and the debt owed to my brother. I would say that I succeeded Sol, who is alive, and she's breathing, although she tried to give me a heart attack last night with that little stunt.

If I get early onset grey hair because of her, there will be hell to pay. Actually...she can make me a genetic modification so that silver never graces my hair.

Now that things are back on track and her downgrade is working, it's only a matter of time before she opens those pretty blue eyes, and then the next phase of our plan will have to be enacted.

I'm indeed going to miss my brother's presence by my side. It's just so much fun to poke Death. I never know how he will react; that's what's exciting. Gabriel and Evander are so predictable. But alas, every one of us must grow up. It's time to change the world. Who better than the Horsemen to do so?

When Evander called a meeting to discuss our future, I felt butterflies in my stomach. I was giddy like a schoolgirl. I felt like a caged animal that had been pacing its confines. Finally, the gatekeeper walked down the hall, jingling his keys, taunting me. Soon, we'll be able to leave this vault, which means we'll have to create a new society. We turned the small lunch hall into a meeting room and were all sitting around the table, just staring at each other. If looks could kill, there would be dead bodies scattered on the floor.

I'm waiting for the big giant to start talking, but his eyes keep bouncing off Gabriel and Wes like a tennis match. Shockingly, Gabriel is here actually joining us at the table after everything we've done. That's the problem with memories; they plague you. My brothers are infested with memories of us together, both the good and bad times. If we killed one another, then there would be no more memories. So we all come together and sit around the table to break bread. The conversation isn't lively now; the butter knives are gripped tight, but it will all settle one day. No storm can rage forever. One day, Gabriel will forgive us.

"Well, I'll kick this show off," I begin, but Evander narrows his eyes at me. "Fine, someone say something other than how they want to kill one another."

"I don't trust you," Gabriel says, then flashes me a 'fuck you' smile.

"Trust can be earned again," I grin back. He snorts and shakes his head.

"Listen," Evander states, "We're all here. Together. We survived, and we have the science. We all wanted the same thing; we wanted the science safe in our hands. We have it. The longer we fight, the more time we give our enemies to gather forces. We need to show a united face." He pauses. "I propose a new council consisting of Gabriel, Kane, Wes, Cody, Zander, Luna, Sol, and myself."

"No," Wes speaks; his tone sounds like the whistling of wind after throwing a knife. "Sol will have nothing to do with any of this."

"But she is a part of it. Look what she created."

"Sol is not going to be a part of this council," Gabriel interjects. "Neither is Luna or you two," He glares at Cody and Zander.

"Gabriel," Evander warns, "If we start to split up, we will form divides."

Gabriel tips his head back and laughs, "You think I'm going to consider Luna's opinions?"

"Yes. I do," Evander replies. He leans forward in his chair like a horse bucking its legs to run a race. "You don't want the politics of it, Gabriel. I know you don't. You want to be in the lab working on the science, and so does Luna. You both can do that." His eyes glance at Cody. "Cody can be the face; someone needs to herd together the masses to inspire hope."

"He does have a handsome face," I add, "I guess he got that from you; the square jaw and curls grab the ladies' attention."

Cody relaxes his shoulders, "I'm not trying to take anything from you, Gabriel."

"I'd like to see you try," Gabriel hisses.

Oh, it's getting interesting now. I sit taller in my chair and prepare to watch the show.

Wes sighs, "I have to report our final plan to my dad." He looks at Gabriel, "Evander has a point. Form the council, you all get a vote; the power is shared, and the weight is lifted off your shoulders."

"You're kidding me, right?" Gabriel roars, "You think after they all lied to me, I would rule Manus Dei with them?" He slams his fist down on the table, causing some metal to dent under his palms.

From the corner of my eye, a new presence appears. Oh my, now the fun is about to begin because the little mouse who should be tucked in bed has woken up.

She's gripping the door frame with all her might, "Luna didn't want Manus Dei to continue. You'll make something new, something better. Please! Please stop fighting. Please!" She cries. It's smart to put on the waterworks. "Don't make all our pain be for nothing. We did it; we took down Manus Dei. We stopped

Astrid! So many Reflections died. If you can't come together, it will all be for not;" Her blue eyes pin Gabriel, "Your pain will be wasted. Please, Gabriel. You once told me to see every angle. I'm asking you to see Luna's angle, and I'll ask her to see yours."

Wes is up faster than my upgraded eyes can blink. He rushes to Sol, who looks weak, but the color is back on her face. "What the hell! Why are you out of bed? When did you wake up?" He grabs her, his eyes roaming up and down her body, searching for an injury. Then he pulls her to him and kisses her with such passion that it silences the room. You can feel his panic, grief, and obsession. His wild need that is now satiated.

"This is why we must work together," I whisper to Gabriel, all kidding aside. "We have to set aside the past and mend our family." I point to Wes, who is still embracing Sol. I should tell him to take it easy on her, but I refrain. "Passion. Life and love. This is what we have been fighting for. I'm not asking you to love Luna again, but we know you still care. She was wrong; we all have done terrible deeds. You killed her Reflections, so she lied to you in order to save her kids."

"They are not her kids!" Gabriel snaps.

From the corner of my eye, Zander flinches, his muscles flex, and I can see how badly he wants to argue, but Cody silences him. This isn't going to be a fast game; fixing our family is going to take time.

"In her eyes, they are," I stress. Gabriel won't look at me. He can move his eyes away, but I'll force him to listen. "We have a blank book we get to write and fill the chapters, brother. Let's write something we all can be content with. A little drama, some suspense, a shit ton of romance because we all need a good lay." I end my plea with some humor because I just can't resist.

Silence feels like a snake slithering around our feet; if we move or inhale too deeply, it will strike. Then it finally does; Gabriel's calculating eyes sweep over Cody, Zander, mine, then Evander's, "Fine. I'll play this new game."

Chapter 38

Sol

Waking up after the downgrade feels like stepping out of a frozen lake. My body feels numb, but slowly, it tingles back to life. It's not without aches and pains, but once I inhale and know I'm alive, I made it; it makes the pain worth it.

I have a deep-seated chill that helps my body force itself to sit up. Apprehension grips me; my fingers curl into the rough sheets when I take note of my surroundings. I'm in a hospital-like room alone.

I've passed this room before; I know where I am, and that settles me.

I rub my eyes and slowly drag my hands down my face. I remember seeing Wes, but I'm unsure if that was real or a lie my mind painted to soothe me.

Pressing my bare toes onto the polished concrete, I feel a surge course through me. I flex my fingers, pumping fresh blood into them. I'm alive.

Did the downgrade work? Was everything stripped from me, or did it backfire?

There's only one way to find out. I need to get to my lab and start running tests.

Stumbling from bed, I keep my hands bracing the walls as I walk down the hallway. The further I walk, the louder the voices grow.

"Wes!" I gasp. I would know his voice anywhere. He is here!

I want to scream and shout, but my throat feels too raw. My steps quicken, and I feel a new vigor surging within my body.

The voices are coming from the mess hall. It isn't just Wes's voice, but Gabriel's, Evander's, and Kane's...where is Luna?

I pause and look the other way, towards the staircase where she is. Should I go to her? But what if I failed? How will I confess that to her?

No, I need to run the tests and see if the downgrade worked, and then I'll confront Luna.

I take three steps but stop and press myself against the wall when I hear arguing.

"You're kidding me, right?" Gabriel roars, "You think after they all lied to me, I would rule Manus Dei with them?"

The slamming of something onto metal makes me jump.

Gabriel...oh, Gabriel, I am so very sorry. I know my words will never be good enough, not after every lie I forced you to believe.

One of my biggest fears has been facing the boy I once knew. How do you look a man who is like a brother in the eye and ask for forgiveness when it isn't due? Maybe you don't. You just let all the emotions run like water under the bridge; it will either surge high and tear down the bridge in its current, or the tides will eventually retreat.

I press my hand against my heart. After everything, it still beats.

I can't bear the fighting. No! I surge forward and step into the entryway; around the metal lunch tables are the men I love. My family, the old and the new additions. They are fighting; the tension is so thick it stinks. If this continues, it will all be for not.

"No," I meant it as a shout, but it sounds no louder than a church mouse. However, every one of them has upgraded hearing, so they all turn to see my pleas. Every single eye blinks in shock.

I fought for this, for their eyes to blink, to be alive, for their hearts to beat. I won, even if the downgrade didn't work, I won. My family is here, and we will mend our tattered bonds.

I grip the doorframe tighter, "Luna didn't want Manus Dei to continue. You'll make something new, something better." I turn desperate, "Please! Please stop fighting. Please!" I cry. "Don't make all our pain be for nothing. We did it; we took down Manus Dei. We stopped Astrid! So many Reflections died. If you can't come together, it will all be for not;" I look towards Gabriel, "Your pain will be wasted. Please, Gabriel. You once told me to see every angle. I'm asking you to see Luna's angle, and I'll ask her to see yours."

A flash of movement catches my eye, and Wes is in front of me before I blink. His shadow blankets me, covering me in his shades of darkness. It feels like home.

"What the hell! Why are you out of bed? When did you wake up?" He grabs me. His strong hands make my knees tremble. I want to collapse and melt into him. Forest green eyes look me up and down as if he were a lost hiker searching for refuge. Then he finds it in me. His lips descend and claim mine in a searingly brutal kiss. His tongue invades my mouth, swirling, sucking, and laying claim to every inch of me.

My breaths are his; my soul is his.

He tastes like life, a pure, hot intensity that makes my toes curl and then push up as I press my body into his. I feel like I've been floating a drift, but now I have his hard body and beautifully twisted mind to ground me.

His kiss turns from frantic to slow, to painful, to tender.

The faint talking behind him is completely drowned out when his hands cup my cheeks. He presses his forehead against mine, "Little mouse," He purrs.

"I'm sorry," I whisper.

"Don't worry, you'll spend a lifetime tied to me to compensate for it." He rasps.

I swallow, "Away from here?" My chin tips up, and we stare into each other's eyes.

"Far, far away, in a tower I built for you."

A tear drips from my eye, "I've never wanted to be locked in your cage so badly."

That makes him smile. I've never seen this grin before; it's so full of satisfaction it's as if he is a ray of sunshine warming every inch of my once numb skin.

"Home." I whisper, "I want to make a home with you."

His smile fades, not from anxiety or anger, not even shock. It's simply bliss like when you're laying out sunbathing, basking in the light as it warms you and kisses your skin with a glow. Utter relaxation.

"You taught me how to navigate the darkness, Wesley. It was so dark without you. I never want to walk down those paths again." Reaching up, I grasp his hands, "I made it; I found the strength to continue for you, for a future with you. You were right; you said I would run, and then I would want to run directly into your arms. Your cage isn't physical; it's mental. You want to keep my mind safe from all the lies and from the darkest part of myself. You're the only person who can. I realize that now."

I interlace my fingers with his. It's difficult for me to express, but it's necessary. You can't simply skip a chapter. For Wesley and me to create our own story, I have to complete this book of games my sister forced me into being a part of. Only then can I start writing my own narrative."But first, I need to see if the downgrade worked."

Chapter 39

Sol

I've told many lies and witnessed just as many shocking truths. I know what anticipation tastes like. It's that odd flavor you're unsure you crave or dislike, much like a Sour Patch candy. It's seductively sweet yet devilishly tart.

Do you like it?

Anticipation has never tasted as potent as it does right this very moment.

Gabriel has just taken samples, and in a few hours, we will all see if my downgrade was truly successful. It tastes sweet, but the time we must wait will turn it sour.

Wes stands so closely behind me that he feels like a cape draped over my shoulders. I find myself leaning back, embracing his presence.

"Are you finished?" Wes questions.

Gabriel nods, not even glancing my way.

"Let's go; you need to rest," Wes nudges me.

"Give me a minute," I reply. I stand and walk towards Gabriel. His back is turned to me as he busies himself with the equipment. I want to explain to him why I did it and how I regret so many things. "Gabriel, please let me-"

"I don't want to hear it, Sol," he growls. Wes clears his throat in a warning.

"But—" I step closer.

He twists in his chair; his blue eyes look thunderous, like heavy rain clouds that want to cry and release their fury. "Let me finish. I don't want to hear why you did it. The 'why' never matters when compared to the aftermath. You begged me to move on, so let me move on."

"What does that mean?" Why does it feel like a punch to my gut?

"That means allowing you to walk away unscathed with my brother." He nudges his head, signaling for Wes to remove me. Wes grips my biceps, but I tug back.

"I don't want you to hate me."

He laughs. It sounds so menacing it makes my stomach drop. "Don't worry, all my hate is focused elsewhere."

"I don't want you to hate her either."

His eyes narrow into slits. "Why? Luna expressed love by saying she hated me. I'm just giving her a taste of her own twisted definition."

"What if we give her the downgrade and it fails? What if her heart stops beating?" I shout. His jaw clenches. Good, that's what I was hoping for. "If she died, how would you feel?"

"I already know how I would feel because you helped me believe she did die."

"Let's go," Wes mutters as he edges me out of the lab.

I grasp the doorframe and shout, "Gabriel. They took a future from her. A future she might have wanted with you. Children. Then Astrid dangled two kids in front of her. They ripped away her choices. Her freedom, Gabriel. They took it from the both of you. I'm not saying what she did was right, but she was backed into a corner. She was just trying to save everyone she loved. You can't burn down the world without love. It's an endless fuel. If you nurture it, it adds fuel; if you worry over it, it adds fuel; if love is threatened, it sparks the fuel. A fire can destroy but also add nutrients to the soil. Please try to understand why she did it; please try to grow something new."

"Stop fucking talking, Sol!" He roars. Wes steps in front of me, but Gabriel's words still penetrate me like arrows. "What more do you want from me? I agreed to continue the science and rule alongside a bunch of liars. Traitors who are less demonic than the old Masters. I chose the lesser evil, but it's still evil. What more do you want from me!" He slams his fist to his chest.

"I want you to fight to make it better! Make Luna better."

***

Wes leads us back to my old room; the bunk beds have been moved and altered since I took the downgrade. All but two beds remain in the center, the rest shoved aside, making it impossible for another person to sleep comfortably on them. The two left have been shoved together, making one larger bed.

"You were planning this," I state, looking at the single bed.

He closes the door. "Was I planning on you waking?" he replies. I feel his warmth as he comes behind me, his arms snaking like chains locking me in his hold, "You bet your ass I planned on you waking up, taking you back to this room, and fucking some sense into you." He spins me so abruptly that my feet stumble, momentarily losing their balance, but his firm grip steadies me. His voice, rough and strained, breaks the tense silence. "How could you?" he barks, his eyes wide with a tumultuous blend of disbelief and hurt.

It's not anger in his green eyes; it's anguish. Such saturated pain. "I knew it would work." I lie. He immediately senses my fib, and his hand curls around my neck like a viper.

"Lie to me again. I dare you."

"Much like Luna," I begin. I try to inhale, but he clamps down, making it wheezy, "I was backed into a corner. I had no choice." That's why she forced me to play; it was the only way for me to understand the absolute fuckery her plan was.

His eyes watch me; it feels like he's slowly carving off the skin of a peach, and then his lips take mine in a bruising kiss. He doesn't break the kiss as he walks and leads us into the bathroom. Then he cruelly rips his lips from mine to turn on the shower.

I'm panting and thoroughly exhausted but eagerly awaiting what this will entail. I just want him; I want him to make my body feel alive.

I grab the ends of my shirt, but he snarls, "Leave it!"

I drop my hands. He turns the knob all the way too hot, but I've been here long enough to know no about of time will get the water to a comfortable level of warmth.

With the slow precision of a surgeon, he strips me bare; then he runs the tips of his fingers all over my body.

"I'm ok," I assure him. His hand glides up between my thighs, to my opening, where he slowly parts my lips and pushes a finger inside. I gasp at the feeling, clenching around him. It's been months without him, making one finger feel invasively thick.

"This is mine. You risked it." He curls his finger, then moves his palm so it circles my clit. He adds another finger, then a third; I feel the pressure building; it's mixed with apprehension. I don't see Wes or Wesley looking at me.

I see Death.

He's incensed.

"Death," I moan as I try to soothe his anxiety.

"Shhh," He purrs in a low, sinister tone. He adds more pressure to my body with each circle of his palm.

"Oh, yes…" I tip my head back, my eyes close. I'm about to come, but then he grabs a fist full of my hair, tugging my head back so my neck is exposed to him. He stops and withdraws his fingers.

"Wes," I cry, but there is no reasoning with him.

He's right; I did risk our love. Love consists of two beating hearts. What I did was selfish. Risking your own heart is one thing, but taking another's and playing a game of life or death is crossing a line.

I become a puppet again. I allow him to pull my strings in whichever way will help him heal. He won't hurt me; his obsession, love, and devotion to me leash his beast.

He spends the next twenty minutes washing me, soaping over every inch of my body, then washing it away. He's aware of the cold water, so he keeps large portions of his body pressed against mine, feeding me his body's heat. He brings me to the edge of an orgasm multiple times; by the end of the shower, I can't stand; my body is wound so tight I feel like I'll explode.

After he dries me, he carries my naked body to the bed, gently laying me down in the center. He covers me with his body as a blanket. "Do you understand how it feels?" He asks.

I'm a trembling mess beneath him. I need him, need a release, or I think I might die.

I nod, then reach up and grab his hips, pulling him further into me. I feel his hard cock as it presses between my thighs. "I understand."

He lowers his head to the crook of my neck; his exhales tickle me. I buck my hips up and spread my legs open so I can wrap them around him. Now, his arousal slides up and down my wet core. One more small shift and his tip begins to nudge my opening.

"It's done, Wesley. These games are finished. Make me yours." I beg as I raise my lips to his and kiss him. I push my tongue inside and swirl it around his.

God, his taste! It's madness.

After everything, I want to be insane, totally lost in him.

I suck his tongue into my mouth, and that's when his restrain is severed. He shoves inside of me in one brutal thrust that shocks me to life. It feels like my heart never beat until now.

This is the beginning, and I can't wait to spend the rest of my life with him.

My back arches, my mouth parts, and I cry out for more.

"You're mine, little mouse." Thrust.

"You ran right into my trap." Thrust.

My body isn't going to make it. I'm going to detonate, tip over into the waterfall of ecstasy, "I'm coming."

"I'm never," thrust, "letting," thrust, "you go!"

Darkest blankets my eyes, a buzzing fills my ears, my heart stops then…thump! Blood rushes through my veins as we both come together. It's like magic, a taste of the forbidden.

I grab him, squeezing my legs tighter around him. "Please don't ever leave me, Wesley."

"I'm still in you," He chuckles. The sound of his laugh makes me want to cry.

We've both done a lot of fucked up shit. That's why we are perfectly imperfect for one another.

"Good," I circle my hips and clench my inner muscles. "Let's keep it that way." I purr, and then we start to make love again and again.

Love can be destroyed, separated, torn apart, and burnt down, but it can also be rebuilt again.

I just hope Gabriel and Luna can figure that lesson out well they still have the chance.

Chapter 40

Sol

"We need to wait six weeks. We will retest it again. If the results are the same, we'll give it to Luna. In the meantime Sol will meet me for daily testing." Gabriel states as he addresses the room. There is a confidence to his stance, shoulders wide, his lungs seem to have a steady inhale as if a wind is constantly blowing in his sails.

I'm not sure I heard him right. My eyes can't move off the screen that shows the results.

My downgrade worked.

I'm me again. Genetically the same as I was at birth. Still upgraded, but not with any modifications Manus Dei forced onto Luna during the games.

It worked.

I did it.

"Why wait?" Wes asks Gabriel. I feel his thighs stiffen since he's position me on his lap.

"I want to make sure no underlying side effects begin to form. Ideally, I'd wait longer, but Klara has been sedated for too long as it is, and," he clears his throat and pauses. He can't say Luna's name.

Kane claps his hands, making me jump, "You did it, little mousey." He grins. "Oh shit, I can't wait to get out of these terrible clothes. Seriously, Evander, why didn't you pack me something that wasn't made of cotton and polyester?" He jokes, but no one laughs.

I feel the weight of every eye on me. Pinning me like a lab mouse they will slowly dissect. I don't know what they want from me.

Should I jump for joy? Not after everything that has been sacrificed.

Should I cry? This is the end. I'm walking away from all of this.

Should I smile? I'm free.

"Hey," Wes whispers. His hand hugs me tighter to his scarred chest. We haven't been able to let go of one another. "What's wrong?"

"Nothing and everything," I state. Like a serene, undisturbed lake, the room's silence seems to hold; Cody, Zander, Kane, Gabriel, Evander, and Wes all focus on me as they wait for me to cause the first ripple.

"I have to leave her. I'd say, 'I don't want to,' but that would be a lie. I want to leave. I just..." I exhale shakily, "I want to know she will be safe. I want to know after everything we all sacrificed that we will make something together and not allow our past memories to tear us apart."

"She will be," Evander stresses. He hasn't been able to sit down, he paced the room as Gabriel went over the results. His mind was elsewhere; on Klara. I didn't just fix Luna I fixed Klara also.

Does saving two people grant me redemption from all the lies I told?

I glance at Gabriel, whose eyes are cast down. There are dark circles making his eyes look like blue glaciers on a pitch black night.

"Listen to me," Wes interjects, "When Luna pushed you to play this game, she wasn't always with you, but she knew you would survive. She knew this would happen if you succeeded; she knew this, Sol. She knows what she is doing."

He's right. Luna plotted everything thing out exactly how she wanted it. She knew one day she would be locked head to head in a game, again, with Gabriel.

I don't know who is going to win this time. There is no crown; the science will be split evenly. Each of my family has a role to play.

Not me.

I played my part. I'm done.

Luna's whole life has been a game. I thought I was ending it, but I realize it didn't end with the downgrade.

It is just getting started.

Luna's about to play the most vital game of her life. Her heart isn't on the line; she already risked her life. This time, it's all about the one thing we thought we had to teach her, the one thing she distorted into her own definition of survival.

Emotions.

She has to make a devil whose soul she stole then traded, somehow see her as a human again. A human he might be able to love again.

Chapter 41

Gabriel

Sometimes, being upgraded isn't always a good thing, like right now. I can hear Wes and Sol proclaim their love for one another as they fuck in their bedroom. No matter how hard I try to focus on something else, their sounds only taunt me, growing louder. I could use headphones to drown them out, but music reminds me of Luna.

I stand up from bed. I'll just go back to the lab. I'm almost there when I hear talking - Evander and the twins. Yes, those twins, Cody and Zander.

"No, you looked where you were planning to strike. You just gave your intentions away," Evander says, his voice gentle, almost parental.

What the fuck is it with these twins! Why does everyone want to help them?

Striding forward, I reach the gym, where I see Evander sparring with Zander. Cody is behind them lifting weights, but as soon as I move, he freezes mid-air. There is a cold, serial look in his eyes that mirrors mine. I used to look at others like that when they got too close to Luna.

You know what's fucked up? I still find my eyes narrowing like that when someone mentions her name. How do I lower my shields when I made them impenetrable?

What's more irritating is they all are right. I still love her, but it's tainted, filled with abhorrence. But it's still love.

Evander glances my way but then moves, keeping his sparring lesson going with Zander. Cody puts the weights back on the bar and sits up, flexing his muscles in warning. I laugh, which catches Zander's attention. His mistake.

Evander advances, his footwork precise and calculated. He feints left, then launches a rapid combination—jab, cross, hook. Zander tries to escape him, but he hasn't taken regard for Evander's size. He's a big fucker, Zander thinks he can beat him using speed, but Evander is deadly because he's also fast. Faster than Zander. In a lightning-quick sequence, Evander seizes Zander's arm, pivots with finesse someone his size shouldn't be able to possess, and applies a textbook hold.

Zander sighs, then taps Evander's biceps. He's tapping out. Is he serious? You don't stop fighting; the minute you do, you die.

"No," I order Evander. "Keep him locked."

As much as I hate to admit it, these boys are a part of my genes. Any weakness in them is going to ripple onto me. When we open those bunker doors, none of us can look feeble. We are about to usher in a new world. I don't want to work with them, but I will because it's the only way to keep the science safe.

"Figure a way out," I bark. "You think of yourself as her child, as her DNA," I state.

"I am!" Zander growls, his pale skin flushing red. I always thought it was a mistake to design Luna to have pale skin. It flushes so easily, showing her annoyance...or passion.

"We're cutthroat, literally. Klara enjoys cutting throats. We don't tap out," I mock. I feel the first surges of adrenaline pumping into my veins.

I don't miss the 'fuck you' look Evander flashes me. He's a fool if he thinks he can tame Klara, but he needs a dose of reality and some karma. Klara will never act civilized, and an untamed beast can't reciprocate love.

Zander struggles as he tries to break Evander's grip. He succeeds eventually, but that's because Evander went soft on him.

"You think others will help him?" I step forward. My bare feet are sinking into the padded mats.

Why the hell do they have padded floors? There is no buffer when an enemy bests you. Luna and I trained outside on the hard, unforgiving soil. I know what it feels like to be thrown against it, the hard thump pushing out the air from your lungs. Roots and rocks digging into your spine trying to cripple you. The feeling of pinning Luna beneath me against that soil is etched in my mind. Trapping her against the earth as I took her, then when she flipped us and rode me. It added pain to our pleasure.

"You think they will make it easy for him?" I challenge Evander.

"No," he snaps, "But I'm not going to throw them into a death match. That kind of teaching produced Luna and you. I'm breaking the cycle."

I don't like the effect his words have on me. I'm too stubborn to admit he's right. I was raised to be this way, and my actions are a cycle. Luna was raised the same; for years, we sacrificed Reflection after Reflection until she stopped the cycle. Risked her life and her mind to save them.

Why the heck did she break the cycle? How did she break it?

I could betray them all, play along until I see the perfect moment to snatch it away from them. That thought keeps me up at night. I've already started plotting how I would do it.

Is that how it started with Astrid?

I'll become the monster I loathed.

Break the cycle. How do I accept members who betrayed me? How do I trust them again?

"I hate you," I shout at Evander. He guides Zander behind him; he's protecting him like a shield.

"I know," Evander nods.

"Fight me."

He exhales and steps forward. "I'm not talking about you," I glare at Zander. Cody stands and enters the padded square that makes the small sparring ring.

"You're not in the right frame of mind," Evander states.

"Trust me," I challenge him. I just cornered the big guy. He wants me to trust them again. Trust has to be shown by both sides. Evander can't back down now. He steps aside and tells Zander, "Remember what I taught you."

"No," Cody yells. He strides forward and shoves me. Hard. Good, he has balls, but they haven't dropped yet. The twins might think they are men, but they are boys. They have no idea who they are messing with. It takes me five seconds to have him pinned in a move that would make it easy for me to snap his neck.

"You're weak. You never would have survived. Luna loves you; I should kill you both, but that would be predictable; just like your moves. Don't be predictable. I'm not. I'm going to keep you both alive; consider this your punishment. I'll be training you."

"Fuck you," he boils. I cut off his air. "What was that?" I mock. He tries to speak again, but I jerk his neck in a vice grip. His cheeks turn from red to cranberry. "Go ahead, tap my arm. See if I release you."

"Gabriel," Evander warns.

Cody's face turns darker. I glance at Zander, "Luna's not here to save either of you. Stop relying on her. Go ahead. Save your brother." I poke. He tries, but it doesn't take me long to get him flat on the mat while still holding Cody.

"False hope leads to a gradual death," I look at Evander. "I'll teach them how to fight." I release Cody and push him onto the mat. "You will train with me for two hours every day. I dare you not to show up." I sardonically grin.

Cody glances at Evander. I laugh, "He's not going to help you. You want a savior, guess what? They don't exist. Welcome to hell, boys. Only the toughest clones will survive."

"Gabriel," Evander starts, but I hold up my hands.

"Don't worry. I won't kill them. I won't resemble Manus Dei, but I'm not going to give them a fool's hope. This new society we are forming will face challenges that will claim many. If you want to give the world genetic enhancements, people will take our science and try to manipulate it for evil. You want to form a branch that polices this. That means they will need to know how to survive, one on one, one against an army." I open my arms wide, "I'm the army; I've got many faces thanks to you. They will face all my sides, and if they really are offspring of Luna and my DNA, then you shouldn't worry, brother," I smirk, "look how far Luna and I have come. We're survivors. I'm going to show them how to be just like us."

Chapter 42

Sol

I don't know how many times Wes and I have made love, it never feels like enough. We're laying naked wrapped in each others arms. He's just told me about his family, not the Horseman but his father and older brother Wade.

He made a deal with them, a deal that took away some of his freedom all for me.

"Why did you choose not to continue working for your father? He had a seat waiting for you. You could have avoided all of this," I ask, my eyes fixed on his scarred heart.

"Then I never would have met you," he purrs, his hands slowly roaming up and down my lower back.

"Seriously," I giggle, "Why?"

"Because, like you said, a seat was waiting for me. I saw that seat as a cage. Like you, I wanted freedom, to forge my path, not have it handed to me. I knew it wouldn't last forever, so I made the most of my time. I helped take down Manus Dei and found a woman who loves my black soul," he kisses the top of my head. This is a new side of him, this lighthearted nature.

"Not one to boast, eh." I push up on my elbow, and his eyes lock onto my breasts, making my nipples harden under his stare. They feel heavy with a tension only his skilled hands can free them from.

"It's not boasting." He palms my breast, gently squeezing it. "It's just facts."

I glance down at his hardening erection, the tip already glistening with pre cum. I can't help myself; I bend down and lick it off, flicking my tongue over his sensitive head.

"Sol," He warns me. I grin as I close my lips around him and begin to suck him off. He's so thick and long I can barely take him, but I force myself to. My eyes water as he grabs my hair and takes control of my movements.

"Fuck, little mouse, yes, just like that," he pushes my head down further till he hits the back of my throat. "Fuck!" He moans. I place my palms on his strong thighs. I feel his cock swelling and twitching with each new thrust.

"Scoot your ass towards me," He barks.

I edge my hips towards him, and his hand snakes out; he slides his fingers into my wet core and begins to match my movements with his hand.

"Together. We will always be together. Always come together from now on." He vows. "Come, little mouse." He orders me. We both come, just as he declared. Together. Always together, never apart.

"I love you," I say as I curl up on his chest like a kitten seeking shelter.

"I love you more than my words can describe." He replies. His arms pull tighter around me like a seatbelt, holding me to him and keeping me safe.

"I'll never lie to you again," I respond. "I'm finished."

He slaps my ass. "Good. You learned your lesson. I will always be there to catch you or chase you."

I feel a surge of wetness seep out from me. "We never use a condom," I state. I'm not on the pill. Unlike Luna, I can get pregnant.

He turns me, pushing me onto my back; his right-hand covers my stomach, "I know." His eyes look down my body, leaving me heated in their wake.

"What if we get pregnant?"

His smile spreads like a flower, making its first bloom on a warm summer's day. It's beautiful, so captivating; you can almost scent a sweet fragrance from it. "It's not a question. It's a fact. You're my life, Sol, my future. I want a family with you."

I can't help but think of Luna. It must show on my face. "I don't know how Luna will take it." I blurt out.

"It doesn't matter how she takes the news. You have to stop worrying about her. It's time to be selfish. This is our future, not hers. She made her bed; she knew what it would look like; she also knew you'd be with me."

I nod, but fear still swells in my belly. "I don't...I don't know if I'll be a good mother."

His hand glides up my body until he cups my cheek, turning my face toward him. "No one does, not until you have a child." He lowers himself and kisses my stomach, "A devil can raise an angel; it's up to the angel's self-control not to follow the same path as its parent. We will make sure our children do better than us. That's all a good parent can hope for."

Chapter 43

Sol

Four weeks later.

I've visited my sister numerous times. That's the truth and a lie because she is drugged, so in reality, it's like I'm seeing a shell of my sister. It's her, but it's not.

Klara is the same, although her robot-like demeanor seems more content. At least she reads and moves around her cell. Luna doesn't. She just sits there, looking at the wall.

It's been four weeks. Gabriel runs tests daily, and everything is working. It's been so flawless that I'm worried it's all a lie, a trick. I think Gabriel thinks that, too; that's why he keeps testing and retesting.

He and Evander have tweaked his AI not just to report how a specific body will react but also to predict the response over a decade out. This technology will change the world of health for the better. Good can come from evil. I've seen it happen now countless times.

Two weeks later.

Dear Mental Journal,

It's been a while since I last spoke to you. I would say I'm sorry, but I'm not. Honestly, this will be the last time I reach out to you. After this, there won't be a need for it.

Everything is coming to an end, and with closure comes the potential for a new beginning. Wes will be a part of that fresh start.

The impending conclusion has put everyone on edge, including Kane, who has had to bite his tongue numerous times in an attempt to lighten the mood. No one wants to tempt fate by discussing the outcome.

We're all still confined within the fallout bunker. While its purpose is to shield us from the outside world, the stress within these walls is so palpable that it feels like the weight of nuclear radiation slowly affecting us all.

My only respite comes from Wes. He's my pause button. I spend hours each day with him, his presence so all-encompassing that when he's deep inside of me, I lose myself in the moment. It's a welcomed escape — a state where concentration gives way to bliss, and the fears that threaten to consume me are temporarily forgotten.

***

The day my life will change for the better and for the worst.

Today, I will give Luna the downgrade that will cure her mind and strip her body of its added strength.

Today will be the last time I play with the science that makes mere men feel like gods.

Today is the day I will lose my sister by saving her. After she recovers, I'm leaving, and she will be on her own. One less puppet in her arsenal.

I step into the cell alone, but I feel the presence of the Horsemen behind me. It took weeks of arguing to convince them I had to do this alone. Just Luna and me. Only twins can understand this odd bond, a connection that can never be fully broken; it twists and molds you, forcing you into unimaginable things. The only reprieve is to put distance between us, but even then, I know I will sense her.

She's partially sedated; we started to wean off the medicine because the way I designed the downgrade was for the nanobytes to put the body into a coma-like state. This way, the patient exerts no added energy, and the body can solely focus on recovering.

To the right, Klara lies on her stomach, immersed in a book, her legs crossed in the air. She will receive the downgrade after Luna has recovered, which should be in the following weeks. She looks so peaceful right now, though. Perhaps we should let her stay in this state?

I sigh; Evander will never allow that. He thinks he can fix everything. Heck, maybe he can. He forced me to create the downgrade, and I succeeded; maybe he can make Klara act civilized and show her what it means to be loved.

Luna is sitting on her bed, legs crossed, looking at the wall. She's so still that she looks like a toy sailboat on a river with no current. It's wrong; the sailboat should have wind in its sails; it should be moving.

I enter her cell; her eyes finally glance at me. Can her upgraded ears hear my racing heart?

Her blue eyes glance down at the needle in my hand. I'm alone here, but Wes and Evander are outside the door. She won't have long to hurt me if she tries.

"Hi, Luna," I whisper as I hesitate. I shouldn't have paused; that gave her the power. She knows I fear her.

"I don't know if you can hear me."

"Of course I can hear you," she deadpans. "You're talking." Her voice sounds distant, her emotions buried under the drugs and failed modifications controlling her mind.

I clear my throat and stand taller. "I mean if you are going to understand me." I correct myself as I take another step inside her cell.

"I did it, Luna. The downgrade worked." I admit as I sit on her bed. The thin, weak coils bend under the added weight and squeaks a cry.

"Should I be happy or mad?"

I shrug and pivot towards her, "Both, I suppose." Her hair is tied back with her red ribbon. I put it there, hoping it would help her remember. Her face is clean, but she looks tired, like someone who existed on coffee and now feels like a sleepless zombie.

"Ok," she keeps looking at the wall.

I take the cap off the needle, "I will give it to you now. There will be a small pinch," I tell her. "Can you lay down? It needs to be injected into a fatty tissue. Your stomach."

She moves without replying, listening to everything I said. I hate it. I want her to rebel, to fight me. She can't, no matter how hard she tries. That freedom has been taken from her; she took it from herself to save us all.

I clean her stomach, and then I press the needle against it. A soft click sounds when I push the button. She doesn't flinch or move when the needle pierces her flesh; she just lies there like the perfect doll.

"You know I love you." I whisper, "But more than that, I forgive you. I have to so I can move on. I can't dwell on the past, or it will engulf me. I have to keep looking forward. Can you do that for me, Luna? Can you look forward and stay positive even when the world might be against you?" *Even when Gabriel can't admit he still loves you.*

I pull the needle out and wait for a reply. Her vacant eyes are on the ceiling now. "Luna," I murmur as I gently touch her forehead, "I know you can hear me even if you can't reply. Just remember my words."

I stand and walk to the cage door's entrance; As soon as I leave, Evander will come inside and take Luna to the medical bay he has set up, then he and Gabriel will monitor the nanobytes and their progress.

I look over my shoulder; she remains lying. Will she stay that way until someone orders her to move? It's too painful to watch, so I turn.

"Did you do it?" She asks. I stop suddenly, turn, and rush back to her side. Her eyes don't regard me, but she continues, "Did you end my games?"

A tear slips free and lands on her cheek; she blinks but doesn't move. "I did," I reply.

She nods.

"I ended your games, Luna, but Gabriel's games are about to begin. I thought I could stop all the games, but they are constant, like gravity. Their pull is too strong; it's what keeps us grounded, stuck to some fucked up moral compass that at times looks utterly insane, but without the competition, we are monsters left to roam with no rules. We need rules; thus, we must continue playing games. I understand that now. We end games just to create new ones."

"You say such silly things, Sol," Her voice is still dead-sounding, like a sack of bones picked apart by vultures. There's not much left to take. But her choice of words tells me deep down she is noting everything. Just because bones have no meat on them doesn't mean they are useless. You have to crack them open and find the marrow inside. That's usually the best part, what's hidden deep, deep inside.

Luna is trapped inside her own mind. "Of course, you can't end the games; that, in itself, is a game." She responds. She's right; to end the games, I had to play a game that affected others who now want to play their own matches.

"So you're ready then? You're ready to play a game against Gabriel?" Because it's going to challenge you and now you're not as strong. Gabriel never said he would take the downgrade. Why would he?

Evander said the downgrade was a way to wipe the slate clean and give Luna a choice at the upgrades she wanted; there's the massive roadblock that is Gabriel. I'm not sure he will allow Luna access to the upgrades. Not without a give and take.

"No," she replies, her knuckles curling, fighting hard to speak through the fog in her mind. Footsteps sound behind me; someone has joined us. "I was never going to play *against* him. That's what Manus Dei wanted. They wanted one winner and a backup. Then, they wanted the winner to train Cody and Zander. It was going to be another competition. Brother versus brother, twin versus twin. The most cunning takes the crown. That's not what I wanted, and that isn't what will happen when Gabriel takes over."

I tilt my head, "What do you want?" How is she so confident she still has control even after she has lost possession of her mind?

"I want to play *alongside* him. Now I will." She replies. Her eyes move slowly, but her body remains still; she looks past my shoulder for a moment, and then she glances back up at the ceiling. I follow her gaze and see Gabriel standing at the entrance to the cages. He heard everything.

"You can go now," She dismisses me. "I can feel it starting. You did what I wanted. You're free."

Chapter 44

Sol

Five weeks later.

What's done is done.

It's finished.

I've sat by her bedside every day, watching and waiting. Unlike my downgrade, Gabriel added more nanobytes so her immune system could not override the downgrade. Luna is awake, sitting up, and I'm waiting for her to say something.

"Why are you still here?" She finally asks me.

Ouch. That's okay; this is her defensive. What she means is I'm happy you're here.

"Where is Gabriel?" She's asking about him. Good.

"He's training Cody and Zander. He's been training them in combat daily. Wes is with them. Evander is right outside the door."

Her eyes narrow at the mention of Cody and Zander. "He won't hurt them." I assure her, "Kane and Evander will ensure that."

She snickers, "I know, you silly fool," She glances at me. Her eyes have life swirling in their depths again. A cloudless horizon is pretty, but it can't compare to the awe of a building thunderstorm. Just like rumbling storm clouds, she's calculating again. She grins an actual smile. This is her way of thanking me. "Gabriel won't hurt them because they are his leverage."

"What do you mean." I edge my chair closer. The screen behind her displays her heart rate which goes up five beats.

"Ten steps ahead wasn't enough. I had to keep plotting. Gabriel needs control; he thrives on it. He never would have been able to give up control like I did. He'd never sacrifice his mind; he relied on it to save us all. Having Cody and Zander as a part of our new society gives him control over me." She swings her legs out from under the sheets and starts to swing them back and forth. It reminds me of when I was in the virtual reality, and she was swinging her legs right before she pounced and managed to make Klara obsessed with her.

"He's going to use them as leverage to keep me in line."

"And you'll let that happen," I reply. I see where she is going with this. "Because the more he grows closer to them, the better he can understand and use them against you." I inhale deeply, feeling my lungs press against my ribs. "The closer he gets to them, the more likely he will begin to accept them as his own."

It's a perfect plan.

"He'll be a good father. It's a father's duty to protect, but a mother's to sacrifice." She states.

Her words hit me like a hurricane, tearing through the carefully constructed walls of my emotions. In an instant, all my hate and anger, all the reasons I thought I could comprehend why she did this, forcing us all to witness such shocking events and turn into monsters, are swept away, leaving me standing in the wreckage of my understanding.

Just. Like. That.

"You should tell him that," I whisper, still shocked by the weight of her statement.

"Why?"

"You ask such silly things sometimes," She rolls her eyes.

"Tell him, then you'll understand why I told you to do so."

I stand but keep my eyes on her face, her makeup free face. We're both a bare canvas, but it won't remain like this for long. I wonder if she will return to using the mask I gave her, red lips and black eyeliner, or try something new. "I hope you know what you're doing,"

"Of course I do. I plan ahead. You should get going. It will get very nasty around here, but don't worry." She pushes up and bounces off the bed, standing tall as if she wasn't just stripped of her upgrades, "I know exactly how it will end." She confidently declares.

***

The hallway leading to the entrance of the bunker feels like a cluster fuck of emotions. Kane is practically running down the hall, excited to get out of here so he can wear a custom suit again.

Gabriel seems eager, leading the pack and the first to reach the entrance door. He should be excited; he's about to get what he has always wanted. Not just the science but Luna. Like she said, they are trapped together; now it's his game. He's making the rules when it comes to their relationship.

Cody walks behind Gabriel, positioned in front of Wes, who walks ahead of me, almost like a guard. Cody doesn't trust

Gabriel, so he sticks to him like glue. He's not going to let Gabriel out of his sight.

Luna and Zander trail behind us. I sense Zander's unease at opening the door and welcoming others inside. Zander isn't fond of newcomers, and once that door opens, Wade and a secret army controlled by Wes's father will make their way inside as they oversee the formation of the new Manus Dei.

Luna's behavior makes me question everything. I don't know what I expected but I did expect some display of emotions. Instead, she hasn't spoken much to me or even sought me out. This is how we will part, and I'm not sure when we will meet again. It's painful, cutting me deep, but she's my twin. When she feels the most, she hides it. She's the strongest woman I know, yet even heroes fear; that's why they wear capes, concealing their anxiety beneath it, like sweeping problems under the rug.

Klara is in the medical wing; we gave her the downgrade four days ago. She is responding to it as expected.

I'm thankful I don't have to see her back in her mind and awake. I understand how she was formed and sculpted, and I know the motive behind her actions, but they are still hard to bear. The memories of her virtual reality will always haunt me.

"Type in that code and get me the hell out of here." Kane chirps as he slaps the metal door. He will be working with them remotely, working as Evander's eyes and ears. That's what he always has been, in invisible force that pushes and pokes sides when needed.

Evander begins to type in the code. Each beep makes my heart rate spike. I'm about to meet my new family. Wade, Wes's brother, is waiting for us. Don't get me wrong, I'm excited to meet Wes's older brother, but I know he is suspicious of clones. The more time I can shove between getting to know him, the better. Right now, I just want to rest. I want a long vacation with Wes; I want to go to a place without technology, so it can just be the two of us.

The huge steel door begins to creek and slide open. Cold fresh air rushes inside. Wes looks down at me and grins, "Soon," he whispers. Soon we'll be free.

In the far distance of the tunnel, I can see a line of soldiers, a tall man with dark hair and similar features to Wes grins. That must be Wade. "Come on," Wes says as he grasps my hand. His excitement is palpable. Kane rushes out, Gabriel and Cody follow them, then Evander, who stands one foot outside the bunker's door. I slip my hands-free from Wes, "Give me one second." I say. He nods as I turn to look at Luna.

Zander stands next to her, but his eyes are ping-ponging off the others as if waiting for something to happen.

"Luna I," What the hell do I want to say? Does it matter?

"You little shit," I hear a deep voice that has a similar accent to Wes. That's Wade talking. "I should kill you." He growls, and then I hear them hug. I glance over my shoulder. I wish Luna and I could do that. Just embrace each other.

Everyone is past the door, waiting for me to join them. Wade slaps Wes on the back, and his eyes flick towards me. They judge me at first, but then he gives me a somewhat friendly grin.

All I have to do is walk out that door, and I'm free. I've got a new family.

I glance at Luna again, "This isn't the end," I painfully voice. I could never say goodbye. This is just time apart that has no limit; then I turn and begin to join the others just outside the door.

"You say such silly things; it's not the end. Not yet," Luna replies. It's her voice that makes everyone turn silent. It's like someone blew out a row of birthday candles. Smoke fills the air; a wish has been made.

Luna has done something.

It's as clear as a flawless diamond. Her voice and the confidence reeking from it put everyone on guard.

She glances at Zander and nods. My stomach drops. I feel like the Titanic; I hit an iceberg, and the water is rushing in, filling my guts; it's pulling me down, weighting me. I'm sinking; the pressure from the cold ocean collapses all my hopes and dreams. Then I hit rock bottom. I'm frozen, like an artifact for others to examine.

What didn't I see? What move is she making that I didn't plot out?

Zander moves; reaching behind him, he grabs a gun and raises it halfway. I hear footsteps running.

"Luna!" Evander roars.

"Sol!" Wes shouts.

"Zander! Stop! Don't do this!" Cody screams.

It's a chaos of panic cries that all ends when Zander starts to shoot.

Chapter 45

Sol

This was a game, purposely planned. Zander shoots exactly where each person would place their next footstep, giving Luna enough time and cover to get to the access panel and seal the door. The others have no cover; it's an open tunnel, leaving only two options: run away or run right into the gunshots.

Wes picks option two. Our eyes lock, and the fear in his gaze cripples me. His green eyes turn into a forest on fire. He's going to run through bullets to reach me. He's done it before, and he will stupidly do it again.

I move, Wes screams at me, but it's too late. I rush towards Zander, arms spread wide; I grab the gun and shove him into the wall. The bullet is deflected and shoots off the cement walls; a heavy thud shakes the tunnel. My hands are squeezing Zander's so tight that I yell in a fury. I only move my eyes to scan my surroundings to make sure Wes and the others are okay, but that's when I see it. I know what the thud was; the vault door closed, sealing me off from Wes and the others.

I'm trapped with Luna and Zander.

My next exhale sounds like a knife stabbed me in the back. My blood is filled with adrenaline yet frozen with shock.

Zander shoves me off him, causing me to fall to the cold, unforgiving ground. For a moment, I stay with my hands bracing the floor. If he is going to shoot me, this is the perfect opportunity.

My eyes land on a fresh bullet hole that tried to dig deep into the concrete. Zander wasn't aiming at them. I keep looking at the floor and see all the shots he had fired marked on the ground.

He was aiming down the whole time. He was just trying to stop them. But why?

"You didn't think I would actually let you leave," Luna says. There's an excited passion in her voice. Like a circus ringleader who is amping up the waiting crowd.

I never thought I'd miss her robotic state, but I do now.

There's pounding on the other side of the door, but it's faint, like church bells in the distance.

I push myself up; my fingers claw into the ground. I face her, and she's smiling, truly grinning a genuine smile.

I taught her how to do that. I taught her everything. When we switched places, it gave her all the lessons she needed.

"You said I'd be free," I state, now I sound like the robot. I'm shocked, rendered useless.

She nods and glances around the bunker's tunnel, "You will be."

"What have you done!" I charge towards her, but Zander comes between us, gun in hand. I shove him once, then twice. He doesn't respond how he once did because he's been cured; he no longer sees me as the clone who tried to kill him.

"I've done exactly what I said I would." She reaches into her pocket and pulls out an auto-injector. "I'm offering you freedom." She uncurls her hand to reveal the injector with her red ribbon tied in a neat bow around it. It's like she's handing me a fucking Christmas gift.

After everything we both have done, we don't deserve gifts. We earned coal.

Maybe her betraying me now is what I deserve.

My lungs finally exhale. It feels like I'm pushing out crushed glass shards. On the other side of that wall is an illusion of freedom.

Will I ever be able to live a normal life with Wesley, or was it a lie I told myself?

My feet stagger back; I feel dizzy like the walls are closing in on me. "What is that?"

She snorts, "Well, from how you're looking at it, you think it's a weapon. Allow me to level the playing field." She looks at Zander, "Give her your gun."

His eyes narrow, resembling Luna's expression when I question her. "What?"

"I said give her your gun." She barks.

I can sense his reluctance, but he concedes and listens. Stepping closer, he aims the barrel down and tries to give it to me. I don't move. If I accept that gun, I roll the dice and play this new game with her.

"I'm not playing games anymore." I roar. I curl my fist in so tightly that my nails cut into my palm. A slight wetness from the fresh blood coats my fingers.

I thought I was done seeing blood, but apparently, I will see my own today.

"This isn't a game. It's your prize. Take. The. Gun." Luna bites.

When I don't move, Zander does, opening my clenched
fingers; I try to fight him at first, but then I concede. It's a weapon,
after all. He shoves the gun into my hand and steps only an inch
away. If he wanted to, he could grab it faster than I could raise it,
but I could still fire a shot.

"There, now we can continue." She breathes as if she has just
taken her first inhale of fresh air. It's filled with hope, as if the
world is in the palm of her genetically engineered hands. "As you
know, Cody tried to fix Zander. He wanted to delete certain
memories; he failed but then fixed his mistake. Cody didn't tell
you that while you were creating the downgrade, I was studying
the science that was being ripped from my memory. I was trying to
help Cody as best I could."

I knew she was studying the science again, but I didn't think to
look at what she was studying. I didn't think it mattered.

Everything Luna does matters. Nothing is without carefully
plotted details.

"After Cody was successful that's when Zander and I started
our own little modification. Zander designed most of it. I still have
a lot of things to relearn, but like myself, Zander is a fast learner."

"You were helping them," I repeat. It feels like the air is being
squeezed from my lungs, like an eclipse is happening deep inside
me, casting out all the light and bathing me in darkness. "You
could have been helping me with the downgrade."

"No, silly. Creating upgrades and downgrades is much more
complex. What Zander was doing was tweaking a single
modification. That's all I was able to help him with, it's all I
managed to relearn when I was sane of mind enough to
comprehend the materials." She shrugs, "Plus you didn't need my

help. You could always do it. Since the beginning, you could have played our father's game. This was your time to shine."

"To shine!" The gun feels hot in my hands. "I've been— " I stammer, my voice trailing off; how do I reply to this?

"Please," She holds up her hands. "Just let me finish this."

My eyes begin to water both from the shock and betrayal of this all. The tears feels like acid. She's begging me. I don't allow her to finish because I'm weak, I do it because I'm stronger than her.

"Thank you." She responds. "Deleting certain memories can be beneficial." She steps forward. On the other side of the wall, I hear gunshots in rapid fire. They are trying to shoot at the door, which is utterly useless, but, when you're desperate you do stupid things.

"You wanted freedom, but it will be plagued with nightmares. However, I found a way to allow you to escape truly." She says, looking more hopeful than I have ever seen her. There is a sincerity that is radiating from her like a halo.

Luna is no angel; her gifts always come with a steep price.

"I don't understand." My voice is no louder than a whisper. The shock is spreading.

"Of course you do." She mocks, "This is freedom," she raises the needle higher, her eyes pleading with me to take it. "I programmed it to block all memories that were too painful; I embedded a virtual reality of events to replace them. You will never see the murders that happened. Don't you see," She comes forward arms open wide. "I knew you'd have to see the murders; there was no other way," She grabs my shoulders, but her touch feels foreign like a stranger is grabbing and trying to abduct me, "but I also knew I would be able to fix it. Erase your nightmares."

"This is wrong, Luna." I whisper, my feet edge away from her and closer to the door but I can't peel my eyes off the needle.

Her lips press into a line as she meets my gaze, it feels like we are five years old again and she is convincing me to allow us to trade places. "It's what you have always done: paint a lie. This is just a more permanent solution."

The dim overhead lights flicker, producing a dance with the shadows. When the flickering halts, it feels like the walls inched closer to us.

Zander glances at Luna, but I've pieced the puzzle together. "How long till Evander hacks his way inside here," I question.

She looks at the door, "It's debatable, but it will be a fun challenge for him." I snort in frustration.

"You should have predicted this," Luna adds. There is nothing malicious in her voice, just blunt honesty. "You said it yourself: the games will never stop."

"I thought I could stop them." I seethe more to myself.

"No, that's a lie you told yourself to give yourself hope, to wipe away the subconscious part of your mind that wanted to remain the hero," she asserts. Her chin dips as she adds, "You can't stop the games, but you can escape. You will, with your Horseman."

My heart beats in a rhythm of uncertainty.

"What are you thinking about?" Luna's voice, like a haunting melody, interrupts the silence.

"If this is another trick?" I respond. I look towards Zander, but his stony face is a mirror of Luna's.

"I never tricked you," she assures; her voice resembles a comforting, cool, calm, and collected melody. A stark contrast to the dissonant chords of my current situation.

"You forced me to be a villain," My hand grasps the fabric covering my heart. I wish I could cut open my chest and show her my heart, reveal to her how the chambers have blacken and formed a thick shield that protects it but also hinders it from beating as freely as it once did. "You told me to deceive those we loved to save them," I accuse her.

"I never forced you." Her fingers curl around the needle.

"I led you to the start of a path, and you walked down it. You always had a choice," She explains, then raises her hand, fingers still curled around the needle. "Here is another choice." She taunts me. She wants me to take it, to uncurl her fingers, so I know it was my choice.

Is this her way of fixing it all, or inside that needle, does another labyrinth of games and lies wait for me to fall into its trap?

I search Luna's eyes for any sign of remorse or sincerity, but the shadows play tricks, revealing nothing.

I blink rapidly, then grab my hair, trying to tug at the roots, but I forget the gun is in my hand until it bangs against the side of my head.

She did it; she played god. She created deep fakes of events, coded into the nanobytes, and wants to insert them into my mind. It is, as she said, an escape.

"What about Wes?" I whisper. What about the memories of the man who is trying to breach that door?

"I considered the details," she scoffs as if offended. "The memories you have of him won't be altered, just the things I knew would haunt you. The deaths of Astrid, Subject 52, Marcus, oh, and Ethan. Memories are like a filing cabinet; I programmed the nanobytes to only insert themselves at certain times when the event occurred."

I lock eyes with her. It's like looking at the most evil version of myself. But even villains feel that's why they do what they do. In Luna's mind, she thinks this is a peace offering.

It is, in a twisted fucked up way. It's a cure many would take without a second thought.

"What about this moment? Did you create a fake to replace this?"

She rolls her eyes, "Yes. I know you. If you knew memories were replaced, you'd start digging as Zander did. You will think you walked out that door and never glanced over your shoulder."

Her choice of words makes me pause, "Why would you want me not to look back at you?"

"Because it's time for you to move on, Sol. Sometimes, if you love someone, you have to set them free. You'll always be my sister but must live your own life. Stop worrying about me."

"This is wrong. It's what Astrid would do."

She swallows, "I'm giving you a choice. She never gave me an option. I'm not her." She seethes. "That's why this is the only injection I created. Zander is fixed; you can be too. Then this science," She shakes the needle, "will be erased."

That makes me laugh. I know a lie when it's spoken. "Until someone else creates it again." Maybe she did delete the way to make this drug, but she could easily create it again.

"We will have a team in place to stop that." She glances at the door as she grows impatient.

I look at Zander. His behavior hasn't been erratic; as a matter of fact, he's been a different person. He no longer looks at me like he wants to kill me. "Did you regain your memories or forget what happened?" I ask. Some of my shock is subsiding; my mind races with questions and a need to escape.

"I got them back." He replies. I knew he would say that. I see the grief in his hazel eyes, eyes he changed so they didn't resemble the woman who tried to kill him. The eyes of a monster.

My eyes.

You see, the best way to survive is to learn from your mistakes if you are lucky enough to survive them in the first round. Zander made a wise choice; he's just starting to enter the games that revolve around the science.

I'm an old player. What decision will I make?

"Why?" I challenge him. I want to hear it.

"It was better to know the truth to prevent the past from repeating. But you're not going to be a part of this anymore, Sol. This is your ticket to actual freedom. You'll know what happened just without the details."

Details.

That's what art is about: details that shout at you, tucked away or hidden.

Can I still be an artist without having all the details of my past?

Luna thinks this will help me move on; it's like painting over a canvas instead of throwing it out and starting over. You can simply paint something new over it or alter the image. It sounds so simple. Peaceful.

Maybe it is.

I won't see any more blood, no details; I'll just have the facts that that person is dead.

I glance at the gun in my hand and then toss it on the floor; it slides until it hits the door. I don't need a weapon. Luna is right; that needle isn't a weapon; she meant it as a cure. "I made my decision."

Chapter 46

Gabriel

One week later.

Luna is back in her cell, but Evander gave me the key this time. I'm in charge, and she is caged.

I should be happy, but this is Luna, after all, she knew this would happen. Why does she want it to play out like this?

We kept her in solitary confinement for an entire week. It was a way to punish her after the stunt she pulled. We separated her from all her puppets. We made Sol's old room into another cell. Zander is locked inside there.

The only positive to their stunt is that everyone questions them and sides with me, giving me more power, which must be what Luna wanted.

It's making my win less sweet. I run my tongue over my teeth as if I can swipe away the sour taste.

She lounges on the small bed with a book in hand. She looks so relaxed, like a Greek goddess, as if this is her temple and we are mere mortals coming to visit her. Her long legs are stretched out and crossed over one another. They used to wrap around me. Her swan-like neck is slightly tilted. I used to kiss that neck and whisper my love into her ear. Her long hair hangs loose. I used to wrap it around my fist like she was a wild creature I was taming when we fucked.

She's the monster I love and the beast I loathe. The wolf and the sheep. You see, wolves can bite or protect. It just depends on which mood they are in. Sheep only do one thing.

They lead.

They will lead you right off a cliff if you aren't looking. It is poetic since Luna led me to believe she jumped off a cliff.

I hear her sigh. "You can't keep me in here forever," she barks. I step out of the shadows and into the light. I hated this bunker, but now it doesn't seem so bad. It's one giant cage, a maze I can roam free in. Luna can't.

"The key in my hand tells me I can," I challenge. I'm happy she is back to being her again. The broken woman slipping in and out of madness was no fun to play with.

She chuckles and sets the book down. It's a book her father wrote on genetics. I shake my head; Evander must have snuck it into her. "Well, the knowledge in my head tells me," she stands from the bed, walks to the fence wall, and pushes her fingers through the holes. "You can't. You still haven't figured it all out, baby. I said we would play alongside each other, not against one another."

"The science is in my hands," I grin. "Evander, trust me more after what you pulled, you're in a cage. Nothing is left to figure out except what I will do with you." I come closer to the cage and look down at her. The darkness from my shadows doesn't make her shrink; instead, she gloats like a rare flower that blooms at night.

"Manus Dei, the science, me," she runs her hands down the curves of her body, "it was all the prize. The crown, if you will. But that's not always what the game is about." She's baiting me, leading me somewhere. Sometimes, it's best not to fight the current; let it pull you off course, and then once it settles, you start to fight.

"What is it about?" I ask. Reaching up, I touch her fingers and trap them with my own. I hate that the feel of her flesh against mine makes me want to burn down the world for her.

"The little people." She replies. "The individuals who may or may not join our kingdom. We won, but we need an army."

I want to laugh, but I mask my feelings. She still thinks she can sway us all. "You will have no option regarding Manus Dei's future." Now, I smile and push my body against the cage. She hates that name. I was sure it would be the first thing she voted to change. Now I think I'll keep it.

"Let me do you a favor and fill you in. You're not on the new council anymore. It's Evander, Kane, Cody, and me. You offering Sol freedom cost you yours. I hope it was worth it." The new council will now vote on the rebuilding and future of Manus Dei. If we can't agree, we will have Wes cast a vote to break it. This keeps Wes involved enough to keep his father happy but distant enough to keep Sol sane.

She tries to hide her anger, but I sense it coming off her in waves. "It was always an outcome I considered."

"Whatever army you thought you were manipulating and building is now useless." I look around the cell, "Much like you. You're useless to me now."

"If I'm useless, then why are you here?" She sardonically beams. "This is our game, baby; we hate to love each other, but," she presses her lips to the fence wall, "we love to hate each other."

I want to rip open the cage door, fuck her, and strangle her.

I step back. That's what she wants. She wants me to open that door. I begin to turn. "Why waste the energy to make an army when you could just take one?" She shouts.

That bitch is so clever. She could trick the devil into giving up hell.

I stop walking, which means she won.

"Did you ponder all the angles?" She taunts. "You know why I disappeared, but you never asked me where I went."

I turn slowly; trying to remain in control with each pivot. "Evander didn't know either, just in case you plan to run to him." She teases, "You didn't think I was laying low and hiding, did you?"

That was an option I considered. That and she was pulling the strings of her puppets.

She steps back, strolling away with an added sway of her lovely hips, goes to her bed, and sits down. Throwing her legs up, she goes back to her relaxed state. "Oh, baby, grief did a number on you." She shakes her head well, eyeing me before she glances away disappointedly.

She picks up the book and looks long at the cover. "If you were smart, a genius, and knew your time was coming to a close, you knew that your deeds created an army marching on your front door. What would you do?" She taps the bottom of the cover. My eyes glance to where her fingers remain, pointing at her father's name.

"What would you do, baby?" She repeats. "What would a coward do?"

I feel my heart sink into a slow rhythm so all my energy can go toward thinking and plotting.

She opens the cover and turns the first page. "You'd make a backup. That's what a coward does. He wants to protect his skin with an illusion."

That's it. In a flash, I'm at the door, key in hand. I swing the gate open and charge her. My hands are around her neck, in an instant, my body pressing against her, trapping her on the bed.

She exhaled like a child just finishing a cupcake they lusted over. Her hands reach up not towards mine, which grip her neck, but rather to my hips.

"It's not what you are thinking. You and I are not cowards."

I snort, "Are you so sure? You did use Sol and Klara as your illusion."

"I didn't create them. I used them as my strength. You would have done the same."

I squeeze her neck slightly. All the blood rushes towards my cock. This was never me. Sure, we fucked like animals sometimes. We just lost control, but I was never rough. I tried to show Luna a different side. Attempted to teach her that love didn't have to be painful.

What a waste.

"Let me explain," she purrs. However, the following words aren't in English, French, or German—languages I knew she could speak. Instead, she speaks in Japanese, a language I'm unfamiliar with. The confusion is evident, knitting my brows as I struggle to comprehend.

That's what she wanted. She's telling me that though I control her air supply, she still has the upper hand.

"I said," she states, now speaking in English. "Let me Explain. I indeed hated my father, but I also respected him. The question is, which man did I hate and which did I respect?" She smiles, resembling God. Like a powerful being that allowed the devil control of the earth, during that time, the devil started to believe he was just as powerful, but then God laughed and cast him into the depths of hell, the kingdom of his creation. It's the ultimate trick, making your prey think they have a chance. I've been her prey all along.

My fingers clamp harder, causing her pale, smooth skin to flush a beautiful shade of red. "Are you saying Dorian cloned himself?" I question.

She manages to grin as her face turns more cranberry. I have to release her neck if I want answers. Finger by finger, I allow her more air.

She glides her hands up into my hair and massages my scalp. "Wouldn't you just love to know?" She giggles, and then she slams her lips to mind.

Chapters 47

Kane

Three months later.

I don't like Berlin; the city doesn't appreciate a custom-made suit like the Parisians or Italians do, but this is where she hides.

She's moved around a lot and tried New York and San Francisco. Settle was the worst; if I saw another person with a poorly knitted beanie on their unwashed, oily head, I might have thrown her over my shoulder and dragged her away. A more caveman approach like my brothers often take.

Unlike my brothers, who have obsessions of their own, I didn't always stalk her. I've tried to keep my distance. I'm not a good man. I'm a Horseman. But attraction makes the mind do funny things; it causes your heart to beat an off-kilter tune that periodically sounds so lovely. That's why I'm here outside a second-hand book store in Berlin that she often visits when she is in town.

I'm not the only one who has tried to fight this chemistry. It's like we both know that we're strong and stable alone, but together, we're nuclear; we can be immensely powerful but deadly destructive.

She knows I'm not good; she knows many of the dirty details. She knew I loved her chestnut hair, so she dyed it pink; she knew I loved to watch her creamy skin blush under my touch, so she covered practically every inch of her body in a Lumenis tattoo. She knew every detail I loved about her and tried to change it. It was her way of running without physically doing so.

She couldn't run. Everyone who was a member of Manus Dei was watched and guarded. She was chained to the society even more tightly than I was.

Not anymore. She helped us take control, thinking it was her ticket to freedom.

The grin that stretches over my face reaches ear to ear. How wrong she was.

I push open the bookstore door, and a quaint bell rings overhead. The nostalgia is cute, but it only lasts momentarily. Once I'm fully inside, the scent hits me first. Stuffy, moldy paper. Hundreds of books have been passed from one germ-infested hand to another. A second-hand books store, otherwise known as my hell.

A cheap air freshener can go a long way, but the owner is either daft and has no sense of smell, or they want to drive customers away by the allergy-inducing aroma.

I tug at the collar of my shirt but then think better and press the material back to my skin. I don't want the dust circulating in the air to cover any more of me than it has to.

It's this smell she loves. I can't understand it, but now I crave it.

Yes, she has driven me to the edges of insanity. I've filled my safe houses with old books so the rooms can have the aroma she loves. That's how committed to her I am.

When I take a step, the old floor creeks from my weight. Another step, another creek mixed with the scent; you'd think this was a haunted house, not a business trying to attract customers.

There is a bookstore in Paris that I do enjoy. It looks like a carved-out room from Versailles. The details and care made me feel relaxed like I could sit down and read a book without having a flesh-eating tick roam off the armchair and onto my flesh.

I'd like to take her there, but if she knew I liked it, she would automatically hate it.

As I proceed deeper to the back, the aisle becomes so overstocked it looks like a house of cards waiting for one deep exhale to blow it down.

A flash of pink hair catches my eye; blood rushes to my cock. Her back is turned towards me, she's holding a book up so high, with such a keen interest that it angers me.

She can't be that foolish not to be aware of her surroundings.

The Horseman took over Manus Dei, but that doesn't means those scorned have been quelled. We have a long road ahead of us that she needs to be wary of. One wrong turn, one pothole could take her from me.

I step closer. She must sense my presence. Yeah, she does. Her fingers grab the book tighter, making the old pages crinkle under the pressure. I take another step.

It's her fault she captured my attention and then chose not to release me.

It's true; I'm addicted to her push, which only makes me claw my way back closer to her.

"Is it that good?" I ask. I'd read the title, but the leather is so cracked that it makes the letters look more like a jumble of dots than actual words.

"It is, so if you don't mind, buzz off." She turns her shoulder, blocking me from seeing her face.

Oh, angel...that was the wrong move. You just poked my demon, and he loves to claim the wings of angels.

The good thing about the old second-hand bookstore is its abandoned nature. It's the perfect setting for me to pounce. I'm quite sure I could take her right here against the bookshelf, spread her legs open, and shove myself so deep inside of her. The only thing stopping me is the poor construction of the shelves. They would topple around us. She might like to be buried under books, but not me.

I strike; as soon as my hand grasps her shoulder, my cock tests the fine stitching of my trouser. I'm so painfully hard; It feels like my cock will burst through the seams. Why does she have this affect on me?

I spin her around and cage her between the shelf and my body.

She looks angry, which only makes her look so adorable. Her pert nose jerks up; her full lips are covered with pink gloss pressed into an even line, and her little round cheeks blush red.

"I'm reading." She hisses. She tries to hit me over the head with the book, but I dodge it. I've spent my life dodging hits.

"And I'm talking to you." I flash a sarcastic grin.

"It's done." She tries to shove me away. I push my body harder against her. I can tell by the widening of her eyes she feels my erection, and I bet if I slipped my hand under her panties, she would be soaking wet for me.

"I'm free from them." She mutters, but I hear the lust in her tone, feel it when she tries to shove her greedy hips against my arousal.

"Oh, angel," I chuckle. I twist a lock of her pink hair around my index finger. It's so short and shiny that it slips free, causing me to catch and twist it repeatedly. "Just because you're no longer 'The Historian' doesn't mean you're free." Her next inhale is sharp. I press a kiss on her lips, tasting her sticky gloss. Her heart is beating so loudly I can hear each thump. "You're mine."

Chapter 48

Evander

Some people say that hope is like a cancer. It spreads and multiplies, making you sick until it takes over your body. It corrupts your thoughts, not allowing you to see the honest picture or the possible outcomes. It makes you terminally ill once it claims your mind.

On the other hand, some people might say that hope is like a cure. It heals all the doubts that make you sick.

I've gambled everything on hope—hope that one day Klara could love me, hope that one day I could trust her, hope that I could take a woman who was abused and teach her that love comes in many forms. None of those forms should be destructive; none should tear down a person.

You might wonder how I could help someone like Luna if I believed all this. Many would say Luna's love was just that— destructive. It wasn't; it just was unconventional. Luna loves as easily as she hates. She loved Sol so much that she wanted her to survive without being her constant shadow. Now Sol will. Luna gave her a new shadow, my brother Wes, but she also taught Sol how to take what she wanted. Sol always wanted; she dreamed but never took. When Luna pulled the stunt that trapped me and my brothers on the other side of the vault, well, that's when Sol learned her final lesson. She took what she truly wanted. She felt no guilt. That gave her the confidence to survive with her actions.

Luna and Gabriel's love, now that's a fucking dark book, but it's an interesting read. Not all of us are content to work nine to five, come home, eat dinner, and chat with our partner before we go to bed and press repeat.

Gabriel's need to protect Luna blinded him. He focused solely on her and the challenges before them. He should have looked behind. Not all storms are on the horizon; some are racing, inching closer and closer to our heels.

That's why I helped Luna. We didn't have a normal childhood. Sometimes, love comes by toughening skin. Making it thicker so others can penetrate it and tear it apart.

I remember the first day I met Luna in the lab. I know a dangerous person even when they are hiding in the form of a child. Luna was deadly.

Klara wasn't.

Astrid just tore and tore; she never rebuilt Klara's confidence the way Dorian did to Luna.

When Luna decided to help Klara, purposely failing a test so she and Klara could tie and Klara would not be punished, I vowed to help her. No matter the cost.

Along the way, I fell in love with Klara. I wanted to save and protect the broken girl I could not reach. I knew if Luna could just teach Klara how to survive, then one day, I would be able to reach Klara.

That day has come. Klara has received the downgrade, and soon, she will wake up.

I never wanted to destroy aspects of Klara, not even the side of her that seeks revenge by killing. Change creates resistance. I don't want any aspect of her to resist me; therefore, I don't want to change her ways. I want to simply re-navigate them. I want to take her off the highway of destruction and put her on the safe road which leads to me. Give her different outlets to release her inner demons.

I will.

It won't be easy, and that's what makes it fun. Just like my name states, I'm Famine. I have to teach Klara what love and trust are. I need to make her starving, salivating for it. Then, and only then, will I be able to tame the beautiful monster that she is.

Epilogue

Sol

Seven years later.

I edge closer to my canvas as I try to add small details to my painting, but my protruding stomach pushes against it. This happens all the time; I forget how big my belly is. This causes Wes to hover over me constantly; his hands have been outstretched for seven months, acting as pads if my stomach gently bumps into anything.

"Mom!" Elara, our daughter, screams, "Mom! Tell Elon to leave me alone."

I grin as I rub my stomach. I'm pregnant with our third child. Our first pregnancy was twins, but we broke the cycle; we had a boy and a girl. I'm not sure what we will have this time. We know it's only one baby, but we wanted to keep it a secret. I haven't thought of a name yet, either.

Names were important to my father; he named me Sol after the sun and Luna after the moon. We were meant to counterbalance one another, a good versus evil, light and darkness fueling motivation. Without both the sun and the moon, humanity would fail. I suppose my father thought that without his high advancement in science and creations like Luna and myself, mankind would fail. Maybe he was right. It's been years later, and the world has vastly changed; it will always change. Man is never satisfied. We always want change, and we get it.

End My Games

Luna would say it's silly, but I wanted to give my twins names that also had a deep meaning. Elara means hope, and Elon means freedom. You can't have freedom without constant hope. Enemies will always linger in the shadows to take your freedom away. It's an endless battle that needs hope as fuel. After everything I went through and did, I needed constant hope and freedom. I have both in numerous ways now.

"Hey, leave your mom alone." Wes shouts. His office is next to mine. We live in the home he built for us; it's a secluded escape on a private mountain peak in Snowmass. It's not a far drive from Hazel's art gallery, which is always filled with my art. Just like Wes said, this home is my castle. I always feared a cage, but he's made these walls my refuge. Sometimes, I never want to leave. Other times, I have to.

Then there are the times Wes and I travel for the kids; I want them to see the world and have a childhood I never had. Wade has been a fantastic uncle to our children; he's so protective of Elara, our little girl. Wes gives our son sparring lessons; he tells him he has to protect his sister, but Wade sneaks Elara into the backyard and teaches her how to defend herself. The first time I watched him teach her, I cried; I knew what he was doing. It's too hard for Wes to admit that one day, his little girl will be an adult; he always sees her as a child. Wade knows better; thus, the lessons so she can keep herself and her brother safe. Twins rely on one another; if one is weak, it makes the other suffer.

I put down my paintbrush, wash my hands, and go check on the kids. When I exit, they are fighting over a tablet. "If you break that, I'm not buying you a new one." I threaten.

"You don't have to. I know how to build one myself." Elon quips with a sassy grin as he flicks his head to move his dark brown hair out of his green eyes. Elara and Elon look more like their father, with dark hair, green eyes, and, of course, strong will. I always kept my intentions hidden, but Elara and Elon make themselves known.

"Hey, you don't talk to your mom like that. You might be able to build a tablet, but I have to buy the parts." Wes rounds the corner. He's trying to act stern, but when his eyes see me then look down at my belly, he grins.

"Uncle Wade gave me a thousand bucks!" Elon mocks.

"He what!" Wes snaps.

Elon nods, "He told me if I punched Deacon, he'd give me a thousand bucks."

"Why?" I gasp. I glance at Wes silently, telling him to have a word with his older brother. I always thought we had to worry about Kane, but it seems Wade is the worst.

"Because Deacon said he liked Elara and wanted to marry her one day." Elon hisses as he sticks out his tongue.

Wes scratches his head then replies, "A thousand bucks well earned then. Keep Deacon away from your sister."

I elbow him, "Don't teach him that." I whisper.

He ignores me, places a hand on my belly, and kisses me.

"Ugh!" Elon moans

"Yuck!" Elara cries.

"How's my little mouse?" Wes purrs in my ear. His fingers flex on my stomach.

"Better now." I grin as I push up on my toes and kiss him back.

"Stop! It's so gross!" Elara stomps her foot, which makes her hands slip from the tablet. Elon strikes, grabs it and snickers. "Loser"

"Don't call your sister that." I warn.

"Hey, give it back. Mom tell him to give it back. He already changed his eye color today. I want to change mine."

I sigh, feeling too tired to stop this argument. This is the world we live in. Genetic modifications are now as easy as pushing a button on a tablet. Of course, many modifications are cosmetic. The kids love to change their eye colors. That's all we allow them for now, but we won't keep them in the dark. This is our world, and learning how to read the shadows is the only way to evolve.

All that remains of Manus Dei's worth is the science; all their principles have been long erased along with their name. Manus Dei meant the hand of God, but men abused God's hand, so now they must deal with Judices Mali. It's Latin for judges of evil. Only evil can judge evil, and the Horseman have been ruthless leaders against those who try to steal, control or manipulate the science they share with the world.

My other family did as they promised. They offered the science to everyone, saving millions of lives. The science is regulated and restricted. Of course, cosmetic changes are not as strict. They don't worry about changing eye color or hair pigment; they fear those who try to recode nanobytes into a biological weapon.

Medical modifications require a permit; treatments are given only by their selected doctors. Every nanobyte in circulation can be switched off if you abused it. Of course, there are the fools that try.

Unlike Manus Dei, Judices Mali isn't hiding in the shadows; they are upfront and honest with the world. That doesn't make them weak. It's made them stronger. They are now a beloved and praised face; millions have rallied around them and the positive impacts they have gifted to the world. It's a fragile line they have to walk, giving and control without thinking they have the power of a god.

***

I go to our bedroom; my feet ache, and my ankles are slightly swollen. I lay down and swing my legs up. My stomach is so heavy that I have to sleep on my side now to keep the weight off my chest. I spot the portrait hanging above our fireplace.

Years ago, I had four paintings when I had my first solo show in Hazel's gallery. One, however, was purchased before the show. It was the only portrait I painted of myself. I questioned Death if he bought it, but he cleverly evaded my question.

It wasn't Death, it Wes who bought it. Yes there are the same person but at the time I treated them as different men. He bought it and hung it in the house he wanted me to make our home. It's remained right where he first placed it, in our bedroom above the fireplace.

I don't even recognize the girl who that painting was of. I'm happy he bought it; those small details keep the past intact. I'm not her anymore; I've grown. Evolved.

Luna once offered me a cure. Why take a cure if you're not sick?

I remember that day I grabbed the needle and crushed it under my shoe.

Once, I was an ignorant girl who wanted to escape. I wanted so many things but I was too scared to chase them.

Luna offered me a chance to escape, a way to be free and ignorant. I probably would have taken that injection at one point in my life.

I never would now.

Yes, I'm haunted by nightmares. I don't often use red paint because it reminds me too much of the bloodshed.

Luna thought of so many details. She plotted so far ahead, but she failed to see that I didn't need the injection. I had a Horseman. I chose him. I took what I wanted.

Death did exactly as his name proclaimed. He killed and vanquished all the monsters that tried to plague my mind.

I'm the freest I'll ever be, locked in a cage of protection with the monster I love. Monsters can be intimidating, but once you tame them, they willfully use their strength to keep you safe. They will go to exceeding lengths to see you happy and watch you thrive. That's exactly what my monster has done; he's released me into his habitat. I'm the happiest I've ever been, but also the wisest. I can see all the shades of darkness and all the blinding light.

I won't change that for one moment of ignorance. You have to take the bad with the good, the hero and villain; it's what makes the scale of judgment. You can't measure one without the other.

I've measured it all and accepted the yoke filled with good and bad memories. I just have to dwell on the positives because watering a negative memory causes sickness to spread.

I cured the sickness from my mind. I have what I always wanted. Freedom, a family, and a sense of normalcy. I have what I always needed, a Horseman who can stop my mind from wondering and thinking about the science.

Life with Wes is like hitting pause and never undoing it.

He rounds the corner of our bedroom. He's taken over bedtime duty with the kids so I have a few extra minutes to rest my feet. "They're asleep. Elara started crying when Elon wouldn't give the tablet back to her. You know he can't stand to see her cry. She's got him wrapped around her finger. She asked him to change his to pink and he did." Wes chuckles.

He comes to my bedside and sits down. "You look so happy." He bends down and kisses me, "You better have been thinking about me and how I was going to make you moan tonight." He purrs. He kicks off his shoes, then peels off his clothes. He's still my strong, deadly Horseman, time only seems to make him more formidable.

He slips into bed spooning me, and starts to unbutton my flannel pajamas. I can feel the warmth of his delicious body as it starts to chase away my chill. "What were you thinking about. Tell me so I can bring your fantasies to life."

"I was thinking about our future." I grin as my hand comes to rest on my stomach.

"I'll put another baby in your belly once you pop out this one." He purrs a deep husky sound. "I'll show you what your future looks like. How ever night, the rest of your life, will be spent." His hand cups my breast, kneading my nipple between his thumb and index finger. His other hand glides down my body leaving a wanting need in their wake. His hand parts my folds and begins to ready my body for him. Then he positions our bodies closer, angling my legs so he can push deep inside of me.

"You're mine, little mouse. Always and forever."

Hey, hold on!

Don't you even think about closing the book yet! Seriously, you don't want to risk upsetting an author. You never know when she might just immortalize you as a character in her next tale. Just saying (wink, wink).

Your reviews are invaluable to indie authors. Whether it's a few words or a star rating, your honest feedback is greatly appreciated. If you'd like, feel free to tag me in your review on Instagram or TikTok—I'd be thrilled to share your thoughts on my pages!

Thank you for taking the time to read my books.

Against Fate

For those of you seeking an escape into the world of fantasy, I've got the perfect book for you. It was an honor when bestselling author Ashley C. Harris roped me into co-authoring a book with her. If you're into faes, shifters, vampires, dragons, hybrids, and a bunch more, our first book, 'Against Fate,' is about to cast a spell on you. It's a coming-of-age fantasy romance filled with young adult drama, rejected mates, magic, sizzling hot shifters, and mysterious fae.

A.G. Harris & Ashley C. Harris

A.G. Harris

Against Fate

Rejected Mates of Magic Borne

"I can help you bring out your inner wolf," the mage whispered into my ear, but she never mentioned the price....

Most wolf shifters my age want two things... to find their fated mates and take a high place amongst their pack. But I couldn't even get close to those goals until I shifted.

That's right, I'm a half-shifter, half-human hybrid, living amongst the strongest wolf pack in all of Magic Borne. Unfortunately, if my inner wolf doesn't surface, I could lose my life.

Only the strongest can survive in pack Sköll, and Carter is the epitome of strength and power. He's also the son of the most prejudiced alpha in my world. I'm not exaggerating... Carter's father believes hybrids shouldn't be allowed to exist, which means the two of us should stay away from each other... but that doesn't seem to be happening.

Everywhere I turn, Carter is there, tempting me to either punch him or kiss him. My plan is to ignore his presence. I need to seek out the magic that can awaken my wolf by any means necessary. Even if that means venturing into the forbidden, exhilarating parts of Magic Borne and rejecting everything I thought I knew.

Against Fate is the first of a heart-pounding, enchanting story.

Chapter 1

ADAIRA

If only I were a mage. I'd open a portal up right now to swallow me from the fate that loomed upon my future. Six foot four and a solid wall of wolf shifter muscle. *In theory, that sounds perfect, a shifter with power and a title, drool-worthy looks that make women stop in their tracks. Sign me up!*

That isn't the fate I was dealt.

Nope.

With each inhale, his shoulders grew wider and curved forward, casting a shadow-like cage that crept closer until it encased and trapped me. It made my ribs constrict with each breath I took. He loved to lure his prey like all shifters, and I was the perfect little bunny cornered by the big bad wolf. I studied him closer; his hair was slightly longer now, the tips of my fingers tingled as they itched to feel the silken strands.

Damn him and his looks! Could fate have lowered the playing field and made him be a bit less panty-dropping handsome?

As I looked back into his eyes, I could see the conflict that swirled within them. They were always filled with mixed emotions when he looked at me. He was always at war mentally when I was nearby. Lately, he looked more stressed, like the weight of Magic Borne was bearing down upon his broad shoulders. He seemed only able to hold the pressure for so long until he snapped.

And snapped he did. I was what tipped him over the edge. I was his relief as well as his misery. I was the victim of his pleasure and pain caught in the cacophony, unable to escape. I have to admit that during times I didn't want to escape. These encounters became more frequent. Each time leaving me more and more confused. I should push him away. *Yeah, right, Adaira, like you could literally refuse him or push away an alpha shifter.*

I was never able to entirely fight him. There was something intangible that halted me from doing so. Maybe it was the flood of hormones when he came close. The perfect picture of the ideal male. He was strong, sinfully stunning, and had a title, money, and power, but he also had his dark side. *So yeah, he was what every girl wanted, right?* The bad boy who taunted us, cornered us like his plaything, and kissed away the pain with pleasure. That's not what I told myself I wanted... *Yet my reactions weren't right, and why wasn't I able to be callous and cunning back?*

No magical portal was opening up to save me, and as my feet tried to take another step back, my heels hit the brick wall of the dark alleyway. My hands flattened against the old brick. The hardness of the stone was nothing compared to the indifference he had shown me at times. The crisp cold air didn't help to dull my senses. Instead, it made everything feel more alive and more menacing. His nostrils flared while my skin blanched with goosebumps.

He could sense that as he visually stripped me bare of my clothing. Like a vampire on the warpath he drank me in. Roaming from my lips which were parted because, what can I say, I felt parched and the only thing to quench my thirst would be his lips. I unconsciously licked them, not the smartest thing in the moment. The reaction taunted him as a growl escaped, a growl that was pure wolf. No trait of his human remained. When his eyes dipped lower and lingered on my chest, I felt the magic swarm in my core, and somehow I know he felt it too because he took the final step closer. Any space between us had completely disappeared.

I forced myself to close my eyes. When he was this close, it was hard to think about anything other than him. Deep down, my body was yearning for everything he was, as my mind was shouting at me to wake the heck up and defend myself. I felt like I was standing at the base of a camp, watching an avalanche cascade right towards me. The situation was bad, ok scratch that. It was possibly unrecoverable. One swipe from his wolf, and I'd be dead.

Yet he always seemed to be trying to keep me safe as the warmth of his finger under my chin caused me to gasp. Such a contrast to the cold night air. He angled my face up to look at him. My blue eyes glanced away, but no escape had become evident to me. Even if I could slip under his arms that were caging me in I'd never make it more than one or two steps. *Hope was a good friend to have, but she could also be a backstabbing bitch when she failed.*

I tried to still my breath as I inhaled. Shifters loved fear. It egged on their animal for a fun hunt. There was no running from an alpha shifter, so I needed to fake my confidence as best I could. I had been faking things for a long time now, so I slipped on the mask and tried to cool my nerves.

His human hazel eyes switched to his wolf irises as they glowed with the hint of his magic. *That isn't good!* Just then, his magic started to leave his hands as his arm erupted with fur before I could even blink. *His wolf is too close to the surface!* The hazel now looked more like burnt gold that was ready to solidify on anything it glanced upon.

Unfortunately that's me. The prey.

His right hand slowly slid down from my chin to my neck as if he was trying to embed the feeling of my skin onto his fingertips. Slowly he settled his hand by the back of my head, where the gentleness evaporated, and his grip tightened. Some shifters preferred humans because they were so fragile. It gave their animal more of a sense of a need to protect what they claimed to be theirs.

I hated being so breakable. I felt like a doll that was tossed around. It was that feeling that forced me to take matters into my own hands. That was why I ended up here in the middle of the city, where I met with a dark mage from time to time. Even though I was told not to. Every decision has consequences, and as I tried to take fate into my own hands, I only hoped for a positive outcome.

My life was literally in his claws. Any shifter could kill someone like me in a blink of an eye. I tried to force down a gulp. "I... I'm tired...." I murmured as I licked my lips, "Of your games." My mind was filled with questions and anger towards him and myself because of how I reacted in the past when he trapped me with his kisses. "I'm not yours, and these—"

His growl caused my mouth to snap shut. It would have cleared a crowd of people if any had been nearby. "You want me to stop?" He leaned closer and smelled my hair. "Then leave Lykos." It was always the same request. Well, he wasn't requesting it, he was demanding it, but as much as he demanded it, he allowed me to stay. He was torturing himself too. If he wanted me gone so bad, he had the power to do so. Why was he waiting on me to make a move?

Knowing I had some kind of power over him, a power that stopped him from banishing me, caused me to gamble with my life. A bet I was willing to wager now. My weight shifted onto my toes yearning for his warmth. As my body pressed closer to his, the last few inches between predator and prey started to vanish. He sensed the shift of my weight, allowing it for a mere few seconds before his hand gripped me tighter. Then the control shifted as he pushed me back into the brick wall and pressed his body more intensely to mine.

I'd need a long cold shower.

His golden eyes darkened even more as if to tell me I would never escape him. "I should put an end to this. You're a distraction." His voice thick with fieriness sent chills down my spine, chills his wolf felt as he licked his lips.

"So do it." I hissed. I know I was poking the wolf. Actually, it was more like a strong kick I delivered to his hind legs. A smile came to my lips as I taunted him. It was a stupid gamble but one I chose to make. Clouds of blue magic started to fill the air as they fogged my vision. The blue was ethereal, like the streaks of blue haze that filled the night sky some nights.

"You're a distraction. One that doesn't listen to a single warning I give you." He pushed his chest against mine, and I knew he could feel my body's reaction to him. Each inhale of my breath was now pressed against his until our breathing became each other's air supply. The tension between us was palpable. It was only a matter of time before an explosion occurred.

His head lowered closer to mine. I closed my eyes, trying to push away what my body wanted. "Why can't you just listen?" With a slight change in the angle of his hand, my face was forced to look at him directly. To make matters worse, my eyes could not resist the pull from his as they snapped open and looked directly into his wolf's eyes.

His thumb grazed my bottom lip, "Just once." He whispered more to himself than to me. It was something he told himself every time, and I knew what was coming next. Maybe he didn't understand the definition of *once*. I should tell him the meaning when he finished.

But then you'll never feel his lips again, Adaira.

His lips crashed down against mine, and then the alleyway faded, and all I could feel was him. His warmth, touch, and scent that smelt of fresh pine after a rain shower. The feeling of his lips against mine as they took control was all my mind could focus on. He always put me under a spell when he kissed me. The way he forced the kiss was like a fight of fire and ice. Passion and hate, melting and freezing each other until ultimately each would be defeated and neither would remain.

For ice could suffocate the fire, and fire could melt ice. There was no chance of surviving for either one of us.

* * *

<u>Two Years Earlier</u>

Glossy white paint coated my fingers as I raised my hand and smeared the paint in a straight line down the canvas. *Finger painting wasn't just for kids, folks.* I needed my art to be tangible. I needed to feel it on the tips of my fingers. Line after line appeared on the canvas. Trees that looked liked the bases were carved of white ivory that littered the landscape mimicking the scene I dreamt of. Thick and haunting, perfectly smooth tree trunks that were unlike the metal buildings in the city I lived in.

I remember how the trees felt in the dream. I could still feel the silky smoothness on my fingers. It was unlike anything I had ever felt before. Behind the rows of white trees was a dark blue sky for contrast, creating a haunting image overall, just like my dream. Grabbing the paintbrush, I thinned down the grey paint, then I started to add the darkness that would consume the pure white trees. The darkness wasn't magic. It was something else, something darker. Like chaos spreading without an end destination, a great ocean storm was something that couldn't be destroyed or stopped, no matter what type of magic a person has in this world.

"You dreamed of this place again." A deep voice startled me from the trance I was in. Setting down my brush, I grabbed a cloth to remove some of the paint from my fingers. A wisp of my red hair broke free from my low bun as I turned to face him.

"It's nothing," I whispered. Liam was a shifter and able to hear me even when I wanted others not to. "Just a silly dream." I smiled at my best friend. His tall muscled body that fit the profile of a shifter male was leaning against the door frame. *I wonder how long he has been watching me.*

The downside of me being a magic-less hybrid, half shifter and half-human, was that I got the short end of the stick. I couldn't shift, and even smaller shifter abilities like accelerated healing, heighten hearing, amongst other badass magic, I couldn't tap into.

Liam's left eye twitched almost too fast for me to catch. This was his signal when he was concerned. I could read him like a book as he could me. *We are all each other has, a pack of two living in one of the most feared packs in Volkovia, the kingdom ruled by shifters.* We'd been together since we were babies who were tossed aside into the foster care home in Lykos City. *Liam had always watched my back, and I...well, I'd like to say I watched his, but a useless hybrid watching a shifter is as comical as it is impractical.*

But hey, it's the thought that counts, right?

After cleaning up, I grabbed my bag and closed the distance between us. My dirty sneakers squeaked across the floor. They were covered in more paint than some of my canvases. "Why are you worried? Seriously you don't want your face to get stuck in that pensive look. You'll never find a girlfriend." I nudged up to his side. It was as natural as breathing.

"I only need one girl in my life," Liam said as he swung his arm over my shoulder. His warmth always calmed me, as did his scent, which smelt like fresh laundry.

I flashed Liam a playful smile, but deep down, I wondered if his words had a deeper meaning. Before I could contemplate more, he added, "The results are out."

Four words I didn't want to hear. It was bad enough that I already knew the answers, but to have it posted in the hall for the whole school to see made it so much more humiliating. That's how my pack did things. There was no coddling. Pack Sköll was feared because of its history during the Great War. A history that was entangled with dark magic and a lust for killing. Not swift killing either, for the darker the magic, the greater the root of evil that spreads.

Pack Sköll was known not to be lenient to other kinds. Even to hybrids like myself, we all knew the alpha would cast us out if he could. Alpha Mason Sköll only allows hybrid shifters and other kinds into his pack's lands to appear more acceptable to the Guild of Creatures. In reality, it was all for show.

I was a sixteen-year-old hybrid who had never shown a single ounce of any magic. I was no more wolf than the average house dog. Heck, in the pack's eyes, a house dog was more accepted than a hybrid like me. *I'm utterly useless.*

Liam must have felt my body stiffen with tension because he pulled me tighter to his chest. "Hey, it doesn't change anything. We don't even have to look if you don't want to." That was Liam, always trying to shield me.

"No, it's fine." Looking up at him, I smiled, "I want to know what rank you are."

We were tested throughout our childhood up until our mid-twenties to see how powerful our magic was and, in my case, what type of hybrid I was. As a child, I was classified as half shifter and half-human, so I was sent to live with the shifters in hopes that my being around a pack would coax out my shifter magic. Liam, on the other hand, was classified as a full-blooded shifter. If he was sent to any other pack, he might have been adopted, but Alpha Mason ranked families by pure blood, lineage, and power. Since Liam had no known lineage or family power, he was left to the pack-run foster home. No one would want to adopt him because it wouldn't further them in society. It would only tarnish a pack's family name.

At thirteen, Liam was able to shift into his wolf. I remember that day clearly. I was being bullied, and right after I took a punch to my shoulder, Liam literally jumped in the air, shifting mid-jump. After that most of the time, the bullies stayed away when Liam was nearby, but Liam couldn't always be my shadow.

As we rounded the corner, I spotted the huddle of kids as they started to gossip about the results. My heart accelerated, a fact the shifters would be able to pick up on. I knew what was coming, Liam did too. I could feel him stand taller. His wolf was fighting to come forth.

Both Liam's and my fate was now foretold on a simple white sheet of paper that was taped up on the wall. I felt like the school should have made more of an effort. Maybe framed the results that would dictate our future. Even if some futures were not as bright, at least give us a pretty wrapping.

My eyes scanned down, looking for my name as I chewed my lip. I read,

Adaira Warg: Classification: Hybrid.

Hybrid Status: Shifter/human.

Power Ranking: Magicless.

Something in me dropped. "I shouldn't have even looked," I whispered under my breath as my heart beat even faster. I knew others could hear my pitiful mumble, but I couldn't help it as I tried to act ok. After all, I'd never felt my wolf before, and that fact was reflected on paper now, permanently. After blinking away emotions, I scanned further down to find Liam's results.

Liam Warg: Classification: Shifter.

Shifter Status: Pure blooded wolf.

Power Ranking: Beta.

My body twisted into Liam as my head looked up with pride. "Holy Fae Liam, you're a beta!" I gleaned. Being ranked a beta was a huge honor, just a step below alpha power. If Liam chose to leave Pack Sköll, he'd have a lot of opportunities open to him.

Liam ran his hand through his thick chocolate brown hair causing it to look like he just rolled out of bed. "It doesn't change anything here." He tried to sound nonchalant, but I could tell deep down that Liam was thrilled. I hated that he felt the need to hide his happiness about his magic ranking. It was a gesture like that, that caused me to question if I was more of a burden to him.

Liam turned us away from the wall, and we started to head to the exit, but we were stopped by the wall of bullies who relished in making my life hell. Front and center was Stella Sköll. Daughter to the reigning Alpha Mason, sister of Carter who graduated two years ago and was next in line to take over. She stood tall and confidently with her shiny black hair that hung around her face like a curtain of doom. Piercing hazel eyes looked down at me with an evil twisted smile.

If only I could channel a bitch face like that when it came to looking at people that displeased me.

"You know, since you're more human than a wolf, I should tell my father to send you out of the pack." Stella stepped closer, her minions behind her followed like magnets. "Why should we have to put you up at our foster home? You're nothing but a useless waste of space. Taking our money, food, and complete advantage of our pack. Let the humans have you. Oh wait, they don't want you either." She laughed.

"Back off." A growl left Liam that was more wolf than his normal voice. I could feel the vibration of his chest as it started to shake against my back.

Stella flashed a pearly white smile as she crossed her arms. "Make me. Oh, wait, you can't because my father would hunt you down. Then he'd make Carter kill her in front of you and save you for last." She glared at Liam as her eyebrow went up like she had an idea, "Actually, that could be fun. Go ahead, beta, piss me off." She taunted.

The sad truth was she was right. Our alpha wasn't fair and just. The Guild of Creatures was always questioning him about the rumors of him meddling with dark mages. That was just the tip of the iceberg. Stella's family came from a line of feared monsters. Shifters who during the Great Wars killed anyone who wasn't a purebred shifter. Although the wars had long been laid to rest, Alpha Mason still thought in the old ways. He only acted civil to hold onto his power and to keep the Guild away from his throne.

"Let's get out of here," Liam said under his breath, he actually took a hold of my hand, — not as a boyfriend, more as a protector— pulling us away from wicked Stella as I wished with everything inside that I had the power to shut her up, but I didn't.

Chapter 2

CARTER

A blood curdling yelp escaped from the back alley. A cry so loud and commanding it would have been clear to even a human that a shifter was getting pummeled to death. My senses smelled blood, so much that I could almost taste it like fresh prey in my mouth. As a shifter, you craved what your alpha wanted, needing to let it be, even if it was wrong, and I knew this was. My father's ways had acted like a poison. It spread like a bleeding wound, tainting the entire pack. Those who were pure of heart would slowly die here over time.

All I wanted to do was change... to lose this human shell, go back behind the giant Sköll skyscraper my father called home and either stop my dad as he drained another shifter of life... or help him.

That reason is why I fought to stay human, because had my mom been alive, knowing I'd help my father claw the life out of someone simply because they weren't a pure wolf or of good lineage, my mom would hate me. Just as she abhorred my father, just as I sometimes hated myself under my father's rule.

Until he died, this was my life. You had to suck it up or crumble under the emotions. *Bury the emotions Carter, bury them so deep you feel nothing.* Numbness was what I sought when I was alone.

After another feral cat-like scream, I heard Laurence, a panther shifter with a low lineage, let out the last gasp of his last breath. I and everyone from our pack nearby knew Laurence had left this world. This was all because of my father's third wife, Darla. She'd found out my father had taken on several new lovers even though he'd been mated to her since my mother ran off.

So Darla had welcomed an affair with the 'alley cat.' Something she knew would enrage her alpha wolf-mate because of his old-fashioned beliefs that different shifter breeds shouldn't mix. My father desired pure wolf breeds and was willing to silence those that argued, which is why my mom had run. But tragically, she hadn't bothered to take my sister or I with her, and now she had a new family.

My father rounded the alleyway with Jackson, one of the betas by his side. He handed my dad a shirt as my father wiped blood from his mouth. Jackson was a year or two older than me and already in college. He was the pure breed who believed in everything my dad professed and was now giving me a look like he wanted to challenge me for rule over our pack one day. If only I, Mason's son, and a future alpha, would get out of his way.

Yeah, in your dreams, buddy. I thought as I felt my own inner wolf want to come out and spar with him. *I'd end him.*

"You were summoned here over an hour ago," my father barked at me. He hardly made eye contact. He resented that he saw more of my mother in his kids than of himself. *How I wish that was true.*

"Yeah, I had this pressing matter called school," I sneered at him and wished our pack's pull wouldn't draw me to obey, forcing me to leave class and come here.

"I help fund that school, if you wish to continue to go to it, then I suggest you arrive on time, boy," He spat hatefully as his eyes darkened when they looked at me. I tried not to remind myself that I could look just as scary when I was angry. My father tossed aside his bloody rag he'd cleaned himself with, the metallic tang of blood hung heavy around him. He expected me to follow him and Jackson as we abruptly heard a female voice.

"My dear Mason, why do you stink of fresh cat," Joana said. She was the only female I'd ever met not afraid of my father and all his wrath. She was dressed in a fiery orange dress that clung to her like a second skin showing off her curves. Thick gold jewelry that she could re-wield into handcuffs was bound to her wrist like iron shackles. Joana had sexy dark skin, long slick black hair that went down to her hips, and wore red heels that made her tower over six-foot-two. She wielded her body like a weapon.

"Sorry I didn't save any for you," my father said back roughly. He may have been filthy rich and of the best wolf shifter lineage, but Joana was on a whole other level of wealth and shifter power. You see Joana wasn't just any kind of shifter, she was a dragon shifter. She stuck out in this grungy part of the city like a sore thumb because dragon shifters usually stayed to their high up homes in Skydome. The isolated island to the north was a perfect fortress for dragons. Surrounded by mountains, most of the top plateau was only accessible by flight or portal. *And trust me no one dared to open a portal in Skydome if it wasn't sanctioned.*

"Ugh, no, thank you, I don't dine on scraps that can hardly defend themselves," she said to my father, disproving of him killing another shifter, even if Laurence was of pathetic lineage.

"Well, I heard you do kill vampires. My sources told me that there was a scuffle and that's why a meeting of the entire Guild has been called," my father snapped at her.

He hated Guild meetings because he preferred to only be around his own. If it was up to my father, there would be no Guild meeting between all the different creatures and races of Magic Borne. *"Us shifters, we are supreme, not the mages, vampires, their pet humans, or those damn other worlders that call themselves Fae.... You know they only come to Magic Borne because it's their ancient power lingering here that all other beings want; power that doesn't belong to them bastards anymore."* I had heard my father say over and over.

"The blood sucker wasn't killed by one of mine," Joana said sternly as she and my dad walked in unison with us trailing behind them. They walked with an air of self-righteousness. Everyone was beneath them. My body reacted with hate as I balled my fist; my wolf wanted out to rip them apart. I forced my eyes away, I could not afford to lose composure.

Looking up to the tops of the city towers around us, switching my sight so my wolf was in control I spotted the shadowy figures perched on the roof tops. Members of Joana's pack always followed her as personal guards. Like our own kind dragon shifters were pack animals. They would protect their alpha and pack just the same as us.

"Rumor is a mage might have killed the vamp." Joanna added.

Dad seemed not to comment for a moment as he thought out his response before he grumbled, "Rumors are hardly worth their weight if they can't be proven... besides, if all the vampires took themselves out it would be all the better for us."

Only I knew he had a silent deal with the Mages and that's why he hadn't verbally accused them. My father had been scheming something behind all the other shifter alphas' backs and the entire guild for a long time, and he was set on not letting me or anyone else, especially the dragons, know about it. After all it was in my very own blood to be deceptive. I bit back my grin. Like father, like son.

Chapter 3

ADAIRA

A precious gem. Something that took years of work to make and tons of pressure to form. Dug from the dirt, then polished and refined, so it sparkled like the sun that burned in the sky of Magic Borne. At least that's what my sketchbook was to me. It was like a rough diamond covered in the dark lines from my charcoal pencil that formed an image.

I smudged the line using my index finger, so it faded into the background. It gave a softness to the columns I was drawing. The image was one I had dreamed of time and time again. A building of my imagination but definitely was influenced by the art history I had studied in school.

If only it were a gig that paid.

I dabbled in figurative drawing, but my passion was architecture, strongly influenced by my dreams of castles and far away lands. *Funny enough, I had never seen such buildings in person. Never even left the city of Lykos.* Yet there was nothing like drawing a castle opposed to a shiny new cage that lacked the history other cities had, but a cage nonetheless. Being trapped in a castle seemed more romantic than the newly built metal and glass buildings surrounded by trees and mountains the shifters had.

I dreamt of escaping from Pack Sköll, but deep down, I didn't think it would ever happen. It was hard for a wolf to leave its pack, and although I never had shifted, Liam had, and I wasn't sure if he'd be able to leave the pack we both hated. *His wolf self was connected to everyone else now, and breaking the pack connection wasn't an easy task.* We hated being a part of something our genetics made us loyal to, well, at least Liam's genetics. Mine still wanted to play hide and seek. They were a no-show, too shy to come to see the world.

Shitty circumstances, but you have to work with the hand fate dealt, and I was just trying to survive. So on the outside, I took all the rumors, swallowed them, and digested the cruel words of other wolves once I was back at our foster home. It was there with Liam that I cried sometimes. I heard whispers that in other packs, fosters were treated as equals. Adopted into families and raised with respect in the pack. They even received a monthly allowance.

I huffed out loud thinking about it as I tucked a lock of my red hair back behind my ear.

Sure we have a roof over our heads, Thank Fae for that! It only leaks when the rain comes down really hard, a meal a day at the foster house and a meal at school. Two meals a day for a shifter was slim pickings. We had to eat for our human side and our animal side. At least the meals at school were a buffet, so we usually ate our fill at lunch. I required more food than the average human but less than a shifter. I was stuck in limbo, unable to define a certain category.

My fingers ground the charcoal pencil into the precious paper as I thicken the lines in the foreground. I had to believe hope was on the horizon, or what's the point of chugging through life? My green eyes look up to the parade of meat currently sparring on the field below. *That's one reason to keep pushing through life.*

Men.

Especially the shifter men that were all fighting for dominance in the after-school sparring session I could see outside. Muscle on muscle. Glistening with sweat under the mid-day sun. What a sight it was too. I might not be in touch with my wolf, but I'd like to touch a wolf. I'd have to be satisfied with looking for now. *Settle down hormones you get the last pick of the pack.*

I didn't have a boyfriend or mate. Heck, my first kiss was my best friend Liam, and we only kissed each other as emerging teenagers wanting to explore. Since then, we hadn't ever kissed again, both of us too worried it would mess up our friendship which went beyond just friends.

Liam and I were also blurred lines, even with him I was stuck in a limbo situation. We were best friends, each other's only family. At times we were like brother and sister, then we were each other's companions. We cuddled and even shared a bed some nights in the foster home as we kept watch over each other. It was perfectly normal for wolves to seek out affection and touch. We were pack animals by nature and longed to be surrounded.

Living with little taught Liam and me how to be resourceful. That brings me back to my sketchbook, which I had now started using the opposite side of the pages for my rough drawings. In just a few weeks, I'd be submitting my drawings as well as a thesis paper to the Lykos Museum of Art, where I planned on getting one of five internships that pay.

That's right, wolves, I'll be making my own money, so take that!

Not only does it pay, but it's my dream internship. I'll be surrounded by history and the art inspired by it. With any luck, I'll get my foot in the door to have a full-time job at the Institution of Magic Borne's Arts Conservatorship. A program dedicated to preserving the history of the world through the arts. I'd be able to travel to all the kingdoms and see art others can only see in books. Work on preservation sites and curate shows.

As a good luck gift, Liam had bought me the premium paper and charcoal that I needed for my drawings submission. We'd each worked summer jobs and saved every penny making sure the money would last the rest of the school year. I didn't have the luxury of wasting paper, so I needed to make sure all my ideas were perfect before putting the first charcoal line down.

I heard a barrage of giggling and whispers from a group of girls that were a few seats down cut through the air. It was the classic tip-off sign that a guy was nearby. Why we changed our voice to high pitch squeaks was beyond me. It made us seem small and weak. It catered to the male wolves who sought to dominate their females.

"Hey, Liam," a girl shouted. At the mention of his name, my eyes snapped up, first in defense, then in annoyance. Yet they continued to reach out to Liam.

I was seated on the training field bleachers as I sketched. Every afternoon Liam wolfed around with the other shifters from the school. It wasn't mandatory to spar in high school, but that would change for those who attended college or military training. The training helped ensure they had control over their wolf and engaged in pack-like bonding and support.

I had noticed the changes in Liam after a few months of this sparring. He now seemed much more alert to what was happening around him. If a pack-mate was upset or agitated, it seemed to have a ripple effect that the others could sense. Liam was always protective when it came to me, but he also was protected now by others in the pack.

When we visited the city, if an outsider came near a pack-mate or us, Liam's physical demeanor would change. He'd stand taller, puffing out his muscles. His wolf becoming more on the surface, as if he was ready to shift and pounce if the stranger was a threat. In weird ways it was as if Liam was becoming slightly more aggressive. Kind of like the head alpha of our entire pack, Mason. All his wolves would show tiny bits of his traits as long as that alpha was alive. And Mason was someone Liam and I and everyone in our foster home certainly feared. Alpha Mason only valued members who were rich, strong and of a higher lineage. Those deemed worthy were able to hunt with him, those who were not could become the hunted.

Liam is too good, too pure for Pack Sköll. However, knowing he was more in touch with his wolf and magic let me sleep better at night. Yet pack bonding was necessary to become a more robust and be a healthier wolf. It made the person more stable and less likely to go lone wolf. Nothing was worse than a lone wolf.

Ok a few things could be worse, like not being able to shift, but socially the title of a lone wolf was like a danger sign hanging above your head. Lone wolves often were unstable. Going against their genetic need to bond with a pack caused most wolves to go crazy. *And I'm not talking about crazy in a hot and sexy way. I'm talking in a lunatic unhinged way.*

As Liam approached, I watched the girls change from their relaxed positions to ones of display. They all sat up straiter and pushed their best assets out. It was a sea of push-up bras, long legs shimmering with lotions freshly applied, and thick and shiny hair. You name it, it was being flaunted on display like peddles at a circus. From a distance, it was comical how hard they tried. None of them needed to. They all were pretty, some beautiful just as they were. They looked more attractive at ease than when they tried too hard. Guy wolves noticed girls without needing the extra effort. Still, nonetheless, the girls all tried to shove their asses in Liam's face. Biting back a smirk, I watched as a girl stood and tried to talk to Liam.

She flung her long brown hair back and pushed her chest forward, which was overflowing in her low-cut skin-tight top. Ever the gentleman, he stopped for a moment before he resumed his approach to me. She, like some of the other girls, had opted out of the fighting part of training, not wanting to break a claw or ruffle her fur. Instead she sat with a group that preferred to sit on the sidelines and ogle the half-naked guys who shifted from man to magical beast.

I can't blame them.

Yet since I had yet to shift, no guys in Pack Sköll would seriously consider me a viable dating option. I didn't want to just be another hookup. So like always, I preferred to stay on the sidelines and observe rather than join the action. But the sidelines were getting very dull. I wanted to live and feel the rush of adrenalin when someone you liked touched and kissed you. *Is that so much to ask for?*

The metal bleachers creaked with each step Liam made as he ascended the steps towards me. His steps were fluid and graceful, even with his body that seemed to add monthly muscle weight. If he took the extra time, he could silently take each step without making a sound. His wolf would be able to adjust and camouflage its sounds too deadly perfection. His chocolate brown hair was slightly damp from sweat, making it shine deeper in the sun. The ends of his hair had a curl to it, little curls I loved to twist around my finger tips when we cuddled.

"So what are you drawing today?" He asked outright as I put my sketch book down and looked up. His light blue eyes looked even lighter as the sun shined directly into them. His pupils adjusted becoming smaller as he watched me.

"I'm still deciding," I said with a shrug.

Behind Liam, I could see all the bitchy looks the girls were giving me, as Liam closed the distance between him and I. Liam was hot. He was fit and built like most shifters, which meant every muscle in his body was sculpted and defined. Liam didn't have family power or money. Yet still, he had charming good looks and a personality you wished every guy his age had. He didn't play around or hook up either. He was the real deal you wanted when you found a mate. Also, did I mention Liam tested as a beta which was terrific considering his family lineage wasn't known? Having the beta wolf title opened many doors Liam could use to his advantage even as a foster kid.

If Liam never found his fated mate he'd still be fine. Liam would have lines of girls waiting to possibly be picked as his mate. That was a semi depressing thought because I wasn't sure if I'd ever have one? I doubted I had a fated mate since my wolf was too shy to even show me her tail. She was worst than trying to coax a scared rabbit out of a hole. So I'd be left looking for a mate the way humans did. Striking up a conversation, and feeling some kind of spark that made two people feel connected.

Liam ran his hand through his curly brown hair. Now it stuck up at all angles but it somehow made him look even cuter. He was shirtless, and the thin coat of sweat glistened over his rippled torso. It was hard not looking at Liam in a different light now that we were older. The boy I grew up with was now a man becoming a powerful wolf. Flashing his goofy smile that leaned more towards his right side had started to make my insides warm.

I bit my inner cheek, trying to quell my hormones. These new feelings of action towards him I'd kept to myself. Liam used to be like a brother to me. He was my only pack-mate, my best friend, and I didn't want to risk feelings for him growing only to ruin our friendship. He felt the same way I think.

He sat down next to me, and immediately I could feel the warmth radiating from his body. That combined with the sun's heat, made me feel perspiration starting to build on my brow. I slyly tried to wipe it off, as he tucked a loose strand of red hair back behind my ear. A finger came up, meeting the corner of my lip. His thumb now was rougher than it used to be. Hours of sparring in human and wolf form made his skin tough like a warrior.

The fire inside my stomach went from an ember to a wildfire. *Oh my gosh, stop this, Adaira! This is Liam.* My mind fought with my body. *But Liam is gorgeous now!* It was a constant battle as I recognized that my body wanted attention, but my mind tried to quell my need.

The touch might have been innocent, but I wondered what his touch might feel like in other ways? Maybe if I had fooled around with other guys, the simple touch wouldn't feel so grand, but Liam was my comfort zone, and only his touch I seemed to welcome. Only his indication I trusted.

"You've got charcoal dust right there." Pulling his fingers away showed the evidence of the dark black charcoal I drew with.

And there's a sexy image Adaira, black smudges all over your face... not. I loved drawing in charcoal because of how intense the black could become. The downside was how extremely messy it was. Charcoal dust littered my clothing and skin constantly. I looked as dirty as the pack assumed foster kids were.

Smiling, I tilted my head down so a curtain of my red hair would cover my blush. Liam laid back on the bleachers letting the sun coat all his exposed skin. You could see every peak and valley of the muscles on his torso. He was always at complete ease with me, as I usually was with him, but my legs squeezed together as I tried to ignore the draw I had towards him.

"Are you tired?" I asked.

"Please, I could go a few more hours if I needed to." He grinned and opened his glacial blue eyes to look at me. I'd read that you could see glaciers so clear they looked like new glass surrounding the island Kingdom of Skydome. That's how Liam's eyes were, pure, pristine, and calming. "But I'm starving. Let's go to Maria's for a burger and shake."

I rolled my eyes and shook my head because I knew he was going to suggest that. That's how well we knew each other. Maria's was a small diner in a rough part of town, but she was famous for burgers and shakes. Even the likes of Mason Sköll would show his face at Maria's for a burger which said a lot since the Sköll family had enough money to portal in food from all over Magic Borne if they wanted to.

Maria was a bull of a lady shoved in a tiny body. Nobody messed with her. She always gave Liam and me food for free. All we had to do was a sink load of dishes which wasn't so bad. She was a foster herself and knew the life of growing up in Pack Sköll. So she took sympathy for us, and in turn, we helped out where we could. I'd fill in for a waitress or Liam a cook if she was short-staffed.

"Fine, but shower first, please." I jabbed his arm, which only made him grab me in a tight hug as he covered me in his scent. His scent wasn't foul. It was the opposite. Liam smelt like cinnamon and cloves due to shifting into his wolf to spar. It only made his scent stronger. It was a scent I loved. It meant protection and safety.

That was Liam.

As Liam went to the locker room, I continued to draw until the clacking of heels on the metal bleachers stopped me. "You think he'd be interested in you?"

That would be Stella.

Every pack had Stella, a queen bitch. She was also the alpha's daughter, unfortunately. I didn't even need to turn around to know that voice that haunted many wolves. So I ignored her, which only pissed her off. She stomped forward in her designer black heels, black leather skinny jeans and blood-red sleeveless shirt right into my view. Red and black were her two favorite colors and were perfect symbols for her wicked personality.

"I'm. Talking. To. You." She emphasizes every word.

I'm sorry I don't speak bitch. That's what I wanted to say, but I also knew when to tuck tail and just let Stella be Stella.

"And I'd rather not talk to you."

"You-" Her hand reached out towards me but retracted when a deep baritone voice shouted from down below. A voice commanded an order that was hard even for Stella to ignore.

"Stella, hurry up!"

My eyes looked around her to land on Carter Sköll. He was the next pack alpha and Stella's big brother. He sometimes showed up to these fighting practices after school. No doubt scouting for the next-in-line pack guards. Where Liam was all charming boy next door, genuine and sincere, Carter was the opposite.

He was like a portal that would take you to a dark, seductive land. Full of sinister secrets, his wolf would chew you up, bones and all. There was no coming back from a guy like Carter. If his family history proved anything, then Carter most likely dabbled in dark magic. His father was rumored to do so. Carter and his family didn't play by the rules. They made them.

Living in Pack Sköll meant you were merely a pawn for what the alpha wanted. So Carter was like poison. If you touched him, you would be tainted. And so many girls wanted to be tainted by him. *Hey, if I judged by looks alone, then even I wanted to be tainted by Carter at times.* He had hordes of girls waiting to be entrapped.

My eyes drank him in from a distance like an unquenchable thirst. As scary hot as Carter was, you couldn't look away from the male perfection he'd been formed into. Carter was the perfect model of what an alpha shifter should look like. He stood so tall, well over six-foot-four with broad wide shoulders, his arms alone could kill a man if they bugged him with the slightest force. From his biceps to his thighs, his muscles were so hardened and well-sculpted that I wondered how he had the power to shift and be limber as a wolf. I'd imagine Carter would be a better fit for a dragon shifter, not that I'd ever seen a dragon shifter. Still, a dragon seemed more fitting for his personality.

Bruiting, fire breathing, and eternally pissed off. *Yeah, that sums up Carter.*

I'd seen his wolf in action. It was the biggest of them all, with jet black fur and golden eyes. When his wolf ran, it was like watching fluid strokes of a paintbrush painted onto a canvas by a master painter. It was perfection. He could change directions at a moment's notice, just as seamless as water running down a stream.

Six foot four, square jaw, and shirts that were always too tight to fit his muscles, and when he threw on that leather jacket... I'll be damned. Every wolf's tongue was wagging. I wonder where he found clothing that fit him half the time? *Then again, as Mason's son he was wealthy beyond measure compared to the rest of us at this school. So all his clothes must be custom-made.*

As much as I hated Carter— *and my hate wasn't petty because he was a rich and a fine as heck looking alpha shifter.* —*My hatred was due to how his family treated others in the pack. Others like me who had no social status.* Yet I loved to look at him just like every other girl here. Love-hate relationships were always the best, or so I have been told. Fiery passion exploded and erupted until it all crashed and burned.

The sun reflected off Carter's jet black hair, making it look shaped and faceted like a polished stone. Carter had the same dark black hair as Stella's and those burnt golden eyes that looked like liquid gems cooling down and hardening from molten lava. When he walked into a room, you could sense his alpha power, and it sent most cowering. I had difficulty not lowering my eyes when he was near, a sign of submission to the alpha.

"You're lucky this time, Adaira." Stella hissed, then she flipped her perfectly straight hair and pranced down towards her brother. My eyes were summoned like a magical pull back down to Carter, who looked directly at me. I didn't particularly like it when he looked at me because I could never decipher what he was thinking. Yet his eyes always found me in the crowd whenever we were in a room together. This was unnerving. Was he looking at me in disgust because I was a foster, a hybrid that could not shift?

Sometimes I believed that because he usually looked so pensive and angry. However, other times he just looked at me as if I was this strange creature. Casting my eyes down and back to my sketch pad, I realized I needed to lock away my hormones and focus on my future. *Which was incredibly hard to do when surrounded by males competing for everyones attention after they'd sparred.*

It's too many male shifters. Pheromones were tainting the air, trying to trick me as I looked away from Carter and his sister, and looked to my comfortable Liam instead.

"Let's go," I told him.

Chapter 4

CARTER

I approach Lykos Grand Central station, where I saw some of my dad's top older beta's guarding the doors. They were easy to spot as they stood with an arrogant pride wearing our pack's uniform. Solid black with our pack's golden crest sewed over their hearts. A thick leather belt with weapons was strapped to their sides, but that was mostly for show since our real weapon was our wolf. Most of them were my grandfather's Betas before he died and now dried up soldiers for my dad. They were assigned to lower ranking positions such as guarding the central portal station. But they were soldiers just the same and took their jobs with pride. Avoiding them, because I was never in the mood to have a conversation with any of my father's men, I swing to my right.

Lykos Grand Central station was full of portals that remained permanently opened. Decades ago we paid mages for the upgraded portals that could get you anywhere within our world of Magic Borne. Some less and poorer cities were not as lucky to have the permanent portals. In the more rural area where mages and roads were few and far between humans and vampires still used horses as modes of transportation. Richer humans and vampires that didn't want to paid mages used the human designed cars or planes to get around. They designed the vehicles to run on the power of the sun. I always wanted to try to drive a car but my father thought anything a human made was for lesser species so I never had the chance to try.

Then there was our world's main portal station located in Ziden, Magic Borne's Capital kingdom. Ziden was the location of the first ever portal opened by the Fae when they first arrived to our world. Those lucky enough to receive an invitation to travel to the Fae world could use the capital's portal.

Rumor had it, that when my mom first ran away from my dad, rejecting her mate to be with Dracos, a Dragon shifter who was engaged to someone else. They'd both hid somewhere outer world with the help of the Fae until it was safe for them to return to the kingdom of Skydome, where the dragon shifters lived. Thinking about my mom always made me feel cold and bitter. I thought I had shut out any need of wanting answers from her but I was wrong. During the last Guild summit, Joana had slipped me a note. It had a message in it that had me breaking all the rules.

I approached Lykos Central station which was across from our campus, near series of parks made for hunting and sparring, and was the center of our city for commuters like me.

"I'm pleased to see you've come," I heard the voice of Joana before I saw her. My senses heightened as I walked through a darker part of the park that was plush with heavy trees. I turned where I heard her voice. I stopped walking when I reached the base of an enormous tree tucked in shadow as it was hidden from the moon's light. The wolf in me itching to come out as if I was being set up for a threat. Yet the note had said it was from my mother as I made a fist and tried to still the beast within me.

Out of the tree, where I smelled what can only be described as something slimy and damp underneath the surface and reptilian, I saw Joana. All Dragon shifters beamed with this scent. She looked at me. Even in the darkness her skin seemed to glow with a rich dark hue, her memorizing beauty was a gift dragons had. Behind her there was a portal that still remained open, showing off its view of Skydome. I could roughly make out the tops of mountains that were framed by snow and clouds.

"This portal is strong enough for you to enter my kind's domain if you really want to make this conversation private. We could even have some fun before you come back," she winked at me with a sexual smile. I remembered Draco, the dragon alpha that she served, he allowed his shifters to have relations with anybody. So to her pack a dragon shifter and a wolf shifter was a very much excepted combination and had been normalized ever since Draco had married my mother.

On the other hand, my father loathed mixed breeds of any kind. He thought that wolves were the first shifters ever. That made our breed superior to other shifters. Our family line was supposedly a direct descendent of the first wolf shifter and the first shifters period. My father said keeping our line pure meant our pack could access ancient powers that other packs and mixed breeds couldn't access anymore.

"I'm fine over here, thanks," I said, my voice coming out crueler like my dad's as I tried not to insult Joana. I would have been attracted to her before my mated bond clicked in with... *someone else.* My mate had exploded into my life, changing my very soul down to the core.

Joanna laughed, clearly not insulted since she had a hundred dragon suiters on her tail. Her full lips that were painted cherry red, grinned, "You're missing out, wolf-man," she laughed then as if my breed, compared to dragons, were a joke.

"Anyway, your mother wrote that note hoping you'd come and see her." She told me.

"Not happening," I barked, knowing my mom's new husband might try to imprison or have me spelled the moment I entered his domain. The way my father wished he could do to his subjects, brainwash them all forever... "You mind as well give me her message or stop wasting my time." I told her.

"That vampire's murder that the Guild is investigating," Joana paused. "Your mother has gathered secret intelligence about it. The vampire was pregnant with a hybrid baby at the time of her murder." There was no sadness in Joana's eyes.

I found myself struggling to hide my true feelings about hybrids that were very different from my father's. My dad wanted them all wiped out. He claimed they were our pack's biggest threat when it came to accessing our ancient bloodline's abilities. "Most hybrids for the past thousand years or so have been born weak and powerless."

"Young wolf," she purred, "Rumor has it something has changed... That new hybrids are being born with more power than even the Fae."

I scarfed, and crossed my arms over my chest. "Some rumors are just rumors. Most hybrids are a nuisance. Many given away before they are even tested. Why kill over it? Unless the vamp was just in trouble and the pregnancy didn't detour her killers." I told Joana.

"Your mom's intel is that the vampire's baby was showing signs of being very powerful, even from the womb. That someone, perhaps a shifter, not a mage, took the mother out to stop the vampires from raising the child and having an upper edge over us," Joana said as I tried to hide the surprise on my face at this theory.

If this was true, while most shifters in my pack would secretly be pleased. The vampires would raise hell at the next Guild meeting if they knew this rumor to be sound. The punishment for our kind could result in an all-out war if we lost the Guild's protection as a result.

"You see what your mother is concerned about?" Joana asked as I tried to act indifferent.

"What if one of your kind was responsible for the death?" I threw back. Did Joana want me to believe my mother was concerned about my sister and I? I tried to respond without an ounce of emotion in my voice.

"No, a dragon would not fear a vampire hybrid," Joana rolled her eyes like wolves were all muscle and had no intelligence. "But she does suspect that a Sköll is responsible. Moreover, that maybe your father had that pregnant vampire murdered. If that's so, the Guild could demand not only your father's death but you or your sisters too, to settle the price," Joana said as I felt a chill go down my spine. Not for myself, but for my sister Stella as I felt my wolf eyes transform, my claws coming out of my hands, my whole body wanting to turn to show this dragon what a Sköll wolf was made of.

"Relax, your mother cares about you and your sister more than you know. She won't let this happen. That's why she wants me and you to work together, covertly. To find the truth, and if it can't be hidden, then you instead should be the one to turn in the true killer before the Guild. You doing so could persuade those in power to make you the new reigning alpha of your pack; sparing the innocent wolves underneath you," she said to me, offering to help me replace my father.

I wondered deep down how destroying my family could benefit Draco, the dragon alpha who also craved control like a life line. That made me want to know more than ever who was really behind this vampire and hybrid killing, Draco, my father, or someone else?

* * *

ADAIRA

"Even poison can taste sweet."

Sunlight casted off the metal pillars of the Cafeteria building, creating a rainbow of blue light. My eyes squinted as they adjusted from the change, as I exited the main hall to the outside courtyard. Sköll Academy was a newer building in the city of Lykos. It was grand and pristine. Paid for by the current ruling alpha's family, the Sköll family. Every building they erected in Lykos reflected their power and wealth. They often chose finishes that mirrored that. Metal and glass. Shiny like a diamond yet hard like the edge of a sword. It was cold and barren, much like the feeling of belonging here.

Of course, there was beauty in the designs if you looked deep. The architectural form was twisted into flowing lines that reached high and mighty. It reminded me of a ballet dancer. The metal was strong and solid like the muscles of a ballerina.Yet, the metal curves were gracefully bent and fluid like the dancer spinning across the stage. Magic Borne, the name of our world, was a mixture of old and new. Some buildings were made from the stone from the very first humans. In contrast, other cities and towns had been utterly destroyed and rebuilt with modern materials infused with magic.

Crossing the central courtyard, I passed a few groups of wolves sparring with each other. It was common to see. The only rule was no shifting inside the main hall. We might be shifters and have an animal inside us, but we had to remain civil. Besides the main hall, the library was also off-limits to a magical shift. No need to ruin the books with fur dander and claw marks.

The grass in the courtyard bore signs of numerous shifts. Full of patches of missing grass with muddy patches from the running and stomping of wolf paws. Balm trees scattered the area, providing shade. Given their name from the sap they produced which healed flesh of magic-less beings in half the time. The trees were infused with the magic that was rooted in our soil. Balm trees were a favorite tree in throughout Magic Borne not only did they have healing purposes but they just looked beautiful. They grew relatively short only reaching heights of about thirty feet. Their branches reached far and wide making them the perfect tree for shade. The branches were covered in bloom that ranged in color of deep blues to vibrant pinks.

Wolfs, especially young wolves loved to test their balance in wolf form and climb the tree. Since the branches were low lying a fall would be less painful. Liam and I climbed the trees often as children. When he first met his wolf, we played wolf and rabbit. He naturally the wolf and I the rabbit. I raced up the tree, trying to escape him. It helped us both, me with speed and Liam with balance in his wolf form.

Taking the steps up to the cafeteria, I reached out and pulled the door open. But I was quickly shoved away before clutching the metal handle. I stumbled back, missing the first step but caught myself before I tumbled down the entire way.

"Watch where you're going!" A catty voice snarled at me.

"You think your are good enough to enter before us?"

Stella's minion's barked at me as they pushed me to the side of the cafeteria entrance. They walked past me as if they owned the place. *Then again, Stella did.*

After they cleared, I stood tall and readjusted my backpack's straps as if it was some sort of body armor. I patted down my long wavy red hair as I flipped it over my shoulder and prepared to walk into a battlefield, otherwise known as the school lunch.

Hopefully, that would be the only attack during lunch today. *Washing food out of my hair wasn't a fun pastime.* The scent of baked breads, freshly cooked meats, and sugary delights assaulted my nose. My stomach rumbled as it always did when I entered the building. It caused a few of the eyes of my fellow classmates to glance my way. With their shifter hearing in tune, they'd hear my stomach rumble easily.

I know what they thought too, here comes the foster kid, a hybrid that can't do any magic. I tried not to let their whispers get to me, but it was really freaking hard to ignore the world sometimes. It felt like heavy chains around my ankles, like I was permanently attached to an anchor of failure since I could not shift or prove anything of worth to the pack.

Numerous circular tables were scattered all over the room except for the one long rectangular table near the far back left wall. That was my table, the table where the outcasts were destined to sit. Unlike the packed tables in the middle, my table was scarce and quiet. We were like a fallen branch off a great tree that slowly crumbled into the dirt again.

After loading up a tray of food, I walked to my seat. Slumping down in the metal chair, I felt its coldness as it pressed into my back. Nothing here was welcoming and cozy. It was cold and harsh and made for tough claws and hardened fur. *Two of which I was lacking.*

Lunch senior year was miserable due to one factor, Liam didn't have the same lunch schedule as me. I was faced with enduring one hour alone, and it was those first weeks alone that I realized how much I relied on Liam. He was my safety net, the blanket you wrapped a child in when they were scared, a shield when I had to go into battle. Stripped bare of Liam, I never felt so vulnerable. I realized then that I didn't know exactly who I was. So much of my identity was tied to him. I didn't want to know what it was like to survive independently. I always wanted Liam by my side like a safety blanket, and sometimes I wanted him in more than a brotherly way. We had experienced all our first together, *well not all...* Deep down, I wanted to explore more of those first.

I must have zoned out for longer than I realized thinking about it, because when I picked up my cheeseburger with sautéed mushrooms and truffle sauce, *yeah, our cafeteria wasn't lacking when it came to tasty food.* It was cold in my hand. Nonetheless, I'd never turn down a meal or cold food as I took a bite. Cold or hot the truffle sauced added something rich and exotic that made my taste buds jump for joy.

At lunch, I tried to eat enough to keep myself full until the following day since the food at the foster house was slim pickings. Now that I was older, Liam and I let the younger kids eat the little food that was provided. Shifters had an endless appetite. They had to feed both human and beasts within. Magic users, in general, required more calories, something humans didn't need to worry about.

Going to a restaurant or home of magic user meant food would always be plentiful. Those blessed with charm and magic were also blessed with a high metabolism. You never saw a magic user overweight. They were always sculpted and fit. Another benefit of magic.

My body was always in limbo. Sometimes I was starved like a wolf, yet other days I ate more like a human needed only one meal a day if that was all I could get my hands on. I polished off my tray of food in no time. Glancing at the large clock that was huge on the far wall. I still had fifteen minutes left to endure. My eyes flicked back and landed on Kevin, who usually sat right across from me.

Kevin was a nice guy, but he also had changed in ways I didn't know how to describe. Kevin wasn't a foster kid, but he was one of the unfortunate students who had a late shift, and by late, I mean eighteen years of age. The stronger the shifter, the earlier you would shift. For example, our Alpha's son, Carter, the next-in-line alpha, shifted at only fourteen. Whereas most other shifters matured into their animal by sixteen or seventeen years old.

Since Kevin was a late bloomer, he endured a few years of bullying and pressure from the pack and his family. The sad thing was we could never win. Kevin had come into his wolf, but he still wasn't entirely accepted because of his late shift. People assumed something must be wrong because it took his wolf so long to come forth that he was weak. I knew Kevin's fate would be the same as my own if I were to meet my wolf. I didn't care about being accepted by my pack. I just wanted to be on level ground. I wanted to defend myself and Liam if I needed to.

"The fries aren't bad today. Extra crisp when Joe is the chef," Kevin said as he picked up a french fries from the mountain still on his plate. I could hear the sound of the crunch when he bit into it, and it had my mouth watering. Kevin had offered me some of his food before, which wasn't just a friendly gesture to shifters. As pack animals, sharing was a big thing. You shared with those you accepted into your closer fold. I never turned down his gestures or others from the rejected table. Maybe I was too nice, but also it was nice to feel accepted.

The fry was still hot between my fingers when I picked it up and brought it to my lips. The taste of the potato was so fresh and lightly salted that I quickly grabbed another. "Thanks. They are good today."

I smiled, and ate a few more fries as I glanced around our table. Everyone here looked the same. We all sat slightly hunched over our food trays. We isolated ourselves and avoided conversations with others. Macey was reading a textbook about organism biology in Lake Caströft, a lake in the kingdom of Arenstad. From the look on her face, you'd have thought it the most significant thing to ever enter her hands. The sad part was every day, she read from that book. The same text, flipped the same pages, every darn day.

Life was on repeat for us.

It seemed like hope wasn't on the horizon. So we numbed ourselves. Macey with that damn book, me with my art, Kevin with... *something darker*.

Looking back at Kevin, I noted how he was different. He wasn't hunched over his tray of food. He leaned back in his chair with ease and confidence as if he was part of the main pack. His chocolate brown hair was buzzed shorter like a military cut, making him look more intimidating. He had filled out into the classical shifter body. Tall, lean, well-sculpted muscles primed for an attack. Tattoos of elder ruins on his knuckles and patterns twisted up both his arms.

"You want to tell me what you're looking at?" Kevin asked.

Blinking, I met hazel eyes that were watching my blue ones. He wasn't mad. In fact, he almost looked happy that I was giving him my attention. Maybe Kevin's gestures of sharing food and always sitting across from me had alternative motives? We were both single, after all. I just had never looked at Kevin that way before.

"Sorry," I whispered, embarrassed I was caught. It wasn't that Kevin wasn't cute, but I didn't see him that way.

"You're always watching, aren't you, Adaira, even when you pretend to have your head buried in a book or your sketchbook. That's the wolf in you, never able to fully settle, always on alert."

"It would be nice if that wolf wanted to show." I huffed.

Kevin laughed, "Watch all you want, Adaira, but you're never going to be able to defend yourself against them in your current state." He relaxed back in his chair, making it look like he was relaxing on a throne, "Let me guess, you know all the exits, you know when and where to run. But every week, something still happens, doesn't it? Every week they keep bothering you. Running only insights our wolf, you are constantly egging them to attack you. You're like a wounded animal leaving a trail of blood all over the woods."

My body caved in on its self from his harsh words. They hurt, but he spoke the truth. I tried countless different attempts to avoid Stella and her minions. I tried to be invisible, but they always saw me. I tried to run, but they found me. I even tried to fight back, which was a complete joke.

"What do you suggest?" I sneered.

Kevin's eyes narrowed as his lips turned up. He looked like a wolf who had just stepped out from the woods as it spotted its prey. The sudden change had me pushing back in my chair, needing space from the darkness that swirled in his eyes. Sensing his prey's retreat, he sat forward in his chair and rested his tattooed covered elbows on the table. The ink contrasted off his smooth pale skin with a dark beauty.

"You're making me uncomfortable," I admitted. I flipped some of my red hair over my shoulder as if it was a piece of armor to shield his eyes from my face.

"You're always uncomfortable in your current magic less state. Now, do you want the answer to your question?"

He stirred a nervousness in my core, causing me to take a prolonged pause before I mustered up the courage to ask him.

"What did you do, Kevin?" By his tone and confidence, I could tell that Kevin had indeed done something? His questions were bait. Dangled in front of me, and I was the little fish in the sea of more extensive, smarter fish. So I bit down on the baited hooked and held on as he responded.

"You are always going to be beneath them, Adaira. *Always*." He stressed. "Your little pack mate is one of them." He spoke of Liam. "But you aren't." He smirked then.

The reaction caused my fist to ball. My nails pinched into the palm of my hand.

His hazel eyes glanced down at my fingers, and he laughed, "It's frustrating, I know, but it doesn't have to be. You can take matters into your own hands. You can go against fate, take the control into your grasp."

Kevin shifted, his eyes looking me up and down and lingering longer on my lips. "Are you going to bite Adaira?" He taunted. His tongue swept out to lick his lips, clearly enjoying his affect on me.

"I don't know what you're talking about."

"Don't play dumb with me. How many nights have you laid awake, hoping that your magic came forth when you woke up the next morning? How many times have you tried to call upon your wolf, Adaira? You feel her a little, don't you? It's a terrible joke, letting us feel our wolf but never shifting into it. They are like figures trapped beneath a frozen surface. You need fire and power to break through the ice, Adaira. I can help you obtain that power."

Kevin's words were like pages from my own inner diary. Too many nights, I stayed awake and researched how to connect with my wolf. Liam had tried endless times with me. It had gotten to the point where I didn't ask for his help anymore because the disappointment and worry on his face when I often got upset at my failure was too much to handle.

Licking my lips, I answered, "There is no magical cure." If it was that simple, humans who wanted magic would be lining up. Mages had tried and failed in the well-known past, and the outcomes were drastic. New creatures were birthed, creatures born of pure greed and evil. So many so that the

Guild of Creatures had teams trained to hunt and track the creatures down.

"Or is there?" He smirked. "There's always something else to try. Failure is never accepted in our world. There are people you can turn to for help. I've seen you with all your art history books. What has history taught us about waging wars?" he paused for a beat, "Follow me." He stood like a warrior that just won a battle, the muscles in his forearms contracted with his newly found adrenaline, "Magic always finds a way to succeed," he said.

Then he turned and exited the cafeteria leaving an invisible trail of bread crumbs that taunted me to follow.I knew what I should do. *Don't you dare, Adaira. Stay seated!*

I should remain seated, but that itch took control of my legs in my mind. I stood and slowly walked out the metal doors, knowing that what Kevin would confess wasn't something I should want to hear. Yet when people are desperate, we sometimes cling to the paths we vowed never to turn towards.

Thank you all for your interest and support. The "Magic Borne" series is set for release in 2024. For the latest updates and news, make sure to follow me on social media. Your engagement and enthusiasm mean the world to me!

Made in United States
Orlando, FL
25 April 2025

60758532R00230